FIDELITY

INFIDELITY - BOOK 5

ALEATHA ROMIG

NEW YORK TIMES AND USA TODAY BESTSELLING AUTHOR
OF THE CONSEQUENCES SERIES

FIDELITY
Book 5 of the INFIDELITY series
Copyright © 2017 Romig Works, LLC
Published by Romig Works, LLC
2017 Edition

ISBN 13: 978-0-9968394-5-7
ISBN 10: 0996839453

Cover art: Kellie Dennis at Book Cover by Design
(http://www.bookcoverbydesign.co.uk)
Editing: Lisa Aurello
Formatting: Angela McLaurin at Fictional Formats

This is a work of fiction. Names, characters, places, and incidents either are the product of the author's imagination or are used fictitiously, and any resemblance to any actual persons, living or dead, events, or locales is entirely coincidental.

FIDELITY

—•○•—

INFIDELITY - BOOK 5

Is it really cheating if you're doing it to yourself?

DISCLAIMER

———●○●———

The Infidelity series contains adult content and is intended for mature audiences. While the use of overly descriptive language is infrequent, the subject matter is targeted at readers over the age of eighteen.

Infidelity is a five-book romantic suspense series. Each individual book will end in a way that will hopefully make you want more until we reach the end of the epic journey.

The Infidelity series does not advocate or glorify cheating. This series is about the inner struggle of compromising your beliefs for your heart. It is about cheating on yourself, not someone else.

I hope you enjoy the epic tale of INFIDELITY! ·

DEDICATION

———————●O●———————

The Infidelity series is dedicated to my readers, to everyone who had faith in me, who believed that after the amazing ride that was *Consequences*, another group of characters could come to life within the pages of an Aleatha book. Thank you for reading this five-book series and taking a chance on Charli *with an i* and Lennox "Nox" Demetri. Thank you for your support and anticipation as their story grew and the saga continued. Thank you for having confidence in another twisted, layered story that was not simply boy meets girl, but an epic tale of love, struggle, and survival through the generations.

I couldn't have brought the Montagues, Demetris, Spencers, and Fitzgeralds to life without you.

To my betas: Kirsten, Sherry, Val, Angie, Melissa, and Kelli, my editor, Lisa Aurello, my cover artist, Kellie Dennis, my formatter, Angela McLaurin, my amazing PR support at Inkslinger with Danielle Sanchez, and my proofreader as well as fantastic cheerleader, Ilona Townsel, this series has been a group effort. Thank you!

To my fellow authors who have held my hand and continually offered me and my crazy ideas overwhelming support, I thank you! Despite what the world sometimes sees, this is a fantastic community. I'm honored to be a part of it.

A special thank you to Mr. Jeff and our family. Your devotion, sacrifice, and patience allowed me the time to create. I love you more every day!

FIDELITY

She thought she could save those she loved.
He thought he could save her.
They'll both learn the truth.

FIDELITY, the dramatic conclusion to the epic five-novel series INFIDELITY, following Lennox "Nox" Demetri, Alexandria "Charli" Collins, the Montagues, Demetris, Fitzgeralds, and Spencers is finally here.

When the vows are complete and the dust settles,
who will be left standing?

No one is safe, and no alliance is above suspicion in the much-anticipated finale to this hot romantic-suspense saga. Our heroine has survived betrayal, cunning, deception, and entrapment... what will happen when she's faced with fidelity?

Infidelity, it isn't what you think.

From New York Times and USA Today bestselling author Aleatha Romig comes a sexy new dominant hero who knows what he wants and a strong-willed heroine who has plans of her own. With classic twists, turns, deceptions, and devotions, this new epic romantic suspense will have readers swooning one minute and screaming the next.

Have you been Aleatha'd?

FIDELITY is the fifth and FINAL book of five full-length novels in the INFIDELITY series.

*This series does not advocate nor does it condone cheating.

PROLOGUE

End of Entrapment...

ALEXANDRIA

THIS WAS IT. Alton and Bryce were busy. It was my chance to escape. The seed of hope I'd refused to water sprung to life, its shell bursting open with anticipation, maybe even expectation. Soon, none of this pretense would matter.

Returning Pat's small nod and with a hopeful grin, I turned toward the limestone steps. A thick layer of fog had settled near the fields, even obstructing the lake. Anything beyond the immediate lawn was masked in a cloud. No one would notice if I disappeared, at least not at first. This was the invisibility cloak I'd hoped for as a child. All I needed to do was make it to the fog. As I handed Pat my champagne flute, his eyes opened wide.

"Uncle Alt—"

A heavy hand landed upon my shoulder. "Where do you think you're going?"

I turned, perspiration dotting my skin as my shoulder shuddered with Alton's touch. Fighting the urge to flinch away, I nodded toward the lawn at the few people standing below and answered, "To talk to the guests out there."

"No, Alexandria. When I summoned Bryce, I meant you also. You're half of a whole now. Get used to it. Your presence is needed in the office too."

1

I wanted to scream for help. I wanted to hold on to Pat.

I couldn't.

Alton's stare took away my protest. Instead, I solemnly nodded to Pat and obediently turned toward Alton's office.

Everything was again happening in slow motion as my mind tried to make sense of the changing paradigm. The terrace outside and rooms inside hadn't changed. The voices of the guests combined with rings of laughter created the same low murmur. But now their song was a mysterious melody seemingly written to keep time with the rhythm of my frantic heartbeat.

As we made our way through the crowd, I reached for my necklace—my connection. Instead of the platinum-dusted cage, my fingertips met the diamond choker.

Oh, Nox. I'm coming, just a few more minutes. I took a deep breath. Please let Chelsea be with you.

It was my silent plea as I smiled politely toward the people we passed. Each one smiled and nodded. Was I paranoid? Had their expressions changed? Were they now somehow different, filled with anticipation, as if they knew the fate awaiting me?

"What's happening?" I whispered to Alton. "Is there something wrong?"

His hand, no longer on my shoulder, grasped my upper arm. As he hastened our progress, he leaned close, his stained teeth and thin lips set in a fake yet sneering smile. It wasn't aimed at me, but at the people we passed. "Keep walking."

With each word a gust of warm, sickeningly sweet, whiskey-ladened breath assaulted my senses, skirting over my cheek, and making my stomach churn. "Don't do anything stupid." His grip tightened as he spoke cordially to the people we passed. Once we were away from the crowd, he went on, "Nothing is wrong, *daughter*. Our schedule has just changed."

My mind was a whirlwind with possibilities.

What had happened? Had he learned our plans?

Was my mother free? Did Alton know? Or was the attempt thwarted?

Did Chelsea make it to Nox? Or was it a trap? Did Alton's men follow her? Had they done something to Nox?

My lungs forgot to inhale as I fought the bubbling panic. Who would I find in Alton's office? What had happened? I had visions of a bound Chelsea, maybe even Nox... my mother... dead...

It was no longer my conscious effort that made my feet continue to step. The cause was either continual motion or the forward momentum in Alton's grip. With each foot forward, my body and mind disconnected. Terror and dread fermented into a bubbling witch's brew. The poisonous concoction filled my bloodstream until oxygen no longer flowed. There was no water near. The lake was hundreds of yards away veiled in fog, and yet I was drowning from within.

All at once the chaotic din of guests faded. Nothingness rang like the fading clanks of a church bell as we crossed the threshold into Alton's office. Bryce had assumed the lead, the drum major to our parade, reaching our destination first. Alton and I were the middle with Suzanna following closely behind. To everyone we'd passed, we were the perfect family unit.

Smoke and mirrors.

I scanned the empty room. There was no one there. No bound Chelsea. No Nox or my mother. The unfulfillment of my fears filled my lungs, giving me the illusion of strength.

"What schedule change?" I asked, pulling my arm free. "What are you talking about?"

Alton's hand moved as his gray eyes blazed. At the same moment, Bryce stepped forward, reaching for my hand and hurling me behind him. I wobbled on my thin heels, balancing on the balls of my feet as I found myself pressed against Bryce's back, his body suddenly my shield protecting me from Alton's intended slap.

"Stop," Bryce proclaimed. His speech no longer slurred. "We have guests. Alexandria's question has merit. Why don't you inform us of what you want and I'll give you my decision?"

"Your decision?" Alton asked incredulously. "You'll give me *your* decision? Isn't that special? This isn't about your decisions. *I* built this..." He gestured about. "...all of this.

"*Your* decisions have gotten us to where we are today, where we are at this very moment. If you were anyone else..."

His volume grew and spittle rained with each phrase he spat.

"As it is, I'm not allowing you to make any more decisions." Crimson moved upward, filling his saggy neck like a cloth-absorbing dye and creeping onward toward his cheeks and ears.

"Alton, calm down. Bryce didn't mean…" Though Suzanna's words faded into the background, her tone seemed to placate his sudden rage.

Had the world lost its tilt or was it suddenly in a tailspin?

I couldn't decide as the scene in which I was captive lost touch with reality.

Even from behind Bryce, I could see the growing glow of his neck, now also red.

The monster I'd created with my talk of his impending power was facing the monster I'd always known. Somehow I was a part of this. It was my life, yet the power was shifting—an alternate universe, one where Bryce and Suzanna were no longer my tormentors but my saviors.

I peered around Bryce's shoulder.

Without another word, Alton pulled out his phone and typed a text message. Once he was done, he lifted his beady eyes and smiled.

I shifted my feet, more uncomfortable with his faux happiness than I'd been with his anger. I was accustomed to his wrath. Bryce gripped my hand tighter. Alton's new demeanor sent a chill through the air that even he could sense.

"Did something happen?" I asked from behind Bryce.

"Something is about to happen," Alton replied.

We all turned to the knock on the door.

"Suzy, get the door and then secure it."

Secure it?

"We don't want to be interrupted," Alton added.

Without hesitation she obeyed, opening the door and quickly shutting it. I recognized the gentleman entering as one of the guests. I'd briefly spoken to him and his wife. There were so many people… I couldn't remember his name. That was all right; Alton was again introducing us as he handed the man a paper.

"Thank you for your service, Keith. Bryce and Alexandria, you know Judge Townsend?"

"This is a bit unusual," the judge said, "but I believe we can make it work." He turned toward Bryce and me. "Your guests will be ecstatic."

I looked up at Bryce. Was there comfort in the fact that we shared the same expression of confusion?

"Alexandria and Bryce," Alton announced, "Judge Townsend is here to marry you. Now."

"N-now?" My knees gave way as my stomach fell to my feet. Yet I didn't fall. My new savior was once again omnipresent. Bryce's arm caught me and pulled me upright again.

My vision filled with the man I was about to marry: his gray eyes, blond hair, and ruddy cheeks. This wasn't right. This wasn't what I wanted. I'd had a plan. My finish line was almost in sight.

"No!" I shrieked. "My momma." I turned to Alton. "You said my mother could be here. You promised."

"I'm afraid that's no longer possible."

What the hell does that mean?

Alton turned to Judge Townsend. "Keith, we need to expedite this process. You can predate the license?"

"B-but the wedding?" Suzanna protested, once again coming to my rescue. "This is just the legal part... right? We can still have the ceremony?"

Alton stopped Suzanna's objections with merely a look, one I'd seen many times.

He motioned for the judge to continue as the noise level from the guests increased. Their low din had grown to a rumbling roar.

What is happening?

"Keith?" Alton urged.

"Er, yes." He looked from me to Bryce. "Today we gather to celebrate—"

"No," Alton interrupted, his neck tensing. "Get to the legal part."

Judge Townsend nodded and looked down at the paper in his hand. "Okay, well, Edward Bryce Carmichael Spencer, do you take Alexandria Charles Montague Collins to be your lawfully wedded wife?"

Bryce's support of my waist increased, pulling me closer against his side. "Yes, I do."

My sinking heart seized as the doorknob to the office rattled.

"It's locked," Alton said as if to reassure us. "I told you we wouldn't be disturbed. Keep going."

Rapid-fire knocks came pounding on the wood. The banging grew louder.

"Keep going!" Alton screamed.

Voices called from beyond the door. "Mr. Fitzgerald! Mr. Spencer!"

Alton reached for Judge Townsend's arm. "Keith, do this now if you ever want to see that bench again."

Judge Townsend's eyes widened as he turned back to us.

"Alexandria Charles Montague Collins, do you take…"

THE END OF ENTRAPMENT

FIDELITY

———●○●———

Infidelity —
it's not what you think

ALEATHA ROMIG

For everyone who stopped believing in fairy tales.

CHAPTER 1

ALEXANDRIA

THE LARGE WOODEN doors rattled upon their hinges as rapid-fire knocking pounded the door, growing louder and louder with each passing second. Alton's and Bryce's names were called repeatedly from the other side, each time with more urgency. Some of the voices sounded familiar while others did not. The pleas blended into a chant as pounding kept a strange yet frantic rhythm.

"Keep going!" Alton screamed.

The voices from the other side were unrelenting in their urgency. "Mr. Fitzgerald! Mr. Spencer!"

Alton reached for Judge Townsend's arm. "Keith, I meant what I said about seeing that bench."

Judge Townsend's eyes widened as he turned back to us.

"Alexandria Charles Montague Collins, do you take Edward Bryce Carmichael Spencer to be your lawfully wedded husband?"

It was increasingly difficult to focus on his question or this farce of a wedding as we all turned toward the growing roar.

I took a deep breath, contemplating my next move. Was Chelsea safe? Had Nox's men succeeded in freeing my momma? Was that the reason for this new rush?

"Why?" I directed my question to my stepfather. "Why can't my mother be here? You promised."

"Dear, she'll be at the ceremony."

As if she weren't present, but simply an ostentatious ornament decorating Alton's office, no one acknowledged Suzanna's response. She didn't hold any more answers than anyone else in that room. No one did, except Alton.

In response, his gray eyes glared my direction. There were volumes of retorts on the tip of his tongue. They hung in the air, just out of reach. Silently, I stared back, clenching my jaw and reading his demeanor. The anger was customary, but the anxiety was not. Somehow, something was awry. Bryce and I may have been dressed for a wedding, but that hadn't been the plan a few hours ago as Suzanna went on and on about the arrangements.

"Judge Townsend?" I asked as the room waited for my answer. "When were you asked to perform this ceremony?"

He glanced from me to Alton and back. The beads of perspiration on his upper lip multiplied. "Miss Collins, do you take—"

"Was this planned?" I asked again.

"Alexandria."

Ignoring Alton, I asked again. "Judge, when did you agree to marry us?"

"Alex," Bryce said, "just answer the damn question."

I looked him in the eye. "Don't you want a real wedding?"

The door continued to rattle, the voices growing louder, telling us they were about to enter. Even Alton's cheeks began to pale, the red fading to gray, a lighter version of his eyes, yet darker than his hair.

"Don't you think we should find out what's happening?" I asked.

"Alexandria, now," Alton growled.

"Miss Collins, please," Judge Townsend asked again, his tone verifying Alton's threat. Not only my future, but also his career depended upon my answer.

"No?" My response was a question, not an answer.

Momentarily forgetting the outside commotion, every eye in the room zeroed in on me.

"No?" Bryce asked, his drunken stupor replaced with shock. The change temporarily loosened his hold of my side.

I freed myself from his grasp. "No... I'm asking, don't you all think we should learn what's happening?" It was then I noticed the darkened window. The fog that had settled in the lower grounds had risen. Beyond the glass was a cloud that made the outside opaque, a strange combination of white with a blue strobe.

"Mr. Fitzgerald?" Judge Townsend asked as I ran toward the window. Alton's office faced the side of the manor, neither toward the driveway nor the lake. The view normally didn't offer much, yet I stood mesmerized by the thick layer of condensation that hung in the air. I'd never seen fog that changed colors. It reminded me of a dance floor as different hues of blue filled my view.

"The ceremony is only symbolic," Alton said behind me. "You *will* secure the license. The marriage occurred yesterday."

"I can get it," the judge said, "but they both need to sign."

Hope at the commotion bubbled and mixed with the doom of its meaning. Were there police cars on the property? Fire trucks? Ambulance? Was this about Momma?

"Someone tell me what's happening?" I demanded.

Suzanna's face paled under the layers of makeup, giving her a strange yet gothic appearance, while Alton's crimson returned, deepening to a blood red.

"The signatures aren't a problem, are they?" Alton asked, expecting—no demanding—obedience.

Before Bryce could answer, I straightened my neck and turned toward my fiancé. "Is this really what you want?" I stepped closer. "What *you* want? Remember, this is all yours, or it will be. Do you want to become my husband in an office behind closed doors? Or do you want it to happen in a church full of witnesses?" I reached for his hand. "Do you want to join the Carmichaels and Montagues in private or in front of Millie and Ian and Jess and Justin?" As he was about to answer, I added, "Don't you want Patrick to be there, to see it as this all becomes real?"

"Bryce." Alton's tone held the same growl it had with my name.

"Alton, really, the wedding, the church, the dress..."

For once I appreciated Suzanna's input; however, as with everything else she'd said, no one acknowledged her.

"Mr. Spencer? Are you in there?" The voice came again louder.

"No, Bryce," Alton said. "I order you not to answer."

"Bryce… it's yours… they probably need your approval." I spoke softly, still holding his hand.

As the commotion continued, Bryce's chest again inflated. Nodding my direction, he let go of my hand and took a step toward the door.

His shoulders squared as he narrowed his gaze toward Alton. "You *order?* You're not going to *allow…*" He stressed the words. "*…my* decisions. I've got news for you, old man. My decisions are all that matter. Your time is about up. Once Alexandria and I are married everything is up to me. It's time you got used to it."

I took a step back as my two monsters collided.

"You fool! Don't open—"

Bryce reached for the door's handle, but before he turned it, he questioned, "Alex, tell me you'll say yes in front of witnesses. Tell me that when you said *no* it was because now isn't the right time."

I swallowed the bile as his hand stilled on the knob. Whatever was happening on the other side of the door needed access. "Bryce, please find out what's happening. It could be my momma."

"You'll say yes in front of witnesses." It wasn't a question, but a demand. "You'll answer the right way so others won't face the consequences as they will from tonight."

His words reached inside and twisted my heart. I needed to know Chelsea was safe, yet by the look on his face and his not so veiled threat, I feared she'd been caught. The incomprehensible possibilities of that conclusion terrified me.

I nodded. "I will, but promise me there'll be no consequences today. If you do as I ask, then I will say yes in front of witnesses."

"Bryce!"

Alton's warning faded as Bryce straightened his lips and nodded my direction. In the next second, he turned the handle. All at once, a wave of people pushed through the threshold.

"Mr. Spencer?" asked a man in a Savannah-Chatham Metropolitan police uniform. "Please confirm that you are Edward Bryce Carmichael Spencer."

I nodded toward Bryce, encouraging him to respond.

Still primed like the peacock I'd created, Bryce replied, "I am and I'm in charge here. What's happening? What do you need?"

All at once the officer spun Bryce toward the wall and patted his jacket and legs.

There were two women accompanying the male officer who was searching Bryce. The plainclothed one spoke. "We apologize for the interruption. I'm Detective Means…" She pointed to the other woman. "This is Officer Williams, and that's Officer Emerson with Mr. Spencer."

"What is the meaning of this?" Alton demanded.

"Mr. Fitzgerald, as I explained on the phone from the front gate, this matter couldn't wait."

"Of course it could wait. Can't you see we have a party going on?"

Detective Means nodded and turned to Suzanna. "Ma'am, are you Suzanna Carmichael Spencer, the current owner of the Carmichael estate off McWhorter Drive?"

"Why, yes. Is there a problem?" She looked at Bryce. "What's going on?"

Before the detective could answer, Officer Emerson pulled a small card from his breast pocket and began to speak. "Mr. Spencer, you are under arrest. I'm with the Savannah-Chatham Metropolitan Police Department. You have the right to remain silent. What you say can and will be used against you…"

Suzanna and I gasped, my hands forgetting to grip as my handbag fell to the floor. The tips of my fingers covered my lips. Bryce's mouth fell open. Alton took a step forward.

"Don't say a damn word, Bryce. Officers, Detective, there's been a mistake."

"Sir," Detective Means said as Officer Emerson continued Bryce's Miranda rights. "As I said, this matter is now a criminal investigation and is out of our hands—"

"Out of your hands? You're the Savannah police. Of course it's in your hands," Alton insisted, each phrase growing louder as the crowd outside the door continued to build. "I told you on the phone we'd be glad to come to the station tomorrow. There was no need for this ridiculous spectacle."

Criminal investigation? I watched in horror as I tried to make sense of the scene.

Alton turned toward the doorway, filling by the second with more sets of eyes. "Close the damn door!"

It was then that Patrick made his way through the crowd. Our gazes met, mine pleading for him to come inside with me. However, my plea was snuffed out as one of the men from the house staff came forward and pulled the door shut.

Alton commanded and people appeared.

Swallowing, I took in the room. Bryce's cheek was against the wall. Alton's fists were balled as he rocked from foot to foot. Suzanna's expression paled in confusion. She appeared to be in shock, standing against the far wall with her arms around her midsection. Part of me wanted to help her, to help my mother's lifelong friend.

And then, my hands dropped and a small smile fought to stay hidden. In the eye of the storm, I imagined her passing out and falling to the floor. The bitch wasn't my mother's friend any more than she was mine. I'd let her fall.

"Mr. Fitzgerald," the detective continued, "as we explained, this case now involves not only our department but also the Evanston Police Department and very soon the FBI."

Officer Emerson continued speaking, "Mr. Spencer, please place your hands behind your back."

I didn't know if I was just relieved or also going into shock.

My shoulders sagged, chest caved, and lungs fought to fill. No longer were my thin heels capable of supporting my weight. Reaching for a nearby chair, the tips of my fingers blanched as I gripped the soft leather and tried to make sense of it all.

Did this have to do with Chelsea? Was this a ploy to save me? Had Deloris helped her file some charge of battery?

And then it hit me: I hadn't heard the charge.

"What's the charge?" I finally managed to ask.

Instead of answering me, everyone's attention was on Bryce.

Backing away from the policeman, he said, "Handcuffs? No! Why? You can't arrest me. I didn't do anything. Evanston police? FBI?" His eyes widened. "I've cooperated. I've given them statements. So has Chelsea."

Alton spoke over him, telling him to be quiet.

"Alex," Bryce yelled. "Go get her. Go get my whor—Chelsea. She can tell them!"

"Shut up!" Alton screamed, stepping closer to Bryce. "Cooperate."

"Call her!" Bryce said, nodding his head toward the floor.

I followed his gaze to my handbag. I did have my new phone, but I couldn't call her, not if she were gone.

The room was a cyclone of voices and activity.

Clinging tightly to the chair, my stomach twisted as I tried not to get lost in the uproar. The world grew fuzzy. Maybe it was the fog. Maybe it was a special effect. I realized it couldn't have been Chelsea who pressed the charges, whatever they were. Her charges wouldn't involve the Evanston police or the FBI.

"Sir, step back," the second officer said to Alton. "I don't want to have to arrest you too."

"How dare you talk to me in that tone, in my home, in Savannah…"

Phrases flowed, their volume growing as I tried to follow. If this were a movie, it was poorly scripted. Too many things were happening. Too much to follow.

I thought back to my classes at Columbia. The Savannah police wouldn't dare enter Montague Manor without evidence. The FBI wouldn't be involved if they didn't know something. Yet in all the chaos, I still hadn't heard the charge.

I cleared my throat. "Excuse me, Officer, what are you charging him with?"

My question caused Bryce to look back my direction. The psychopath from yesterday was gone. In his place was my childhood friend, the boy who was afraid of the fictitious monster living in our lake. The man who'd asked for my help. He looked down at my purse and back to me.

"Alex, you're a law student. Do something."

I shook my head. "Evidence?" I asked. "Do you have evidence?"

"Miss," a female officer said, "we're not at liberty to discuss anything at this time. Just know that if there weren't sufficient evidence, we wouldn't be here tonight. We're taking Mr. Spencer to the Savannah-Chatham station where he'll be formally charged."

"Charged with what?" I tried again.

Detective Means turned toward Alton as Officer Emerson again instructed Bryce to place his hands behind his back. "If there's another way out of this office rather than through that crowd, we'll be happy to oblige. We don't want to make this worse than it is."

"You don't want to make it worse," Alton mocked.

"No, you can't…" Suzanna cried. "Are the handcuffs really necessary?"

Neither officer responded. It was as if only I heard her words. Maybe she'd slipped into another of Montague Manor's dimensions.

"Give me a second." Alton lifted the receiver from the phone on his desk and pushed a button. Almost immediately he started barking orders. "Move everyone to the rear of the house. Clear the hallway and entry. I don't give a fuck how you do it. Do it now!"

His commands had momentarily sucked the air from the room. We all stood in silence as the receiver slammed against the telephone.

With his hands now secure, Bryce turned toward Suzanna. "Mom, I didn't. You know I wouldn't." He turned my way. "Alex, you know me. Remember what I told you about the last time I was arrested. I can't do this again." His pleas went toward Alton. "Get me out of there. Don't let me spend the night."

Each time Bryce spoke, Alton's complexion became a deeper shade of red. "Shut up!"

It was then I noticed Judge Townsend. He'd quietly moved as far away from the mayhem as possible. My guess was that he didn't want the police to notice him. I waited until the phone on Alton's desk rang again before I made my way toward the judge.

"The exit is clear," Alton announced, his entire demeanor seemingly resigned.

"No," I whispered to Judge Townsend.

His eyes met mine.

"My answer is *no*. I do not take him as my husband."

The judge's lips thinned as he nodded before quickly returning his gaze to the scene before us.

"Alton!" Suzanna pleaded.

"We'll have Ralph Porter at the station before you get there," Alton reassured Bryce. "Don't worry and for God's sake, don't say another damn word. Keep your mouth shut. If you do that, you'll be home tonight with your new wife."

As Officer Emerson opened the office door to lead Bryce away, the detective turned my way. "Oh, new wife? Mrs. Spencer, I'm so sorry."

I shook my head. No, this couldn't be happening.

As her apology faded away, with my arms around my midsection, I leaned against the wall and slid to the floor. Behind my closed eyes, the chaos dulled and the footsteps disappeared.

I thought of Nox. I remembered my escape.

Maybe it wasn't too late. Maybe I could still slip away. I imagined easing into the crowd of guests, my presence going unnoticed as they murmured amongst themselves, the rumors growing by the second about what had happened.

"Alexandria, dear," Suzanna said as she touched my arm.

My eyes sprung open and I looked up. "What?"

She held out my handbag. "Come on, dear, we need to go."

I shook my head. "Go? No, I can't leave."

"Alexandria, come with us."

Alton's demand hung in the air. I scanned the office, now relatively empty. Only Alton and Suzanna were there, both staring down at me.

"Where are we going?"

"To the police station, dear," Suzanna responded. "Your husband needs you."

CHAPTER 2

—●○●—

NOX

THE IMPACT TRANSCENDED my fist, sending shockwaves throughout my body. The crunch of breaking bones became music to my ears and the scent of blood a delicacy to my nose. One solid punch to the man's cheek was all it took. Unlike the anxiety brought on by the tranquil sounds of the Georgia estate, the brutal connection focused my attention, taking me back to the octagon, to the combination of exertion and satisfaction. With one clean hit, adrenaline flooded my bloodstream and the guard dropped to the hard Georgia clay.

Flexing my fingers, I took a step back and surveyed his limp body. Damn. He fell too fast, too easy. Every nerve within me craved more.

From the moment I received news that Charli had gotten into that damn limousine with her stepfather, I'd wanted to hit. My fists itched with the need to collide with something—with anything. I'd longed to hear the whoosh of air as it was expelled forcibly from someone's lungs and sense the impact as bone met bone, and even to witness the spray of blood as a nose broke.

That euphoria brought on while watching someone fall to their knees, as their muscles lost tension and their brain switched off, was second only to the best and most satisfying orgasm. Both were powerful drugs to my system. I could do without them—abstain—but once the high was within my grasp, like

20

an addict I needed more.

My head whipped from side to side as I sought out another victim. Through the low-lying fog, only stripped stalks of tobacco were visible in one direction and clusters of trees in the other. To assure myself of the guard's unconsciousness, I kicked his side with the tip of my shoe, the dust upon the leather leaving a mark on his dark jacket, the one with the Montague emblem. He didn't flinch or even groan as I reached down and moved his battered face from side to side. Two fingers to his neck confirmed his pulse was strong. It was then as I leaned down that I heard a soft static-filled plea coming from his ear.

Reaching inside his pocket, I pulled out the transmitter and then removed the Bluetooth device from his ear. Holding it near, I listened as the plea came again.

"Stan! Stan! Can you hear me? Did you see someone?"

I cleared my throat and spoke, elongating my words with a hint of a Southern accent. "No. Damn fog. All's clear."

Holding my breath, I waited for a response, praying that I hadn't fucking blown my chance to free Charli from the manor. I glanced up toward the house. From the lowland of the field, it was a blur of warm yellows and cool blues. The strange combination created an impressionistic masterpiece that I didn't have time to interpret. All that mattered was that the manor was within reach.

I should have expected sentries. How had Chelsea made it undetected—or had she? Had they watched her? Did Fitzgerald know what was happening?

"Keep watching," the man on the other end of the two-way radio said. "All hell's breaking loose up here. We don't need more."

What kind of hell? I wanted to ask. Instead, I replied in a voice unlike my own, "Yes, sir."

The airway went silent.

Under the fog, even the sliver of moon did little to illuminate the transmitter in my hand. I swiped the screen and checked for other stations, other information.

What had he meant by all hell breaking loose?

As I squinted toward the red numbers, I noticed the blood smeared on my knuckles. I flexed my hand, assessing if the blood was Stan's or mine. Though my hand was tight, my bones were intact. The breaking I'd heard was most definitely his cheekbone and the blood undoubtedly came from his nose.

One last look at Stan and I took a deep breath. He'd wake in a few minutes or a few hours. Either way, I needed to be sure he wouldn't tell anyone about me, not until Charli and I were far away.

Another search of his pockets yielded a phone and wallet. I threw both items out of reach. I removed his jacket, and then with the help of his shoestrings, I tied his wrists behind him. His belt worked well to secure his ankles.

When Mr. Fitzgerald's top-notch security guard woke, he'd be propped against a tree at the side of the path, his phone and wallet out of reach with no way to stand or walk for help.

After one last check of his pockets, I turned back toward the manor. This time I was wearing a Montague Manor security jacket, courtesy of my friend Stan.

Instead of running full force as I had after the shock of having Chelsea, not Charli, in my grasp, I moved quickly but cautiously, watching the perimeter, looking for movement, and listening.

The closer I got to my destination, the thicker the fog became. All I could make out was a lake to my side and the manor looming overhead. The condensation continued to distort my vision. I imagined Charli running toward me as Chelsea had. I longed to call out to her, but feared alerting more of the Montague security.

The invasion I planned was solo. Though Isaac had wanted to come along, I'd refused. If this were to fail, I was the one who'd breached the property. I sent him back to the car with Chelsea. If all went as I wanted, I'd call for him to come and pick us up. My Charli didn't deserve to be sneaking off her own property.

When I'd first seen Chelsea, I was too shocked to look at her, really look at her. But as Isaac reached for her, telling me to let her go, I saw what Charli had told me, what Deloris had discussed. I saw Chelsea's bruised cheek. Granted in the dim light, I hadn't seen it as well as I could, but I knew that everyone had been right. Edward Spencer had done that to her.

Though I'd released some fury on the security guy who'd tried to stop me, I had plenty pent up for the asshole up at the manor. He deserved to get some of, if not more than, what he'd given.

Step by step, I moved closer to my goal. My ears were tuned to the world around me. For a city boy, I had a sense of nature. As long as the frogs and crickets made noise, the coast was clear. It was when they stilled that I did too. It was part of how I sensed Stan.

Now that our encounter was past tense, I was relieved I hadn't found a gun. Even if I had, it wouldn't have stopped my determination. I told myself to proceed with caution. Just because Stan had no weapon didn't mean that all of Montague security went unarmed.

The crickets stilled as voices began to register. I stepped in the shadow of the tree line and moved slowly toward the light. No longer was the path hard-packed dirt. It had morphed into a thick, lush lawn beneath my shoes. The moist grass muffled my steps as I progressed slowly forward.

In the near distance were people, many people, all dressed in their finest. They were clustered in groups, their voices hushed yet anxious.

It was then I heard someone coming from behind. Spinning, I saw his jacket, the same as the one I now wore.

"What the hell—"

Crack!

I shook out my right hand as another guard hit the ground. This one at least had cushy grass, which was more than my friend Stan had. I knelt beside his wilted body, making sure that he too was unconscious. He was, but fuck. I didn't have time to keep tying them up. And lucky for him, I'd missed his nose. I grabbed him under his arms and dragged him back into the trees. Same routine, phone and wallet. I plucked the Bluetooth from his ear and found the transmitter. The lake I'd noticed earlier was only a few yards away. Casually, I dropped the transmitter and phone into the water, the ripples fading into the mist as they sunk to the depths.

The house—fucking *mansion*—was huge. For a brief moment I recalled my earlier assumptions about Charli. How could I have been so wrong? Looking up at this place, my dad's assessment had been right. It was a palace and Charli was American royalty. In this world of old money, her blood was blue.

I pushed those thoughts away, not giving a damn about her heritage. All that mattered, more than the air needed to fill my lungs, was that she was safe and in my arms. We'd work out the rest as long as we were together.

The guests were gathered in clusters on the upper patio and the lawn below. Their sheer numbers created a rumble while the blue flashes I'd noticed earlier illuminated the thick air. Barely audible above the din of collective murmurs was the whirl of propellers. It wasn't loud enough to be helicopters. No, weaving in and out of the fog were drones, filming, recording whatever was happening.

Some of the guests pointed to the sky while others seemed unaware. Mindful to stay out of not only the people's sight but also the drones' cameras, I moved quietly, making my way away from the crowd and around the far end of the mansion. With each step toward the front, the flashing lights grew brighter, saturating the fog with an omnipresent blue. Peering around the final corner toward the front driveway, I saw them: one, two... I continued to count. There were seven police cars with their lights flashing in front of the mansion.

My heart raced as I contemplated various reasons for their presence.

Was Charli all right? Did this have to do with Adelaide? Had Magnolia Woods tipped off Mr. Fitzgerald?

Taking a step back into the shadows, I removed my phone from my pants pocket. I'd had it on silent.

I swiped the screen.

The red number alerted me of my numerous text messages.

First message from Oren: **"WE'RE TAKING OFF NOW. SHE'S STILL UNCONSCIOUS. LET ME KNOW ABOUT ALEX."**

Text message from Isaac: **"CHELSEA SAID IF ALEX HASN'T LEFT, SHE IS STILL ON THE MAIN LEVEL. CHELSEA IS SCARED BUT SAFE."**

Text message from Patrick: *"FUCK. SOMETHING HAPPENED. ARE YOU SURE YOU GOT AUNT ADELAIDE? ALTON JUST TOOK ALEX AND SPENCE TO HIS OFFICE. FIRST FLOOR, EAST WING. SHE'D BEEN JUST ABOUT TO LEAVE."*

I held my breath as I scrolled.

Text message from Patrick: *"POLICE ARE HERE. THEY'RE ASKING FOR SPENCE AND UNCLE ALTON. THE STAFF IS TRYING TO KEEP THEM AWAY. GUESTS ARE GOING CRAZY. THIS IS FUCKED UP."*

Text message from Patrick: *"I SAW HER. SHE'S OK. SHE'S STILL IN HIS OFFICE. POLICE ARE THERE."*

Text message from Deloris: *"DON'T GET ARRESTED. USE YOUR HEAD."*

Fuck her. Fuck them all.

At least I knew Charli was still there, seemingly safe in her stepfather's office.

I sent a text to Patrick: *"I'M HERE. WHERE ARE YOU?"*

Patrick: "THANK GOD. THEY CORRALLED US TO THE BACK. SOMETHING IS HAPPENING UPFRONT."

Me: "THERE ARE SEVEN POLICE CARS."

Patrick: "WHERE ARE YOU?"

Me: "NEAR THE FRONT OF THE MANSION."

Patrick: "OUTSIDE? I'M COMING AROUND."

Me: **"LEFT SIDE IF FACING FRONT."**

With my back against the side of the house, I gripped my phone tighter. I was prepared to walk into a party, but not past a shitload of policemen. And then it hit me.

I sent another text. To Deloris: **"HOW DID YOU KNOW THERE WOULD BE POLICE?"**

Deloris: **"IT'S ON THE NEWS."**

"Shit, I almost walked right past you." Patrick's voice stopped me from replying to Deloris.

I stood taller as Patrick slipped into the shadows.

"What the fuck is happening?"

"I don't know. Are you sure Aunt Adelaide and Chelsea are safe."

I nodded. "Yes, I just read the texts. Now I need Charli."

We both stepped quietly from around the corner of the house at the sound of voices. Still within the shadows, the scene played out in our full view. Edward Spencer was being led toward a waiting police car with his hands secured behind his back.

"Fuck!" Patrick whispered.

"Take me back around," I whispered. "With all the chaos back there, I can slip inside the manor with you."

Patrick nodded. "Take off that security coat. I'm not going to ask how you got it."

"Good," I said as I shrugged it from my shoulders.

He eyed me up and down. "I think this is the first time I feel better dressed."

Only Patrick would think about our attire during a time like this.

"Follow me…" he began.

Suddenly we both stopped as the police cars began to move. One by one, like a parade, they drove away from the manor and toward the front gate.

"I wonder what in the hell happened," Patrick said. "This place is a madhouse."

"Just get me inside…"

Before we took off toward the back, the LED-blue cast of headlights skirted the front of the mansion. With our backs against the limestone we stood and waited as a long black limousine came up the driveway.

Patrick tugged at my sleeve. "Come on."

"No," I growled. Whatever was happening, it was big. I felt it in my soul.

Patrick sucked in a deep breath as another *fuck* flew from his lips.

Fuck was right.

I'd seen the pictures, the surveillance. I knew these damn people better than I knew my own family. The woman leading the way, the first to descend the front steps, was Suzanna, Edward's mother. Dabbing her eyes, she was a step ahead of the other voices as they made their way toward the bottom of the steps. Slowly the car came to a stop and an older driver walked to the rear and held open the door.

It was as the others came into view that my blood heated, going from ninety-eight to 212 degrees in a second flat. Heat radiated from my skin as my fists once again clenched.

Alton Fitzgerald had Charli's arm in his grasp and was leading her toward the car. Her steps were tentative as if she were resisting his intentions.

"No fucking way this is happening again," I vowed.

Her voice was strong. "I shouldn't be going. We have guests."

My teeth clenched as my hands balled tighter. Charli's pleas were the last bit of fuel my body needed, the spark to my already combustible rage. No other sounds registered as I ran toward the limousine.

CHAPTER 3

———— •O• ————

OREN

THEY HAD PLANES specially made and outfitted for medical transport. There were companies that included air ambulances, who boasted of their competence with such perilous dealings. I wasn't a stranger to risks or dangerous encounters. I also wasn't stupid when it came to announcing our intentions.

A medical transport would require names and medical records. They would need clearance and authorization. We were without any of that.

The last thing I planned on doing was alerting anyone that I was transporting Adelaide Montague Fitzgerald in an unconscious state across state lines. It wasn't that I'd ever balked at breaking the law, but this was a federal offense. Even that wasn't new to me. Murder was a federal offense. If we were to be apprehended, officially this was kidnapping.

Unofficially, this was a rescue.

"*Amore mio,*" I whispered in Adelaide's ear as Clayton pulled the ambulance onto the tarmac of the private airport. "Soon you'll be safe."

Adelaide didn't move, even as I smoothed her hair away from her beautiful face. To me, she was gorgeous. She always had been; however, as I stared at her, it was clear to me that her ordeal had made its mark. Her once rosy complexion was now gaunt. Her cheekbones had become too prominent

28

and her skin loose. Since the time I'd last held her in my arms she'd lost too much weight. I knew from the doctor's notations it had mostly occurred recently. It had been evident as I helped to lift her from her bed to this gurney. Her shoulder and arm bones protruded. My fingers easily surrounded her dainty wrists as I sought the thump of her pulse.

The rhythm was present, though rapid and faint. Maybe it wasn't faint. Maybe it was that mine was thundering in my chest. I held my breath and counted the beats as my fingers pressed against her frail wrist. I wasn't a doctor, even if I'd pretended to be one. In fifteen seconds I counted twenty-eight beats—or 112 per minute. Her breathing was shallow. Since we'd left Magnolia Woods each breath seemed to come quicker, yet be less effective.

"Mr. Demetri," Clayton said from the front seat. "Mrs. Witt said the plane is ready and Dr. Rossi is here, ready to accompany you back to New York."

I nodded. With each passing day I gained new respect for Deloris Witt.

Eva Rossi was the one physician I could implicitly trust with regard to both Adelaide's care as well as discretion. She was family. As I'd told Deloris, family is family. The physician Deloris had consulted had proven trustworthy. She'd scoured Adelaide's records and ordered tests. She was the one who told us how to trick the monitors at Magnolia Woods. She was still on the case, but she wasn't family. I couldn't ask her to assist me in transporting Adelaide to New York.

Eva was a Costello, the daughter of another of Angelina's cousins. Being related to Angelina, she was also related to Vincent.

Angelina's cousin was still in charge.

I should have hesitated to call. I should have known the repercussions. Vincent and I had made our peace. We'd completed our deals and granted each other space. The world was different today than it was twenty years ago. But it still existed.

As a young man I'd worked hard to belong in the Costello world. Then as an older man, I'd worked equally as hard to earn my freedom as well as Lennox's immunity. There were few people who were worth the reintroduction to the family life. Adelaide was one.

During my conversation with Vincent, I'd emphasized one thing: I would be the one in debt, not Lennox.

Clayton brought the ambulance to a stop. Though it was night, the tarmac was well lit. The pilots flying our plane needed flight plans and a manifest with names. Even on private planes the FAA had requirements. It wasn't like we were taking off from a privately owned airstrip.

Our timeline had been tight. I did what Lennox had done. I trusted someone else to make it all work. Now it was time to learn if my trust had been misguided.

As Clayton got out of the vehicle and walked around to the back, I stayed at Adelaide's side. The holster of my gun rested against my hip as I blindly waited for the back doors of the ambulance to open. My pulse increased with each tick of the clock. I wasn't sure what I anticipated, but as the rear doors of the ambulance opened, my solemn gaze met that of the woman standing at Clayton's side.

"All the paperwork has been cleared," Deloris said.

I took a deep breath and nodded.

The identifications she'd provided were false, even mine. It would be too easy for Fitzgerald to follow the plane I hired back to New York, back to Rye. Part of me wanted to change the flight plan and continue east across the Atlantic. I imagined having Adelaide in London. Medical care there was equally as advanced. Though we'd be much more difficult to find, there was one huge unknown that wouldn't allow me to take her to my home in the United Kingdom.

When the woman on the gurney beside me woke, I wanted her to have the option to return to her life. I wouldn't really kidnap her. She was free to do as she'd done before and tell me to leave, to tell me she wanted to work on her marriage.

If she chose that option, though it would kill me, I would let her go. But not until she was well. In the meantime, in Rye she would have access to the one person I believed she wouldn't turn away—Alexandria.

I made a mental note to check my phone after Adelaide was secure. It would be best to have confirmation that both Chelsea and Alexandria were safe before we took off. However, it wasn't essential. Getting Adelaide into the air was my number-one concern.

Once we made it to the home in Westchester County, we'd be safe. The house wasn't only a fortress, but I'd made another deal with my devil—with Angelina's cousin. There was no expense or freedom I wouldn't sacrifice for the woman I loved. Not only was it protected on the outside, the master bedroom suite had been converted into a top-of-the-line hospital room. Silvia had been charged with the transformation. I had no doubt it would be done.

Family.

Clayton reached for the end of the gurney and pulled. As the makeshift bed hovered above the tailgate, the scissor legs and wheels fell into place. I quickly followed the gurney, supporting the foot as Clayton lifted the head and we carried Adelaide up the steps and into the cabin of the plane.

Once she was aboard, I lifted her petite body to the long leather sofa. With only a nod of understanding, Dr. Rossi inspected the bags of fluid as she moved the attachments to the improvised hospital bed she'd constructed.

As soon as the gurney was empty, Clayton moved it back toward the door.

Deloris had followed a step behind. Watching from the side, she said, "Get the ambulance back to Magnolia Woods as soon as you can. Be sure the inside is clean."

Clayton nodded as he took one last look at Adelaide. "Is she going to make it?"

"Yes." I couldn't comprehend another answer.

Leery of using anyone's name, I asked Deloris, "My son?"

She shook her head. "The last I heard, he was making his way toward her."

My chest tightened. "Damn, she didn't make it to the rendezvous point?"

"No. The other did."

I nodded. I'd gotten the mass text message about Chelsea. Our mission was two-thirds complete. It wasn't enough. It wouldn't be for Lennox. "Message me, even if we're out of communication. I'll get it as soon as possible."

"Sir, may I examine your wife before we take off. It won't take long."

My eyes met Eva's. "Yes, Doctor."

My wife. If only.

Deloris handed me a paper as I stood. Together we stepped down the stairs to the tarmac. As the night breeze blew in gusts around us, I read the small piece of paper.

Marco and Laura Ferrari

Stuffing the paper into the pocket of my jacket, I asked, "Those are the best you could do?"

She shrugged. "Two of the most common names, difficult to trace." She reached into her pocket and handed me an envelope. "Identification for each of you. The doctor already has hers. I'll stay here and get the next plane lined up and ready."

I ran the smooth envelope between my fingers. "I rarely depend upon someone else."

Her lips that had been set in a straight line of concentration shifted to an almost smile. "I'm aware and honored." She tilted her head toward the plane. "Maybe one day you or your son will share the reason why she means so much to you, but sir, you're like your son or maybe he's like you. His fidelity is rarely given, but when it is, it's fierce. I don't understand why or how, but you are the same. I'd never witnessed it before. I'm sorry I never knew Lennox's mother, not really. She was very ill by the time I came around."

"It is my observation that you wouldn't hesitate to kill in order to save that woman."

I didn't respond. She was one hundred percent correct.

"I'd rather work with you than against you."

"Thank you. I never forget a debt," I said.

"I'll message you as soon as I hear from your son."

"Until we're together again."

Deloris nodded as I again ascended the steps. Once I was inside, the copilot closed the door, retracting the stairs.

"Mr. Ferrari, please take a seat. The airport is unusually quiet this evening. We can take off immediately."

"Thank you." I turned back to Adelaide. Dr. Rossi was tucking a blanket around her body. Her exam seemed to be complete.

"Once we're in the air," the copilot said, "you're welcome to help yourself to the bar. Your assistant insisted that you have only the flight crew, no attendant."

"We're quite capable. Thank you."

Eva and I waited for the copilot to disappear behind the cockpit door.

"How is she?"

Years of medical training gave people the ability to mask their feelings. I knew the facade well. It had come in handy in many of my endeavors.

"Before we take off," Dr. Rossi began, "I'd like to make a call and arrange for a few additional things at your home. Unless you'd reconsider a hospital? In a hospital I could—"

"Make the call. Hurry. We're about to take off."

Eva nodded and securing herself into one of the seats opposite Adelaide, spoke softly into her phone. She rattled off medications and instructions. I tried to listen, but it was a foreign language. Hearing the name of a six-syllable medication and knowing what it was used for were two different things.

I sat closest to Adelaide. "*Amore mio*, stay strong. You always have been too strong, too unwilling to let me help you. Now, I will help. It's not too late. I refuse to allow that."

My heart ached at memories of Angelina. Perhaps it was what Deloris had said, but I recalled her illness and my helplessness. There was no price I wouldn't have paid to make her well again. God had other plans. As I held Adelaide's petite hand, I prayed that this time God's plans would be different.

The plane began to move as Dr. Rossi turned off her phone.

"Talk to me."

"I won't know until I run a few tests."

"Know what?"

She took a deep breath. "The medication, the Versed, is a benzodiazepine. It's relatively safe when used as intended but it isn't meant for repeated use, especially not in a patient who is suffering from alcohol and opioid withdrawal. Repeated use of the drug is a lot for a healthy body to take. If that body is compromised, it's more difficult."

"Tell me what you're worried about."

"I didn't say I was worried."

I brought my lips together and stared.

"Her breathing is irregular. The sedative can cause respiratory depression.

From what I've seen, she hasn't been on oxygen. Lack of oxygen can cause irreversible damage."

"Damage?"

"To the brain, to the heart. We won't know for sure until she fully wakes. I know the doctors at the clinic were preventing her from waking—the chart said the order was to help her through her DTs, but I advise that she be eased off of all medications. If it becomes too difficult for her to endure, there are less potent pain suppressants to take off the edge. Without blood tests we don't know the level of toxicity in her system."

"But she'll be all right." It wasn't a question.

"Sir, I'll do all I can."

We both looked to Adelaide as the plane lifted off the ground.

"I wish we had oxygen on board, but an FAA regulation requires that the crew and aircraft on private flights be certified."

I looked around. "But what about the masks. Isn't that oxygen?"

"Yes, an emergency supply. Let's hope we don't need to try to access that."

CHAPTER 4

ALEXANDRIA

PANDEMONIUM PREVAILED AS my heart beat faster. The world around me was falling apart, and I was again powerless. I'd said I didn't want to leave the mansion. I'd protested, but here I was, being ushered, forcibly, toward the front of the house. Though I couldn't see the guests, their voices were audible over the sharp click of our heels as Suzanna and I stepped upon the marble floor.

"Dear, you'll need to fix your makeup."

I joined the others in ignoring Suzanna as panic bubbled in the depths of my stomach, creating a sour concoction. I needed to get away—not go with them. I'd done all I could to stall, slowing my steps, claiming I needed to go up to my room, anything. Each moment I searched for aid, for Patrick, for Jane, or for anyone who could offer me a lifeline. Even Judge Townsend had disappeared. Now as we made our way to the front door, the corridors and foyer were exactly how Alton had ordered them to be—empty.

With each step, memories flashed in front of my eyes of my recent return to Montague Manor. Nine days ago as I walked these same hallways, the walls had been lined with Alton's soldiers—his show of power. Their absence was the same display. Alton Fitzgerald could make people appear and disappear. Maybe I'd been wrong about my stepfather's ability to entertain. He wasn't a

35

singer or dancer. He was a magician.

There wasn't even a staff member present to open the front door as we approached. They'd all slipped into the secret dimension that only they could access. For a moment I wondered if they could see us and then I realized they couldn't. Nor could they hear. They were paid too well for that.

Suzanna reached for the large handle and pulled the massive door inward. As we stepped onto the porch, the cool night air blew wisps of my hair about my face. My skin prickled with goose bumps as a chill raced through me.

"I need a coat," I tried.

"Nonsense. The car is warm," Alton said as a limousine pulled up the drive.

A sense of déjà vu filled me with the same doom I'd felt at Magnolia Woods.

I tugged my arm free from Alton's grasp as the autumn leaves danced, creating a trail in the car's wake. I wanted to push Alton for answers, but weighed my words. Over the last few minutes, his panicked sense of urgency had turned into a quiet resolve. The new demeanor gave me no sense of security.

As much as I despised the thought, I missed Bryce.

The realization of his arrest had yet to register fully. Instead, the knowledge that I was again alone at Alton's mercy was gnawing at me. Despite Bryce's bipolar psychotic episodes, he had protected me from my stepfather more than once.

I tried not to think about how I wasn't protected when he and I were alone, or how he'd treated Chelsea—his whore. Even his title for her made me ill. As we waited I longed for a phone with the blue dot app. It hadn't been necessary when I'd been the one to wear the necklace, but now, I wanted to know that Chelsea was with Nox. If she and my mother were safe, I could break free.

My fingers trailed the diamond choker around my neck. Panic at the loss of my tracker necklace was suffocating. I reassured myself that it had been the right move. If for any reason Chelsea had been detained along the way, the beacon on the necklace would have led Nox to her.

Shivering, I wrapped my arm around my midsection and turned toward my stepfather as the car approached. "Please tell me about my mother."

"Really, Alexandria?" His warm breath reeked of whiskey as he looked up from his phone. No doubt his time spent with the VIPs in his office had been filled with the best alcohol in the mansion. "Your husband was just arrested and you're asking about your mother. She's probably sleeping peacefully, still detoxing."

"Probably? You don't know? And Bryce and I aren't married. Do you know about my mother for sure?"

Suzanna didn't speak as she turned her attention to Alton.

He shook his head. "Your mother is being taken care of. But, daughter, you're mistaken about your marital status. You were married *yesterday*. Tonight's party had been to announce your surprise nuptials. I just received confirmation. Ralph Porter will have the paperwork drawn up and Judge Townsend will make it all legal." His thin lips formed a strained smile. "Congratulations, Mrs. Spencer. Today is your one-day anniversary."

"I didn't sign anything and neither did Bryce. He's in jail. How do you plan on forging that?" I looked down at his phone. "And do you know why? Why he was arrested?"

"Now that's the question a concerned bride should be asking."

"Tell me about my momma and why you said her presence was no longer possible, and then I'll talk about Bryce."

Patrick had promised that Nox's men were in place. Did this mean that Alton was unaware that she'd been freed, or was she still at Magnolia Woods?

"You promised she'd be with me when…" I hated to say when Bryce and I married, but it was the end to that sentence. "…we married." *Which we haven't done.*

"No. I said it was up to you." He reached again for my arm. "And she wasn't well enough yesterday to attend."

"Yesterday?" Though I struggled, his grip was iron. "Let go of me. I can walk."

He yanked me toward him. "Don't push me, Mrs. Spencer," he threatened. "I'll force you in the damn car and by God, if you don't sign that license, when Adelaide wakes—*if* she wakes—she'll be in indigent care."

"You're a monster."

"Come on, daughter. Do you doubt me?"

My skin crawled with his touch while my stomach twisted at the stench of his breath.

Through it all, it was his threats that propelled me forward. "I don't doubt you. I won't agree to the wedding until I know my mother is well. I won't marry Bryce until she can be with me."

"It's too late," he growled. "As I said, the paperwork is complete. You two were married yesterday."

I sucked in a deep breath, hoping for a way to avoid going to the police station. "I'm not agreeing to anything right now, but..." I motioned toward the sound of the guests. "...even you must see that this is a public relations nightmare."

The limousine finally came to a stop. Though Suzanna began to descend the steps, I continued to speak, "You and Suzanna should go to Bryce. I should try to explain things."

Brantley appeared, opening the rear door.

"Nonsense. The world needs to see Bryce's new wife at his side." With my arm secure in my stepfather's grip, he pulled me forward, following after Suzanna.

Once we reached the driveway and Suzanna stepped into the car, I tried again to think of any way to avoid the limousine. Despite my efforts, my slender heels gave little resistance upon the cobblestones.

"I shouldn't be going. We have guests. Let me explain—"

Alton's grip loosened as we both turned. In a second—or was it longer? Time moved with no sense of reason—Alton and I both pivoted toward the unusual noise.

Other than Brantley, the staff had been sent to their other dimension. We'd been alone, and now we weren't.

Determined footsteps echoed upon the driveway, drowning out the evening noises.

Steady breathing.

A domineering presence.

"Let go of her."

My lungs forgot to breathe. The autumn breeze ceased to blow. The leaves no longer swirled. My heart stilled and the world stopped spinning at the deep, demanding voice.

Only a few feet away stood the most handsome man I'd ever known. The one who owned not only my body but also my soul. I wasn't married to Bryce Spencer. I never could be. Not as long as Lennox Demetri existed. I was his.

"Charli, come here."

My entire body electrified. Even before I had visual confirmation, the moment before he appeared, I knew he was here. I *knew*. In my heart and soul I knew that my Batman had found me, saving me. I'd told him that I wasn't a damsel in distress. I'd resisted his hands-on approach and I'd done my best on my own.

However, as disbelief turned to shock on my stepfather's expression, I wanted to take back everything I'd said.

In that second I welcomed Nox's presence, his demands, and his rescue.

Before I could move, Alton spoke, "Alexandria, get in the car."

I didn't hesitate as I turned and stepped toward Nox. He was there, right in front of me. But before I got my footing, Alton tightened his hold upon my arm.

The next few seconds happened in a strange space-time continuum. I watched as Nox moved. His body became fluid, effortlessly flowing to my side. Simultaneously, Alton let go of me and fell backward against the car, stumbling.

It took a moment to realize what had happened. Nox hit him. Punched him.

"Oh my God," I whispered as my hand covered my mouth. "Oh my God."

As Alton reeled and steadied himself, Brantley's movements caught my attention. Faster than I'd ever seen him move, he reached inside his jacket. In his hand now, reflecting the lights from the mansion, was a gun.

Gasping for breath, I screamed, lunging toward Nox, "No!"

If it had been a movie, it would have all occurred in slow motion. My scream would have been elongated beyond what is humanly possible. The bullet would have been in the camera's focus as it flew through the air while at the same time the world was a blur.

This wasn't a movie. My scream was quick and so was another voice—a new demand.

"Put down the gun, asshole, or die. The choice is yours."

Thankfully, the bullet never left the chamber. Brantley's eyes moved from Nox and me to somewhere behind us.

While Alton steadied himself and rubbed his chin, Nox pulled me close, tucking me safely into his side. If only he had his cape. Then I could wrap myself inside of it and disappear. Instead, I turned to see whose growling voice we'd heard.

"You?" Alton said, glaring toward Isaac. "From Magnolia Woods!"

It took me a second to realize he meant the alias Isaac had assumed—the concerned son of a patient.

"Put the fucking gun down," Isaac repeated, his gun pointed in Alton and Brantley's direction.

"Son, you will regret this," Alton said to Nox. "I'll have you arrested for assault and kidnapping."

"I'm not your son," Nox said. "Be glad you're not unconscious. I did you a favor."

Moving his glare to me, Alton asked, "Alexandria, what are your two questions?"

I didn't answer, but looked up at Nox. "My mom?"

"Trust me." It was all he said, his angry stare never leaving Alton.

My heart nearly seized up at the ultimatum. Trust him. I had and I hadn't. Patrick had said there was a plan. I swallowed my uncertainty and held tighter to the man asking me to do what I'd done more times that I could remember.

"Chelsea?" I asked.

"Yes," Isaac answered.

In their responses, neither man had revealed the meanings. In this new high-stakes game, neither had shown their cards. But in my heart, I knew that Nox and Isaac, and probably Clayton and Deloris too, had done as they'd promised. Despite the hell of the last ten days, the family that I had in Nox had done more for me and those I love than my real family ever would.

The tension that had kept me standing and moving one foot in front of the other drained from my bones, leaving me as limp as the fallen leaves. My knight, my Batman, steadied me as Isaac came to our side.

"One more time," Isaac demanded. "Put the gun down."

"You'll never get away with this," Alton warned. "You won't make it off this property. If you take her, that's kidnapping."

I shook my head. "No, you kidnapped me. He's saving me."

"You should tell this criminal what happened yesterday, *Mrs. Spencer.*"

Nox didn't turn, but tucked against his side, I felt his body stiffen against mine.

I reached for the diamond ring on my left hand and threw it to the ground at Alton's feet. "My name is Miss Collins. Take the damn ring. The farce is over."

"Apparently you don't care about your mother."

Though Brantley had lowered the barrel, the gun was still in his hand.

Nox stepped closer to Alton. "We're leaving. Try to stop us and next time you'll be on the ground."

Through the open door to the limousine, Suzanna's terrified stare penetrated the night. "Alton, Ralph just texted. He's there, but Bryce needs us."

Nox spoke over his shoulder to Isaac, "I thought I told you to stay with her."

"Clayton has her and the car. I missed the shooting in the park. I wasn't missing this one."

"Her?" Alton asked.

Nox's glare was still on Alton and Brantley. "Charli is the rightful heir here. She's not sneaking out the back. We'll leave through the front gate."

"Yes, sir," Isaac said. "I thought you might say that. Clayton can be here in minutes."

Alton stood taller. "You're delusional. How do you think Alexandria will feel when she learns you just lied and will be responsible for her mother's continued illness?"

"Allow my car to enter—now," Nox demanded.

When Alton failed to respond, Nox said one word. "Infidelity."

CHAPTER 5

———•O•———

NOX

INFIDELITY. THE WORD hung suspended in the dense air.

Charli's golden eyes widened in question as she gripped my hand tighter.

"I've never been a client of that damn company," Fitzgerald said.

Was that true? Hadn't Deloris said that his secretary was an employee? Now didn't seem like the time to question. Instead, I said, "Maybe not, but..." I tilted my head toward Spencer's mother. "...her son is."

I turned to the old driver. "Place the damn gun on the ground and call the gate. I have a car waiting." I turned back to Fitzgerald. "If anything happens to Alexandria or to anyone who she cares about, that information will be front-page news. I'm sure it will add nicely to whatever the reason was he was taken away from here in handcuffs."

His face reddened. "How the hell do you even know about the company... unless you're involved too?" Charli's stepfather turned toward her. "I warned you. He's a criminal, just like his father."

"He's not."

An unusual sense of pride washed over me. The emotion was both unexpected and surprisingly welcomed. I squeezed her hand. "Princess, I'd break any law for you. Remember, I'm Batman, and when it comes to comparisons..." I shrugged at my own realization. "...I'll take that one as a compliment."

Holding tightly to Charli's hand as she leaned against me, we all stood and stared in silence waiting for the other to blink. Fuck that. I was leaving with Charli, and I didn't care whose body I left on the cobblestone driveway in my wake. Of course, I wasn't the one holding the gun; it was Isaac. The barrel hadn't strayed from its target of Fitzgerald's driver. Finally, Charli's stepfather whispered to the driver who begrudgingly popped the safety into place, slid his gun back into his holster under his jacket, and spoke into his shoulder.

No one said another word as a big SUV pulled up the driveway. The headlights skirted the scene before it stopped beside the limousine.

"Don't come after me. I'll send for my things," Charli said, her neck and shoulders straight.

"We'll see about that," Fitzgerald said as he crouched down and picked up the diamond ring that Charli had thrown at him.

Her breasts lifted and fell as she took a deep breath. "Sell it and pay for this ridiculous party. I don't care." She turned toward the house and back to Fitzgerald. "Goodbye." With that she let go of my hand and walked toward the rear door of the SUV.

"Alexandria, you'll regret this…"

I didn't listen as his words mixed with the rustle of dead leaves, their sound lost to the Georgia breeze. My mind was too full of her—of my Charli. She was a fucking dynamo, oozing with poise and strength. I may have stormed the castle, but she was the force. All she'd needed was support to stand up to her own devil.

The magnitude of her exit overwhelmed me. Yes, there was the codicil to her grandfather's will, but she didn't know about its existence. In her mind she was walking away from all of this. Forever.

As Clayton stood next to the still-closed door, I reached again for Charli's hand. "Princess, are you sure?"

Turning her face up toward mine, her golden eyes sparkled. "Of what, Nox? That I love you more than I despise this place? Because the answer is yes, and that's a tall order, because I despise this place with every bone in my body."

I nodded to Clayton. It was as he opened the door that her composure disappeared. Her eyes widened and the sparkle turned to moisture. Her hand in mine began to tremble.

"Shhh," I whispered as I helped her into the backseat. Against the far door was Chelsea.

Charli looked up at me, and then her gaze moved behind me. I turned in time to see Patrick obscured by shadows, standing where we'd been. Charli lifted her hand and wiggled her fingers in a small wave.

Once inside, she scooted all the way across and wrapped Chelsea in a hug. "It's over…"

I tried not to eavesdrop as their voices soothed and reassured one another.

Theirs were the only words spoken as Clayton drove us down the long lane back to the main road. With each inch, foot, and yard, I scanned the perimeter, searching the shadows of every tree and the veil of dangling moss. Both Isaac and Clayton were armed. Isaac passed a small revolver to me.

"Safety's on, boss. Just in case."

I nodded as I flipped the safety and held the gun on my lap.

"Nox?" Charli asked, her attention now back on me.

"Princess, I don't trust your stepfather. We're not leaving here without you."

She reached for Chelsea's hand and exhaled, leaning back into the seat and against my shoulder. As she did, the scent of perfume filled my senses and her hair tickled my cheek.

When the large iron gate moved to the side, we all took a deep breath. The open country roads blurred as Clayton sped toward the airport.

It was then that Charli inclined her face toward mine. "Thank you."

"Princess, if you ever get in another car with that man, your ass is mine."

Despite all that had just happened, my Charli was stunning. Having her near me, her hand enclosed in mine, was greater than the high from cold-cocking the guards or even hitting her stepfather. Obviously, I'd only meant to daze him. If I'd wanted him laid out on the ground like his top-notch security, he would have been. I needed him alert to understand that Charli left his clutches of her own free will.

As I held onto her hand, I longed for more. I had barely noticed as we stood outside the mansion, but now with her thigh against mine, her presence electrified each and every nerve. She was a vision. Even under extreme duress, she exuded class and culture. Her dress was elegant but the ivory lace covered up her sexy body. In my imagination, I was ripping off the buttons that lined her side. One by one they fell to the floor until the lace joined the remnants. I'd threatened her ass, but as she stared up at me, all I longed to do was hold her and make her world right.

What had she endured over the last ten days? I needed to know, but that would wait until we were alone.

I leaned close to her slender neck. The choker she wore was made up of diamonds. No doubt it was worth more money than her Infidelity contract, yet I didn't care.

"Take off that necklace. Chelsea has yours."

Her golden eyes peered my way before her fingers untwined from mine and reached for the clasp. The thick band of stones glittered as she dropped it to her lap. Without speaking, Chelsea pulled Charli's necklace from her pocket and placed it in Charli's hand.

As soon as it was secure, Charli looked up at me again with the cutest, shiest grin I'd ever seen. I wanted to take her in my arms and hold her forever, but first, we had some rules to discuss.

Narrowing my gaze, I found my most direct tone. "Rule number one, entering one of that asshole's cars, ever again, is forbidden."

Charli nodded.

"Rule number two, if that necklace ever comes off your neck for any other reason than swimming, you won't be sitting for a week. Is that clear?"

The intelligent response would have been 'Yes, Nox.' A wise person would have sensed my need for control in this out-of-control scenario and bowed to my demand. My Charli wasn't that person. There was no fear or intimidation in her beautiful eyes. On the contrary, there was the spark that my life had missed since the moment she'd been gone. There was a playfulness that knew how to push me, not to anger, but to devotion. Her lips quirked upward.

Alexandria Collins was my drug and I would never again let her go.

Momentarily, her lips brushed mine. With our faces only millimeters apart, she looked me in the eye. "Mr. Demetri, I've missed you and your stupid rules."

The kiss had been shorter than either of us wanted. That too would wait until I had her alone. Her ass, her lips, her entire body were mine for reclaiming.

I tried to concentrate on the subject at hand. "Charli, I understand why you gave the necklace—"

She shook her head. "I don't think you can."

"What?"

She reached for Chelsea's hand and turned back my way. "I have a lot to tell you. Chelsea has things to say too—either to you, Deloris, the assholes at Infidelity who allowed a monster like Bryce to purchase an agreement, or to the police. That's up to her. They're her stories to tell, but Nox, you don't understand. There's no way you could."

My pulse increased as I tried to decipher her meaning. Why would she say I didn't understand? "You wanted to be sure she made it out. She's your friend." I didn't mean to speak about Chelsea as if she wasn't there, but I needed Charli to know that I did get it.

Nevertheless, Charli was my only blue dot.

Charli shook her head. "You just punched my stepfather."

"So?"

"So… you don't know what it's like to be terrified of someone. You're always in control. That's not a bad thing. It's who you are."

Terrified. The word burned like acid in my already-twisted gut.

The SUV was turning. By the lights on the streets, I knew we were back in downtown Savannah. "You're wrong," I corrected.

She didn't speak.

"I fucking know what it's like to be terrified. That's how I felt watching him manhandle you into his car again. I didn't see it the first time, but seeing it earlier tonight, I was petrified."

"And you handled it, because that's who you are. Nox, I love you for that. Imagine not being able to handle it. Not because you don't want to. Not because you're not smart enough or brave enough or even mentally strong enough, but because you're physically outmatched. Imagine knowing that if you're caught leaving the manor, the consequences will be more dire than anything you've ever known or experienced, and you've already lived in hell."

My gaze darted between Charli and Chelsea. Though they were both sitting tall, the ambient light shining through the windows showed Chelsea's cheeks glistening with visible tears. I may be a monster, but her silent crying didn't bother me as much as Charli's words.

They were those of an advocate. She'd make one hell of an attorney one day.

My teeth clenched as the realization struck: Charli wasn't only talking about Chelsea. She was talking about herself as well.

She'd been terrified too.

"What about you? The necklace was for *your* protection—"

"I was safer than Chelsea. That's all I'll say right now. She needed the reassurance that you would be there for her." Charli intertwined our fingers. "I knew you would be for me. I needed to know you would be for her."

I fucking needed to know what that animal did, not only to Chelsea, but also to my Charli. Jail was too good for him.

Before I could ask, Chelsea spoke. "Alex, where was he? I thought he'd be there. Was he in the limousine?"

Charli turned her way. "Oh, you don't know."

Chelsea sucked in a breath. "Know what?"

"The police. They arrested him."

Chelsea's eyes widened with panic. "What? Why? I-I didn't..."

"I don't know," Charli replied. "They never said what the charge was."

My phone buzzed with an incoming call.

"Yes," I answered after reading Deloris's name.

"I'm sending you all a link."

"Where are you?"

"I'm at the airport where Clayton is bringing you. The plane is ready. Watch the news clip and call me back."

I hung up the phone as Clayton handed his phone to Charli and we all opened the link.

I pushed the small triangle. We all did.

It was a local news broadcast.

BREAKING NEWS read the crawl at the bottom of the screen. The video behind the words was an aerial view of Montague Manor. The place was fucking huge. Even on the small screen the guests were visible on the back patio. Those on the lawn were obscured by fog. The blue lights of the police cars flashed as the camera from one of the drones zoomed in on the top of Spencer's head as he was led away from the front door.

BODY FOUND. CARMICHAEL HEIR ARRESTED.

Chelsea and Charli gasped. "Body?" they both questioned.

"Fuck!" I whispered.

I turned up the volume.

"…received a tip from a concerned employee. The Savannah medical examiner is examining the body. No identification has been made; however, unnamed sources within the police department have confirmed that the arrest could be in connection with the disappearance earlier this year of Melissa Summers, Edward Spencer's one-time girlfriend."

I turned from the screen to Charli. One of her hands held Clayton's phone, while the other held tightly to her best friend.

"Nox, call Deloris back. When did they find it? Where did they find it?"

"I was there," Chelsea said. "I was at Carmichael Hall."

I then remembered the telephone call Deloris had recorded and spoke to Charli. "He wanted you there today—this morning, didn't he?" I asked.

Charli's gaze narrowed. "How do you know that?"

"It doesn't matter. But he did, right?"

She nodded. "He did, but I stayed with my mother." Her back straightened. "Where is she?" Then she sucked in a deep breath and turned back to Chelsea. "Oh God, he said he'd make you…" Her voice trailed away.

Chelsea shook her head. "But he didn't. I was all over Savannah doing things for the party. Things Jane asked me to do. Then I went back to Montague."

I swiped my phone. Deloris answered on the first ring, and I put it on speaker.

"You're on speaker. Tell us what you know."

"Nox, my mother?" Charli whispered.

Deloris's voice filled the SUV. "There are members of the Savannah-

Chatham police here. They want to question Miss Moore and Mrs. Spencer."

"What?" Charli said. "Bryce's mother isn't with us."

"You," Deloris said. "They're waiting."

I hung up the call as the name Mrs. Spencer rang in my ears.

"Sir?" Clayton asked. "We can drive to another airport?"

"How do they know Chelsea is with us?" Charli asked.

I reached for Charli's hand. "I don't know. Maybe it was an assumption."

"Different airport?" he asked again.

I shook my head. "No. You heard what we said. We have nothing to hide."

I didn't want to mention my concern, but I needed to. "What if the body has been there for a while? What if it didn't happen recently? Chelsea, how long have you been there, a couple of months?"

Chelsea's head moved back and forth. "I have, but the police have been there multiple times. Wouldn't they have found it before now? Is it her?"

"My mom?" Charli said again.

"She's safe, ma'am," Clayton said.

"Thank God."

"Mr. Demetri took her back to New York. It's been a few hours now."

"Alton must not know." And then she looked up at me. Her brow furrowed. "Mr. Demetri? Your dad has my mom?"

I nodded. "We have a lot to discuss."

Clayton pulled the SUV through the open gate at the airport. The fog from near the manor was gone. We'd driven out of it many miles ago. But as we neared the hangar, an uneasy sense of déjà vu came over me. The blue flashing lights of two police cars illuminated the tarmac. Speaking to the officers was Deloris.

Just before the SUV came to a stop, my phone vibrated. I wasn't the only one to get the text. Pulling my phone from my pocket, I handed it to Charli.

"Look at this, princess. I'll go speak to the officers first."

"No, Deloris said they want to question us." Her rebuttal ended with a gasp.

At the same time, Isaac spoke, "Sir, it's a group text from your father."

"Nox," Charli said, looking up from my phone, "it's my mom."

CHAPTER 6

—●◯●—

OREN

TWO HOURS. I looked down at my watch. The flight plan called for two hours and eight minutes from wheels up to wheels down. It had only been thirty-five minutes and already Eva was leaning over Adelaide and fidgeting with her IV. Though the physician in her refused to tell me her thoughts, her expression and concentration did little to hide her concerns.

A blood pressure cuff was secured around Adelaide's arm and Eva had her stethoscope in her ears, but I wondered how the doctor could possibly hear anything over the roar of the engines.

I contemplated the bar the copilot had offered. A few fingers of whiskey would ease the sharp edge of my anxiety. My pulse raced as the doctor took Adelaide's.

Instead of a drink, I leaned toward Adelaide and rested my hand on the blanket covering her legs. It was the connection that I sought, the one I'd missed. Just touching her calmed my nerves. My thoughts volleyed between elation that we'd rescued her and terror at her condition. At first I'd attributed her movement to the plane, but the longer my hand rested, the more apparent the trembling became.

"She's shaking," I said when Eva removed the earpieces.

One by one, Eva lifted Adelaide's eyelids and shone a light into her eyes. I took a deep breath remembering her eyes, bright and blue like the New York sky. Though it had been a lifetime ago, I recalled the way they stared into mine as we'd made love and the way they'd sparkled as we talked and laughed.

"What are you seeing?" I finally asked.

"Her pupils are dilated."

"Because you're shining a light on them. That's normal."

Eva's bottom lip disappeared as she turned my way. I had a knack for reading people, sensing fear and resolution. Without a word I knew when a man was resolved to his future—or the lack thereof. Carmine once called it a gift. In this moment, I considered it more of a curse. There was more that Eva wasn't saying.

"Talk to me, damn it!" My demand came out louder than I intended.

"Ore-Mr. Ferrari, I'm afraid your wife may be going into shock. Pupils contract to light not dilate. Her pupils have enlarged since my initial exam. The cause could be a combination of the medication and her withdrawals."

"None of that's changed since we took off."

"I'm concerned that the move has been difficult for her."

I sprang the latch on the seatbelt and stood. "No, that's not it. Whatever's happening, make it stop."

Though I'd felt Adelaide's trembling, when I looked down into her face, I looked past her ghostly complexion. She was the woman I loved. It was then I noticed the perspiration dotting her forehead and upper lip. I reached for the blanket and pulled it back.

"Why the hell is she covered if she's too hot?"

Dr. Rossi stood, meeting me face-to-face, and reached for the blanket. "She's not hot. Feel her skin: she's cold. Too cold."

Before I could respond, we both were silenced. The cabin filled with Adelaide's breathing as it sputtered and gagged as if she were gasping for breath.

Eva fell to her knees and placed the stethoscope over Adelaide's chest.

Spinning in place, I pulled at my hair, closed my eyes, and silently prayed, "I know I'm not a good man. I can't change that. I've made deals with the devil, but that's *me*. Please don't take it out on her. She deserves so much more than she's had."

Eva reached for the bag she'd brought onboard. "Her pulse is erratic—quivering. I'm getting more saline to help flush her system. Search the cabinets for an AED, just in case."

My eyes wildly roamed the interior of the cabin. "AED? The defibrillator thing?"

"Yes. Now. It's better to be safe."

I opened cabinet after cabinet, cursing myself for not being better prepared. I should have called one of those medical transports. Fuck, I'd spend the rest of my life in prison as long as Adelaide was all right.

The planes we contracted were top of the line: Cessnas, Beechcraft Bonanzas, and even Learjets for transatlantic flight. The service was reliable and always at the ready. The interiors of the different models varied with one common denominator—luxurious. At this second, I didn't give a damn about luxury. We could be flying in a tin can. I just wanted to find the AED. There had to be one, didn't there?

As I searched, I found that many of the cabinets were empty—for storage, I presumed. Near the wet bar, most of the cupboards were filled with trays containing packets of snacks, sweet or salty. They were both there. The way each one was sealed, they probably had enough preservatives to last another ten years. I continued to open each little door.

I finally found what I'd been searching for in a shiny cabinet with a gold handle under the bar. *AED* was printed on the exterior of a red nylon bag. "Here it is."

As I turned back around, I gasped. Adelaide's nightgown was opened and her breasts were exposed. Eva again placed the stethoscope against her chest. I held my breath as I watched, uncertain of what I was seeing. Was her chest moving?

Paralyzed, I remained motionless, praying that I would see movement. My feet forgot how to step as the plane glided through the night sky. I was transfixed by the vision of my own life coming to an end. Because if the woman on the couch died, I would too.

As the possibility of losing Adelaide forever began to seep into my consciousness, my own blood pressure skyrocketed. My heart pumped forcefully, ready to do the job for both of us. Regret and anger swirled within me, becoming the accelerants racing through my system.

There were too many years that we'd missed and too many apologies to ever voice. But that wasn't what gave my feet permission to move. It was the rage growing within me. It wasn't directed at the woman fighting for her life or even at myself. While the scene before me tinged with red, I made myself a vow. I would not rot in prison for kidnapping one of the only women I'd ever loved. Hell no. I'd walk into prison with my head held high for the uncontested murder of Alton Fitzgerald.

"Oren!"

Had Eva been speaking?

I snapped back to reality.

"Bring it here and look for an oxygen tank."

"Is she…? Can you…?"

She extended her hand. "Give me the AED. I can't detect a pulse." When I didn't move, she repeated herself louder and with even more authority. She was the doctor and taking charge.

Her tone was a technique I'd used myself, but not one I could recall having been used on me. I'd always been the one in control. Not now.

"Concentrate. Bring me the AED and look for the oxygen."

"But you said the FAA—"

I slowly moved forward, handing Eva the bag.

"You were right. Every plane has emergency oxygen. On a plane this size…" She continued speaking as she hurriedly pulled a box with wires from the red zippered bag. "…it could be as simple as a small tank and mask. Keep looking. Ask the pilots if you have to."

I can't detect a pulse.

The words repeated on a loop, growing louder in my mind despite my attempt to silence them.

With shaking hands, I reached for the cabin's ceiling. It was a futile attempt to steady myself and halt the growing nausea. Bile and acid bubbled from the depths of my stomach as Eva untangled the contents of the nylon bag. At the end of wires connected to the box she unsheathed two large pads, stickers really, and placed one on Adelaide's side and the other above her breast. It was all happening merely a few feet away, but somehow I'd developed tunnel vision. With each second the tunnel grew longer, taking Adelaide and Dr. Rossi farther and farther away.

The box began to speak. "Assessing patient. Stand clear."

Eva sat back on her heels allowing the AED to do its job.

"Shock needed."

I held my breath.

As a high-pitched whine filled the cabin, the doctor's eyes met mine. "Find the oxygen."

I nodded, tearing my gaze away from the scene. The box's voice joined the loop reminding me that Adelaide's pulse had stopped. Together they were a sickening chorus, mocking my vain attempts at good.

Numbers filled the air as the pitch grew even higher. "Shocking patient."

It was an audible zap. The muscles in my throat clinched, keeping the bile at bay as Adelaide's body jumped. I hadn't seen it, but I'd heard it, her weight falling back to the leather seat. It was worse than any TV show or movie as we waited for the box to reassess.

My teeth ached as I clenched my jaw, afraid to turn back around, afraid to know what Eva and the box were doing. Fuck, I'd been around death more times than I could count. But this was different, even different than with Angelina.

My ex-wife had fought a good fight. I hadn't been with her as she took her last breath. The last time I'd seen her, we'd talked. I spoke more than she, but in her eyes I saw her answers and her truths. She'd made peace with her life and her death. Though losing her too young left a hole that can never be filled, knowing that she was ready for what awaited her gave me comfort.

Adelaide wasn't ready. I'd seen her on the footage from Magnolia Woods. The last time she'd truly been conscious, she'd pleaded with Jane to speak with Alexandria. Adelaide Montague had more life to live. This wasn't right.

"Help me move her to the floor."

"The oxygen…"

"I need her on a hard surface to do CPR."

"CPR?" I asked as I cradled Adelaide's slack body and moved her to the floor.

"Yes, the shock didn't work."

I took a step back as Dr. Rossi fell to her knees. With her hands locked she leaned over Adelaide and pushed on her chest, counting aloud. I contemplated helping, but didn't know what to do. I felt completely helpless as the box began to speak again.

"Stop CPR. Analyzing."

My knees weakened and chin dropped to my chest with the sickening realization that both of Alexandria's parents would be dead because of me. The love of my son's life would hate me forever. Why shouldn't she? It wouldn't only be her: Lennox would hate me, too. Moisture that refused to stay contained trickled down my cheeks as I imagined my confession.

Each of their deaths had been different, yet I was the common link. Russell had been business—duty—and Adelaide's was unintentional. Yet if the move from Magnolia Woods was the trigger, it was my doing.

Could I ever make our children believe that if I'd known, I never would have moved Adelaide? I never would have forced this trip.

The cabin again filled with the high pitch.

This time I watched as her petite body jumped, landing upon the hard floor.

The doctor and I both sat motionless, waiting for the box to talk.

"Shock ineffective. Begin CPR."

Eva turned my way. "Come here. You do the chest compressions while I administer epinephrine."

I didn't know what the medicine she mentioned would do, nor did I know what I was doing. Nevertheless, I did as she instructed. Kneeling where Eva had been, I held my hands together and placed them over Adelaide's sternum. Before I compressed, I turned to the doctor. "I don't want to hurt her."

Her expression was solemn. "She can't feel it." Eva reached for my shoulder. "Fast and hard. She needs you to do this."

I did as I'd seen, using my own weight to depress her breastbone. I understood the science, the necessity to compress the heart muscle enough to express the blood and give her body the oxygen it needed. But as my body pushed, noises like cracking cartilage and breaking bone filled my ears. With each snap and crack, the bile I'd tried to hold back rushed upward.

Swallowing quickly and repeatedly, I pressed with all my might, bouncing up and down as Eva filled a syringe.

My count had only gotten to the number ten when Eva injected the contents of the syringe into the port on Adelaide's IV and the box spoke again.

"Stop CPR. Analyzing."

In the few seconds that followed I recalled my vow. Alexandria could hate me forever, because it wouldn't only be her father and mother whose deaths would be on my hands. It would be her stepfather's too. Singlehandedly, I'd be responsible for the loss of her entire family.

We both scooted back as the high-pitched noise rose higher and longer, echoing throughout the cabin. Again Adelaide's body flopped. I poised myself to continue the CPR. The procedure was more taxing than I'd imagined, but I didn't give a damn. I'd keep doing it until we landed if I needed to.

"Shock successful. Monitor respirations."

My eyes opened wider as I looked to Dr. Rossi. The box had spoken a different message.

"What does that mean?"

She lowered the stethoscope to Adelaide's chest as her facade shattered and she let out a long sigh. "She has a heartbeat." The doctor inclined her head lower, her cheek near Adelaide's face.

Without missing a beat, Eva plugged Adelaide's nose, tilted her chin upward, and blew into her mouth. Two breaths and she'd stop. With each breath Adelaide's chest rose and fell.

"Go get the oxygen."

"I-I didn't find it."

"Look!" she shouted just before her lips again covered Adelaide's.

Near the front of the cabin was a slender closet. If I'd been thinking in my right mind, I'd have assessed that it would be the obvious location for oxygen. After all, the tank was tall and slender, a green cylinder. Attached and wound together in a plastic bag was a clear mask with a big ball and plastic tubing. The cylinder was on a stand with wheels and a handle, similar to a one-handled wheelbarrow.

As quickly as I could, I moved all of it to Dr. Rossi. She was no longer breathing into Adelaide. Instead she concentrated on listening with the stethoscope. I waited until she removed the earpieces.

She reached for the plastic bag and freed the mask. As she placed it over Adelaide's mouth and nose, she said. "She's breathing on her own, but the oxygen will help. We should get her back on the couch. It's safer in the air. We can seatbelt her in. Her heartbeat is steady."

I nodded. "Do you want me to lift her?"

"Yes. Let's get her secured."

For minutes upon minutes the doctor adjusted the IV fluid, only to listen and readjust. It wasn't until she was satisfied that we both sat back in our seats and I looked her in the eye.

"There aren't words. I wouldn't have known what to do."

Her cheek rose in an uneven smile. "I became a doctor because saving lives has never been the focus of our family." She shrugged. "I thought maybe it would be good if the next generation changed that."

I remembered hearing how Eva's father had thought it unnecessary for his daughter to attend medical school. That hadn't lessened his pride in her success.

"You've made this member of the family proud and thankful."

She looked at her watch. "We should be landing in another hour. Tell me you have an ambulance scheduled to meet us at the airport."

"I do."

"I'd like to stay with her for the next twenty-four hours, at least. If that's all right with you, Mr. Ferrari?" Her smile lifted both of her cheeks with the use of my fake name.

"My wife and I would appreciate that."

CHAPTER 7

⬤O⬤

CHARLI

THOUGH THE PEOPLE on the tarmac were waiting, we all sat transfixed, reading the text message from Oren.

"LANDED. SHE HAD A DIFFICULT TIME IN FLIGHT. I'LL EXPLAIN LATER, BUT FOR NOW SHE'S STABLE AND EN ROUTE."

Dread filled my stomach as Chelsea reached for my trembling hand. "What does it say?"

I looked to Nox who'd been reading the screen with me.

"It says she's stable," he said.

"Your dad said she had a difficult time during the flight," I refuted. "What does that mean?"

"She's stable," Isaac repeated.

"Is she with someone, like, is there a doctor?"

"Yes, princess," Nox said, kissing my cheek. "She has better care than she had at Magnolia Woods."

I took a deep breath and tried to concentrate on the positive. I wanted to ask more, but Nox was no longer looking at me, or the phone. His attention had moved to the scene outside the window.

I turned that way too, noticing a police officer walking toward the SUV.

"Sir," Isaac asked, "do you want me to—"

"No," Nox interrupted, opening the door. He tilted his head toward his phone still in my grasp. "Keep that in case my dad texts again."

I nodded. The loss of his warm leg against mine combined with the whoosh of cool evening air brought on a shiver. I scooted toward him.

He reached for my knee. "No. Stay in here until we get you."

"But…"

"Princess, I love you. Now is not the time to argue."

It wasn't Nox's tone or even his words. It was the determination in his light blue eyes that kept me silent. In this frenzied scenario, he was telling me to trust him. Though his demand was similar to the ones Alton had made, telling me not to fight his proclamations, Nox's intent was completely different.

Taking a deep breath, I nodded and reached for his hand. "I love you too. Please don't get arrested."

"I don't intend to." With that, he and Isaac stepped from the SUV and closed the doors.

I leaned my head back against the seat and took in the scene. Inside the car, Clayton stayed at the ready, still in the driver's seat with the engine running. Chelsea squeezed my hand. For a few moments, we all sat mute, watching through the windows as the silent movie played out in front of us.

Beyond the tinted glass, blue lights continued to swirl, giving the tarmac a classic colorless hue. In this scene, the police cars were merely props as Nox and Isaac approached the officer. With Nox's suit coat missing, his white shirt glowed with the lights of the cruisers.

Their heads moved as if they were speaking, yet we couldn't hear their words. My eyes widened as Isaac pulled back his jacket and revealed his holstered gun. I expected him to hand it to the policeman or for the policeman to take it. Neither occurred. I looked toward the floorboard, wondering what Nox had done with the gun he'd been holding.

"What do you think is happening?" Chelsea whispered.

I shook my head. "I can't even guess."

"What if they ask us about Melissa?"

I shrugged. "I'll be honest. You should too."

"Alex, I've already lied to them. I told them that Bryce and I were a couple when we weren't."

My stomach churned. "If I were your attorney, I'd advise you to be honest now. This isn't just a missing person. Chels, the news broadcast said they found a body."

"Can I... will I... get in trouble?"

One semester of law school hardly made me the best one to give advice. "I think you should talk to a real attorney before you say much more." I looked her in her hazel eyes. "I'm so sorry you're messed up in this."

"I know he's capable..." Her voice was low, barely a whisper.

Letting go of her hand, I wrapped my arm around her shoulder.

"I-I," she began, her voice cracking. "I-I just want to leave."

"Neither one of you is going back."

Both of our faces—Chelsea's and mine—popped up as the two of us stared toward the front seat. Clayton's gaze met mine in the rearview mirror.

"Is that why you haven't turned off the car?" I asked.

"Ma'am, I have my orders."

For a moment I wondered who'd given Clayton his orders, and then, I didn't care. In the last two hours Nox and his team had done everything I'd needed. My momma was stable, though I didn't know what had happened. She was out of Magnolia Woods and in New York with a doctor and Oren Demetri—another connection that was still a mystery. Chelsea and I were away from Bryce and hopefully on our way to New York.

Outside the vehicle, Deloris was now beside Nox and Isaac as two officers continued to speak with them. There was a third man standing back from the discussion. By his lanyard I believed he too was with the police. He was the only one not in uniform. Every now and then, the officer who seemed to be doing most of the talking would point toward our car.

My breathing hitched as that same officer walked beside Nox and came closer to the SUV. Pushing a button, Clayton lowered the front-seat passenger's window.

"Alex and Chelsea," Nox said, coming close to the open window. "This officer needs to speak with you."

My heart beat faster as I deciphered his unspoken meaning. He'd called me Alex. That meant the policemen knew who I was. I nodded toward Chelsea. "Remember what I said."

The door opened and we stepped outside. My party dress was little covering for the cooled night breeze. Immediately I wrapped my arms around myself as goose bumps prickled my skin.

"Mrs. Spencer?" the officer asked.

"No, Officer, I'm Miss Collins, Alexandria Collins."

Under the tall tarmac lights, he eyed me up and down. "You appear to be dressed for a wedding."

"For a party, actually." My teeth chattered. "I was told you wanted to speak to me. I'm assuming it wasn't about my attire."

"No, ma'am. We need to speak to you about your husband."

"Officer, I'm not married."

"She's not—"

"Ma'am," the officer interrupted both of us as Nox and I spoke simultaneously. "He's very upset, demanding that you…" He turned toward Chelsea. "…both of you come to the police station."

It was then that he took a step back and scanned Chelsea. "Ma'am, are you Miss Chelsea Moore?"

"Yes."

"What happened to you? Did someone harm you?"

"Do you have the authority to stop these two women from leaving Savannah?" Deloris asked.

"Not at this time, but the court can demand they return. Wouldn't it be easier to stay?"

It would, but I didn't want to. I turned to Nox. "I want to leave. If I have to come back, I'll come back."

"Mrs. Spencer," the officer said, "we'll need your contact information."

I wasn't willing to argue my name any longer, but unfortunately, I didn't know my own contact information. I wasn't sure where we were going and the only phone in my handbag was the one Alton gave me. I didn't know the number. I turned toward Deloris. "Can you please provide him a way to reach both of us?"

Deloris nodded.

He spoke again. "It wouldn't take long, if you would reconsider. Your husband has been very insistent."

"Officer, for the last time, I didn't marry Edward Spencer. Besides, the last I heard, the last I witnessed, he was being arrested. How can he possibly be making demands of the Savannah-Chatham police?"

"It's that there is press. Your father—"

I stood taller. "Officer..." I looked to the pin above his badge. "...Michaels, the man you're referring to is my stepfather, not my father. I'm not married and even if I were, I'm an adult and capable of deciding where I will and won't go. Right now, since you obviously don't have the legal ability to retain me, I plan to accompany my friends onto that plane." I motioned toward the waiting craft. "I appreciate your position, but I am leaving Savannah of my own free will and will voluntarily return when I must."

Nox moved behind me. "If there isn't anything else..."

"We're paying the pilots, and this discussion is costing us by the minute," Deloris added.

Nox's hand settled in the small of my back as he led me toward the plane's steps.

It was as my thin heel touched the second stair that the gentleman with the lanyard who'd stayed back came forward. "Mr. Demetri?"

We both stilled.

"Yes?" Nox replied.

"Sir, Mrs. Spencer—or Miss Collins, whoever you are, ma'am—is right. We cannot stop her or Miss Moore from leaving; however, you may not leave."

"What?"

"Sir, there has just been a warrant signed by the judge." He took a step back. "Come down the stairs peacefully."

"On what grounds?" Deloris asked.

"Mr. Lennox Demetri, you are under arrest."

"No!" I reached for Nox's hand and turned toward the police. "For what? He's innocent." As I spoke I looked at the hand in my grasp. In the car I'd noticed that Nox's knuckles were swollen and lacerated. I doubted that it happened with the one punch he'd given Alton, but nevertheless, it could be used as evidence.

"Princess," Nox said, "go with Deloris. There's someone who needs you."

My momma.

The thought tore at my heart. She was stable. That was what the text said. I couldn't... I wouldn't make this decision again.

My head moved from side to side as tears filled my eyes. "I need you." Turning toward the police. "Please, I'm Alexandria Montague Collins. Surely that means something. I'll personally vouch for this man. He's innocent of whatever charges my stepfather wants to drum up."

The man with the lanyard removed the gun from his holster. "Mr. Demetri, step down from the plane."

Nox pulled me close until our lips touched. The connection created a peaceful stillness within the eye of a hurricane. All around us the perilous winds blew, destroying lives with their vicious lies and betrayal, yet with just the two of us, the world was right. As our lips separated, he said, "Go."

"No. I won't leave without you. Not again."

We both took a step down.

As soon as Nox's shoes hit the tarmac, the officer who'd been speaking with him earlier came forward with a pair of handcuffs. The pressure in my chest was suffocating. In the course of a little over two hours, I'd watched two of the men in my life be handcuffed and taken away.

"Mr. Demetri," Officer Michaels began, "you have the right..."

I reached for Nox's arm. "No! Please!"

It was Deloris who grabbed my hand as the Miranda rights continued. "Alex, come up the stairs now."

I'd been strong too long. I didn't want to be strong any longer. My knees buckled and chest heaved. "No!"

All three officers escorted Nox toward one of the waiting cars as Isaac reached for my hands. "Ma'am, I'll stay here in Savannah with him. We'll pay the bond and have him in New York before you wake."

My head continued to shake. I didn't doubt Isaac or Deloris. I just didn't want to leave Nox. "I'm a Montague. I should stay. I can help him."

Isaac spoke softly, "Ma'am, go to your mother."

"Alex," Deloris said, "we need to get you out of here. Don't you see? This is all a ploy to get you to stay."

I shook my head and swallowed my tears. "But…"

It was then my gaze met Nox's. As he ducked his head to enter the backseat of one of the cars, we connected again. Though his lips never moved, I heard his plea: "trust me, princess. I'll come back to you."

I gave into the pressure. The world lost its tilt. Lost its color. Lost its sound. A sob escaped my throat as I reached for the railing. My bones were no longer rigid. I sank to the stair. The movie we'd watched was over. The blue lights disappeared as the police cars drove away.

"Oh my God. They took him!" My words were barely audible between sobs.

The rest of my party was functioning—moving and talking—as my face fell to my knees.

"Isaac," Deloris said, "take the SUV. Go." She took charge, giving orders and typing on her phone. Chelsea was beside me and Clayton was coming closer. Yet my life was incomplete.

"Ma'am," Isaac asked, kneeling before me. "Do you need help to the plane?"

I reached again for his hand as my tear-covered face met his. "Please stay with him as close as you can. I don't trust my stepfather. He's up to something. What charge? Find out. Oh, God, Isaac, please." I looked at Deloris. "Do you know?"

She pursed her lips. "At this moment, I can't venture to guess."

If I didn't know better, I'd say there was a hint of unusual concern in her voice.

My legs wobbled as I forced myself to stand, to move, to reach the top of the steps. This time I was leading the parade. In seconds Deloris, Clayton, Chelsea, and I were all in the cabin. The luxurious interior meant nothing as I rushed toward a window. Placing the palm of my hand against the glass I searched for the police cars, for my love, for my life, but everything was gone.

"Alex, you need to sit."

I hadn't noticed that the door had been shut or that everyone else was seated.

"How?" I asked Deloris. "How can you leave him? You're supposed to take care of him!"

She shook her head. "I thought they were after you, trying to make you stay. When they arrived, I regretted sending you the news video. Shock would have been your best reaction." She leaned forward. "I also tried to convince them that you're not married." She paused. "You aren't, are you?"

"No!"

"It didn't occur to me that the entire scenario was a ploy."

"A ploy?"

"It was a diversion," Clayton said, the two of them seated across from Chelsea and me. "They were keeping us here until the warrant for Mr. Demetri was signed."

I closed my eyes and fell back against the seat. "How does he always win?"

Deloris reached for my knee. "The war isn't over."

CHAPTER 8

—●○●—

NOX

MY GAZE MET Charli's only briefly as the policeman guided me into the backseat of his car. Guided was a kind way to say that he pushed. That wasn't my concern. Connecting with the golden-eyed love of my life and making sure she was safely out of Savannah was.

"Go!" I silently willed. "Get out of here. Do it before they suck you back in!" Though the words had never left my lips, I sent them with all the urgency I could muster.

Closing my eyes, I recounted the devastation in her expression and anguish in her tone.

Fuck!

We were so fucking close. Two more minutes and the plane would have been moving. We would have been gone.

Then it hit me. The police knew they couldn't keep Charli or Chelsea here. It was all a sham, a stall.

My shoulders ached at the pressure on my wrists as the police car bounced along the Savannah roads.

I willed my muscles to relax, to not fight the handcuffs. I'd have them off soon enough.

My mind filled with everything I knew and all we'd learned. If the two officers in the front seat spoke, I wasn't listening.

The memory that fought to consume my thoughts was of Charli. I'd had her in my grasp, feeling her warmth next to me, inhaling the scent of her perfume, and holding her hand in mine. I exhaled, pushing those thoughts away as the car bounced along Savannah's roads. I needed to concentrate. What was the charge?

I assumed it was battery. I'd punched Alton Fitzgerald. I expected more of a fight from him at the estate. That wasn't the way he played. He'd never make it in an octagon. His technique was slimy and backhanded. Give us a little taste of freedom and pull it all away.

I reached for my own fingers and rubbed. My hand was obviously injured, not severely, but my knuckles were scraped. It could be used as evidence. More than likely the manor had surveillance footage of me punching Fitzgerald. I wouldn't and couldn't deny the altercation. The guards, I could. Without proof, there was no way I'd admit to hitting them.

After what seemed like forever, the police car pulled into the back of the police station. I deduced our location by the chain-link fence and multitude of police cars as well as the crowd of people near the front. Thankfully, I didn't appear to be the main attraction.

No one outside the fence seemed to care as the two officers escorted me up a ramp and through back doors. As a new officer booked me, I took in the scene. My location was relatively isolated, yet I could hear the buzz.

Melissa Summers.

Edward Spencer.

"What the hell is going on?" I asked as they took my final photograph.

"You'll learn more as soon as the detective comes to question you."

I tilted my head toward the large room of desks filled with people. "I mean over there. It seems like a busy Saturday night."

The officer led me by the arm. "It's not like we never have murders. We do." He leaned closer. "But this is a big deal. The FBI is here. It's a shit show."

The handcuffs were gone. They'd come off during the booking. Unceremoniously, the officer deposited me in a small room with a metal table and four chairs. "The detective from the scene will be in here in a few minutes to ask you some questions."

"I refuse to answer any questions until my attorney arrives." I knew it was the right move; nevertheless, I wondered when that would be. Demetri Enterprises had a slew of attorneys, none of whom were in Savannah, Georgia.

"Mr. Demetri, we've been informed that your counsel is on his way."

Truly all I wanted was to hear the charge, make a plea, and pay my bail. "After he arrives, when can I see the judge? I have places to go."

"I wouldn't hold your breath. More than likely your case won't be heard until morning. It's already after midnight, the detective needs to question you, and as you saw, this place is hopping with a case much bigger than yours." And then he was gone, behind the solid door. I'd watched enough crime shows to guess the large mirrored surface was really a two-way window. Did anyone ever not know that?

After midnight. Really?

I couldn't even remember what time it was when we drove away from Montague Manor. The whole night was a blur of scenes like pieces of a puzzle that didn't quite fit. I looked to my watch, but it was gone. The policeman had taken that and most of my other personal belongings during the booking. Though they hadn't taken it, I didn't have my phone either. The last time I had it, I'd handed it to Charli.

I didn't want to make a call—I was confident Deloris was on this. What I wanted was to open the necklace app, to see Charli's blue dot flying toward New York. If I could be reassured that she'd done as I wanted, I could concentrate on the shitstorm around me.

Just then, the door opened and I stood, stunned and surprised that I recognized the first man to enter. I'd spoken with him only a few days before.

"Mr. Demetri."

I extended my hand. "Mr. Crawford. I didn't expect you."

He tilted his head to the left. Beside him was a tall man with dark skin and intelligent eyes. "This is Daryl Owen."

We shook hands.

"As you may recall," Stephen Crawford said, "I'm a law student, not an attorney, yet my new internship is with the practice of Preston, Madden, and

Owen here in Savannah. When I received the call from your assistant, Mrs. Witt, I called Mr. Owen, one of the partners. He agreed to take your case."

"Mr. Demetri," Mr. Owen said.

"Lennox," I corrected. "Thank you, Mr. Owen. I appreciate your coming out at this time of night."

The two men sat across from me at a small metal table.

"I'll be frank," Mr. Owen said. "Before the detective comes in, you should know that aggravated battery, in the state of Georgia, faces between one and twenty years in prison and a fine up to $100,000. No one has claimed that you used a firearm, which is in your favor."

"Aggravated battery? I hadn't been told my charge."

"They read you your rights?"

"Yes."

He nodded and jotted down a few notes. "The detective is going to ask where you were this evening at approximately nine-thirty?"

"I'm not sure of the exact time, but I was at Montague Manor this evening. There was a big party."

"Were you on the guest list?"

I smirked. "Most certainly, I was not."

"Yet you were on private property?"

"I was."

"Lennox," Mr. Owen said, "we need you to be one hundred percent honest with us."

"I am."

"Why were you at Montague Manor?"

"To rescue my girlfriend."

"Your girlfriend?"

"Yes."

Mr. Owen and Stephen exchanged looks.

"Would your girlfriend be Mrs. Alexandria Spencer?"

The muscles in my neck tightened. "No. My girlfriend is Miss Alexandria Collins."

Stephen opened a folder he'd placed on the table and retrieved a paper. Sliding it across the table, he said, "We wanted you to see this before the detective came in. Would this be the signature of your girlfriend?"

I bit the inside of my cheek as I read. Starting at the top, it read:

State of Georgia, County of Chatham. To any Clergy or any other person authorized to solemnize: You are hereby authorized and permitted to join the persons named below in matrimony.

Edward Bryce Carmichael Spencer and Alexandria Charles Montague Collins according to the Constitution and Laws of this State, and for doing so this shall be your sufficient...

I scanned down.

I hereby Certify, That Edward Bryce Carmichael Spencer and Alexandria Charles Montague Collins were joined together in matrimony on this 6th day of November...

My stomach knotted as I read yesterday's date. Wait, it was now after midnight. That made it not yesterday, but two days ago.

The officiant named was Keith Townsend. It contained the court's seal, and under his signature were both Edward's and Charli's signatures.

Taking a deep breath, I pushed the paper back across the table and looked Mr. Owen in the eyes. "I understand how that may look, but I promise you, they are *not* married. That's not her signature."

"And you know that because...?"

"Because she told me and I believe her."

The door opened and the detective from the scene came in.

"Mr. Demetri, do you remember me? I'm Detective Holden."

I nodded.

"I heard the answer regarding the marriage license of Edward Spencer and Alexandria Collins. Tell me, how do you explain her signature on this license dated yesterday?"

I didn't look at Mr. Owen nor did I correct Detective Holden on the number of days since the signature. I looked directly at Stephen Crawford and said, "I think it was forged just like many other signatures that I've seen recently."

"What other signatures?" Detective Holden asked.

"Detective, how is that relevant to the charges against my client?" Mr. Owen asked.

Detective Holden pulled the empty chair away from the table, flipped it around so he was straddling the back, and sat. "Well, it appears as though, despite your assault, Mr. Fitzgerald has graciously agreed to offer you a deal."

"A warrant has been issued," Mr. Owen said. "The ball's no longer in Mr. Fitzgerald's court."

The detective shrugged. "True, but he can decide to drop the charges and refuse to testify on behalf of the DA. I'm sure the state of Georgia will take Mr. Fitzgerald's recommendation very seriously. They're a little overwhelmed at this time with other issues, as is Mr. Fitzgerald."

Mr. Owen lifted his hand, silencing my rebuttal. "What does he propose?"

"Mr. Fitzgerald agreed not to pursue the charges of aggravated battery if you agree to honor the marriage of his daughter and accept the limitations set forth in a restraining order restricting your contact with Mrs. Spencer."

I shook my head.

"Mr. Demetri, we should talk about this offer," Mr. Owen said.

"Are you representing me or Mr. Fitzgerald?"

"You, sir."

"First, someone tell me who I supposedly assaulted."

"Mr. Fitzgerald," Detective Holden said. "At this time we're waiting on the video evidence; however, he does have the contusion to support his claim." He looked at my hands resting on the table's surface. "And I will recommend photographs of your hand."

I looked down and shrugged. "Yard work. I work in an office. My hands are soft."

"Mr. Demetri…" Darryl Owen began.

"No. Tell the all-powerful Alton Fitzgerald that I'll take the charge. I'll pay the bail and he can take his offer and shove it up his ass." I leaned forward as my palm slapped the metal table. "Oh, and tell him that I won't be the one contesting this marriage; his stepdaughter will. I'll be the one standing by her side, right by her side, as she hands him his ass in front of a judge and on the front page of every newspaper."

"Mr. Demetri?" the detective asked.

I leaned back and looked at my attorney. "He was manhandling Alexandria. He was forcing her into a car where she didn't want to go. If you have video footage proving his accusation, you'll also have footage of his assault. Let him know: I'll encourage his stepdaughter to press charges."

Though Daryl Owen seemed displeased with my outburst, Stephen's smile grew larger.

"So you're admitting to battery?" Holden asked.

"My client has not admitted to anything except rescuing his girlfriend."

"The wife of another man."

Though I was certain the vein on my forehead was ready to burst, I swallowed my retort.

"Mr. Owen, there are *multiple* charges," Detective Holden continued. "It wasn't only Mr. Fitzgerald who was assaulted tonight on the grounds of Montague Manor. Two of his guards were found unconscious. One was bound." He turned toward me. "You wouldn't know anything about those men, would you, Mr. Demetri?"

I shrugged. "It was a big party. I assume you've questioned each and every one of the guests? I saw a few who looked pretty shady."

"What evidence do you have connecting my client to any of these charges?" Mr. Owen asked.

"He was there. He admitted that."

"Circumstantial," Stephen said. "So were over a hundred other people."

"He just admitted to rescuing a woman from Mr. Fitzgerald, the CEO of Montague Corporation and the owner of the private property where he trespassed. The same Mr. Fitzgerald who was assaulted."

"There was no admission. At the most you have circumstantial evidence for simple battery. My client can post bond and be out of here in less than an hour."

"We're getting the video footage from the mansion."

Mr. Owen nodded. "Fine, and when you do, be sure to watch for the evidence that my client mentioned—that against Mr. Fitzgerald. You heard Mr. Demetri: Miss Collins could very easily follow through on her charges."

"And let him know," I said, "that she will also be filing forgery charges for falsifying her signature on a legal document."

Detective Holden stood and pushed the chair back under the table.

"I'll speak to Mr. Fitzgerald's attorney and be back with you."

"Mr. Demetri," Stephen asked, "are you able to post bond tonight if necessary?"

"Yes."

The detective stopped with his hand on the doorknob. "You were at Montague Manor all evening?"

I shrugged. "I'm not sure of the exact time."

"Were you there by eight o'clock?"

"Detective," Mr. Owen said, "why are you asking?"

He looked at me. "Do you know Mrs. Spencer's mother?"

"I don't know a Mrs. Spencer," I replied.

"Mr. Demetri, what do you know about Mrs. Fitzgerald?"

Stephen's gaze met mine.

"I know she's been ill and her daughter's been very concerned. That's why she came back to Savannah."

"Yet she was willing to leave Savannah with her mother in grave condition?"

"She was willing to go to our home and away from Mr. Fitzgerald." I squared my shoulders. "Between Miss Collins and myself, we're capable of affording her transportation to visit her mother as often as necessary."

The detective nodded as he opened the door.

Nearly an hour later, Detective Holden returned. "Mr. Owen, Mr. Crawford, if your client will agree to an off-the-record conversation, perhaps we can get this unfortunate situation resolved?"

Mr. Owen looked my direction and back to the detective. "Off-the-record conversation with whom?"

"A private, off-the-record conversation with Mr. Fitzgerald."

Mr. Owen shook his head. "Lennox, I would advise against this."

"Detective, can you guarantee this is off the record?"

"Yes."

"Lennox…"

"Gentlemen, please step outside for a moment. I would be happy to speak with Mr. Fitzgerald."

CHAPTER 9

CHARLI

IT WAS ALMOST three in the morning by the time we pulled up to the house in Rye. Exhaustion had taken over long ago. My body and mind were running on adrenaline and even that had begun to wane.

"Alex, do you need me to go in with you?"

I squinted my eyes, trying to understand Deloris's question. "You're not staying here?"

"I can but I'd like to go home."

The door to the house opened as Silvia stood, wrapped in a robe.

I forced a smile. "I guess I never think of you as having your own place."

"Since you've come along, I seem to see it less and less."

"Go," I said as Clayton opened the car door. The offending wind reminded me that I was no longer in Georgia. Despite the onslaught of goose bumps, Silvia's tired, welcoming smile filled me with warmth. After Chelsea and I were out of the car, I turned back to Deloris. "We'll be fine. Besides, Nox is on his way."

We'd all received a text from Isaac just after we'd landed. We didn't know the particulars, only that the charges had been dropped and Nox and Isaac were New York bound.

As we started to walk toward the open door, I added, "Thank you,

Deloris, and I'm sorry."

"Sorry?" she asked.

"That I've kept you away from your home." I tilted my head. "Why did you come all the way out here if you're going back to the city?"

"I promised Lennox I'd get you to this property. I wasn't stopping until you were here. Go see your mom."

"Clayton?" I asked.

"He's driving me back. He'll be here tomorrow and soon Lennox and Isaac will be too. Don't worry. You're well protected."

My lungs filled with the cold night air as I scanned the grounds around the driveway and front of the house. Images of men in black clothing hiding behind trees came to mind. No doubt, delirium had begun to set in. Shaking my head, I stepped inside. As soon as I did, Silvia shut the door and wrapped her arms around me in a welcoming embrace. "Alex, I'm so glad you made it."

I smiled as we separated. "My mom?" I still couldn't comprehend that she was here, in Nox's home.

"She's upstairs."

I reached for Chelsea and introduced her.

The shine in Silvia's brown eyes reminded me of what it was like to be welcomed home. Slowly, I took in the foyer, the bleached wooden floors, light beige walls, and white woodwork. My cheeks rose at the fresh flowers arranged on the large oval table in the entry. "Is it wrong that I always feel like I'm at home here?"

"Not at all," Silvia said. "I think that's wonderful, because you are. Would either of you like something to eat or drink before you retire?"

"I want to see my mom before anything."

"She's asleep. I believe the doctor is too, but Mr. Demetri was awake a few minutes ago."

"I'm still awake."

We all turned toward the deep baritone voice. Like his son, he was a domineering presence.

"I see you left Georgia without my son."

My pulse quickened and shoulders straightened. "And you have my mother. Why?"

Not for the first time, I noticed the family resemblance as Oren smiled and small lines formed around his eyes. Not only were they the same shade of blue as his son's, they held the same silent power of communication. He seemed amused by my response.

"Miss Collins, I admire your fortitude. For the record, I always have."

Silvia spoke to Chelsea. "Let me show you around, and I can get you something to eat or drink if you'd like."

Chelsea shrugged questioningly in my direction.

"Wait," I said. "Mr. Demetri…" I began introducing the two of them.

"Alex, that's very polite of you but unnecessary. Miss Moore, you're welcome here as long as you'd like. I promise you're perfectly safe in my home."

I bristled, wondering how much he knew about Chelsea. Did he know about Bryce? About everything? It wasn't only his knowledge that bothered me. The way he referred to this home as his made the small hairs on the back of my neck stand to attention. I wanted to correct him and say it belonged to Nox, but instead I held my tongue as Chelsea accepted his kind gesture and disappeared with Silvia.

"My son?" he asked.

"Is in flight."

Oren nodded. "I received the same text. I was wondering something else."

Talking to Oren Demetri put me on edge. Each phrase, each word made me feel as if I were constantly trying to make sense of a riddle. At three in the morning, I didn't have the energy. "Mr. Demetri, I'd like to see my mother."

"Call me Oren, Alexandria. The doctor is asleep, but there's a nurse monitoring Adelaide. She'll have around-the-clock care."

"Why?"

"She needs it."

"I don't understand."

"Before we go upstairs, I think we should talk about what happened on the plane."

I took a deep breath. "Can't we talk in her room?"

"I'd rather not."

"I'm sorry. This is rude, but I've had a long day. My mother is upstairs. I left Nox in Savannah to get to her. I'm going to go find her."

He motioned toward the sitting room. "Hear me out. Please, this won't take long. They say that patients can't hear what is said around them while they're unconscious, but I'd rather not take the chance. My house, my rules."

My feet stopped. "Lennox's house."

Oren nodded. "Demetri."

I took a deep breath and held my lips together.

"I'm not insisting on much," he said. "Positivity. What happened today needs to be discussed, but not in your mother's presence."

I swallowed my resistance and tried to hear his intent. Something in his tone tugged at my heart. "You care about what is said around her? I'm going to ask again, why?"

He sat on the edge of the long sofa and leaned forward. It wasn't the confident stance of the man I'd last met in this house months ago.

"First…" He gestured toward the sofa. "…please sit. You need to know about the flight."

I didn't argue as I settled at the far end of the plush couch. "Nox?"

Oren's gaze met mine. "What about him?"

"You wanted to know something about him, what?"

He waved his hand. "It's rather obvious." Taking a deep breath, he sat taller. "As you should know, your mother has been given what some might consider an inappropriate amount of tranquilizers."

Tranquilizers was a broad term. I assumed he was referring to the Versed or midazolam that Dr. Miller prescribed. "They said it was to help her withstand the DTs."

"That's what they said. The doctor who's been with her tonight and I both believe that it was to keep her from talking."

I narrowed my sleepy eyes. "Talking about what?"

He shook his head. "Alexandria, I think we need to get further into the *whats* and *whys* tomorrow. Tonight, as you said, has been very long. The point I want to make is that the excessive use of that medication has affected her body."

My neck straightened as tears I couldn't fight filled my eyes.

"I wanted to get your mother out of that poor excuse of a hospital as much as you."

"Why—"

"Please," he implored, "let me speak."

I nodded.

"Our doctors couldn't examine her until we had her safely out of there. They scanned her records. They made their assessments, but their assumptions were based on the information we could obtain. Unfortunately that isn't as accurate as having the patient in their grasp."

The dread that had filled me at his text message was back. "What happened?"

"Your mother went into shock after we were in the air."

I bolted to my feet. "I need to see her."

Oren stood too, blocking my way. "She's fine, as fine as she can be, but she wasn't. I take full responsibility for forcing her removal. Another twenty-four hours. Hell…" His volume rose. "…another two hours… that fucking excuse for a nurse." His lips shut tight. "Pardon my language."

"What happened?"

"We got her out of Magnolia Woods. We got her to the plane. She was mumbling when we first got to her, but then her vitals began to weaken." He ran his hand through his hair. "Her heart stopped."

I gasped as my knees loss tension and stomach fell. Giving way to gravity, I slid back to the sofa. "Stopped?"

"There was a doctor, Dr. Eva Rossi, on board. She's the one who's still here. She was monitoring her. She must have anticipated… there was an AED."

"AED?"

"Defibrillator."

"My mother's heart was shocked?"

He nodded. "It didn't work at first. We had to perform CPR. She has multiple broken ribs. I'm sorry."

"She's alive."

He nodded again.

"Her ribs will heal. They wouldn't if she weren't alive."

"Dr. Rossi has numerous concerns, her greatest being your mother's brain."

"Why?"

"The medication they used can affect the oxygen level to the brain. For some reason, despite the constant use, they didn't have her on additional oxygen."

"She is now?" I asked.

"Yes. But that isn't all. Her heart stopped. I can't tell you for how long. It seemed like hours, but it wasn't. Nevertheless, during that time, before the CPR, her brain and organs were deprived of oxygen."

"No. This isn't happening." I stood again. "Take me to her."

Oren stepped in front of me. "Alexandria, I don't believe in sugarcoating things. I never have. Dr. Rossi is concerned that she may never wake, and if she does, there could be irreparable damage."

His words squeezed the muscles of my throat, making any response difficult. "W-when will we know?"

"Time will tell us."

The warm, welcoming feeling I'd enjoyed upon my arrival disappeared into the cloud of fear his news delivered. I didn't speak as he led me up the stairs. My only thought was of my momma. I didn't think about Nox or our past as we passed the door to the room Nox and I had shared. I ran Oren's words and phrases over again in my mind. With each step they sank deeper and deeper into my psyche. We didn't stop until we reached a set of double doors.

As Oren reached for the doorknob, I reached for his arm. Something he'd said stood out. "Why do you take responsibility?"

"What?" His voice sounded dazed as if he too had been lost in thought.

"By getting my mother, you were doing what Lennox asked, what I wanted. It was my doing, not yours."

He stood taller, his chest inflating. "Absolutely not."

Before I could respond he went on, "Adelaide will wake. She will be the vivacious, beautiful woman she always was. I believe that with everything in me. However, if I'm wrong, which you should take comfort in knowing is rarely the case, but if I am, her fate is not your doing. You did the best you could. You were willing to sacrifice your own soul for her. She didn't want that, and neither do I. If things don't go as planned, it is on me."

"How do you know about what I was willing to do?"

"The responsibility is mine."

There was a tone of finality in his speech that I recognized, the authority that left little room for argument. He was Nox, or Nox was he. If it weren't for the thicker accent, I could close my eyes and believe that Oren Demetri was his son.

In that second, I wanted to do what Nox continually asked of me. I wanted to trust. This time it wasn't Nox I was trusting. It was Oren. It felt wrong, but at the same time it felt right.

Was this what it was like to have someone who shielded me from life's tragedies and responsibilities? Was this what it was like to have a father? Though I knew he and Nox had their difficulties, I wanted to believe that Oren was sincere.

We'd both been right about the night. It'd been incredibly long, and my emotions were on overdrive. I leaned forward and wrapped my arms around Oren's waist. "Thank you."

His reaction was delayed, so much so that for a moment I regretted my show of emotion. And then, his arms surrounded my shoulders as my cheek fell against his chest. I didn't understand the connection. I didn't try, but for a moment, I was a little girl finding comfort and security in the arms of a man who somehow understood my difficulties, who shared my fears.

When I stepped back my cheeks were again wet. "You do care about her? It's not just about Nox and I, is it?"

"I do." He reached for the handle. "Shall we?"

CHAPTER 10

UNKNOWN

BLOCKED NUMBER: **"I FOLLOWED HER."**

Blocked Number: **"BRING HER BACK. I DON'T CARE HOW YOU DO IT."**

Blocked Number: **"SIR, IT'S NOT LIKE BEFORE. THE SECURITY HERE IS TIGHT."**

Blocked Number: **"THEN WAIT IT OUT. EVENTUALLY SHE'LL LEAVE. WHO ELSE IS THERE?"**

Blocked Number: **"THE WOMAN AND DRIVER LEFT. SHE AND HER FRIEND STAYED. I HAVE NO WAY OF KNOWING WHO ELSE IS INSIDE."**

Blocked Number: **"DID YOU RECOGNIZE HER FRIEND?"**

Blocked Number: **"YES, SIR, THE SAME ONE FROM... FROM BEFORE."**

Blocked Number: **"DEAL WITH THEM BOTH."**

Blocked Number: **"I WON'T LET YOU DOWN, SIR."**

Blocked Number: **"NOT AGAIN YOU WON'T."**

CHAPTER 11

—•O•—

OREN

BEYOND THE LARGE windows of the office, blackness prevailed, thick and chilled. It seeped through the cooled air, rattling the branches of the nearby trees and stirring the waters of the sound. I should have been concerned about the men outside, protecting the estate, but I wasn't. It was their job.

The thick windows held out the wind, but just beyond the windows I could see its effects in the whipping vines on the veranda beside the house. Winter was coming and the chill was all around me. It had been a long time since I'd wintered in New York.

I pictured my apartment in Knightsbridge. It wasn't warmer in London. If anything, it was cooler. Nevertheless, even during my self-imposed isolation, Knightsbridge was anything but. There was no dark lawn or daunting perimeter. The entire hamlet bustled day and night. It was filled with culture, fashion houses, and famous restaurants. Perhaps subconsciously I'd purchased the flat with Adelaide in mind. Now that she was here, upstairs, my desires were no longer subliminal. I wanted to take her there.

I prayed that she'd walk the sidewalks, shop in Harrods and Jimmy Choo, and dine with me at any of the clubs and bars. With her appreciation of art, she could browse the museums or redecorate the flat with priceless antiques.

My dreams were at hand—literally at my fingertips—and yet a million miles away.

The concerns I'd explained to Alexandria were real. Eva insisted that I listen, that I comprehend. At first I was unwilling.

Adelaide would wake. I knew it. Until…

I didn't.

And now the damn newscast.

The body.

The arrest.

This conversation shouldn't occur over the phone, but I refused to leave Adelaide, and I had to know. I had to confirm my suspicions. It was probably the reason she didn't come into the house.

"I could tell you to come here. To talk to me in person," I said when she picked up.

"Or you could trust me that no one will hear this conversation. I provided the house with the burner phone for a reason. I was expecting your call."

I squeezed the phone tighter. "Your name?"

"My name?"

"Standard insurance." If she said her name, we weren't being recorded. Her years as an operative would have taught her that. I shouldn't have to explain it any more.

"Deloris Witt."

I exhaled. "Now," I said, "tell me why."

"You're not asking first if I know who did it?"

"I wouldn't be risking this call if I doubted that answer. I know. You just confirmed it. Now tell me why and if my son authorized it."

"I think you know why."

"My son?"

"No. He didn't authorize it, but he did mention he wanted it. Not her death," Deloris clarified. "He wanted the consequences that would accompany it. He never knew she was being kept safe. He'll never know what happened."

I fought to respond. She was his employee. It wasn't her place to go rogue. However, at the same time, I was thankful he wasn't involved. "Yet you're willingly telling me?"

"You aren't him. He isn't you."

That had always been my dream.

If secrets were stars I could light a galaxy. If they were stars they wouldn't be affected by gravity, not as we know it. Instead, they're weights, each one heavier than the last, each one pulling me down until I fought to breathe, to live. Each one replacing the starry sky with drowning regret.

Could I continue to keep them to myself?

All of my dreams were so close. And yet each weight pulled me further and further away.

I closed my eyes. Murder had been in my past. I'd given it all up, moved beyond, and now I was there again. "Details?"

"Do you really want to know?"

"She was innocent." That simple statement was what ate at me. Then again, I'd seen other innocents die. They'd died for power, for revenge, and for love.

"Her death took precedence over her existence," Deloris said matter-of-factly. "Sometimes the saying is true: the end justifies the means. She was available. Besides, her fate was sealed when she reneged on her obligation to Infidelity and attempted to blackmail Spencer."

"Blackmail?" I tried to understand. "Her accusations were false? He didn't harm her?"

"He did, but from what I learned from her, he'd done it before. She realized she'd messed up with Infidelity. She knew his inclinations and intended to profit from his depravity."

I shook my head. "Not as innocent as I previously thought."

"Her plan would have worked if she hadn't involved the authorities. Fitzgerald would have paid her to go away. I'm most certain the payout would have been short-lived. Her fate would have ultimately been the same."

"So in saving her, you prolonged her reprieve?"

"That's a nice way to look at it."

"Did you lie?"

"No, sir."

"You don't need any more qualifiers? You can answer unequivocally to never lying?"

"Can you?"

"I didn't ask me. I asked you."

"I used a qualifier," Deloris admitted. "I've never lied *to your son or you*."

"Only a few days ago, you told me to my face that she was safe."

"She was and things changed. Spencer was too close to winning. Mr. Fitzgerald was determined to make their marriage legal. Mrs. Fitzgerald's health was getting worse. Mr. Fitzgerald was desperate. If his wife died, the entire will, including the codicil could have come out. If Alex and Edward were married, he could keep the codicil hidden and go on with Article XII."

"And you knew this how?"

"I listen. I watch. It's what I do. Those weren't my primary concerns. My primary concerns were Alex and Lennox. I was with him when he lost Jocelyn."

She let that statement hang in the air, reminding me that I wasn't. "Your point?"

"I wasn't going to do that again.

"Edward's total disregard of Alex as nothing more than a step on his climb to American nobility was only surpassed by his brutality aimed at Melissa and then Chelsea. Do you believe that after their marriage Alex would have been exempt?"

I didn't respond. Instead, I recalled discolored patches on Adelaide's porcelain skin. I recalled her countless excuses—clumsiness and medications. I remembered threatening her ass of a husband and her begging for his reprieve. If Edward Spencer were anything like his father—yes, Adelaide had shared that secret with me too—then I knew that Alexandria wouldn't have been exempt.

She went on. "How would that have affected Lennox... and Mrs. Fitzgerald?"

I knew how it would. It would have devastated them, just as it had me. Lennox had already lost one love in his life. I'd done my part to give him another. Would I have been able to sit back and watch her taken from him? Watch her be abused from afar? Had Deloris authorized something that I wouldn't have, given the opportunity?

Love.

I could categorize Melissa's death… this murder… as done for *love*. There were three people I loved: Angelina, Lennox, and Adelaide. Melissa's death helped two of those people.

I couldn't argue with her logic.

"Lennox can never know."

"I agree."

"Will you lie to him?"

"As I said, I've never lied to him, to either of you. With him, for him, I can omit some information. Will I be the only one who's done that?"

"Mrs. Witt, tread lightly."

"I'll take that as your answer."

"You should. You said the last time we spoke about Melissa that he asked you to *take care* of her?"

"No. He said he wanted the problem *gone*. She was the cause of the problem. I helped her be gone. After listening to the demeaning and demanding way Spencer spoke to Alex on a telephone call, he said he wanted Spencer to suffer. I told him I was thinking about a solution. I never gave him the entire story."

"Two birds. One stone," I said.

"Yes, sir," Deloris confirmed. "We'll never mention this?"

"One more thing. The charges, will they stick? Will my son get his wish?"

"Will he suffer?"

"That's what I'm asking," I said.

"I'm most certain of it."

Why did *most certain* fail to pacify me? "My son will never take the fall for this."

"That goes without saying."

"You have a plan B?"

"I always do."

I exhaled. She was good.

"Tomorrow."

"Yes, sir, I'll be there tomorrow."

"And this conversation never happened."

"What conversation?" she asked. "Good night."

Efficient and deadly. It seemed that Lennox did know how to pick them.

I removed the battery on the disposable phone. The house was quiet as I slipped through the rooms and hallways until I reached the kitchen door, the one that went out onto the pool deck. A cold chill ran through me as I stepped outside onto the concrete. One slip from my fingers and the phone fell to the hard pavement. A misstep of my shoe and my heel smashed the plastic to dust.

I scooped the remains into the palm of my hand and eased back into the dark kitchen. Opening the large cabinet that housed the trash and recycling, I dumped the plastic shreds into the recyclables. Even monsters can help save the planet.

CHAPTER 12

CHARLI

MY EYES BLINKED, staying closed longer and longer with each passing moment. The mug of warm tea teetered precariously in my grasp as I fought the impending sleep. Even the constant beep of Momma's monitors had become a lullaby, the rhythm lulling me to a dream state.

My mind was too full to sleep and too troubled to want to be awake. I couldn't stop thinking about Melissa Summers and Chelsea and even myself. How close had Chelsea and I come to being Bryce's victims? When did Melissa die? Had her body been at Carmichael Hall while Chelsea had been there? If I'd gone there Saturday morning, would he have shown her to me? Would she be another example of his power as striking Chelsea had been?

My skin prickled and stomach twisted with the possibilities.

Then there was Nox. I wanted him to get back to me. I needed him. I needed to rely upon someone besides myself.

Lastly, my momma.

The room where we were had all the essentials of a hospital room but encased in luxury. I'd never before been in the master suite of this house. Once I realized the room we were in, I did my best to suppress the images Nox had described to me of finding Jocelyn. This was the room where she'd died, where he'd found her, and yet it was the room where my mother was sleeping.

I chose to use the word *sleeping*, doing as Oren had said and concentrating on the positive.

It was also the room where Oren stayed when he was here. His bed was still present. I found it more than a little odd that it was where he'd chosen to create her makeshift hospital room, but after what he'd told me about the flight, moving her to another room didn't seem like the appropriate course of action.

After his story, I wasn't sure what I'd find when he opened the door. The reality was better than my imagination. My mother appeared peaceful, her hair brushed and nightgown fresh. Her complexion had a hint of pink and her wrists weren't tethered. The constant beeping provided comfort as the monitors confirmed her heart was beating and a small tube delivered oxygen through her nose.

On a shiny silver pole hung a bag of what I'd learned was simply saline solution. A thin tube delivered the hydration to her arm. Hanging from the bed was a clear bag to monitor her fluid output.

The nurse explained that they'd need to resume intravenous nutrition if she didn't wake soon. In the meantime, they were working to keep her hydrated. I'd been pleased to hear that the doctor believed that most of the opioid hydrocodone and alcohol should by now be purged from her system, decreasing the likelihood of future DTs.

Liz, the nurse, confirmed that my mother did have three broken ribs. Apparently they'd been able to see with some kind of portable x-ray machine. The length to which Nox's family had gone to help my mother utterly amazed me. The doctor or nurse had taped my momma's sides to ease the pain. She also explained that not much could be done about broken ribs. Only time. Perhaps it was the doctor I was waiting for, or maybe it was Nox. He should be landing soon. For whatever reason, I found it difficult to leave my mother's side despite the fact that soon the sun would rise on the other side of the draperies. During my exploration I'd discovered that, like the room I shared with Nox, this one also had a balcony overlooking the sound.

"Miss Collins, do you mind if I go to the kitchen? Everything is stable. If you need me or Dr. Rossi, push the button on the intercom."

I forced a smile. "Thanks, Liz. I'll stay with her."

After the door shut, I placed my tea on a table and walked to my mother's side. I stood silently holding my breath, watching as her chest rose and fell. Then letting out the air, I reached for her hand.

"Momma, I'm here." My voice choked with emotion. "You're going to get better. That's what Liz said. She's your nurse, yours. I don't know how they did it, but the Demetris got all of this for you."

I looked around the room again, taking in the spacious suite. Oren had stepped out earlier and now with Liz in the kitchen, for the first time my momma and I were alone.

"I think you'll like it here. It's not Montague Manor and that's a good thing. It's a home, a lovely home. Wait until you meet Silvia. She's so welcoming. Things have happened here..." I thought again about Jocelyn and wondered about Nox's mom. "Yet it feels warm. Not a temperature, but the way it makes me feel, as if I belong." I took a ragged breath. "I'm sorry if... I-I wish..."

I wasn't sure what I wanted to say.

"Momma, please get better. Don't think about Montague Manor. We don't need anything from any of them ever again. Let them have it all. There's so much to tell you. Bryce was..." I stopped, remembering Oren's request for positivity. "It doesn't matter. Nothing is worth what that place has taken. What Alton..." Damn, it was impossible to stay positive and tell her what had happened.

I took a deep breath. "When I finish school I'll work. I will. I don't want Nox to feel as if he has to, but he's promised that he'll help us until then." I wiped away the tears that wouldn't stop. "Please get better and when you do, stay with me, with us."

I let it all out—the last two weeks. That was such a short time in the span of a life and yet in even less than that, in only ten days, so much had happened. I didn't know if she could hear me, but I wanted to tell her. Part of me was afraid that this would be the only chance I had.

"Oren, Nox's dad, wants us to say only good things and not upset you. I don't want to upset you, but there are a few things I need to say." My breath stuttered as I gulped air. "I know I haven't been a good daughter, but you haven't been a good mom." My eyes closed, forcing more tears to fall. As they dripped from my chin, I imagined her living the last twenty years as I had the last ten days. My childhood hadn't been good, but it hadn't been the hell I faced marrying Bryce, living with his cruelty day after day. The anger I'd allowed to fester inside of me morphed to empathy. "I think I understand. I think you tried. I get that. I can see things differently than I used to. I'm sorry."

The ivory dress I'd worn earlier was gone. I was wearing a sweatshirt and yoga pants. I wasn't sure if they were Silvia's or if Deloris had arranged for me to have clothes. I didn't care as long as I was out of that dress and heels. I knelt beside the bed, still clinging to my mother's hand and rested my forehead on the edge of the mattress.

"Don't leave me. I know I left you, but I wasn't really gone. I was away. I-I don't know what I'd do…"

The words stopped forming as hiccups sabotaged my speech.

Letting go of her hand, I clung to the edge of the mattress. With my head down I cried. I cried because I was scared that she wouldn't live. I cried because I was scared of what would become of us if she did. We were breaking my grandfather's will. I couldn't ask Nox or Oren to support both of us. It wasn't right.

I cried for the little girl who missed out on a mother's touch. More tears fell at the realization of her sacrifice, at our sacrifice. I'd missed out and so had she. Maybe it wasn't that she didn't notice, but that she'd been too busy keeping the monster away. I felt it in my soul. Things Jane had said. Things I didn't understand now seemed clear.

I cried the tears I'd held back at Montague Manor.

I cried for Chelsea and all she'd surrendered on my account.

With time, my tears slowed and breathing began to steady. As it did, I felt a touch to my head, a smoothing of my hair.

"Shhh. Don't cry."

The voice was weak, scratchy, but I'd know my own mother's voice anywhere.

My head popped up. She looked exactly as she had. Her eyes were still closed. But her hand was moved. Had I moved it? Did I imagine it?

"Momma?"

She didn't answer.

"Momma?"

The monitors continued their steady rhythm as the door opened.

Oren stepped around Liz. "Alexandria, are you all right?"

Liz hurried to the monitors. "Everything is stable. Did something happen?"

"She spoke."

Oren looked from me to Momma and back. There was a skeptical expectancy in his expression as if he wanted to believe me, but doubted my sanity.

"Adelaide?"

I took a step back as he reached for her other hand.

"Adelaide, it's Oren. Alexandria is here."

The intimacy in his touch made my skin prickle. It wasn't right, yet he didn't hesitate as he bowed forward and lifted her hand to his lips.

"*Amore mio*, rest. We're not leaving you."

"Not real."

We all looked up, Liz, Oren, and myself. It wasn't a sleep-deprived hallucination. She'd spoken again.

"Miss Collins, that is a great sign," Liz said. "Dr. Rossi will be in here soon. She's not leaving the estate. We will want to run some tests, see how she's responding. There's nothing more for you to do right now. Why don't you get some sleep?"

"I-I don't want—"

The door opened wider. There was something in the expression of the most handsome man I knew. It only lasted a millisecond as he entered this room. His step stuttered and then he strode through, my confident, domineering Batman. "Did I hear something good happened?"

I nodded and swallowed more tears. "She's talking."

Nox reached for my hand. "Princess..." He kissed my forehead. "...you're the most beautiful woman I know, but," he said, pausing to wipe the tears from my cheeks, "you look spent. I'm spent. Your mom is doing better. Let's get some sleep?" He looked to Liz. "If you need her, she's in the suite down the hall. Don't hesitate to wake us."

"Yes, sir."

He nodded toward Oren. "Thank you."

"Tomorrow we'll talk."

"You didn't?"

"No. One thing at a time."

Nox took a deep breath and tilted his head toward Momma. "They know she's gone."

Oren nodded. "I've been following the chatter."

"Wait!" I said. "What? Do you think they'll come here? Do you think they'll try to move her?"

"Eventually," Oren replied. "But no one is entering this property without a warrant."

I reached for Nox's hand. "Alton has people. He got in our apartment."

Oren smiled. "Get some sleep. *Our* people are watching."

Nox's eyes blinked in acknowledgment as he smiled at his father. And then the light blue stare was back on me. "Come on, princess. I have plans."

CHAPTER 13

——●○●——

NOX

IT HAD BEEN years since I'd stepped foot in the master suite at Rye. I know that sounds crazy. I didn't sell the house after Jo died. I couldn't. It was my mother's. She loved this house. I had to separate myself from my loss.

I stayed away. I avoided my childhood home like it was the plague. In my mind it'd killed not only my mother but my wife too. For all practical purposes I gave it to Silvia. She deserved it more than me. She cared for it and honored it. I probably wouldn't be here now, nor would Oren or Adelaide or Charli, if Silvia had taken me up on the offer I made her.

Despite what I knew would become an argument with Oren, I had the deed ready to sign over to Silvia. Everything was there except my signature. Deloris was the one who convinced me to take the paperwork to Rye, sit down with Silvia, and let her know that the house was hers. I was ready to do it from New York City and forget about it.

The conversation that ensued was one that only siblings can appreciate. Charli called Chelsea her sister. Silvia was mine. Fuck blood. Siblings weren't defined by blood, but by life, by triumphs and heartbreaks. My mother had told me that Silvia came to live with us because she needed a family. I don't think I really appreciated that until I needed one too.

With my mother and wife gone and father halfway around the fucking world, I made an interesting discovery the day I came back to Rye. I learned that Silvia shared my loss. My mom was like her mom. My wife had been like her sister-in-law. Yes, Silvia had maintained the house, but not out of obligation to me. She did it out of love and devotion to the women who loved this house and who loved us both.

I handed her the papers. She had the ownership in her hands and in classic Italian-family reverence, she threw them at me and told me to grow up. I'll never forget the look on her face as the papers scattered all over the kitchen floor. "I don't need this house. I don't need the money you say I can make by selling it." She pointed directly at me. "I would never sell it. It's not mine to sell and, Lennox, it's not yours either. It's Angelina's. She loved this house because it represented her family. Face your ghosts and man up. This house needs you."

She challenged me to stay one night. Dared me. Like a fucking sister would dare her brother and because that's how my mother wanted us to be, I accepted. It was one of the longest nights of my life.

To this day, I don't know if Oren knows that I wanted to rid myself of the house. I still don't think it's his concern. Nevertheless, I made peace with it. The next day, Silvia and I made our peace too.

She's my family—blood or no blood.

I started making an effort to visit more often. It was usually only for dinner, but when Oren was in town, occasionally I'd stay. I told myself it was to keep him away from my apartment in the city. Perhaps that was true.

We never discussed it, but Oren always took the master suite. I admit that at first it pissed me off, thinking of my mother there alone while he was off doing whatever in the hell he was doing. However, with time, I secretly appreciated his saving me from reentering that room. Over the years I'd avoided it.

The room down the hall was perfectly acceptable.

When I arrived tonight, I imagined finding Charli asleep in the bed we'd shared. I assumed that would be the room Silvia would give her. I'd only just opened the door to the darkened room when I'd heard her voice—not only her voice, her despair. It flowed down the hallway in a cloud, emanating from where she was and reaching out to me.

Stepping through that doorway to the master bedroom suite… there was so much at once. Though my eyes immediately went to Charli, I couldn't help but see my father holding the hand of another woman. My teeth clenched knowing that this was the same room he'd at one time shared with my mother. In that millisecond, I took in Charli's mom. It was the first time I'd seen her in person, and yet I'd barely noticed her. My Charli had dominated my vision and needed my attention.

Ghosts no longer registered. My father was no longer relevant. All that mattered was Charli—her swollen eyes, tearstained cheeks, and broken expression. The woman in the bed had her attention. That woman wasn't someone taking my mom's place: she was Charli's mom.

I was running on fumes. We all were.

If her devil of a stepfather and even the law couldn't keep us separated, memories wouldn't.

I closed Oren's door and left him, the nurse, and Adelaide behind.

I held tighter to Charli's hand as we began down the hallway. It was time for *us*.

I needed to hold her, comfort her, and do everything in my power to ease the tension surging through her beautiful, petite body and emanating from her.

Pulling her close, I brushed my lips against hers and sighed. Damn, it didn't matter where we were or who was fighting against us, as long as I had her in my arms, life was right.

"*Amore mio?*" she asked.

"Always."

Her golden eyes opened wider as I opened the door to our suite. "What does it mean?"

Closing the door, I pulled her against me. "It means *my love*. And you are. Seeing you, holding you, having you here, makes the hell of the last nearly two weeks worth it."

As her arms encircled my neck, she buried her cheek against my chest. "I don't understand. Why would your dad say that to my mom?"

"Princess, can we save all other topics for tomorrow… after we sleep?"

She nodded, her earlier broken expression melting into one of surrender.

It wasn't me that she was about to surrender to, but sleep.

"Sleep." She elongated the word like it was a pipedream.

"Yes, you and me…" I tilted my head toward the large bed. "…there."

Charli hummed. "Don't let me go."

"Never."

She tugged my hand. "I mean it. I don't think I've slept, really slept. I want to know—no *need* to know—you're with me."

"I'm with you always. It sounds like your mom is doing better. Now it's time for us to rest." I smirked knowing it was already tomorrow. "And later today, once we're awake, we'll talk."

She nodded against my chest before looking up. "How did you get away from the police? I got Isaac's text on your phone, but it just said you were on your way."

"Later."

She shook her head as she pulled away and walked toward the bed. "I hate to leave my mom, but I'm so tired."

As Charli pulled down the covers, I turned on the light in the bathroom. "Give me a minute. I'll be right there."

I'd spent most of the day waiting for the damn party and then hours waiting along a dirt road. Then I ran on the same dirt road, knocked the shit out of two guards, and punched Alton Fitzgerald. That was all before I was arrested. All in all, it was a fucking long day.

I turned on the shower and as it warmed, shed my clothes, leaving them in a pile upon the tile as the room filled with humidity. Just before I stepped inside, the most beautiful image filled my vision. Coming from around the door, walking through the cloud was Charli. She'd lost the clothes she'd been wearing, leaving us both dressed, or undressed, to match.

"Fuck, princess, I thought you said you were exhausted?"

Her small hand rested upon my bare chest and her fingers splayed. She tilted her head toward the shower as her long hair hung in waves and flowed over her shoulder. "If we get in there, can we wash it all away? Like the time with my makeup… when you made it all go away… can you do that again?"

I kissed her forehead. "We can give it a try."

The hot water prickled like small needles on my skin as I stepped under the spray. Using my body, I shielded Charli, turning down the heat until the temperature adjusted and we both could comfortably step under the warm waterfall. Just as she'd asked, each drop eased the tension, washing it away until it swirled on the tile and disappeared down the drain.

Behind the glass doors the mist filled with the aroma of fruit—something citrus—as I massaged shampoo into Charli's long silky hair. In the light of the shower, her red tresses darkened, bringing out a rich, beautiful mahogany hue. With her hands on the side of the shower, her head bowed forward as I covered her, cleaning away the last week—the last two. The conditioner, the body wash… each step removed a little more of the edge. When we were done, Charli turned in my arms, wrapped her arms around my waist, and under the still-hot spray broke down.

It wasn't the reaction my body had been hoping for. I knew we were both tired, but having her naked body next to mine had an effect that my brain could do little to control.

Instead of taking the woman I loved, I held her shoulders as they shuddered.

"I love you."

She shook her head. "I'm so sorry. There's so much I need to tell you."

Did she know about the marriage license? Had she signed it but didn't want to admit it? Did this have to do with Spencer? She'd kissed him to distract him. What else had she done? What had he done?

Turning off the water, I reached for her chin.

"I need to know just one thing."

Her tear-filled eyes lifted to mine.

"Do you still want to be here with me?"

Her entire body lost tension as she exhaled. "Oh God, yes. If you still want me. You thought you were getting a cash-strapped girl—at worst, an opportunistic girl—who signed with Infidelity and you thought that was a mess. I'm not that person. I'm so much more of a mess than that."

"I had no idea who I was getting when I spoke to you in Del Mar. I only knew that there was something about you, something I needed and wanted. On that first night, when you walked out of my suite, I knew I had to get you back. When I figured out why you walked out, I knew you weren't only beautiful but so much more—strong, driven, and honorable. You're my princess and always will be."

Her golden eyes glistened.

I went on, my tone changing, "But as I said earlier, if you make me come after you one more time because you do something like get in that man's car…" I reached for her bare ass. "…this ass is mine."

"You don't regret it?" she asked. "Coming after me?"

My grin grew. "Regret having your ass in the palm of my hand, your sexy body against mine? Never."

She shook her head. "Nox, my life is so fucked. My mom almost died tonight." She looked up. "She did. Her heart stopped. I'm so much more of a mess than just needing to pay for law school." She stepped back and reached for a towel. "And now, what if Alton sends the police here? My mom and I shouldn't be here. We're putting you and your dad at risk."

As she tucked the towel around her breasts, my cheeks rose higher and I untucked the towel, letting it drop to the floor. "Did my dad seem concerned about anything your stepfather can do?"

"No, but he doesn't know—"

I eyed her beautiful body from her toes to her dripping hair. "He does. We'll talk. Now, I'm tired of talking."

Charli's eyes veiled as her nipples hardened.

I reached for her hand and encouraged her to turn completely around. "So fucking beautiful." After all we'd been through, I needed to know she was really here and safe. As she slowly spun, a faint yellowness showed on her forearm. When I reached for her, purposely touching the spot, I hoped I wasn't seeing a bruise… that maybe instead, the lighting was playing a trick on my tired eyes.

Her flinch was quick, almost imperceptible.

Almost.

My smile disappeared. "What happened?"

She shook her head and took my hand. "No more talking. I believe, Mr. Demetri, that was your rule."

I bit my cheek, wanting to know which asshole was responsible. I'd seen Chelsea's cheek. It was obviously worse than what I saw on Charli's arm, but that didn't make Charli's bruise less significant.

Our bare feet padded across the wood floor, finally landing upon the soft rug surrounding the bed. Charli's lips brushed mine before she climbed onto the bed, her perfect ass bringing my dick back to life as she crawled toward the headboard. She fanned her wet hair over the pillow as she lay back. With her eyes glued to mine, her breasts rose and fell in anticipation as I followed suit and crawled across the mattress toward her. As I neared, her legs fell farther apart, silently inviting me toward her core.

With my body suspended above hers, I said, "I thought you were exhausted."

"I am," she confirmed, her hand caressing my cheek. "And so are you."

I was. I'd brought her to bed not anticipating anything but sleep, but having her with me in the shower and now in our bed ignited a need I couldn't hide. My hard dick rubbed slowly over the soft skin of her legs as they willingly spread wider to accommodate me.

"Charli…"

She pulled my lips to hers, opening hers and encouraging our tongues to glide and tangle. Separating our kiss, she demanded, "Make love to me. You helped wash away the past, now fill me with the future. I'm tired of being trapped in a life I hate. I want our life back."

"You're not trapped anymore. Never again. And no matter where we are, the future is ours."

As we kissed our bodies connected, my cock finding her entrance, welcomed by her essence. Inch-by-inch, we came together. The deeper I plunged, the more her back arched, pushing her tits toward me. With each thrust her warm core stretched and surrounded me.

It may have only been a few days since we were together, but this union was different. In the hotel there had been a sense of urgency. We'd been in the eye of the storm. This morning we were home, where we belonged. The storm had passed and we'd survived. There would be damage to repair and retaliation yet to claim, but for the moment, we could savor the present.

With the shutters closed and the dawn's early light seeping in from between the slats, we climbed our personal mountains. Time stood still, no longer demanding our attention. Getting closer to one another became our greatest need.

Our bodies knew what our tired minds may have forgotten. We were two pieces of a whole: as I filled her, as she accommodated all of me, we fit perfectly together, like one. And like one, we moved in sync until her golden eyes closed, neck stretched, and lips formed a perfect O.

We tasted and touched. She wasn't the only one to be filled. Our senses were too. Our tongues feasted on the sweet concoction of bodywash mixed with the salty taste of exertion. The air around us clouded with the scent of shampoo and musk. The sounds of breathing filled our ears, becoming the melody while Charli's moans and whimpers created the lyrics. The rhythm increased until together we stiffened. A deep, reverberating growl filled the crescendo as our dance ended, leaving my muscles slack. Contented and satiated, I caged her lovely face between my arms unwilling to move away.

Time stood still as we clung to one another, her arms around my shoulders and my face buried in the crook of her neck. Instead of releasing me, Charli held tighter, pulling my chest against hers, flattening her breasts until our hearts found the other's beat.

When our eyes met, she confessed, "I haven't felt this good or safe since I left for Savannah."

My lips quirked into a knowing smirk. "And after we've slept, your ass is mine for putting yourself in that danger."

The way her eyes veiled and she fidgeted her hips brought my tired dick back to life.

"Nox?"

I kissed her forehead. "Oh, princess, you knew it was coming."

Pink filled her cheeks. "When we're rested and when I know my mother is all right."

"The longer you make me wait…"

Her chin rose, bringing her confident expression to view. "Yes, Mr. Demetri, bring it on."

My dick twitched again.

"Fuck."

As I pulled out, Charli's smile morphed to a pout.

"Oh, princess, sleep." I rolled to my back and pulled her close.

With her head on my chest, Charli said, "Whether you want to admit it or not, you are Prince Charming."

Stroking her still-damp hair as the scent of flowers filled my senses, I wished I was, but I wasn't. For her I'd do my best, but I wasn't the pure-hearted Disney prince. I knew evil.

I also knew that she did too. I'd stared him in the face earlier tonight when he entered the room at the police station. He'd been unhappy with my answer, sure that I'd take his offer. Not only didn't I take it, I pushed him on showing the video footage of the mansion—of him manhandling Charli into the car. By the time the detective returned, the video footage was no longer available and the charges were dropped.

I wasn't naïve enough to believe that Alton Fitzgerald was done with me, but I took the opportunity to leave Savannah.

As Charli's breathing began to even, I whispered, "No, I'm not Prince Charming. I'm Batman."

She rolled into me, wrapping her soft leg over mine. With the sunlight that was peeking through the slats of the blinds, I watched her cheeks rise just before she fell sound asleep.

CHAPTER 14

ADELAIDE

I BLINKED MY eyes, trying to make sense of the unfamiliar surroundings. It was as if each time I opened my eyes, the scene was different.

I scanned the room, careful not to move my head, apprehensive of where I was or who was watching. From what I could see, once again I was in a room I didn't recognize. It wasn't my suite at Montague Manor, nor was it the blue walls of hell. Slowly, I turned my head. The movement hurt. Not my head—it wasn't a migraine—but instead it was my body. Everything hurt.

Each breath tugged at my midsection as if I were wearing something tight—a bodice? I couldn't comprehend the pressure or pain, but with it my breathing came faster and shallower. Each breath hurt more than the last.

Biting my lip, I consciously slowed my respiration. Again closing my eyes, I tried to remember what had happened. There were sporadic recollections, but nothing with enough detail to fill in the blanks. The memories were a hodgepodge of faces and voices. Past and present intertwined and interspersed until chronological order ceased to exist. Putting it together was like making sense of a mound of puzzle pieces that could create a thousand separate finished pictures. The sizes were too similar—their appearance, scent, and even the feel of them in my hand. I couldn't possibly decipher which one belonged to which puzzle.

What was recent? What was past?

I recalled Jane. She'd been with me in that terrible blue room. My pulse thumped in my veins, accentuated by beeps, as our conversation came back. She'd said something about Alexandria, that her presence hadn't been a dream. Having my daughter near me wasn't what had upset me. It was when she'd said something about Bryce Spencer and Alexandria's engagement party.

My eyes snapped open again.

I wasn't sure where I was, but I needed to stop Alexandria from marrying Bryce. It wasn't right. Though I'd asked her to do it numerous times, I couldn't let her sacrifice her life as I had mine. My parents had encouraged me to do what was needed for Montague, but now that I knew the truth, I wouldn't do that to my daughter. I'd been wrong to try. She deserved a better life than what I had.

I remembered the codicil. She didn't need to. Alexandria could be free as I never had been, as Alton had never wanted her to know.

A sense of relief came over me at the clarity that accompanied my thoughts. They were more precise than they'd been in ages, and yet I still had glimpses of the past.

Oren, to be exact.

It had been years since I'd seen him and yet it seemed as if it were more recent. Had it been my dreams? In that terrible blue place, I'd dreamt about him. Not only had he been my refuge for a short time in life, but apparently he also would be forever in my subconscious.

The beeps increased as I contemplated Alexandria. I needed to call her. I needed to move. I painfully twisted my body from side to side. First, I needed to sit. Squinting my eyes, I searched for the buttons to raise my bed. My hand rose, seeking the controls. It was then I realized it wasn't bound. Had I imagined that? Had someone really restrained me?

My fingers fumbled for the railing.

Wherever I was, I was still in a hospital bed.

As I searched for the button, I noticed the large window to my left. The room around me was bright, filled with light—not just light but sunshine. It was yet another clue that I was out of the terrible place. In that horrible blue room the drapes had always been closed.

"Ms. Montague?"

I turned toward the woman's voice.

Was this heaven, what I'd prayed for? Had God finally granted my wish and changed my name in the process?

Tears filled my eyes, spilling over onto my cheeks as both relief and grief swirled through me.

If this was heaven, my life was over. I was dead.

I recalled the pills. Death had been my wish, what I'd planned. In death I would no longer need to fight… but I wanted to fight. Alexandria needed me to fight.

"No," I begged, though my words were garbled. "I can't be here. I need to help my daughter."

The woman stepped closer. She had the shining dark eyes and kind smile of an angel. There were no wings. Was that a misconception? Were they reserved for the Victoria Secret models?

"Ma'am, did you speak?"

I tried to swallow, but my mouth was dry.

"Water?"

In a few seconds my angel was back with a cup and a straw. Pushing the button to lift me to a sitting position, she placed the straw at my dry lips. Before I drank, I sucked in a deep breath at the movement of the bed.

"Yes," the angel said, "I'm sorry. You're going to be sore."

"Sore?" I was sore in heaven?

She encouraged me to drink. "Drink slowly. Only a little. We need to take it easy. Your stomach hasn't been accustomed to anything for a while."

I nodded as I sucked and listened, enjoying her gentle tone.

When she pulled the straw away, she smiled. "Ms. Montague, it's nice to meet you. I'm Eva Rossi, your doctor."

"M-my doctor?" I tried to recall. Dr. Beck was my doctor and then the other one… Dr. Mills or Miller. I couldn't remember. "You're not an angel?"

She laughed a joyous melody. "No, thank goodness, we kept you here on Earth with us for a little while longer."

As she checked the monitors, I truly looked at the room around me. It was beautiful with beige walls and lovely woodwork. There were wooden shutters over the large windows, opened slightly, allowing sunshine to enter between the slats. There was even another bed, a big one and chairs. It was a suite, not like any hospital room I'd ever seen. When she came back around to me and nodded, I asked, "Where am I?"

"Ma'am, I think I'll let your husband explain that to you."

The beeps near my bed accelerated. "My husband? Where has he taken me? What's happening?"

Dr. Rossi reached again for my hand. "Ms. Montague, no. I'm sorry. I know you're not married. It was our story. I'll let him explain. Before I get the others, who I'm certain will be happy to see you awake and talking, can I ask you some questions?"

"My husband brought me here?"

"No, not really. How are you feeling?"

I took a deep breath and winced. "I hurt." Although I did, a smile crept over my face. I was talking. My mind and lips were working together in a way they hadn't done in what seemed like weeks. I went on, "I'm sure you know from my records that I have a history of migraines, but it isn't my head that hurts." I tilted my head toward the windows. "Even the sunshine isn't bothering me. It's my sides, my ribs. They're tight."

"Ma'am, what do you remember?"

I pursed my lips, trying to fill in the blanks. "I was talking to Jane. That's the last thing I remember... Oh, they made her leave."

"Jane? Was she someone at Magnolia Woods?"

I scrunched my nose. I'd heard that name before. "I'm not sure what that is, but it sounds familiar. No, Jane is my..." I suddenly worried what had happened when they made her leave my room. "...she's my friend. I want her. Can she come here?"

The doctor shrugged. "I'm sure she can."

I shifted on the bed. "My mind seems clearer."

"Clearer than...?"

I shook my head, recalling the memories of Oren. "I think I was hallucinating or recalling a time long ago, but now things aren't as fuzzy."

"That's very good to hear," she said as she reached for her phone and typed. "I'm also not surprised you don't recall anything more recent. That's very common."

"More recent?" I asked. "What happened?"

"Ma'am, during transport from Georgia, your heart stopped."

From Georgia? My heart?

"I-I… I'm not in Georgia?" I reached for my chest. "My heart. I died?"

Dr. Rossi's smile widened. "You're here. There are different definitions of clinical death. While your heart stopped, your brain continued to work. We shocked your heart and performed CPR; that's why you're sore."

It was so much to comprehend. "This is real? If I'm not in Georgia, where am I?"

The door opened. In that second, my reality and fantasy collided. Dreams became real as the most handsome blue eyes I'd ever known met mine. In less time than could register, his expression went from urgency to adoration and finally to anguish.

"O-Oren?" His name fell from my lips as I prayed I wasn't hallucinating.

Hesitantly he took a step toward the bed. He seemed real. The doctor was still there, but then he asked her to leave us. His deep voice reverberated through the suite. I sighed as Dr. Rossi answered him, confirming he wasn't in my mind.

She answered questions and nodded toward me. Their words weren't registering as I fought to understand and then the door shut and we were alone.

"*Amore mio*, I'm sorry."

My sore chest clenched, not only at his endearment, but also at hearing the voice I hadn't heard in years. Just as it always had, the timbre rumbled like thunder from his lips to my soul.

"Oren, is this real? Are you really here? Where am I?"

He took another step closer and stilled. In his characteristic gestures, he motioned about the room. "It's not what you're used to, but this is my home."

I tried to comprehend. "Your home? I haven't seen you—"

He came closer, each step slower than the one before as if he were afraid I would tell him to leave. "I've seen *you*," he said, "every night in my dreams, every night since we parted."

I again looked about the suite. "H-how did I get here?"

"I took you."

I tried to swallow. "T-took me? Why?"

"Adelaide, you don't have to stay with me. I just couldn't let that monster..." His hands balled to fists at his side. "...Alexandria... you almost..." His strong, confident demeanor fought to overtake his emotions as his words came in fragments. "I-I know you told me to leave... I respected your wishes... I understand that you hate me... You should... I just... I've told you..." He took another step closer. "Once I love, I can't stop. Those I love, I must protect."

Tears streamed from my eyes as each of his declarations twisted my heart. The man I'd loved since the first time I met him teetered before me on the balls of his feet.

During our affair he'd been a powerful man in his own right. I presumed he still was. Yet at this moment he was waiting for me, giving me what no man had ever given me, the power to make or break him—us.

I couldn't move or speak as I took in the handsome face of the only man who'd ever loved me unconditionally. He'd aged, but each year had only made him better looking. Now in blue jeans and a button-down shirt, with more salt in his dark hair than pepper, he was still the same man who'd made me laugh, smile, and love.

I shook my head. "No, Oren. I never hated you."

He lowered his chin. "You should."

I lifted my hand, beckoning him closer. As we touched a renewed surge of energy zapped through me. "I didn't hate you. I hated me. I told you to leave because I didn't want you to waste your life with me, asking for what I couldn't give."

Releasing our touch, he lowered the railing and sat beside me. Reaching again for my hand, he kissed my knuckles, his warm lips reigniting the spark he'd lit long ago, decades ago, at a Christmas party. "I did what you said. I left, but *amore mio*, I never stopped loving you."

"You deserve so much more." I tilted my face toward the warmth of his palm as he caressed my cheek.

"No. I never deserved you. I still don't, but I can't fight it anymore. I kidnapped you."

My eyes widened. "Kidnapped me?"

He nodded. "We stole you from Magnolia Woods."

"Is that where I was? That terrible place?"

"Yes."

Memories came and went. "There was an awful person. I can't remember much, but he scared me."

"He'll never hurt you again. No one will."

I bristled at his words. "What about..." I didn't want to say his name; however, honesty between Oren and I had always been our strength. "...Alton?"

Oren's shoulders widened. "Leave him for good. He almost killed you. You can't deny it. We have medical proof."

My chin fell forward. Shame and disgust veiled my vision as I refused to look into the blue eyes I adored. I'd allowed everything that happened. I'd willingly married Alton Fitzgerald. I'd stayed with him despite his vile ways. Sitting with Oren, I didn't want to remember the beatings or belittling. I'd been too weak to leave. The only strength I'd shown was for Alexandria, but even that hadn't been enough. I didn't hate Oren for what he'd done, but I was certain my daughter hated me for what she perceived I hadn't done.

Oren lifted my chin. "I don't know what you're thinking, but let me explain. According to a hair follicle test we recently ran, a few months ago your alcohol and opioid use increased significantly. Yet according to the records from your doctor, he didn't increase your prescription. He had months before, but the levels in your blood exceeded all that had been prescribed. Our people traced a connection between one of the staff members at Montague and a local drug dealer."

"What? Who?"

"OxyContin is a synthetic opioid, chemically similar to the Vicodin your doctor prescribed for your migraines. I'm not a chemist, but we've had doctors working on this. By giving that to you, it appeared as though you were overusing your Vicodin. The OxyContin is much stronger. Its use has similar side effects as a Vicodin overdose. When combined with alcohol, especially in large amounts, the result can be lethal."

The small bit of water I'd drunk sloshed about my otherwise empty stomach as his words seeped into my consciousness.

"You're saying I didn't do this to myself. It was done *to me*?"

Oren nodded. "Unless you tell me otherwise."

I shook my head. "I can't remember. I recall trying to cut back on wine. I even stopped drinking the white during the day. I wouldn't even have a glass until…" I recalled Alton's newfound attention in the evening, spending time in our suite before dinner. "…oh my God."

He again caressed my cheek. "Do you see why I needed to save you?"

"But how? How would you know?"

"It's a long story. Let's just say it involves many more people."

"Who?" I asked. "Who was the Montague staff member?" I'd lived my entire life at Montague. I knew from experience that the staff was sycophantic to Alton's every wish, but this was different. Who would assist in poisoning me?

"A Brantley Peterson."

Tears again formed. "Brantley purchased drugs?"

"That's what the connection said."

"That's what you meant about his trying to kill me? Alton drugged me?"

Oren sat back. "Is there more?"

I shook my head. "Everything has been fuzzy for weeks. I don't remember." I looked up to his caring blue eyes, swirling with questions. "Do you believe what you just said? Do you believe that I wasn't drinking as much, that even though the tests say otherwise, this wasn't my doing?"

"With all my heart."

I took as deep of a breath as I could. Pushing past the pain, I let his answer sink in.

He believed me.

"Why did you bring me here?"

"Because I had the opportunity to help you and you didn't tell me no."

The tips of my lips moved upward. "I couldn't tell you anything in the state I was in." I squeezed his hand. "Though we spoke often."

His blue eyes silently questioned me, perhaps my sanity.

"Reality has been bad," I began. "I don't even remember that much of it. But when I'd fall asleep, I'd go back to the one time in my life when I was happy." I lifted his hand again to my face, relishing the warmth against my cheek. "I went back to you."

Oren leaned forward. "I want to kiss you."

"Kiss me?"

"Last chance, Adelaide. Say no, or it's going to happen and once it does, I'm never letting you go again."

I swallowed. "I-I remember something—my father's will. I'd finally learned something that I'd never been meant to know."

"Yes, the codicil."

I leaned back. "How do you know this?"

"Because I do. Now you can leave him. Even without it, I wanted you to leave him. Now you can walk away and the future isn't up to him; it's up to you."

"Me?"

"*Amore mio*, the kiss?"

My eyes opened wide. "Oh! Oren, I want that kiss, but first I need to reach Alexandria."

"She's sleeping."

I couldn't comprehend. Looking to the sunshine, I asked, "Sleeping? Where are we?"

"We're in New York and so is she. Last night was long. She's sleeping down the hall."

"Wait? She's here in your home?"

He leaned toward me. "Adelaide, I've only ever professed my love to two women. I'm not a man who can walk away. I have you here and I can't wait any longer. Tell me no or I'm going to kiss you."

My memory went back to a seedy motel outside of Savannah and I smiled. "Kiss me?"

"Yes," he said with a grin. "I've spent the last months—no, *amore mio*, the last years—remembering your taste and the feel of your lips against mine. You're so close. I'm losing control. I need to know if my memory is close to reality. Say no."

I lifted my lips near his. "Never have I wanted to say yes more."

As our lips touched, Oren's presence gave me hope for the future. I didn't know what would happen with Alton, but I knew in my soul that without Oren's intervention, I wouldn't be clearheaded, my heart wouldn't be full, and the man I'd loved more than any other wouldn't be holding me in his arms.

CHAPTER 15

CHARLI

THE LAST FEW weeks created a drowning sense of exhaustion. Being with Nox, in his arms, was the haven I desired most. Totally spent, I expected to sleep for hours. I expected rest and rejuvenation. That wasn't what either of us found. From the moment we finally closed our eyes, our rest was anything but peaceful.

Over and over dreams interrupted the serenity of Nox's embrace. I'd wake, my body tossing and turning. Screams that were supposed to be hidden by the cloak of sleep became audible, echoing throughout the bedroom and waking us both. Perhaps it was the sense of security I had while with Nox. My mind told me that feeling safe shouldn't bring out my fears, but it did. Each time my eyes closed, the floodgate opened, washing me away.

While in Savannah, I'd kept my personal concerns suppressed, concentrating on my momma and her health. Selfishly, lying in Nox's arms, my night terrors weren't about my mother. She was safe, as safe as she could be. The nurse promised that she was through the worst. After all, what could be worse than death?

Each time my eyes closed, the scenes were personal—much more personal.

Though Alton and Suzanna weren't without blame, costarring as villains in my dreams—or were they nightmares?—their physical slaps were but blips on the radar compared to the fear evoked by Bryce. On Friday night at Montague Manor, he'd morphed before my eyes and now he was doing it again, this time in my sleep.

My childhood friend was gone. I saw him for the monster he was. Figurative claws became real as I surrendered to his tightening grip upon my knee. I shuddered, meeting his cold eyes as excruciating pain radiated from his vicious grasp. His smile chilled my blood as he looked toward his mother, forcing my lies of love and devotion.

Streaks of pain emitted through my nervous system until I'd wake, certain it wasn't Nox beside me but Bryce. Even the millisecond of believing that Bryce was in my bed set my heart to hammering against my breastbone and accelerated my breathing.

The woodsy scent of Nox's cologne mixed with the musk of our union would then lull me back to sleep until other scenes infiltrated my night.

The waves lapped the shore, creating a rhythm. The hand holding mine was strong and protective. I stared up at the light blue eyes as Nox and I strolled along the beach in Rye. My flat shoes morphed, their heels growing. I stumbled, each step more difficult as my shoes slid upon the pebbles. When I looked up from our intertwined fingers, the eyes were no longer swirled with love, but were infused with contempt.

As my heart again thundered, I tried to pull away from the now-iron grip. The scene had changed, erasing the beach as the song of waves faded into the mist and sadistic laughter rang in my ears. The laughter wasn't for me, but for the other person with us. Bryce's grip vibrated as he laughed at the desperation of his whore.

"Run," I whispered to Chelsea. She couldn't, paralyzed not by Bryce's grip as I was, but by his stare.

I searched for the house, for Nox, or even Oren. They were gone. Chelsea, Bryce, and I were back in Chelsea's room at Montague Manor. My stomach lurched at the whack of Bryce's knuckles as his hand left mine and collided with Chelsea's cheek. The sickening crack reverberated against the walls mere seconds before she crumpled to the floor.

I fell to the ground by her side, but the room was gone. My best friend was upon the floor, no longer in Savannah, but in our apartment in Palo Alto, her face battered. Though

115

I reached for her, I wasn't actually there; I was simply a bystander—a voyeur. My screams went unheard as a perpetrator rolled Chelsea's body over and moved her hair from her face. His head shook as recognizable sadistic laughter only momentarily stalled his abuse. Just before resuming his attack, he muttered, "Wrong one."

I woke with a start, knowing his voice. I'd known it all of my life.

Hugging the man I loved, I pushed the thoughts away. They weren't real. They weren't memories. I'd been in New York when Chelsea was attacked. I hadn't seen it. It was my mind playing tricks on me.

She was safe, like my momma. Slowly, sleep resumed and so did the dreams.

Tension filled the Georgia night as my shoes slid upon the damp grass.

It wasn't Chelsea paralyzed by Bryce's cold eyes: it was me. I tried again to wake, to find Nox, but no one was near. Alton had gone to his office and Suzanna had bid us goodnight.

When had I looked to either of them for help? And yet in my desperation, I was.

Bryce's words cut through the autumn air, his touch a jolt of dread diving deep to the pit of my stomach as my mind shifted from concern to panic. No longer in Rye, I was back in Savannah. What had I done? Why had I gone back?

The dread leached through me, from my stomach to my heart, and I knew what I hadn't the time before. I knew that this time I couldn't stop him.

"Darling, I'm getting off with you tonight, in your mouth, on your tits, or inside your cunt, I don't care. It's happening."

The contents of my stomach lurched upward as I managed my reply, "Why?"

His initial response was without words, each answer turning my body to stone. Gentle at first, he brushed his thumb against my lips. The squeeze of my breast was harder, but it was the way he grabbed my core that registered as violation as well as pain. My heart thumped against my chest as his erection probed my stomach.

"Do you need to ask? You asked me to 'take it out on you.' Your wish is my command, darling. Over there, by the tennis courts... I'm going to take it out."

His iron grip pulled me across the wet lawn. I pleaded, called out to Nox; I said no. I proclaimed and then begged. I reminded him of our childhood friendship while digging my heels into the grass. I silently pleaded with myself to wake.

Bryce's voice was ice, freezing my will with the cold, hard reality. My pleas wouldn't help me. They did the opposite, fueling his power and need for control. My childhood friend was a monster whose only concern was his own desire. He was a psychopath and his words were but the prelude to my future.

"Wrong," he said. "You want it. Say you do."

"Please, Bryce."

"Close. Begging is acceptable. Now, tell me you want me to take you. No, tell me you want me to fuck you. Come on, darling. No, I know! Tell me that you want to fuck me and you'll do it better than my whore."

"No!" My shouts were no longer contained to my dreams. They echoed through the room, waking both Nox and me.

Nox pulled me close to his chest. The woodsy scent settled in my senses, replacing the aroma of the damp Savannah night air. With time, my breathing slowed as his steady heartbeat calmed my own. With both of us fully awake, he rolled me to my back. Hovering above me, he brushed his lips over mine. "I'm only going to ask you this once, but princess, I need you to be honest."

Closing my eyes, I nodded. It hadn't been our first awakening of the night. Nox wanted honesty. I'd give it, even if it meant he'd hate me.

"What's your name?"

My eyes blinked at his strange question.

"Alexandria."

He kissed my nose. "You're my Charli and you always will be."

His words washed through me, so simple and yet so poignant.

"Did he do more than kiss you?"

How to answer that? I took a deep breath and swallowed my tears. "Yes."

Nox's body hardened as every muscle tensed. In the dim morning light, the bulging vein in his forehead pulsated. His lips pressed together as emotion emanated from his every pore, momentarily souring the air between us. I tried to look away, but his contrasting tone kept my eyes on him.

"Was it consensual, more diversion, like the kiss?"

I shook my head and lowered my chin to my chest.

"Tell me." The control he was exercising was waning.

With my face still hidden, I shook my head again. "He didn't. We didn't... sex." More tears interrupted my words. "He threatened. I told him no, but... if..."

I shouldn't have gotten in that car.

"If?" Nox encouraged.

"If I hadn't gone with Alton..."

"That was done. What more? What *if*?"

"If it weren't for Pat and Cy... showing up... Bryce said he would... he said he was going to... he threatened..."

Nox pulled me close. "Fucking bastard."

"Do you hate me?" I asked. "I'm sorry..."

Nox rose to his elbows hovering above me, his eyes meeting mine, forcing our stare, our connection. I searched the blue for answers. What did I see? Anger and regret, yes, but also unquestionably love.

"Be sorry you got in that car," his deep voice commanded. "Never do it again. Anything beyond that is not your fault. It's not you who should be sorry. It's me. I'm sorry I didn't storm the damn castle sooner." His volume rose. "Fuck Chelsea and your mom. If that makes me a monster, so be it. You are and will always be my biggest priority.

"I'm sorry you had to fight off that asshole by yourself. I'm sorry Pat was your savior when it should have been me. I'm sorry that douche bag is still walking the earth. As it is, he's a dead man walking.

"No one and I mean *no one* should scare you like that."

The tears were back, coating my cheeks as Nox kissed me again.

"And yet you asked me to make love to you last night?"

I nodded as my answer came in phrases. "I did and it felt right... I love you, Lennox Demetri... I don't ever want to be with anyone else... I'm sorry I put myself—"

His finger touched my lips. "No more apologizing. I promised to punish you for getting in that car and putting the most important person in the world in danger. I promised that when we spoke on the phone. But," he added, "not for anything else. There are others who will be punished. And I promise you, when I'm done, your ass will be sore, but others will be dead."

"You're not being literal, are you?"

"Yes, your ass will be sore."

I shook my head. "Not about that."

"Sleep. I'm here now. No more nightmares."

I clung to Nox's chest, allowing his woodsy scent and hard muscles to be my new blanket. Did I want Bryce dead? I couldn't wish death on anyone, not even Alton. I wanted them both to suffer. I wanted them to get what they deserved for treating my mother and me the way they had. I wanted to be rid of them—forever.

Was that the same as wanting them dead?

As time passed, Nox's breathing evened and I accepted his promises.

I didn't fully understand the way he made me feel or the blind trust I had in him, but that didn't mean it wasn't real.

I wanted it. I craved it.

I craved the release that I knew would come with accepting his punishment, delivered not in anger, but in love.

I also understood that his punishment wouldn't be for getting in the car, but for disobeying him, for breaking the promise I'd made to him—the promise to keep myself safe, the promise Jocelyn had also failed to keep. He'd punish me because I put the one person he loved in danger.

He'd be right. My nightmares confirmed it. I'd been in danger.

CHAPTER 16

---•O•---

NOX

CHARLI'S GRIP FINALLY loosened as her breathing found a steady rhythm. It was possible that I'd slept at some point during the night. I'm confident that I had when we'd first surrendered to sleep. After that, it was only for minutes at a time. Even when Charli wasn't fully awake, her body twitched, her head shook, and she mumbled words.

I couldn't make sense out of it until she began screaming. Her protests were loud and clear. My name even infiltrated her monologue. At first I assumed she was telling me no, but that wasn't it. She was calling out to me, for me, and I wasn't there.

As the sleepless night continued, with each of her outbursts—whether done in her sleep or causing her to wake—I saw red, blood red. Deep, dark crimson filled my vision as it flowed over my thoughts. My fists clenched, aching to connect, to seek vengeance, to mutilate Edward Spencer.

Charli had broken her promise to stay safe. I wasn't blaming the victim. Like I'd said, no one deserved to be scared like that asshole had scared her; however, she'd made me one promise, the same one Jo had made, and by getting in that car, she'd broken it. I'd promised her consequences for her actions, and when the time was right she'd experience them, but her consequences weren't what kept me from sleeping.

It was *his* consequences that kept me awake—and her stepfather's too.

Slipping from our warm bed, I eased into a pair of jeans from the closet, grabbed my phone and opened the door to the balcony. A gust of cool late-morning air made me turn, hoping I hadn't woken Charli. I hadn't. Buried under the covers, her only movement—the rise and fall from her breathing—verified she was finally sleeping.

Sighing, I made my way outside and quietly closed the door behind me.

With the sun fully up, the breeze showed itself on the sound as white caps dotting the surface and muting the colors. The bright blues of summer were fading. To the side of the property I took in the dense line of trees. Some stood bare like skeletons of their former selves, the seclusion they'd granted with their leaves now gone. The former shields were now dried, brown, and dead, their useless bodies scattered over the lawns. The few leaves remaining kept the grayness of winter at bay, holding tight to the autumn colors—the oranges, yellows, and reds.

A little farther south from my house was a yacht club. On a Sunday during the summer, the water would be alive with activity. But November in New York didn't lend itself to sailing. Stepping to the railing I inhaled, expanding my chest and filling my lungs with the brisk air. The cold burn was the wake-up call I needed. As my thoughts volleyed with the recent and not-so-recent past, the chilly surface of the decking made itself known under my bare feet.

Soon enough I'd go downstairs for coffee. First, I had a call to make.

"Lennox," Deloris answered on the first ring.

"Tell me what's happening."

"The Montague lawyers are doing their best, but Spencer is still in jail."

"What did you learn about the body?"

"Not much. They still haven't confirmed it as Melissa Summers. They've called her family to identify her."

"Identify? So the body is identifiable?"

"So it seems."

Wouldn't that mean she was recently killed? I ran my hand through my hair as the autumn scene before me disappeared and Alton Fitzgerald's face came back to my memory. "Fitzgerald came to the interrogation room at the police station last night. He accused me of being behind this whole thing—some mastermind plot to incriminate Spencer. He said he knew Melissa Summers was connected to Infidelity. When I saved Charli, I'd mentioned that Spencer was a client. Fitzgerald threatened to figure out the connection and told me that my plan wouldn't work."

"He accused you of planting the body?"

"Not in so many words, but yeah, he did."

"He's grasping at straws. He and his crooked police and judges can't ignore a dead woman on Spencer's property."

My teeth clenched. "This is going to be a nightmare. If he exposes Infidelity…"

"As I said, he's desperate. Before yesterday everything was circumstantial. Now they found a body. That combined with Melissa's earlier statements… Lennox, you didn't even know who she was when she went to the police. There's no connection. Alton Fitzgerald is grasping. I've been listening to their phones," Deloris went on, "and audio from Montague Manor. The surveillance was set up in the manor during the chaos as guests left the party last night. The crew was in and out dressed as part of the catering staff. Mr. Demetri also secured audible surveillance at Montague Corporation and Hamilton and Porter. I can't listen to everything at once, but I have a team working on it. We'll know what they're thinking as soon as *they* do."

"It's Sunday. The law and corporate offices should be closed."

"The law office has been buzzing. Are you kidding?"

"Is Fitzgerald there?"

"No. He was at Magnolia Woods and now is back to the police station. The poor man hasn't gotten any sleep. I've listened as he's yelled at Mrs. Spencer about it all morning."

Mrs. Spencer. The name reminded me of Charli instead of Edward's mother.

"What do you know about the marriage license they showed me yesterday?"

"Have you talked to Alex about it?"

"No, she's still asleep."

"I'm glad someone is getting sleep."

"Neither of us got much."

"I've told you… too much information."

I grinned, remembering Charli's sexy body in my arms. "That's not where I was going. We should have moved faster. I never should have left her there for that long."

"And have left her mother and Chelsea in harm's way? Alexandria wouldn't have allowed it."

Fuck her approval.

I swallowed my response and went back to what Deloris had said earlier. "You already had Magnolia Woods bugged. You said Fitzgerald was there. Are you on it?"

"Yes. The nurse, Mack?"

"That big guy," I said, recalling the video feed from Adelaide's room.

"He woke with a whopping headache. Though his memory is fuzzy, he's certain there was a doctor who came in to get Alex's mom, but the video footage doesn't corroborate his story. If they'd do a toxicology screen, they'd know he was drugged. They haven't and pretty soon it will be too late. They seem to have taken the footage as unaltered. Not surprisingly, the facility administrators are more concerned about their reputation than his story.

"Before Fitzgerald was consulted about his wife's disappearance, Magnolia Woods contacted the Savannah-Chatham police. They've taken Mack in for questioning. If I'm to interpret the chatter correctly, they're currently holding him under suspicion of aiding and abetting in Mrs. Fitzgerald's kidnapping. They're waiting for a ransom demand."

"That won't last when they learn it wasn't a kidnapping."

"No, but they can hold him for up to seventy-two hours. It's a nice diversion and makes the police and Magnolia Woods feel like they're doing something."

"None of this has made the news? No leak at all?" I asked.

"Fitzgerald demanded radio silence. Porter, his attorney, claimed that at the very least the facility is negligent. Magnolia Woods wants it kept quiet and handled internally. They boast the wealthiest clientele. Losing one of them, especially one who was last seen unconscious, isn't good for business. And the police want it kept quiet until they hear from the kidnapper. They're concerned that media coverage will bring out false demands."

I nodded. "Well, at least for now, that seems to be working."

"From the feed at Hamilton and Porter, I'm expecting Alex and Chelsea to be subpoenaed back to Savannah sooner rather than later."

The cool air was forgotten. "I'm not allowing her to go alone."

"I didn't expect you to."

My mind went to Demetri Enterprises. I never thought I'd be happy to have Oren back in New York, but I was. I was relieved to know that he would be where I should be while I was away with Charli.

My bare skin prickled as the cold wind picked up. At the same moment, a rustling in the tree line caught my attention. My voice lowered. "Oren's men are out here." It wasn't a question.

"Yes, we've spoken. You're better protected right now than the president."

"You've spoken?"

"Many times."

"You still work for me."

"Lennox, right now, we're all working together."

I let out a long breath. "I never thought I'd want that, not after he left and moved away, but now…"

"Be thankful."

I nodded. "I am. I'm going inside to talk to him now and to find out how Charli's mom is doing, before Charli wakes."

"One more thing that you should know," Deloris said.

"What?"

"Just because Edward Spencer is still behind bars, that doesn't mean they won't allow him to post bail. I'm sure there'll be restrictions to ensure that he doesn't flee, but I'd venture to guess that Mr. Fitzgerald will stop at nothing to get him out."

"Even with a body?"

"Out until trial. If he's convicted, which he should be, no one will be able to keep him from going behind bars."

"I want him dead," I confessed. "I want them both to be, and I want to be the one to do it." I flexed the knuckles of my free hand. "I want them to know fear."

"For a minute or for twenty years?"

I gave her question some thought as the waves blurred, giving the illusion of snow covering frozen water. "Twenty years."

"Then let him hang himself," Deloris said. "Without Chelsea's corroboration, his defense is shaky at best. He does have the travel records. He was in California the night Chelsea was attacked, but let's find out when Melissa was killed. Let's see if he has a defense. That's why they want the ladies back in Savannah. Ralph Porter is betting that they can vouch for his whereabouts."

"You still have nothing on the ME's report?"

"I'm waiting. I should learn as soon as Porter does."

"Let us know."

"I will. I'm driving up to Rye soon. I hope to convince Chelsea to allow me to take pictures of the abuse. They can be used to get her out of her agreement. Perhaps they could even be leaked to the press."

"As with Melissa, there's no way to prove that Spencer was the culprit."

"No, but with the smoking guns stacking up, someone will eventually believe there's a fire."

"When do you plan to be here?"

"I want to get back to the discussion at Hamilton and Porter. Isaac is there in Rye. Since your father has the security taken care of, Isaac's been concentrating on the manor's surveillance. My computer pings every time Fitzgerald or either of the Spencers uses their phones. Clayton is listening too. We also have others. I know I can depend on them, but I personally want to hear the ME's report."

As I turned toward the windows, my own reflection became visible. I pulled the phone from my ear and looked at the screen. Lifting it back, I asked, "How did you access all their phones?"

"They all called the phone Alex was given. Once I had their numbers, the rest was easy."

"I don't say it enough, but damn, I'm glad you work for me."

Deloris's laugh made my cheeks rise. "You should be."

I hung up the call as I eased back into the bedroom.

Charli hadn't moved. Every bone in my body ached to climb back under the covers with her, to smell her sweet scent and bask in her warmth. My cock twitched, knowing she was completely nude under those blankets.

Instead, I tiptoed across the wood floor and out into the hallway.

Silence echoed through the corridor. Should I go to the master suite or downstairs? Where would I find my father?

I took one step toward the bedroom he used and remembered my attire, or lack thereof. *"Hello, Mrs. Fitzgerald. Nice to meet you."* Yes, I thought that sounded better coming from a man wearing a shirt.

Feminine voices came into range as I descended the stairs and neared the first floor. At the base, I turned toward the sitting room, but stopped short, hearing Chelsea's voice. Still hidden, I listened.

"...like I'm intruding. Honestly, it's how I've felt since this whole thing started."

"Don't be silly. You're a friend of Alex's. The Demetris have welcomed you here. You can stay as long as you'd like."

"They scare me, Mr. Demetri more than Nox."

"Nox?" Silvia asked. "You call him that too?"

"Only in third person. It's the name Alex called him from the beginning. I was there when they met."

Visions of Del Mar scattered across my memories. I turned the corner as both Chelsea's and Silvia's gazes turned to me.

"Did you forget your shirt?" Silvia smirked.

"I'm looking for Oren. I figured formal attire was optional."

"Now, I suppose, but I'd suspect this place will get busier as the day progresses."

"Is Alex awake yet?" Chelsea asked.

"No, she was up late with her mom." I turned my conversation to Silvia. "I think I'd like to take her some breakfast."

Silvia lowered the mug she was holding, placing it on the table. "It's after one. How about some lunch?"

I nodded. "What do we have?"

She waved me away. "Go talk to your father. He's in the office. I'll make both you and Alex something."

"You don't—"

Chelsea lowered her mug. "I can help. Please, Silvia, let me feel like I'm doing something."

I turned back to Chelsea. "I owe you an apology. This thing—Infidelity—was never supposed to end up…"

She shook her head. "I'm a big girl. I signed the agreement."

"I have a question. Did you write the note that the guard gave me at Montague?"

"Yes," she answered softly.

"The *rules*. You were giving us a clue."

"I tried."

"I just heard you refer to me as Nox, yet the note was addressed to Lennox?"

"I hoped that would let you know that it wasn't Alex who wrote it."

I nodded. "Thank you."

"I'll go help Silvia." Her big hazel eyes looked up. "Thank you. I'm sorry too. I wish I could have done more to help her."

"You're her best friend. I'm glad that hasn't changed."

I didn't wait for her response. Instead, I made my way through the rooms and corridors to the office. The door was slightly ajar. For only a second I began to hesitate, but then just as quickly, I pushed it open.

Fuck this. It's my house.

Oren's chair was turned, facing the windows that overlooked the pool. "…yet you were there? If the conversation will affect Demetri Enterprises, then I should be informed."

Who is he talking to?

His chair spun toward me as I approached the desk. "Doyle, I'll call you back. Something just came up."

"Doyle Carroll?" I asked after he hung up.

"Yes, he heard some interesting things at the Montague party."

CHAPTER 17

CHARLI

THE CLATTER OF dishes pried me from my slumber. For only a moment, I scrambled for the blankets. My modesty quickly faded as the handsome man delivering my meal spoke.

"No, princess. Don't pull those blankets up. I want to see that beautiful body."

Nox's deep voice rumbled through me, tugging a lazy smile from me. With bright sunshine from the windows as a backlight, his features were muted. Despite the halo of light, Nox's mussed hair, wide shoulders, and bare chest sent a tingle of electricity through me. As my eyes adjusted, my gaze lowered, taking in his defined abdomen and the V that disappeared into his low-hanging jeans. I pushed my thighs together as I again reached for the blanket.

My smile blossomed as I scooted toward the headboard pulling the cover with me. Tucking the blanket around my traitorous breasts with their hardened nipples, my attention went from Nox to whatever was hiding below the silver dome. As my imagination filled with breakfast delights, my stomach growled in a very loud and completely unsexy way.

Nox's lips parted with a big smile. "Hungry?"

I shifted, wondering how the sound of his voice could stir a desire deep in my core, a hunger rivaling the one for food.

"I am. What time is it?"

Nox lifted the cover of one tray revealing a sandwich, soup, and vegetables. It must have been the soup, but the way its spicy aroma filled the room made my mouth water.

"Almost two," he said. "I figured it was time to wake my Sleeping Beauty, and since breakfast is long past, Silvia suggested lunch."

The sweet scene, his caring gesture, and even the delicious aroma washed away in a wave of panic. "Two? What?" My legs flailed as I worked to untangle myself from the sheet. "How's my mom? Have you seen her? How could you let me sleep so late?"

Leaving the tray on the bedside stand, Nox lowered himself to the edge of the bed and seized my hand, stopping my escape before I could free myself from the blankets. "She's fine. I haven't seen her but I spoke with my dad." Nox looked down at his bare chest. "I'm not exactly dressed to introduce myself to my girlfriend's mother."

His words registered: she's fine. *She's fine.*

Warmth filled my cheeks as I again studied his lack of clothing. "My mom's old but I'm pretty sure you'd make quite the impression."

"How about on her daughter?"

"On me?"

"Yes, princess…" He scooted nearer until our noses touched. "…have I made an impression?"

With a slight tip of my chin our lips came together. The sheet that had thwarted my escape dropped to my waist as his muscular chest pushed toward me. My moan filled the room as his touch roamed my side, grazing my breast and skirting lower. With Nox as my puppeteer by way of invisible strings, inch-by-inch my legs willing opened, exposing my ready core.

"Oh, Nox."

The food he'd delivered was forgotten as my neck strained and back arched to his touch. With a kiss to my lips, his fingers plunged and thumb made magical sparks as he strummed my swollen clit. I reached for his jeans, wanting to free what I needed.

"What do you want?"

My breathing quickened as my smile grew. "You're such a dick."

"But you love me."

"I do."

"Say it."

"I love you."

His head moved back and forth. "No, tell me what you want."

"I want your cock." My declaration was much softer than it had been in a gas station months ago.

"Enough that you're willing to wait on lunch?"

I looked at the tray and then back at the eyes above me, devouring me. His erection strained against his jeans and pushed against my leg. My hunger for food wasn't gone, but unquestionably, my desire for him was greater. "Yes."

"Oh, princess, I want you too." His hand trailed the inside of my thighs. "I want to give you my cock." He teased my clit. "And I want to make you my lunch."

"Nox."

He sighed. "But my dad said your mom will be downstairs soon. I'm still working on that first impression. *Sorry we're late, I was busy fucking your daughter* probably isn't the way to go."

I giggled. He was right. "Okay, but… maybe we could work on that lunch part. I mean, I don't want you to starve."

Nox laughed. "And Deloris is on her way, and…"

I waited, not sure what the *and* meant.

"And?"

"Deloris thinks we'll need to head back to Savannah soon, possibly tonight."

My pulse quickened as the idea of a quick afternoon delight faded away. "No. We just got here. I finally slept. I don't want to go back."

Nox brought the tray of food over to the bed. "Eat."

I shook my head. "No. I just lost my appetite."

He lowered the tray to my lap. "I don't think you ate the entire time you were gone. I swear you've lost weight."

"After all Lana's cooking, that's probably a good thing."

"No, it's not. Eat. Besides, if you think Lana's a good cook, you need to eat Silvia's food."

I wanted to argue, but the feast before me wouldn't allow it.

"While you eat," Nox said, "let me explain what my dad and I were told earlier by a member of the Demetri legal staff."

I shook my head. "I've thought about it already. I think I know."

"Okay, tell me what you think—after you've eaten."

I lifted a piece of the sandwich and took a bite. As I began to chew, my stomach did the loud growling thing again. Shaking my head, I took a drink of the iced tea. "Fine. I'm still hungry."

"They were talking about you and Chelsea making a statement," he said.

I swallowed. "They think it was a mistake to refuse the police last night?"

"Yes and no."

"I don't want to go back, but they're right. It would look better if Chelsea and I were willing to make statements. And I'm nervous that the policeman called me Mrs. Spencer."

Nox exhaled. "At the police station they showed me a marriage license dated Friday. Your stepfather offered me a deal if I agreed not to contest your marriage and obeyed a restraining order to stay away from you."

Blowing on a spoonful of soup, I shook my head. "Alton won't stop. He won't." And then my mind filled with the last twelve hours and I met Nox's gaze. "I'd say if you accepted his offer, you're definitely in violation of that restraining order."

"I told him to stick it up his ass."

"You what?"

"Not directly, though we did speak."

"Mmm," I hummed as the spicy broth warmed my mouth, bringing my taste buds to life. "That is amazing."

"I told you," he said with a grin.

"I promise, Bryce and I weren't married. Remember when I told you that Bryce threatened to…" I didn't want to say the words again.

"Yes." The vein in his forehead throbbed.

"That was Friday night, the same night Pat and Cy showed up at the manor. Do you think it would have only been threats if we were married?"

Nox covered my hand. "No, and even thinking about this makes me want to kill the motherfucker."

"Stop saying that. Besides, I'm not sure if it would be better to speak to the detective or the attorneys."

"The police can't make you talk to them. A subpoena would come from the attorney of the court."

I nodded, again dipping my spoon in the soup. "It could come from either side. But I doubt it's been long enough. Today's Sunday. A prosecutor probably hasn't been assigned. Not officially," I added.

"On a case like this, I'm sure the state is mounting its offense," Nox said. "Nevertheless, the attorneys told us that Spencer is stuck in jail until after his first appearance. Assuming they still believe they have enough to convict, then he'll officially be charged. They're waiting on the report from the medical examiner."

My hungry stomach twisted. "I can't help wondering where they found her. How long was she dead?"

"We don't know anything. My guess is that they don't either or it'd be all over the news outlets." He reached for my hand. "Deloris is concerned that no matter what they find or come back with, he'll be released on bail. It could be high, but his mother or your stepfather will more than likely pay it."

I exhaled as my shoulders sagged. "I don't want to see him."

"I don't want you to. If we go to Savannah tonight, you and Chelsea could speak to the police and even his attorneys if you want to. Then we can be back here before he's out on bail."

I lowered the sandwich to the plate. "Chelsea's face."

Nox nodded. "It will help the prosecutor's case. If the attorneys see it, they might realize the uphill battle they have in front of them."

"Wait a minute," I said. "You said *we*... if we go to Savannah?"

"Oh hell yes. You're not going on your own. We're taking the Batplane and flying as low under the radar as possible."

"Thank you." The delicious soup and sandwich churned as I contemplated Savannah. "We won't be under the radar if we show up at either

Hamilton and Porter or the police station."

"No, but we don't have to announce our presence until we arrive."

My gaze went behind Nox to the windows, bright with sun through the now-opened shutters. I took in the clear blue sky. I couldn't see anything else from my angle, but the blueness reminded me that today was another day. Yesterday was finally over. "Thank you."

Nox leaned over and kissed my forehead. "For what?"

"For everything."

"Don't you get it?" he asked.

"Get what?"

"Alexandria Collins, I want to be your *everything*. There's nothing you can tell me or confess to change my mind."

My cheeks warmed. "You are my everything. That doesn't mean that I'm not still mad at you and Deloris for involving Chelsea."

"It wasn't supposed—"

I touched his lips. "I know. Chelsea and I have talked about it."

"Deloris will help her get out of Infidelity. Once she does, we can find something for her at Demetri."

"I'm not sure if she'll—"

This time Nox touched my lips with his. "How about we let her decide? There are a few other things we need to talk about, things I've recently learned."

I took the last carrot stick from my plate and eyed the empty bowl, wishing for more of whatever kind of soup I just ate. It reminded me of vegetable soup, but spicier with some noodles. "I would love more soup, but first, I want to see my mother."

Nox reached for the tray. "Maybe it would be better if she explained some of the things."

Wrapped in a towel after a shower, I entered the closet. It was the same place I'd found Nox's belt so many months ago. Built-in dressers and racks lined what could be a room. One section was filled with my clothes. They weren't mine from New York or Savannah, but they were all in my size. "When did these get here?" I asked.

"Earlier today. Deloris had them delivered. I brought them in here while you were sleeping."

I shook my head as I searched the nearby drawers. "Did she send me any underwear?"

Propped against the doorframe with his arms crossed over his wide chest, Nox's blue eyes sparkled as he watched me search. "What if I told you that I told Deloris you didn't need any?"

I spun toward him. "What?"

His laugh rumbled through the small room as he took two steps and reached for my towel. I swatted his hand. "Stop. I want to see my mom."

"I'm never letting you out of my sight again."

"That may make your work and my school difficult."

He reached for the platinum diamond-dusted cage. "This never comes off."

I nodded. "Underwear?"

He pointed to one of the drawers. After I finished dressing in jeans and a soft white sweater, I braided my hair, pulling it all over one shoulder. For a moment I stared at the woman in the mirror. For the first time in nearly two weeks, my eyes weren't filled with worry.

"You're beautiful," Nox whispered, his handsome face coming near my ear.

I spun toward him. "Did your dad really say my mom would be downstairs and out of the hospital bed already?"

"That's what he said."

I shook my head, recognizing an emotion I hadn't felt in nearly two weeks.

Happiness.

In this home, under Nox's protective gaze, and with my mother safe, I was happy.

More than happy. I was excited—almost giddy. It was as if sometime during the morning, a seed of anticipation had cracked open deep inside my soul. Its roots were spreading through me, pushing away the stress and gloom. No longer entrapped, I was like a young girl on Christmas morning, eager to go downstairs and see what was under the tree. "I can't believe she's that much better. I was so scared."

A strong arm surrounded my waist and Nox pulled me against his chest. "Never again. No more scared."

I leaned back, our hips touching, and my lips in a full grin. "What if I told you there's something else that scares me?"

"Tell me and I'll make it go away."

"That's the thing. I'm not sure I want it to go away."

Nox's brow furrowed as his lips quirked to the side. "I'm confused."

I lifted myself up on my tiptoes and brushed my lips to his. "Me too. That's what you do to me."

As I began to pull away, Nox brought me closer. "Tell me what scares you."

"You."

His embrace stiffened. "Me?"

I looked down and ran my fingers over his belt buckle before looking back up through my lashes. "This… last night you said…"

"I said your ass is mine," he said, finishing my sentence. "And it will be. Is that what scares you?" His question was laced with concern.

"Part of it."

"Princess, if you want to go see your mom, stop talking in riddles."

"The idea scares me…" The warmth I'd felt earlier in my cheeks burned hotter. "…because as much as I shouldn't want what you described, I do. I trust you."

His smile returned as his phone vibrated.

"I want so fucking bad to ignore that," he said as he pulled it from his jeans.

DELORIS flashed on the screen.

"Where are you?" Nox asked.

I started to walk away when he stopped me. "Charli, where's your handbag from last night?"

Spinning a full circle, I looked about the room. "I'm not sure. I had it when we got here. Why?"

"Deloris wants to know if the phone your stepfather gave you is in it."

The happiness that had sprung to life evaporated as dread filled its place. "Shit, it is."

"She's been listening to audible surveillance. They know where you are and are speculating that your mom is with you. She believes they've tracked your phone."

CHAPTER 18

——●○●——

OREN

"YOU DON'T NEED to carry me."

Adelaide's voice might be weak, but the sparkle in her eyes wasn't. The blue was glowing—electric—as if her eyes were telling their own story. They were saying that her body would still need to heal, but inside she was alive.

The reality was that I'd carry her anywhere—everywhere. As it was, I was only carrying her down the steps to the first floor. Dr. Rossi had said it was good to get her out of bed. I'd told Lennox that she'd be downstairs.

This morning, after she'd awakened, after we'd talked and kissed, I gave her privacy. It wasn't that I wasn't willing to be with her as Dr. Rossi disconnected her from the different tubes and helped her bathe. But I hadn't earned that right.

Stealing a woman—even one I love—didn't give me the right to take what she wasn't willing to give. With her in my arms and the memory of our kiss, I was content to accept anything she offered. Who was I kidding? I'd push for more, as I had the kiss, but not too much. She deserved to make the decisions. After all, she'd been the one to send me away.

While Liz and Dr. Rossi helped her, I'd made my way to another room and showered. Through the night and morning, sleep had only come in small snippets, but I wasn't complaining. Having Adelaide safe and with me gave me more energy than hours of rest.

After Adelaide was disengaged from her connections and showered, I'd joined her again as she tried to eat. It wasn't much, just broth and Jell-O, but it was food, it was in her stomach, and thankfully it stayed there.

With each passing moment and instance, I appreciated Eva Rossi's candor. Subjects I would have preferred to avoid to shelter Adelaide, Eva attacked head-on. She was straightforward about Adelaide's heart stopping and the CPR. Then as Adelaide nibbled her first meal, Eva explained that the DTs should be done but her body needed help to heal. She recommended daily vitamin shots and lots of rest. She also emphasized that from this point forward, Adelaide would need to consider herself a recovering addict. She didn't beat around the bush. She said no wine. No alcohol of any kind. Even painkillers were discouraged. The high dosages of alcohol and opioids her body had been forced to metabolize had left her liver enzymes too high. The only way to a full recovery was without further assault.

As the doctor spoke, I noticed Adelaide's grip of her spoon tighten. In that moment, I vowed to join her on this journey, if she'd have me. I'd give her the encouragement and support she needed.

Though that was my desire, I was a realistic man. I didn't have the illusion that we were finally a couple or that we could even pick up where we'd left off. Besides, I didn't want to pick up where we'd left off. I wanted to go back further to before she told me to leave and never contact her again.

Adelaide's arms tightened around my neck with each step.

"Just down the stairs," I said. "I'm sorry if this hurts your ribs."

Her shoulders moved up and down. "It does, but apparently pain medicine is out of the question."

I brushed my lips over her forehead. "Just squeeze tighter. Give it to me."

Adelaide's chin dropped to her chest. "Oren, you don't need to…"

I stopped with only a few steps to go. "I don't *need* to. I *want* to."

Her eyes met mine. In that moment I hoped she could see the sincerity in my stare, the same way I saw the wonder in hers. Perhaps the first time I looked into the life of Adelaide Montague was out of a sense of obligation, but that pretense ended once I truly knew her. Obligation was not the reason she held a place in my heart. Having her there, keeping her there, wasn't something I could control. She was there and always would be, because of the woman she was, because at one time she'd loved me too, a poor boy who'd worked the docks in the city, someone who'd never dared to dream of a lady like Adelaide.

She'd loved me when I'd thought myself unlovable.

Maybe it wasn't gone?

Adelaide settled her head against my shoulder as I stepped as gingerly as possible. She was light, too light. We were on our way to the dining room so Adelaide could eat whatever it was that Silvia had prepared. Dr. Rossi had said to take eating slowly, but damn, I wanted to find lasagna. I wanted bread. I wanted ten courses of never-ending food. I wanted Silvia's cooking to return the fullness to Adelaide's cheeks and pad the bones I was able to feel through the nightgown and robe she wore.

Liz smiled up from the bottom of the stairs with her hands upon the back of a wheelchair.

As I turned, Adelaide saw the chair. "Dr. Rossi said I should walk."

"Ma'am, we don't want you to overdo."

I lowered Adelaide to her feet near the chair. As I did, her hand reached for mine and tightly gripped. Trembling rattled through her as she fought to stand. Though I knew her unused muscles added to her shakiness, I feared it was also the pain of her ribs.

"Maybe you should sit," I encouraged.

"No. I'm tired of being an invalid."

My grin broadened, taking in her strength. "You heard the lady. We're going to walk to the dining room."

"Yes, sir," Liz responded, dropping behind, but not going away.

She needn't worry. As Adelaide and I walked slowly, step by step, through the house, if Adelaide so much as faltered, I wouldn't hesitate to scoop her back into my arms.

"Your home is beautiful," Adelaide said as we navigated the hallway. In front of us was the back of the house, my favorite view, the reason I'd built this house here. It was one of the things Angelina adored.

Through the windows, the sound sparkled with the beauty of a million diamonds.

It had been years since I'd appreciated the view, but now, with Adelaide's petite hand gripping mine, I did. "I've always loved the view."

"We're in New York. What is that?"

"It's the Long Island Sound. That's Long Island across the water."

She shook her head, her freshly washed and dried hair skimming her shoulders.

I helped her to a chair in the formal dining room. The house as a whole was rarely used by anyone but Silvia. The dining room was one of the safest rooms. Though the pocket doors at each entrance were ajar, the room was interior. The windows and sound were a distance away.

"I can't believe I'm here and we're here," she said, gazing up. "But I'm beginning to doubt that my daughter is here. I still haven't seen her."

"She is. I wouldn't lie to you."

Silvia appeared. "Ms. Montague, it's nice to meet you. I'm Silvia."

Adelaide reached out, cupping Silvia's hand between both of her own. Her eyes glistened as she spoke. Immediately, I knew she was thinking back to the stories we'd shared. "Silvia, please call me Adelaide. It's so good to finally meet you. My dear, you are as lovely as I'd heard."

Silvia's eyes fluttered from Adelaide to me and back as her voice stuttered. "A-as you've heard?"

There was so much about me that even those closest didn't know. I usually wasn't the sharing type. Adelaide brought out another side to me.

"Yes," Adelaide said, her honesty bringing our past to light. "Oren always spoke highly of you. And seeing you, I understand why he loves you like a daughter."

Silvia took a step back, her lips forming a straight line. Never could I recall seeing her speechless.

"Ma'am, I believe I'm at a disadvantage." And just like that, she was back. Silvia leaned closer. "But I say we kick him out of here and you fill me in on what I apparently was never told."

Still standing, I found my tone, the one that hid the fact that I was overwhelmed at seeing Silvia and Adelaide together, of witnessing what I hoped would be a budding friendship, perhaps like the one Silvia had shared with Angelina. "I'm not going anywhere. Silvia, I've been talking up your culinary skills. Don't make a liar out of me."

"As if I can impress with the diet restrictions Dr. Rossi gave me."

"Let's give it a try."

She shrugged, sending a smile to Adelaide as she walked back to the kitchen. Once she was gone, Adelaide's gaze met mine. "I'm sorry. Did I say something out of turn?"

I shrugged as I sat. "Maybe I've never actually said those words to her."

She reached out to my hand. "But they were true?"

I nodded. "I've never lied to you."

"Then it's time. Life is too short. Now, you were still trying to convince me that my daughter is here and yet it's after three and I haven't seen her."

"She is," Silvia said as she brought us glasses of water. "Lennox took lunch up to her about an hour ago."

Adelaide's back straightened. "Lennox? Your son?"

I nodded.

"Oh," she sighed more than spoke. "I'm relieved to hear that. I had memories of something about someone else." She shook her head. "I don't know what was real."

"We have a lot to sort out," I said. "I spoke with Lennox before he took Alexandria her lunch. He said she didn't sleep well. The last few weeks at Montague have been difficult. According to him, she may be married."

Adelaide's eyes widened and she set the glass of water back on the table as the liquid sloshed upon the shiny table. "No, please don't tell me she married Bryce."

"He doesn't think it's legal. She's denied it."

"Then why would he think she was?"

"Your husband had a marriage license shown to him while they detained him in Savannah."

"They detained him?"

Silvia came back in with bowls of soup, something with noodles and a wonderful aroma, and then just as quickly, she stepped away.

"He's here now. Everyone is."

"A marriage license?" She shook her head. "Surely Alton has realized that I'm gone."

I nodded. "Yes, that happened sooner than we'd hoped."

She paled. "Does he know *where* I am?" She wasn't only asking about location but also about with *whom*. We'd successfully kept our affair secret through the years. Once he learned where she was, that would no longer be the case.

"Not yet," I said. "They've hypothesized that you are with Alexandria. Your husband is wisely not making a big deal out of your disappearance. So far there's been no news coverage. According to Lennox's assistant, the police believe you were kidnapped. They're waiting on a ransom demand."

Adelaide's smile bloomed. "You did say you took me."

"And I'm not letting you go. There's no amount of ransom I'll accept."

"But what about Alton?"

"His hands are a little full with the murder investigation and bogus marriage."

We both turned to footsteps as Chelsea stopped at the doorway.

"Miss Moore."

"Chelsea?"

We both spoke simultaneously.

"I'm sorry. I don't want to interrupt," she said, her eyes wide, one bordered by a sickening brown and green discoloration.

Adelaide's hand went to her lips. "Chelsea... what happened?"

The young woman's fingers went to the bruise on her cheek as her face tipped forward. "I heard voices and thought maybe Alex was awake."

"See?" I said. "She's here."

Adelaide's shoulders straightened. "Why are *you* here?" It was a tone I wasn't accustomed to hearing come from her lips.

"Because she's my best friend." This time we all waited as Alexandria appeared behind Chelsea holding Lennox's hand.

I took a deep breath. "Well, *amore mio*, this is what we'd wanted."

Alexandria dropped Lennox's hand and raced around the table to Adelaide. "Look at you!" she cried, wrapping her arms around Adelaide's neck. "You're sitting here. You're eating."

When the two separated, both of their eyes were moist with emotion. After Lennox pulled out a chair for Chelsea and another for Alexandria, he came forward offering his hand. "Mrs. Fitzgerald, Lennox Demetri."

Her blue eyes scanned my son up and down. "My, my... you are the spitting image of your father."

His lips quirked upward. "It's very nice to meet you."

"And you as well. Please call me Adelaide." She turned to Alexandria and cupped her cheeks. "We need to talk."

"We do, but right now I want to relish the fact that you're talking."

"You visited me?"

"I did."

"You were in Savannah?"

Alexandria swallowed. "I was."

"How did you know? Did Jane call you?"

It was as if they were alone in their own bubble until Alexandria answered.

"No, Momma, Chelsea told me that you needed me."

Adelaide turned toward Chelsea, her expression souring and neck straightening as it had when Chelsea first entered the dining room. "I suppose I owe you my gratitude."

"No, Mrs. Fitzgerald, you don't owe me anything. Alex needed to know what was happening with her mother."

"Thank you."

As the women spoke, my eyes met Lennox's. Adelaide was right. My son was the younger reflection of me, the better parts of me, the parts before I'd sold my soul. In his eyes was my prize. He'd been spared so much.

"We're all here—" Lennox began.

"Who else needs soup?" Silvia asked. "I may have made it a little spicier than the doctor recommended and for those of you not on restrictions, we have bread and..."

"I wish," Alexandria said. "Silvia, it's amazing, but..." She looked to Lennox. "...Deloris just called. I need to find my handbag."

"And Chelsea, the three of us need to head back to Savannah," Lennox added.

"No." The word came from nearly everyone besides Lennox and Alexandria.

"Why?" Adelaide asked.

"It would be better to give our statements and get out of Savannah before Bryce makes bail."

Adelaide's head shook back and forth. "Alexandria, Oren was just saying something about a marriage license?"

"I didn't marry Bryce. Alton tried to force it. He had a judge in his office. I didn't say *yes*. If there's a license, it's forged."

"We can't let him get away with ruining any more lives," Adelaide said. She looked at me. "Too much time has been wasted."

Alexandria sat between Lennox and Adelaide. "We have a few minutes before Deloris gets here. Momma, help me." She motioned between Adelaide and me. "How do you two know one another?"

Silvia was still standing. I reached for her wrist. "Let's not worry about the food yet. Sit with us. This involves all of us."

Chelsea began to stand. "I'm intruding."

"No, Miss Moore. You're here because you chose to help Alexandria. Sit." I took a deep breath as all eyes turned to me. "We have too much to discuss to ease into any of it. Let me start. I first became acquainted with Adelaide—"

She reached for my hand. "It was a Christmas party..." Her smile shone, telling me to begin our story there, not years before. She turned to Lennox. "...your father's first Christmas as a single man."

"What?" Alexandria said before Lennox reached for her knee, pulling his chair closer to hers.

"Let them talk. I heard this from Oren about two weeks ago and it still hasn't sunk in. Just listen."

She nodded, turning back toward us. "Okay. I'm sorry. Can you define *acquainted*?"

Pink returned to Adelaide's cheeks. "No, dear."

"Holy shit," Alexandria murmured.

"We *spoke*..." I emphasized the word. "...for the first time at that party. We were surrounded by other guests. I'd planned all these fantastic business pitches. That was why I was there. The guest list was exclusive. However, fate had other plans." I turned to Adelaide. "Everyone else disappeared. It was only the two of us. I'd never been so attracted..." My eyes closed in memory and reopened. "…I had, but I never believed that I deserved to know that same kind of love for a second time in my life."

Adelaide squeezed my hand as Lennox tensed. The muscles of his face flexed as he clenched his jaw, just as he had in his office when I'd explained this for the first time.

"It was a few months later before I tried to contact Adelaide again. I couldn't get her out of my mind."

As had happened decades ago at the Christmas party, the rest of the table disappeared. I was recounting our story to the only woman whose opinion mattered. In her gaze I saw the love I'd feared was gone. Was it because we were walking down memory lane or was it still there?

"He tracked me down at a luncheon," Adelaide said. "Of course I hadn't gotten him out of my mind either, but I never thought… when he stood there at that restaurant for a moment I thought he was a figment of my imagination." She reached out and caressed my cheek. "But he was real, just as he was when I woke this morning."

"*Amore mio.*"

"My love."

CHAPTER 19

CHARLI

NOX'S HAND ON my thigh kept me seated, kept me quiet as I listened to one of the most unbelievable stories I'd ever heard.

How is this possible?

How can it be true?

After the shock eased a bit, I tried to take in the scene. I focused not only on their words but also the way my mother and Oren stared at one another. They were well into their private history and stories of stolen moments and secret rendezvous when it hit me—my momma had an affair.

My mother screwed around on Alton.

I suppose that should have upset me. After all, shouldn't I look to my parents as a moral compass? But the reality didn't upset me. I'd known most of my life that Alton cheated on my mother. After the last two weeks, I believed it had happened right under her nose. What I never imagined was that my mother had done it too—that she'd actually experienced happiness.

"I couldn't do as he asked." Momma's chest heaved. "Telling Oren to leave me and going back to you and Montague…" She looked at me. "…was one of the hardest things I've ever done." She turned back to Oren. "I wanted you to find someone else."

"That's when you moved to London," Silvia said to Oren matter-of-factly.

Oren turned toward her. "It was. You all had each other."

Nox's grip tensed. When I looked up, his jaw was set, hard and rigid.

"I didn't know who you were," Silvia said to my mother, "but I knew about you."

"You did? How?" Nox asked.

"Angelina."

His lips pursed.

Silvia nodded. "Get that look off your face, Lennox. She approved."

Oren shifted in his chair. "I didn't know that she told you."

"It really is nice to finally meet you, Adelaide."

My momma's eyes glistened with moisture. "Thank you, Silvia, that means more than you know."

A stillness fell over the dining room, a calm like that following a storm. Maybe that was what it was. The storm had passed and we were all here.

"Now it's my turn," Momma said, "to thank you. I don't know who all is responsible for saving me..." She smiled, her eyes sparkling in a way I couldn't recall witnessing. "...*kidnapping* me but thank you."

We all turned toward footsteps on the wooden floor.

"Good afternoon," Deloris said. "It appears you're all having a party and I wasn't invited."

"Mrs. Witt," Oren said, with a grand gesture. "Please, join us."

She sat between Chelsea and Silvia, nodding at each and scanning our grouping. The dining room table was large, but in its current form we were nearing capacity. Deloris looked at my mother. "Mrs. Fitzgerald, I'm Deloris Witt. Nice to meet you."

"Witt?" Momma turned to me. "Is she the one who spoke to Alton and me after the incident in the park?"

"Yes." I looked from one to the other. "Momma, Deloris. Deloris, this is my mother."

Momma nodded. "Nice to meet you, Deloris. You're a strong woman. My husband was not impressed."

With a slight smile Deloris continued as she scooted her chair forward, "I've been working on many different things and different avenues. I'd say the most important bit of information right now is that the medical examiner just released information on the body found at Carmichael Hall."

She had the full attention of everyone in the room. Six sets of eyes opened wide in anticipation.

"Her identity has been confirmed as Melissa Summers. They haven't said specifically how she was killed or where exactly she was found, only that a concerned employee called the police. They are estimating the time of death as only hours before discovery."

The lunch I'd eaten earlier churned. That meant she was killed on Saturday, hours before our party.

"Hours?" Chelsea said. "Had she been there all along? Was he holding her there somewhere?" Her cheeks paled with each question.

Deloris shook her head. "They haven't said."

"He wanted me to come to Carmichael Hall on Saturday after I visited... you," I said, turning to Momma.

She stared in silence waiting for more.

"But you had complications. Jane and I stayed with you." I turned to the rest of the table. "He was angry. I mostly avoided his calls, but we did speak a few times."

Chelsea nodded. "He wanted me to come over when Alex couldn't. He blew up my phone, but Jane had asked me to help with things around town. Everywhere I went, I was afraid he'd be there. But he wasn't. Was he with her... killing...?" She tucked her hands on her lap and looked up at me with round hazel eyes. "Do you think? Did she die because of us?"

"What?" Nox said. "She died because of that animal. Why would you say it was because of you?"

I covered his hand, the one that was still on my leg. "Not because of us, but in place of us..." Nox's hand tensed. I looked to Chelsea. "...one of us."

Pushing my chair back, I hurried around the table and wrapped my arms around my best friend. As she trembled in my embrace I looked up to Deloris. The anger I'd felt back in the hotel with Nox, learning that they'd been the ones to bring Chelsea into this mess came back to life. "This is your fault." And to Nox. "And yours. This is your doing!"

"Alex," Deloris said, "this is Edward Spencer's doing. Chelsea, we'll get you out of your agreement. You don't even need to speak to anyone at

Infidelity. I'll take care of it."

"Like you took care of her before?" I asked, my skin prickling with rage.

"There was always an out," Deloris said.

"So instead of owning up to your part, you're blaming Chelsea for not leaving him, for not walking out on her agreement, the one you told her to take?"

"No. That's not what I'm saying. I take full responsibility for my role. As you both know, Chelsea's agreement was meant for someone else. I turned away in a crisis and when I looked back, it was too late." She looked at Chelsea. "Financial compensation will never take away what you went through, but you will get it, as long as you don't press charges against Edward Spencer."

"What?" Nox and I said together.

"It's part of the Infidelity agreement. If Chelsea makes a statement against him that includes Infidelity, it will null and void her agreement and risk exposing Infidelity. She can report him to the company, but she can't break the nondisclosure or confidentiality portion of her agreement. If she abides by it, Infidelity will pay its full one-year obligation."

"B-but you said we were going to Savannah to make statements," Chelsea said, looking up at me.

"I thought we were."

We all looked to Deloris. "Now that they know the time of death, they'll want to know where you both were on Saturday. Were you in contact with him? Did you ever see Melissa during the months you lived at Carmichael Hall?"

"I didn't," Chelsea said. "I never saw her. Oh God. The place is big, not as big as Montague, but there are other buildings, places I never went." Chelsea turned to me. "Do you really think he had her there all those months?"

We both knew the answer. He'd made it perfectly clear that he intended to keep the two of us. We just hadn't realized he'd not only had two, but three women at his disposal.

"Can I answer those questions? Will it hurt Infidelity?"

"You can. You can do whatever you want. I would suggest you do only that. Answer the questions. Don't make accusations. Answer questions in regard to Saturday, to Mr. Spencer in general. Avoid the nature of your relationship from a legal perspective. Speak about it in general emotional terms."

Chelsea's hand moved to her battered cheek. "But they'll see."

Deloris nodded. "Which could be the nail in his coffin. Pictures speak louder than words."

"What about me?" I asked.

"Technically, you don't have to make a statement. A wife can't be made to testify against her husband."

My gaze met Nox's as the small hairs on the back of my neck stood to attention. "I'm not married."

"Then that's where we need to start. I believe we have proof that the marriage is illegal, at the very least that it was signed without the knowledge of either of you, thus fraudulently." She shrugged. "However, there is the slight problem that our proof was not legally obtained."

"What proof?"

"I bugged your phone."

My nose scrunched. "My phone? The one Alton gave me? How?"

Oh, shit. I still need to find it.

Deloris tilted her head. "The *how* isn't as important as the audible recordings. Saturday morning Edward Spencer called you. I recently replayed the conversation."

"That would have been before he…" It was hard to say it out loud, to say *before he killed Melissa.*

"During the call," she went on, "Mr. Spencer specifically states that the two of you *are going* to be married. He doesn't say that you're already married."

"That's right! Can the recording help?"

"Not in a court of law. In the state of Georgia they're only admissible if one of the two parties is aware of the wiretap."

"I could say I knew."

Deloris shook her head. "I'd rather not. However, I suspect we can stop this farce from ever getting that far. I can send the recording to Fitzgerald's attorney. It will show him that we have evidence to fight the claim. That should help as well as a few other loopholes."

Oren repeated, "Loopholes?"

Silvia laid a phone on the table. Though it wasn't making noise, the screen was bright. "It's the house phone," she said, explaining how it was attached to her cell phone. "The caller ID only says Georgia."

At first no one responded. How many times would it ring?

Finally, Oren nodded to Silvia, who connected the call.

"Hello?"

We all hung on each of Silvia's responses.

"Yes."

Her eyes darted to my mother. "Mrs. Fitzgerald?"

Momma's head moved back and forth.

"I'll talk to them," I volunteered. Deloris had already said they'd tracked me down.

"No," Nox said. "Give me the phone."

Silvia asked the person to please hold before she pushed something on the screen. "It's a Ralph Porter, representing Alton Fitzgerald. He's looking for…" She bobbed her head toward Momma. "…Mrs. Fitzgerald."

Nox reached for the phone. "This is Mr. Demetri."

A familiar concoction of anger and fear stewed inside me, simmering below the surface.

"If we hear from her, we'll let you know… Yes…" He looked at me. "…*Miss Collins* is here." The way he emphasized my name made me worry Ralph had referred to me as Spencer again. "No, she's unavailable at this time… I'm not sure. Perhaps you could try again tomorrow?… We'll be looking forward to that… Yes, I understand you're concerned. I hope you locate her soon… Goodbye." Nox handed the phone back to Silvia.

"Even after we're gone, if they call, only say that we're unavailable." He turned to my mother. "No one will give up your location until you're ready."

Momma's eyes were closed. One hand was near her neck while the other was on the table, encased in Oren's.

"You don't have to talk to anyone you don't want to," Oren confirmed.

Her neck straightened. "I do and I will. Just not now."

"When you're ready, *amore mio*." He searched her expression, his eyes narrowing. "Do you want to go back upstairs? Is this too much?"

Momma's head moved back and forth.

"Shall we move on to the will?" Deloris asked.

Heavy footsteps approached. "Mr. Demetri."

"Yes?" Oren and Nox answered in unison.

I reached for Nox's hand, unsure who the man was who'd entered the dining room.

He was tall and dressed similarly to Isaac with a nondescript dark suit. "Sirs, there's a guest who demands your presence."

Oren stood. "I said no one was to be allowed on the property." His eyes flickered to Deloris. "No one not already approved."

"Sir, it's—"

It was then the voices came from the front of the house. I didn't know who it was but the man's Brooklyn accent was thicker than Oren's.

CHAPTER 20

OREN

"EXPLAIN WHY YOU'RE here in this house!"

Who was he speaking to?

The voice bellowed from the front of the house like baritone thunder. Each rumble brought back a memory. With Adelaide right in front of me, the most prevalent recollection turned my stomach, taking me back to a bar in California. I purposely avoided Alexandria's stare. Her red hair wasn't as copper as her father's, but her damn eyes were his.

Even without visual confirmation, Vincent's image danced through my mind, a slideshow commemorating the years. I recalled the accompanying glare, the bulging veins protruding from his wide neck, and the color that filled his cheeks.

As a younger man, Vincent Costello had been the voice of reason. His influence while his father Carmine was alive and immediately following his father's death, was instrumental. He understood the changing world and climate. His visions worked to move the family forward, evolving as technology advanced and recognizing the importance of legitimate investments. He'd ensured not only the survival of the Costellos but also the continued dominance of the family.

Time and power had a way of clouding what was once clear. Though I hadn't been directly involved with the Costellos for years, the ties were never fully severed. With both the role of family leader and time, he'd changed. That was evident the night he'd almost sentenced both of our sons to death, but from what I'd heard, it wasn't the only time his decisions were impulsive.

Arrogant was a term often whispered in the darkest of corners. No one dared say it aloud or to his face.

From what I'd heard, everyone was watching and waiting for the time Luca assumed his father's role. No one questioned Luca's birthright. He'd paid his dues, some of them to the federal penitentiary. But like many before him, nothing stuck. His incarcerations were short. Even from behind the walls, Luca retained his position as underboss.

Things had quieted in the recent past. Legitimate businesses comprised the main revenue stream. However, it was Vincent's boisterous temper and growing waistline that caused many to project that the transition of power could happen sooner rather than later.

"Tell me," Vincent Costello demanded.

"I'm here to help," Eva replied.

My eyes met Lennox's as we both jumped to our feet heading straight to the pocket doors closest to the entry and quietly enclosing the dining room. Though we couldn't see the people in the foyer, we could hear them, loud and clear. I eyed the other two doorframes before turning to the guard. "You let *him* in?"

"Sir, he insisted."

My jaw clenched as Vincent's voice continued to boom, each phrase as loud as the last, oblivious to listening ears. Then again, perhaps it wasn't that he was unmindful, but rather that he didn't care. I turned to Lennox. "Get them all upstairs." I motioned toward Adelaide. "She's tired and can't manage the stairs without help."

"I'm fine. I can," Adelaide countered. "What's—"

"Is that Vince—" Lennox asked interrupting Adelaide.

"As soon as I distract him—them," I said, "I want everyone upstairs."

"You're not facing him alone."

"I am," I contested. "After all, I'm the one who called him."

"What? You called *him*? Why?" my son asked, eyeing the people at the table. "You did it for them."

It hadn't been a question, but I nodded in return.

"Then it's my responsibility," Lennox said.

"No. I called. I'll talk to him."

The only thing on my mind was keeping Vincent Costello away from Adelaide Montague. The history was too real. Adelaide didn't know it, but Vincent would. He'd connect the dots and I couldn't predict his reaction.

Once a job was done, it was done.

What would he say or do if he knew that I'd pursued the wife of my first job?

It wasn't a confrontation I wanted to experience. As my pulse raced, my only goal was getting Adelaide Montague, the widow of Russell Collins and daughter of old man Montague, upstairs and away from Vincent. If I could sweep her from the chair and carry her upstairs myself, I would. Unfortunately the path would take us straight to Vincent.

I turned as Silvia eased the other two entrances to the dining room closed.

Safest room.

That's what I told myself as I exhaled and prepared for the inevitable meeting. Never in all my life had I seen Vincent or his father when he'd been alive, alone. Undoubtedly there was someone else out there with him watching his back. I suspected it was either Jimmy or Luca.

God, let it be Luca.

Stepping forward I reached for Lennox's arm. "It would be better if you and I discussed this situation with our guest or guests in the office." My words came clipped. "After you make sure everyone is upstairs."

Lennox's eyes narrowed. Within the blue I searched for understanding and too late, realized its absence was my doing. I'd spent most of my life keeping my son away from this part of his heritage. Even though Angelina and I'd shielded him, he was an intelligent man; innately, he had to know that it was serious.

Deloris stood. "Lennox, Isaac is here. I can contact him to come inside."

My son's jaw clenched as he gazed from me to her. He looked from Adelaide to Alex and exhaled. "No. The *guest...*" He emphasized the title. "...will listen to Oren and me. Let's not complicate this any more than it already is." Again his eyes narrowed, lengthening his brow and silently admonishing my decision to include family.

At the moment, his approval wasn't my concern. Protecting Adelaide and concentrating on the impending meeting was. That family reunion sure as hell wasn't happening in the dining room, and if I didn't move soon, Vincent would come to find me.

"Give me a minute to escort them to the office before you go upstairs."

"Sir, I can take them to the office," the guard offered. I think his name was Paulie. He was part of the crew I'd borrowed from Vincent. It was no wonder he'd bowed to Vincent's demands. Everyone within the organization did and most people outside of it would too.

"Accompany me," I said.

It wasn't that I didn't trust the guard. I did. I had. He wouldn't be here if I didn't. My concern was Vincent. Angelina's cousin came to see me. He wouldn't be deterred without accomplishing his goal.

Right before I reached for the dining room door, I turned back to Adelaide. Her expression was the one I described as *plastic*. I'd seen it many times in pictures and videos. Adelaide Montague had spent too many years perfecting the perfect shell. Her ability to mask her thoughts and feelings was one of her greatest defenses. It had been the times I'd broken through that mask that had melted my heart. Seeing the plastic smile in my home brought an ache to my soul. I didn't ever want that expression, but right now it wasn't meant for me. She too was intelligent. She knew something was happening even if she didn't understand the particulars.

In three strides I was before her; squatting near her chair, I reached out to her knee. "Rest, please. Let Lennox help you upstairs. I know you can make it on your own. You can do anything you set your mind to. There has been a lot happening and discussed today. Now, rest.

"This doesn't concern you or Alexandria," I went on. "Let Lennox and I handle this. We can resume this conversation later." I tilted my head toward the now-closed door, the one that if open would face toward the windows at the back of the house. "Besides, it's getting dark."

"Adelaide," Silvia offered, "let me bring you some fresh soup upstairs."

Deloris nodded as Lennox whispered something to Alexandria.

"Thank you, Silvia," I said with a nod and a feigned smile. Had my lips actually curled upward or was it more of a grimace? I wasn't sure.

Silvia's gaze met mine. In her brown eyes was the understanding I wanted from everyone. That wasn't possible. Understanding took a base of knowledge that only Silvia and I shared.

With a squeeze of Adelaide's hand and a kiss to her cheek, I took a step in front of Paulie and pushed back the door. As soon as we cleared the threshold, he began to explain.

"Sir, I couldn't—"

With the uplift of my hand, I stopped his words. I didn't want to hear his apology or reasoning. It wasn't necessary. Turning from the attached room toward the entry, our footsteps echoing upon the bleached wood floor announced our arrival. Vincent, Luca, and Eva turned our direction.

"Oren," Vincent's voice bellowed through the entry.

"Vincent…" I turned toward his son. "…and Luca, welcome." Luca had matured since I'd seen him last. How long had that been?

"Well, you see," Vincent said, "we weren't sure how we'd be greeted. We weren't invited."

I reached out my hand and shook each of theirs, firm and solid, the same as they did in return. "You're always welcome." I looked to Eva, appreciating her fortitude as well as her medical skills.

Though she'd been in a verbal power match with her cousin, the head of the family, in that moment she reminded me more of my Angelina. There was nothing docile or submissive in her stance. Her arms were crossed over her breasts, neck straight, and lips held tightly together.

There were many things I could say about the Costellos, many issues I'd had, but how they respected and adored women wasn't one of them. That was why Angelina could argue with Vincent when I couldn't. She was one of them, as was Eva. Though their voices had been raised, there was no real hostility, simply a desire to be heard.

I doubted I'd be afforded the same concession.

"Eva," I said, nodding toward her, "has been a tremendous help as I'm sure you understand."

Vincent shook his head. "No, Oren, I don't. We spoke, you and I, but I don't really know what's happening. When Luca here told me that Eva was staying with you, well, for her father's sake, I offered to learn why."

Eva huffed at the mention of her father. "My father could have called me."

I smiled her direction. This wasn't about her. She was his excuse. "Thank you, Eva. We seem good. Are you staying longer?"

"I want to check—"

"The patient," I interjected, keeping Adelaide's name out of the equation.

"Yes. And then I'll decide."

"Is someone ill?" Vincent asked. "Tell me it isn't Lennox or Silvia."

I shook my head. "It isn't." I extended my arm toward the long living room that separated the front door from the back hallway. "Please, come with me to the office. We can talk."

Each step resonated in the silence as we crossed the floor. As we neared the door to the office, Luca spoke. "It's been a long time since I've been here. It hasn't changed."

Though the sun had set, the lights near the pool deck were on. Beyond the pool and lawn, the sound appeared as black as ink, a span of nothingness bordered by a horizon of lights as across the water Long Island shone in all of its glory.

"It hasn't changed, not much," I agreed. "Not since Angelina left us… and then Jocelyn," I added, realizing as I spoke that I rarely said or heard her name since her death. "As you know, I'm not here often."

"Lennox?" Vincent asked.

My skin crawled at the sound of my son's name on his lips.

"Memories. You understand. He spends most of his time in the city."

"Brooklyn," Vincent said. "That's where he belongs."

His words twisted my already-knotted stomach.

I opened the door to the office and motioned for them to enter. "He belongs with Demetri Enterprises. It requires most of his time."

Near the windows overlooking the pool were a leather sofa and chair. It didn't surprise me that they both sat on the sofa. The windows were behind them with another wall of windows to their side. The door was in front of them. They knew enough about this house to know that the windows were bulletproof. Besides, ninety percent of the security on the grounds was Vincent's men. They were as safe as babies in a cradle with their back to the window. Watching the door for whomever I had in the house was more of their concern.

"And yet there have been reports of him with a new woman. His time appears divided."

I shrugged. "My son doesn't share much with me."

Vincent leaned forward. "Shame. That's what families should do—share." His round head rolled on his wide neck. "It's what I did when you asked."

I took the chair opposite them. "Thank you."

"You were in a hurry during our call," Vincent said, "but for family, I was happy to help. How long do you think you'll need my men?"

The air burned my lungs with each inhale.

Quid pro quo. Did a day equal a year?

I sat tall and met his gaze. "Vincent, as I said on the phone, this is between us. Lennox isn't involved. He'll be here in a minute, but the debt is mine."

Luca stood and walked to the windows facing the pool. With his back to us, he said, "I haven't seen my cousin in years and he couldn't meet us at the door?"

"I asked him to do me a favor."

"You seem to be in the asking mood a lot lately." Vincent leaned back against the sofa and unbuttoned his jacket. "Which is interesting, considering we haven't spoken in what…? Help me remember, Oren. My memory isn't what it was."

"It's been a few years."

"A few?"

"It was after Angelina's passing." Hell, I couldn't give him the exact date. Did he think I had it circled in red on a calendar in my drawer?

He nodded. "How is business? Is there a problem, a concern? Is that the reason for the added security?"

Before I could answer, Luca turned. "Who's ill?"

Shit!

"Excuse me?"

"Eva is an excellent doctor with a sharp tongue," Vincent said. "She has patients of her own and yet here she is in your home."

The door opened and just as quickly shut.

"My home and welcome."

I didn't need to turn to know Lennox was the latest addition to our family gathering. I hadn't had the chance to brief him about not saying the name Montague or Collins. I should have, but I didn't expect the personal visit. I didn't brief Lennox because if I had, he would have asked questions. Explaining the Collins connection that Vincent and I shared wasn't on my list of things to do.

Lennox came forward, offering his hand. With a hardy shake, he greeted his family. "Vincent. Luca."

He and Luca exchanged a prolonged stare as they shook. No matter what had happened or would in the future, having both of these young men healthy and strong and shaking hands was a blessing, one that I hoped Vincent recognized. It could have all changed one night, long ago, in Jersey.

"Lennox," Luca said, patting Lennox's shoulder. "Long time. Sorry about your wife."

Lennox stood taller. "Has it been that long? Thank you. We need to catch up. How's Gabriella?"

"She's good. We have a son."

"You do?" Lennox answered as he pulled a chair closer to the grouping. "Congratulations. I am out of it. What's his name?"

"Carmine."

Lennox and I nodded.

"How old?" I asked.

"Only six months."

I turned to Vincent. "You're a grandfather. Congratulations."

"You?" he asked me as Lennox shifted in his chair.

"No."

Vincent leaned forward. "They're better than having your own. You can spoil them and hand them back."

I took a deep breath, thinking of a million responses, none of which Lennox wanted to hear. As the silence grew, I said, "This has been nice. We should do it more often."

It was total bullshit, but the pause in conversation made me uncomfortable. I was used to being the man on the other side. I made the awkward silence—I didn't suffer through it.

Luca sat again by his father. "You were just talking about Eva's patient. I missed the name."

Before Lennox could speak, I jumped in. "I didn't offer… but I should have. Her name is Chelsea, Chelsea Moore."

I had to give my son credit. He didn't flinch, not a sigh, or even a blink. Maybe he did understand more than I thought.

"And what happened to this Chelsea Moore?" Vincent asked.

Lennox shook his head. "She got the shit beat out of her. She's scared to death and has the bruises to show for it."

Both Vincent and Luca sat forward. "And you know for sure who hurt this woman?"

Lennox nodded. "I know for sure."

CHAPTER 21

NOX

"THE SECURITY?" VINCENT questioned. "You're concerned for this woman's safety." He eyed me up and down. "Surely the Lennox Demetri I remember can handle the situation?"

"I'd like nothing better."

"As I said," Oren interjected, "I'm the one who called. I'm the one who asked for help. The girl was employed by a company under the Demetri umbrella. If the connection were to be made public, it could affect Demetri Enterprises." My father tilted his head toward me. "Lennox is capable. It's the repercussions I'm trying to avoid."

"This woman?" Luca asked. "Is she special?"

"As a friend, nothing more," I answered truthfully.

"You see, not worth jeopardizing our good name or that of our company."

Vincent pressed his lips together and sat back, eyeing Oren and me back and forth. "What company?"

I wasn't sure where my father was going with this, but I hated the damn company. I was more than willing to have it implode. Fuck, I'd light the match and warm my hands over the blaze. I just didn't want Chelsea, Patrick, or Cy to be left in the ashes. "Infidelity. I was the one who got Demetri involved. I even played a part in getting this woman the job. I should have called you for help, not Oren. It's my doing that got us here. Thank you for your assistance."

Though Vincent seemed to be mulling over my answer, Luca nodded. "Infidelity, the website? Was she one of their models?"

"Not exactly," Oren replied, his eyes narrowing my direction.

"Yet," Vincent asked, "her safety is important enough for you to bring her here, to ask for my men to help keep her secure? I'm sensing more."

Before I could speak, my father leaned forward. "*I made a promise. I keep my promises. I pay my debts and my share. Just as I have in the past.*"

"My father may have asked," I interjected, "but only because he could. Vincent, we haven't spoken in too long. I've neglected my family, you, and Luca. And even so, here you are. Your men are outside my doors. My father asked and you came. Thank you. It's time for me to take responsibility for myself and recognize the ways you've helped me."

My gaze met Luca's. There were too many unspoken acknowledgments.

"No, Lennox," Oren protested, "I called."

I turned back to Vincent. "May I?"

"Call?" Vincent asked. "Of course! You're family. Angelina's boy. Her pride and joy. We're here for you as it should be—as you are for us."

"No—"

Vincent's hand rose. "Oren, let the man talk. It appears that finally he has become one."

I couldn't look at Oren. I knew this wasn't what he wanted, but at the same time, he'd broken free of the Costellos. They were my blood, my family. I couldn't let Charli's family be the reason he was dragged back. No matter what history he had with Charli's mother, Charli was my responsibility.

"You're dating?" Luca asked.

"I am."

He nodded. "I've seen pictures. I recall one from Central Park."

My stomach suddenly twisted. "Wrong place, wrong time."

"Ten millimeter. Most likely shot from a Glock 20. Automatic with a magazine that holds fifteen rounds, yet only one shot was fired."

Oren and I stared at Luca. None of that was common knowledge. "How? How do you know that?" I asked.

"Family," Vincent replied.

"What are you saying?" Oren asked.

"When family, even those we haven't seen in years, is threatened in our backyard, we look into it."

"Look into it?"

"We have friends. We have enemies. Sometimes threatening the most unlikely of targets can have the desired ripple effect."

"You think Lennox was shot at because of the Costellos?" my father asked.

Vincent shook his head. "Not anymore. We had to be sure."

"The woman you're dating," Luca said with his elbows now on his knees. "She's from a good family?"

"I suppose that's subjective," I said. "Good as in wealthy. I don't give a fuck about her money."

Luca's lips pressed together. "Not what I meant. I meant good as in sneaky as fuck."

Adrenaline raced through my veins as my fists clenched. "What do you mean?"

"You've also been working with some high-powered people on some interesting drug deals."

I scoffed. "You make it sound like I'm selling coke on the corner. It's legal drugs."

"Like alcohol," Vincent interjected.

"Similar."

"Not legal everywhere, not for recreational use," Luca responded. "We were worried about our enemies, but Lennox, you have your share."

"The shooting was aimed at me? You're sure?" Part of me was relieved to know it wasn't meant for Charli. Another part of me was furious as fuck. Who had the balls to shoot at me, especially with Charli present?

"Not without the shooter can we be sure. The shooter was a gun for hire. Not someone from around us. If it were, we'd know. The money trail has gone cold. The operation was well done—a professional. The entire operation. They knew your location. Their only mistake is that you're still here."

Oren stood. "Is that a threat?"

Vincent waved my father back to his seat. "No. It's a relief. We're still looking for the shooter. The bullshit on the news about the husband was genius."

"Diversion," I said.

"It was a good move."

"Where do you think the money came from? Who put this plan into play?"

"I'm not sure about the money," Luca answered. "As I said, the trail went cold. But that level of expertise can't be found on Craigslist. Whoever hired the shooter knew who to contact, knew your schedule, and your vulnerability. My first area of concern is your inner circle. Do you walk through Central Park every day?"

I shook my head, my mind going through everyone on my personal security detail.

"Do you know anyone with those kinds of connections?" he asked.

I shrugged, mulling over my list of suspects. At one time I'd thought maybe it was Charli's family, trying to scare her back to Savannah. It wasn't only my concern, but one Deloris had mentioned. That was before we really knew Charli. Now that I do, I doubt that Alton Fitzgerald has those connections, and I was confident that Spencer wasn't smart enough to pull it off.

And then I recalled advice Deloris had given me, telling me that around Severus Davis, a bulletproof vest was warranted. His expression when I appeared at the Senate Finance Committee had been one of surprise. It wasn't enough proof, but it warranted investigation. "Let me give it some thought."

Luca changed the subject. "This Chelsea Moore, was she seriously injured?"

"No broken bones, but her injuries aren't all physical," I replied.

"She's a friend of your girlfriend, yet you're responsible for her recent employment?"

"I've made mistakes."

Vincent abruptly stood and extended his hand, first to Oren. "We will go now. My men are your men as long as you need them."

Oren met him as we all stood. "Thank you."

Vincent turned to me, extending his hand again. "My men need a name."

"Vincent," Oren began, "I think we're working on it."

With our hands still clasped, he said to Oren, "You're not the only one who repays debts." And back to me, "I've watched you. Despite the accomplishments you've achieved, the ones the world considers important…" His wide shoulders shrugged. "…those your mother surely thought important, college, business school, and even your fighting, I've not until tonight seen the man Angelina wanted you to be." He nodded as a thin smile graced his thick lips. "She was proud of you, but I believe that she is even more proud now. Tonight, Lennox, you impressed me. Whatever you need, ask, call. Keeping your company scandal-free benefits us all. This woman, this girl, should not have been hurt. Give me a name."

My gaze met Oren's. If I did this, I knew what I was doing. I knew what it meant. I also knew I wanted Edward Spencer to pay.

"For a moment or for twenty years?" Deloris's question came back.

Edward Spencer was in jail. Assuming the charges stuck, he would suffer for years to come. Did I want him to suffer for only a moment? Removing him from the equation wouldn't be difficult while he was out on bail. We all knew that was coming.

Then again, was he the only one I wanted to pay?

Charli had argued that her devil was more evil than mine. Perhaps she'd been partially right—if Oren were my only devil, but he wasn't. Mine was an entire family. Maybe it was time for the showdown.

CHAPTER 22

—•○•—

CHARLI

A DAY LATER, I was pacing the living room of the hotel suite. Outside the open draperies and stories below, Savannah bustled. Even though it was November, the tourists continued to walk the cobblestone streets and browse the shops. As a child I'd never understood the fascination. Now after traveling and living elsewhere, I did. Compared to New York, the Georgia air was balmy and the historical heritage that I'd taken for granted gave visitors days of sightseeing opportunities.

There were even Christmas decorations beginning to line the streets and sparkle in windows.

The new phone in my hand vibrated with the text I'd been waiting for.

Deloris: **"TWO O'CLOCK AT THE SAVANNAH-CHATHAM POLICE DEPARTMENT. YOU'RE MEETING WITH DETECTIVE PAMELA MEANS. DARYL OWEN WILL ACCOMPANY YOU AND CHELSEA."**

I exhaled. I'd prefer Nox by my side, but legal counsel would be best. Other than having Mr. Owen beside me, I planned to appear the naïve heiress until the time was right to show my hand.

Deloris and Nox spent hours on the Batplane and again in the hotel suite last night explaining my grandfather's will. I needed to learn to accept their information instead of question it, yet at times like this it was difficult. It took me time to wrap my mind around the idea that Nox, Oren, and Deloris had secured a document that I'd never seen and my mother hadn't seen until recently.

Granted, the implications of the document were far-reaching, going way beyond my marriage and inheritance. There were pages, articles, and sections devoted to Montague Corporation, the structure and divisions. I wasn't the naïve girl Alton made me out to be, but quite honestly, it was beyond my understanding. My undergraduate degree in political science and business gave me some foundation, but what my grandfather had engineered was not a typical business structure.

As a family-owned-and-operated company, there was a provision that allowed the subsidiaries to be publicly traded. That was a substantial portion of the corporation. As publicly traded commodities under the Montague umbrella, news of Bryce's arrest in connection with our marriage would most certainly affect the value of the stock. Nox and Oren had people watching the numbers.

I'd never expected to care about Montague Corporation, but knowing now that my mother had the right to the company, I did. Unfortunately, the arrest of Edward Carmichael Spencer was the headline on many cable financial networks as well as publications questioning his connection to Montague Corporation. Even the Montague machine couldn't keep the news hidden. After all, a body had been found.

The bit of news we didn't see on either TV or the Internet was talk of my marriage. They discussed the engagement party on the night of Bryce's arrest but that was the extent of it. Nox, however, had seen the license. Even the police had referred to me as Mrs. Spencer, but sometime since Saturday night, that information seemed to disappear. No doubt it would be considered less significant than Bryce's arrest and the discovery of Melissa's body. There was even one broadcast that showed protesters outside the gates of Carmichael Hall.

Perhaps Deloris had been right and we wouldn't need to fight the marriage.

It was the infrastructure and the governing board of directors of Montague Corporation that interested Deloris and Nox. I'd been surprised to learn that the board was elected. That was until they explained that the structure currently in place only allowed the shareholders to vote upon and elect the board.

Montague Corporation had few shareholders. Nearly ninety-percent of the stock was owned by my mother and me. All of our shares were managed by Alton. While on his own he had no rights, he held the legal power of attorney as Momma's husband and my fiduciary guardian. With that power, he'd elected the board of directors. That board of directors had named him CEO.

Quid pro quo at its finest.

If my marriage to Bryce never occurred or was annulled, without the codicil Montague Corporation and all Montague assets would revert to Fitzgerald Investments—Alton would be financially set. With the codicil, Montague assets would revert to the rightful heirs, Momma and me. However, the corporation was different. With the codicil in effect, the board of directors would be dissolved and Montague Corporation would become a publicly traded entity.

According to Nox, the news of Bryce's arrest, in conjunction with our engagement party and being named heir apparent of Montague Corporation, could most likely produce one of two possible outcomes. First, when the stock became public, Mother and I could purchase the shares at a seemingly reduced price and maintain control. As the primary stockholders, we would receive the right to any remaining assets after liquidation. In essence, we would buy Montague Corporation from ourselves and reap the profit as well as the loss.

In the second scenario, we could lose control of the corporation to investors ready to pounce on a wounded but historically profitable entity. Theoretically, anyone, including Alton, could purchase the controlling interest.

Both Nox and Deloris wanted me to understand my grandfather's will in its entirety before meeting with Ralph. They were convinced that Alton would try to manipulate things to his advantage. We just had no idea how far he'd go.

DARYL OWEN WAS a tall, handsome man with dark chocolate colored skin. He appeared younger than Ralph and Alton, but older than Nox.

"Miss Collins, it's nice to meet you."

I smiled at his greeting, thankful to hear Collins instead of Spencer. "Thank you for helping us."

A little after noon, he joined Chelsea, Nox, Deloris, and me in the hotel suite to prepare us for our meeting. While we knew from the chatter that Deloris had heard that Ralph Porter wanted our statements, it was decided that our help could be best given to the state in building its case.

Mr. Owen wanted Chelsea and me to know that his presence was specifically to help us stay on topic and avoid giving more information than necessary. Our statements weren't under oath nor were they testimony. Neither of us was on trial. We were simply witnesses who were both in contact with Bryce on the day before the murder. I was also with him on Saturday night. The police were working on establishing a timeline before the arraignment.

Undoubtedly, Hamilton and Porter would want to speak to us too. Mr. Owen advised we wait until after the meeting with the detective. More than likely, it would be the prosecutor who could benefit from our testimony. Ralph just didn't know that yet.

The unofficial nature of this meeting was why our voluntary appearance at the police station was important. It was why we'd flown back to Savannah.

"I've verified that Mr. Spencer will not be present," Mr. Owen said.

My pulse quickened as I looked to Chelsea.

"We thought he was still in jail," Nox said.

"He is; the arraignment is tomorrow morning."

"Tomorrow? We assumed it would be today," Deloris commented.

Mr. Owen nodded. "The state requested time. They have up to seventy-two hours to file. Even Hamilton and Porter can't force them to file faster. There won't be a bail hearing until after the arraignment."

I thought about Melissa, something I hadn't done before. It was probably the news coverage. I'd seen her picture multiple times. She was young and pretty, a simple Midwestern beauty. The newspeople were playing that up: an innocent college freshman who made the mistake of getting involved with an older man. The assumption was hilarious. They were painting Bryce as the older man. It was the same argument I'd used when Bryce first asked for my help, when I'd been appalled at her youth. In reality, Bryce was eight years her senior, but she'd been living with a much older man.

It wasn't that man's primary residence. That was with his wife. According to the news, this unnamed man was a family friend who traveled to the Chicago area routinely for business. Since his apartment sat empty when he wasn't there, he allowed Melissa to stay there. Though the media tried to make more out of it, nothing had been uncovered.

"You expect there to be bail?" I asked.

"Given the defendant and his connections, yes."

"But surely the severity of the charges…"

"Miss Collins, this is still Savannah. He is still being funded by Montague money. All Hamilton and Porter needs to do is convince Mr. Spencer to plead not guilty and persuade the judge that he's not a danger to society…" He looked at Chelsea; her bruised cheek had faded to green and yellow, but it was still evident. "…nor a flight risk. If they can do that, they can request bail."

"What if he is a danger?" Chelsea asked.

Mr. Owen nodded. "That's what can be discussed today, unofficially."

We'd hoped to slip into the police station unnoticed. As we pulled up to the curb, it was obvious that wouldn't happen. The sidewalk was lined with reporters and along the street were various large trucks with station letters painted on the side.

Clayton brought the limousine to a stop in front of the chaos.

Nox reached for my hand. "Princess, I want to go in there with you."

"I think it'll add to the rumors. After all, we still don't know if I'm supposedly married."

"I know you can do this."

I took a deep breath, filling my senses with his woodsy cologne and my vision with his blue gaze. "I'll be fine." I looked over at Chelsea. "We'll be fine."

"Deloris and I will be with you the only way we can."

He was saying they'd be listening to every word, but with Daryl Owen in the car, he couldn't be that blunt.

My necklace had been improved. Actually, I now had two. One with and one without an audible connection. The feature I'd requested not be present was now available on my new necklace. It looked identical to the first, a platinum diamond-dusted cage holding a glistening pearl. Just like the first one, the pearl wasn't a pearl, but a translucent transmitter. In the necklace I was wearing, it transmitted not only my location, but included an audio transmission. The range was impressive.

"And while Mr. Owen is beside you," Nox said, "Isaac will be too."

I nodded. Hadn't there been a time when I didn't want Nox's men with me?

"You won't be getting in any cars besides this one when this meeting is over."

I leaned forward and brushed my lips to his. "I believe that was rule number one on your most recent list, Mr. Demetri. I just want to get back to New York."

"Hopefully tonight."

"Before that bail hearing," Chelsea added.

Reaching for her hand, I smiled. "Girl, are we ready to get this dog-and-pony show going?"

The remnants of an old spark shone in her hazel eyes. "And then it's a jail break back to New York."

I squeezed her hand. "Damn right. I seem to recall you kick ass at those."

"I did. Just maybe I will again."

CHAPTER 23

―●○●―

ALEXANDRIA

WITH MR. OWEN LEADING the way, we walked the gauntlet. Reporters pushed toward us as Isaac kept them at bay. Questions filled the air.

"Did you know he was a murderer?"

"Did you know that before you agreed to marry him?"

"Do you think he's guilty?"

"Did you see her?"

By the time the front doors to the station closed, the din of voices within was merely a murmur compared to the roar outside.

"Miss Collins and Miss Moore," Detective Means said, meeting us at the front desk. "Let's get you to a more private room."

Every eye turned our direction and the whispers stilled as we walked through the large room filled with desks. It was unnerving as people stared. Once we finally made it to the plain room with gray walls and a gray metal table and chairs, Detective Means escorted us inside.

"I know it's not much, but please have a seat. Thank you for coming in today. You can understand how surprised we were to get your assistant's call."

Isaac nodded and stayed outside as Mr. Owen, Chelsea, and I entered the room.

Mr. Owen offered his hand. "Detective Means, I'm Daryl Owen, Miss Collins and Miss Moore's attorney."

She motioned to the table. "This isn't that formal. We just have a few questions for you."

"And we hope we can answer them," I said. "Mr. Owen is our moral support."

The detective smiled. "Can I get you something before Officer Emerson joins us?"

Though we all declined, she was out and back with plastic bottles of water. Through the open door as she reentered, I watched her hand one even to Isaac. Within a few minutes, the five of us, including Officer Emerson were seated about the small table.

"Miss Moore," the detective began, "I'm Detective Means and this is Officer Emerson. We were present during the arrest of Edward Spencer. You weren't there?"

"No," Chelsea said.

"Yet you wanted to answer questions?"

Chelsea sat taller. "I wouldn't say I want to. I'm here."

"Please tell us about your relationship with Mr. Spencer."

I squeezed Chelsea's leg and gave her a smile. Mr. Owen had talked to both of us about the possible line of questions. He'd advised us on what to offer and what to omit.

"I dated Bryce... Edward Spencer from September until a few weeks ago."

"Dated?"

"Yes."

"In fact, you lived with him. Isn't that correct?"

"Yes, ma'am. I lived at Carmichael Hall. However, for the last week I've been staying at Montague Manor."

"Those are nice addresses. When did you first meet Mr. Spencer?"

"Shouldn't we concentrate on Melissa Summers?" Mr. Owen asked.

"Miss Moore, living at Carmichael Hall for... what would that be... two months? How often did you and Melissa Summers cross paths?"

"We didn't."

"You didn't?" Detective Means asked. "Do you believe she was living at Carmichael Hall?"

Chelsea shook her head. "I can't say. I can only say I never saw her."

"Did you eat meals there?"

"Yes."

"Who joined you for meals?"

"It varied. Sometimes I ate alone in my room. Other times I ate with Bryce or Suzy." She looked at Mr. Owen and added, "Mrs. Suzanna Spencer, Bryce's mother."

"Was there additional food prepared for someone you didn't know was there?"

"I-I don't know. I'd never lived like they live. I never saw the food prepared. They have people who do that. People who serve it." She shrugged. "Not as many as at Montague, but it wasn't like we all hung out in the kitchen."

"So you started dating Edward Spencer and immediately moved into his house?"

"Yes."

Detective Means leaned across the table. "That seems quick."

"I didn't have anywhere to live. I got a job at Montague Corporation, in their human resources department. And I was going to get an apartment when Bryce offered me a room in his home."

"A room? Your own room?"

Chelsea nodded. "Yes. I can tell you which one. Some of my things are still there."

"You didn't share a room with Mr. Spencer?"

"No."

"Did you ever enter Mr. Spencer's suite?"

"Yes."

"Did you ever see another woman in his bedroom?"

"Of course not."

"You said there were a lot of people there. Maybe Melissa was there and you didn't know she was?"

"It's possible," Chelsea said.

Detective Means opened a folder and pushed a large glossy picture of Melissa across the table. "Look at her. Does she look familiar?"

"Only from the news."

"Only from the news? Haven't you accompanied Mr. Spencer and made statements regarding her disappearance?"

Chelsea nodded. "I have, but the first time I saw her picture was on the news."

"Miss Moore, where were you this past Saturday?"

"I woke at Montague Manor. Jane, the house manager, asked me to help with the engagement party."

"That must have been awkward," Officer Emerson said.

"What? No. I was happy to help."

"You were happy to help with the party celebrating the engagement of the man you were dating to your college roommate?"

My stomach knotted listening to their questions. From the outside it had to look twisted. Hell, from the inside it was twisted.

"I was," she said confidently. "Jane gave me a list of places around Savannah. I went all over: florists, caterers. I even met with the quartet to go over music selections."

"That was very helpful of you," Officer Emerson said. "I'm sure we could see you on the surveillance footage of these establishments to determine a timeline."

"I'm sure you could."

"Why weren't you at the party?"

Chelsea's fingers grazed her cheek. "I wasn't feeling well."

"Miss Moore, the guests were catalogued as they left. You weren't at Montague Manor after the party."

"No. I'd left during the party, before all of this."

"Left? Why?" Detective Means asked.

"I'd decided to move to New York."

"And give up your job?"

"Yes."

Officer Emerson scrunched his nose. "It was embarrassing to be in Savannah with Mr. Spencer engaged to..." He nodded my way. "...her?"

"I was ready to leave."

"Thank you, Miss Moore." Detective Means turned to me. "Miss Collins, are you and Mr. Spencer married?"

"No."

"Yet at the scene, your stepfather referred to you as Mr. Spencer's wife. There was a license filed and then voided in unheard-of rapid succession. Can you explain that?"

My eyes widened. They'd voided it? "I can't. I wish I could, but I can't."

"So it is *Miss Collins*, not Mrs. Spencer?"

"Yes."

"Now if our notes are accurate, you've known Mr. Spencer for most of your life."

"That's correct," I said.

"Where were you on Saturday during the day?"

"I also woke at Montague Manor. Next I went with Suzanna Spencer to Magnolia Woods where my mother was a patient. I was there with Jane, the house manager Chelsea mentioned, until late afternoon. I'm sure I'm on their surveillance. I had a meeting with Dr. Miller, my mother's doctor."

"But your mother is no longer there?"

"She was there on Saturday. I was with her."

Officer Emerson looked down at his notes and back up. "You don't seem concerned or shocked about your mother being missing."

"Does this have to do with Mr. Spencer and Melissa Summers?" Mr. Owen asked.

Officer Emerson shrugged. "We aren't sure. We're just covering our bases."

"Miss Collins and Miss Moore are here to answer questions about your timeline. Are they done?"

"Miss Moore," Detective Means began, "what happened to your cheek?"

Chelsea looked to Mr. Owen.

"Is this about Mr. Spencer and Miss Summers?" Mr. Owen asked again.

"I don't know, Miss Moore, is this about Mr. Spencer or Miss Summers?"

Tears filled Chelsea's eyes as she maintained her posture. "Bryce has a temper."

Detective Mean's eyes widened. "Are you saying you received that bruise from Edward Spencer?"

"I-I'm not pressing charges."

"But you will testify to his temper?"

She looked again at Mr. Owen. It was the subject we all expected. It was the picture worth a thousand words on her cheek. It was proof of Bryce's violent outbursts.

"I will," I volunteered.

"Miss Collins?" Officer Emerson asked.

"I witnessed the altercation." It was the loophole in Chelsea's agreement. She wasn't pressing charges, nor was I. But I could testify as to what I witnessed, what I experienced.

"You saw Mr. Spencer strike Miss Moore?"

I took a deep breath. "Yes. I was in the same room."

Officer Emerson and Detective Means exchanged looks.

"Miss Moore, we'd like to take a photograph of your cheek, if you'll allow it?"

Her lip disappeared behind her teeth as she looked at Mr. Owen and then to me. We both nodded.

"Yes, but I'm not pressing charges."

Detective Means continued her questions. "Did either of you see Edward Spencer on Saturday?"

"I did," I said. "It was after six o'clock. He'd called me multiple times during the day. He wasn't happy that I spent the day with my mother. You can check my phone records. He'd wanted me to go to Carmichael Hall. I'd agreed, but then my mother took an unexpected turn. As I said, I spent the day with her and her doctors.

"Once I got back to Montague, I had to get ready for the party. People were supposed to arrive at 6:30."

"You saw him before the party?"

"Yes. He came to my room."

"Was he still upset?" Officer Emerson asked.

I shook my head. "No. He was the complete opposite. During his calls he was angry, but by that evening he was calm and even nice."

"Nice." Detective Means repeated. "You say that like it was the exception rather than the rule."

"I wasn't sure what to expect."

"Miss Moore, did you see Mr. Spencer on Saturday?"

"No. Like I said, I was at Montague Manor and then all over Savannah for the party. I didn't attend the party and decided to leave during it. I never saw him."

"Do you have a phone?"

"Yes," Chelsea said.

"Did Mr. Spencer know your number?"

"Yes. You can check my records too. He called many times. I even let some of them go to voicemail."

"What did he want?"

Chelsea took a deep breath. "He wanted me to come to Carmichael Hall. He was very upset that I was not available."

"Available?" the detective asked. "But he was about to go to a party announcing his engagement in front of Savannah, Georgia... well... nationwide society, and he wanted you to be *available* to him before that?"

Chelsea nodded. "That's why I wanted to leave. That's why I left during the party."

Officer Emerson and Detective Means turned to one another. After a prolonged stare, they turned back to us. "Ladies," the detective said, "thank you for your cooperation. Today's statements weren't made under oath. Would you be willing to testify to the information you shared with us today?"

My tongue darted to my lips. "I will." It wasn't up to me to speak for Chelsea.

We all turned to her. Finally her head bobbed. "Yes."

A knock at the door echoed through the small room.

CHAPTER 24

───●○●───

ALEXANDRIA

OFFICER EMERSON STOOD and opened the door as we all began to gather our things.

"Alexandria!"

I turned to the familiar face of Ralph Porter. He'd been at the party Saturday night; however, before that it had been years since I'd seen him. Most of the contact I'd made with Hamilton and Porter regarding my trust had been with Natalie, one of their assistants.

I nodded. "Ralph?"

Granted, in proper society, a man Ralph Porter's age, probably older than Alton, deserved the respect of the use of his last name. Nothing I'd discovered about Ralph Porter, from the archaic will of my grandfather to the loss of my trust fund, deserved my respect.

He lifted his hand toward me, beckoning me out of the room.

When I didn't move, he said, "Officers, if you'll excuse us. I need to speak to my client."

Standing directly behind Ralph was Isaac. His head and shoulders loomed higher, dwarfing the man who'd forever been my mother's as well as Alton's and Bryce's counsel.

"Are we done?" Mr. Owen asked Detective Means and Officer Emerson.

"Yes, thank you," the detective said as they both stepped from the room. Mr. Owen, Chelsea, and I had yet to move.

After a backward glance at Isaac, Ralph stepped inside and shut the door. "My dear, I saw your picture on the news and rushed over. You shouldn't be here without counsel."

My smile grew. Tilting my head toward the side, I said, "Ralph, I'm sure you know Daryl Owen. I'm represented. Thank you for your concern."

His wrinkled face paled, or was it grayed? Confusion clouded his eyes. "I don't understand. I dropped everything when I saw you enter this place. Dear, you're a Montague. Hamilton and Porter has represented the Montagues exclusively since... well, since your grandfather."

Perspiration dotted Ralph's upper lip. He had thinning gray hair that was thicker toward the base of his head, wrapping around like a white horseshoe. In the fluorescent light of the interrogation room, even the top of his head seemed to glisten.

"Actually, Ralph," I said, "Mr. Owen has been a big help, not only to Chelsea and me but also to my friend Lennox Demetri." I pursed my lips. "Seeing as you represent Bryce and well, my stepfather, I didn't want there to be a conflict of interest."

"No conflict of interest. Dear, we're all on the same side. We all have the same goal. We all want to see Bryce acquitted of this ridiculous charge. As his wife—fiancée, that is your goal?"

I took a step forward. "What happened to the marriage license you showed Mr. Demetri?"

"I-I," he stuttered. "I didn't show anything to that man."

"No, you gave it to me," Mr. Owen said. "Complete with the court's approval. Yet now it seems to have been voided. Was there a problem?"

Ralph looked at me. "Alexandria, please, we need to talk privately. There is more at stake here than a marriage license."

I lifted my brow. "Forgery?"

"No, dear." He turned to Chelsea. "Miss Moore. We're so pleased you've returned to Savannah. Seeing as you have testified on Bryce's behalf in the past, we'll need your continued support."

When she didn't respond, he added, "We'll require it."

"Thank you, Ralph, for hurrying down here. As you can see, we're fine and now we're done."

"Alexandria, come to Hamilton and Porter and talk to us. Let's get things straightened out. Don't leave Georgia without learning your options."

"My options? What are you talking about?"

"Dear, you've seen the will." He leaned close. "I can't let Montague fall from the rightful Montague heirs without a fight. As I said, I represented your grandfather... your father, Alexandria. I was with Adelaide when he died. I'm here for you now and for her."

"I know where you were in New York. Please tell me that Adelaide is there or at least that you know she's safe."

He deserved an Academy Award for the performance he was giving. It was heart-wrenching and sincere—and it was total bullshit. However, years of addressing a jury had served his acting skills well.

We'd talked about this with Nox and Deloris. The fire was burning hotter under Alton's world. Since he didn't know that we knew about the codicil, we'd expected a power play. Was this meeting it?

"Ralph, I really need to get back to New York. Despite all of this, I'm still a student. The semester will end soon. Once it does, I'll have more time."

He reached out for my hand. "I remember you as a little girl. Always so inquisitive and so intelligent. You'll make a wonderful attorney. Perhaps there's a future for you at Hamilton and Porter?"

As if that should be enticing. I pulled my hand away. "Goodbye, Ralph."

"I can't make you stay, but we can make her," he said, nodding his head toward Chelsea.

"What?"

"You've testified. You've given information under oath, Miss Moore. Bryce is going to need you to continue to corroborate his story. Perhaps," his voice slowed, "you were with him on Saturday? I believe you two have an agreement."

"Mr. Porter," Mr. Owen said, "Miss Moore is now my client. She is free to travel until she receives orders from the court saying otherwise. I hope you're not suggesting that you have the authority..."

Ralph's hand went in the air. "I only need a signature."

"Make sure it's legal," I said.

"You're correct," Ralph nodded toward us. "Let's hope it doesn't come to that. Miss Moore, please come to my office tomorrow and I'm sure we can get a statement. I'm sure we can come to an agreement that will allow you to leave Savannah until the time is necessary for you to return to testify."

She looked to Mr. Owen.

"You are under no obligation to cooperate," our attorney said. "However, the court can insist on your return."

"What kind of statement?" Chelsea asked.

"The truth," Ralph said. "Just as you've done in the past, just as you did in Evanston. Just as your agreement articulates."

RETURNING TO HAMILTON and Porter required another night and day in Savannah. I didn't want to be there, but at least it allowed me a chance to speak with Jane. She met me at Leopold's, just the two of us—and Clayton. Slipping under the radar—me in a baseball cap, wearing jeans and a vintage *Bill Elliott* t-shirt—we met at a table near the back.

With my bodyguard at the table to my side, I nibbled on a bowl of chocolate raspberry swirl and scanned the crowd. It didn't take long until I saw her, working her way through the tables to me.

Her big brown eyes glistened as we hugged and she sat across the table. At her place setting I had a bowl of lemon custard. It was the flavor she always ordered when I was young.

She shook her head. "Child, you remembered?"

"Of course I did!"

"I'm so glad you got a message to me."

"Yeah, Aunt Gwen has been more of a help than I ever imagined."

She nodded toward my shirt. "He was your daddy's favorite."

"Awesome Bill from Dawsonville," I said with a grin. "I really don't know anything else about him, but I saw the shirt in a shop and decided I needed to have it." I shrugged. "I remember your telling me that he was my dad's favorite NASCAR driver."

"You safe? Your momma, she's safe?"

I nodded.

"Oh praise Jesus." Tears spilled onto her round cheeks as I reached across the table. "Child, I prayed all night and day. It was a mess here." She shook her head. "I just kept thinking, what would Miss Adelaide say about this spectacle? Oh, Lordy, what would Miss Olivia say?"

I squeezed her hand. "Momma wants to see you, but we think we need to wait."

"Wait?"

"She needs to get stronger before she faces… him."

Jane nodded then leaned across the table. "He didn't do it, Mr. Spencer." She looked up from the custard. "Did he?"

I lifted one shoulder. "I don't know. I was with you most of the day."

"He wasn't happy when he called you. I heard his voice. Not his words," she clarified, "but his tone. He was mad." She took a bite. "I wasn't trying to listen. That room, it was small."

"It was, and he was."

"But not mad enough to do that?"

"Jane, I don't know. I really don't. If the police question you, please be honest. It's all we can do. If he's not guilty, then honesty is his best defense. If he is guilty, Melissa deserves our honesty."

"I can't. I can't say nothing about what I see. It's part of my job. It always has been."

"I think," I said, keeping my voice low, "they can still call you. I think they can still question you."

"But I can't say nothing. If I do, Mr. Fitzgerald will be angry."

"The law is more powerful than Mr. Fitzgerald." Even as I said the words, I heard my uncertainty. Legally what I said was true. No private agreement could supersede the law. The law always won. Just like the song said. And then I recalled another old song, one Jane used to listen to. The singer had red hair, Vicky someone. She sang about a 'backwoods judge in Georgia who had bloodstains on his hands.' I even believed that Reba McEntire did a cover of the song. Suddenly it had new meaning.

"I think you should talk to my attorney."

Jane shook her head. "I'll just keep quiet." She feigned a smile. "Will you come back to the house, or can I bring your momma some of her things? I know she'll be missing them." She clutched her chest. "I miss both of you. I ain't never had you both gone."

"No, I'm not going to the manor. I can't. Especially after Bryce is out on bail."

Her eyes widened. "They're going to let him out?"

"Probably. You know Alton. If he wants it."

"But if Mr. Bryce done that to that girl, he shouldn't be out."

My eyes continued to flit around the room. Though the restaurant was busy, no one seemed to be paying any attention to us.

"My attorney? If you get a call from the police or Mr. Porter, will you please call my attorney?"

"Mr. Porter?"

"No. Mr. Porter is Alton's attorney. He's Bryce's attorney. Daryl Owen is my attorney's name. Please don't talk to Mr. Porter without him."

CHAPTER 25

—•○•—

ALEXANDRIA

I COULDN'T RECALL the last time I'd been to Hamilton and Porter. It had been years ago, accompanying my mother as she signed something or did whatever it was they asked.

Similar to yesterday, we were all together as Clayton stopped the limousine in front of the beautifully constructed building in the heart of the historic district.

"This time I'm not letting you two go alone," Nox said.

"I don't want you to."

"I don't trust these people, not one of them."

"They're questioning Chelsea, not me." I looked over at my friend. "Are you sure you're ready for this?"

"I don't want them to call me back here tomorrow. I don't want to risk seeing Bryce without you." She looked around the interior of the car. "All of you. So yes. Let's get this over with."

With my hand in Nox's, Mr. Owen leading the way, and Chelsea and Isaac behind us, we all entered the front glass doors of Hamilton and Porter. The historic exterior blended nicely with the more eclectic interior. Classic and modern at the same time.

"Miss Collins," the dark-haired receptionist said, standing, as Isaac opened the front glass door and we entered.

"Yes," I replied confidently.

"I'm Natalie, Natalie Banks." She came around the large desk. "We've spoken." Her step stuttered as she looked up at Nox.

"You're...?"

Did her complexion pale? "He's my boyfriend, Lennox Demetri. He's here to support me. I remember. You helped me with my trust fund." She was also the one who'd mentioned Del Mar to me.

Pulling her eyes away from Nox, she asked, "How is your mother? We're all very concerned."

"Thank you for your concern. Natalie, this is Chelsea Moore."

Natalie took a step back as Chelsea removed her large sunglasses.

"Hello," Chelsea said.

"H-hello. Um..." Natalie looked to Isaac and Mr. Owen.

"And this is Daryl Owen of Preston, Madden, and Owen. He's here today to represent Chelsea and me."

"Represent you? Miss Collins, you've always been our client."

"I've already been through this with Mr. Porter. He said he needed information from Miss Moore? That's why we're..."

Before I finished speaking, Ralph Porter entered the reception area.

"Natalie..." He stopped in his tracks. "Miss Collins, look at you."

I'm the same as I was yesterday. I didn't say that. I only thought it. Instead, I offered my hand. "Ralph..." I took continued pleasure in the way the use of his given name caused his lips to thin.

He turned his attention to Mr. Owen. "Daryl, so nice of you to join us again. You must not have any other clients."

They shook hands as Mr. Owen spoke, "It's good to see you too, Ralph. I'm sure you understand that some clients require more of your attention."

Ralph turned to Nox. "Ralph Porter."

Nox shook his hand. "Lennox Demetri."

"Yes, you're the man who was arrested Saturday night."

"Detained, the charges were dropped," Mr. Owen corrected.

"Fortunate for you, Mr. Demetri..." He looked to Mr. Owen. "However, it does cause a problem in the billing department."

Mr. Owen didn't crack a smile at Ralph's poor attempt at humor. "From what I understand," Daryl said, "it was fortunate for everyone that a resolution was found. Our hope is that today the same can be accomplished for Miss Moore."

I scanned the office as we followed Ralph. If I were honest, I'd admit that I was nervous that Alton or Bryce would sabotage this meeting. It was why I was clinging to Nox's hand like a life raft.

My fears weren't without merit. Bryce's court appearance had been earlier this morning. Deloris informed us that he was charged with felony murder and granted bail. It was exorbitant at ten million dollars and included surrendering his passport. Nevertheless, it was granted. The last we heard, he was still at the court dotting the *i*'s and crossing the *t*'s. That meant it was just a matter of time before he was a free man.

As soon as we turned the corner, I recalled the old-fashioned elevator from my childhood visits. It was still the same, quite possibly the same as it had been when my grandfather visited this office, maybe even a century before that. The black iron scissor gate opened and closed manually, and the floors were reached with the turn of a crank, not the push of a button.

Ralph closed the gate and began to turn the crank. Slowly the floor moved upward, the interior of the shaft, cords, and wires were visible as we ascended. And then, we were at eye level with the second floor. He continued to crank until the elevator's floor and the second floor met. Ralph unlatched and opened the gate, motioning toward the hallway. "Watch your step. We're going to speak in a conference room. Let me show you the way."

Mr. Owen followed behind Nox, Chelsea, and me as Isaac took up the rear. When we reached the conference room, Isaac tapped on Nox's shoulder, causing us to stop. He followed Ralph into the room. I wasn't sure what he was doing, but soon he exited and announced he'd wait in the hallway.

"Making sure there were no unwanted guests," Nox whispered near my ear.

Apparently, I wasn't the only one who was concerned.

The room we'd entered was plush with a long, shiny table and comfortable cushioned chairs. With its ornate trim and cherry bookcases filled with legal volumes, it was a far cry from the interrogation room at the police station. After we all entered, Ralph pushed a button on the wall. "Natalie, can you bring us some water, please.

"Unless anyone would like something stronger?" he asked turning to the room.

"No," Mr. Owen answered for us all.

"Just water," Ralph clarified to the intercom.

Her response came through more as a crackle than words.

He pointed to the corner. On a tripod was a small camera. "We would like to videotape this session."

"Why?" Mr. Owen asked.

"It's to help me remember."

"No."

"No?" Ralph repeated.

"Miss Moore is here to answer your questions, clarifying previous statements. If you want to recall her for a deposition, do it. That's not what you requested today."

Ralph's gaze flitted between Chelsea and Mr. Owen. "I'm certain, considering appearances, we won't want to use the video as evidence. It is only a means to help us prepare for Bryce's future defense." He turned toward Chelsea. "Miss Moore, surely you want that?"

"I'm here, Mr. Porter."

"Yes, fulfilling your agreement."

Though Infidelity was the elephant in the room, it wasn't invisible to anyone, not even Mr. Owen. As our attorney, Nox and Deloris agreed that he needed to be informed.

Mr. Owen placed his briefcase on the table. The latches clicked, opening and echoing as he gained everyone's attention.

"Mr. Owen?" Ralph asked.

He looked up at Ralph. "As you seem to enjoy referencing the *agreement*, I brought a copy of said agreement. I thought it might be helpful to expand your vocabulary beyond the word."

"Excuse me?"

Mr. Owen placed a manila folder on the table and removed a copy of an

Infidelity agreement. It wasn't Chelsea's nor was it mine; instead, it was a blank agreement of intent. "I'm not sure if you've seen the actual agreement of intent from Miss Moore's employer? They're not easily obtained." He didn't wait for Ralph's answer as he turned to page two and pointed to a clause. "As you've probably been told by your client, the agreement was for a one-year relationship, one year from the date the employee was contacted with his/her assignment, with the name of his/her client. This time period is set in stone with one exception.

"The only way the agreement can be voided is if there is physical abuse."

Mr. Owen looked up, first to Chelsea and then to Ralph. "Tell me, will your vocabulary now expand beyond the use of the word agreement? I believe it's clear that your client broke said *agreement*."

The light from the window made the perspiration again dotting Ralph's lip glisten and brought a shine to his forehead. He turned from Mr. Owen to me. I was now seated at the table between Nox and Chelsea.

"Alexandria, once this is complete, I'd like to speak to you privately about your grandfather's will."

"No," Nox replied.

"Mr. Demetri..."

"Ralph," I said. "There's nothing you can say that Lennox, Chelsea, or even Mr. Owen isn't privy to."

He shook his head. "You were only shown a small portion of the will. There's much more you need to understand."

Mr. Owen, who was still standing, removed a flash drive from his briefcase. "You're going to need to trust us on this one. As you know, the document is lengthy."

"What are you saying?"

"He's saying," I said, "that I've seen my grandfather's will in its entirety. I've studied every line from the first to the last."

"That's impossible."

Mr. Owen shrugged and turned to me. "I guess he doesn't believe us."

Ralph turned toward Chelsea. "Miss Moore, if you'd like to complete this interview in private, I would understand. It makes sense that some of what might be said could be embarrassing to you."

Chelsea sat taller. "I want it over. As Alex said, everyone in here knows the score."

Ten minutes later, glasses of ice water at each seat, cameras off, and Mr. Porter staged in front of a large legal pad and seated at the head of the table, he began.

At first Ralph asked Chelsea about Bryce's character. That line of questioning didn't last long. He then turned to facts. His questions were similar to the detective's. Leaning across the table, he asked, "Just so we have our dates right, how long did you and Bryce date?"

Chelsea took a deep breath. "I met Edward Spencer for the first time in August of this year."

Ralph made a spectacle of riffling through some papers. "Of this year?"

"Yes, sir."

"But here, Miss Moore, I have your statement to the Evanston police stating that you and Mr. Spencer had a relationship that dated back to your freshman year of college." He peered up from the page, looking over a pair of wire-rimmed reading glasses he'd recently donned. "You were a student at Stanford University, isn't that correct?"

"I was a student at Stanford my freshman year, yes."

"And Miss Collins's roommate?"

"Yes, sir."

"Mr. Spencer took…" He looked again at his papers. "…a total of five trips to California during your freshman year. He had the receipts to verify his travel."

I sucked in a deep breath as a chill rattled through me. Five. Bryce had traveled to California five times and never spoken to me. Was he there watching me?

"Was that a question?" Mr. Owen asked.

"Are you now saying that you never saw or spoke to Mr. Spencer during any of his visits?"

"That's what I'm saying: I did not."

Ralph turned to me. "What about you, Miss Collins. Prior to your departure to Palo Alto, you and Mr. Spencer were dating."

"You asked to question Miss Moore, not Miss Collins," Mr. Owen reminded him.

I shook my head. "It's fine. Bryce and I dated while I was in high school. That's common knowledge. I broke it off after I moved away."

"You broke it off until you agreed to marry him."

"I didn't—"

"Yet he visited," Ralph interrupted. "Bryce flew to San Francisco commercial and Palo Alto private on multiple occasions. I mentioned your freshman year. His visits weren't limited to that year; they continued for all four years. They continued even after he began dating Miss Summers. There are even records of him staying at a hotel on Stanford Avenue. You're familiar with Stanford Avenue?"

"Yes," I said, "I'm familiar with Stanford Avenue."

"How far was that from your residence?"

Nox's body tensed beside me. We weren't touching, yet I could feel his temper growing. I wasn't sure if it was directed at Ralph or Bryce.

"It's a long road. I'd need a point of reference."

Ralph went on, "How did you feel knowing your ex-boyfriend was seeing not only your roommate but also another woman? His picture was in the media with Melissa."

I answered, "I didn't know he was in Palo Alto. I wasn't following his whereabouts. He wasn't seeing my roommate. It's true that he attempted to contact me a few times when I first moved west during my freshman year, but I blocked his number. I even blocked him from social media."

"Why?"

"Because I broke up with him."

"Did your dorm room or apartment have a telephone, a landline?"

I tried to recall. "Yes, our first dorm did."

"Miss Moore, did you ever answer that phone?"

"Of course."

"And you never spoke to Bryce Spencer? You never flirted with him? You never encouraged him to give up on Alexandria and see you instead?"

"No, Mr. Porter, I did not."

"Ralph," Mr. Owen said, "Miss Moore is not a suspect. She's here to give you a statement about Edward Spencer. Perhaps we could concentrate on Saturday?"

"This line of questions goes to witness integrity," Ralph explained, turning back to Chelsea. "Did you lie to the Evanston police or are you lying now?"

"I met Edward Bryce Spencer in August of this year while I was hospitalized at the Stanford Medical Center. I have no recollection of speaking to him or even seeing him before that date. Recently, Mr. Spencer and I were in a relationship. He asked me to help him, to lie for him. I thought he cared for me. I wanted to help him."

"So you lied?"

"I helped him with an alibi."

"Miss Moore, you do realize that if you admit this in a court of law, you will be admitting to perjury? Do you know what perjury is?"

"Yes, sir, I do. I will tell the truth if I'm required to speak in a court of law. I will tell them what I just told you: I met Mr. Spencer in August."

"And you moved in with him when? In September?"

Her face lost color as she leaned across the table. "Mr. Spencer told the world I was nothing more than his whore. Nothing you or anyone can say to me on the stand can make it any worse. I have nothing left but the truth. I won't hesitate to speak it."

Ralph made a note and looked up. "So this is retaliatory?"

"Ralph, she isn't on trial," Mr. Owen said.

"Miss Moore, he paid for your relationship, isn't that true?"

"We had an agreement as you've so frequently mentioned. I cannot nor will not say more than that. If you mention it in a court of law, you are violating his side of the agreement, and I will walk away with my entire year's pay."

"Isn't that your intention now? That violation clause that Mr. Owen mentioned?"

A pregnant pause settled over the room. Finally, Mr. Porter continued, "Tell us, how did you feel when he called you a whore? How did you feel when he and Alexandria became engaged?"

"Used. Cheap." Her answers were clipped. "Are there any other words you'd like me to use?"

"And how did you feel when you found out that not only was he seeing Alexandria, but also Melissa?"

"I didn't know about Melissa except in past tense."

"Yet you shared a home?"

"I never saw her."

Their responses and rebuttals came lightning fast. Multiple times Mr. Owen intervened. I offered my perspective, but each time he concentrated on Chelsea.

"Miss Moore, you never saw Melissa, just as you never saw Bryce Spencer before August of this year?"

Chelsea stopped answering, crossing her arms over her chest as her eyes filled with tears.

"I think we're done," Nox said, beginning to stand.

"Fine," Ralph said. "Let's talk about Saturday, about the day Miss Summers was brutally murdered." He narrowed his gaze. "Where were you?"

She gave the same answer she had to the detectives. Waking at Montague and running errands for Jane.

"All day?"

"Yes."

"Did you have a driver?"

"No. I was given a Montague staff car to use."

"And you knew where to go?"

"I had a list with addresses. The car had GPS."

Ralph sat straighter. "Miss Moore, your cheek. When did that happen?"

"That is enough," Mr. Owen said.

"Melissa appeared to have been a healthy young lady. Did she put up a fight before you killed her?"

CHAPTER 26

— ●○● —

ADELAIDE

THE CRACKLING FIRE soothed me as I drifted in and out of sleep. I was growing stronger with each day, but I'd still spent nearly two weeks in bed, mostly drugged to the point of unconsciousness. As the hours and days passed, I recalled bits and pieces of the detoxification.

More than once I'd woken with a start, my ribs screaming out in pain as my body jolted awake. There were memories of the nurse, a burly man. I also recalled insects and vines. The memories weren't as real as when it had happened, but they were enough to keep me away from painkillers or alcohol. I wouldn't risk going through that again.

Oren had done his part too. Silvia informed me that the house was completely alcohol-free. Every bottle of anything had been removed. Though I had no intentions of searching, I appreciated the knowledge.

It wasn't that I didn't long for a glass of wine. I did. I could close my eyes and see the wine cellar at Montague: walls and walls of shelves lined with bottles. The vision made my mouth water and pulse race.

It wasn't only the thought of alcohol that sped my heartbeat, but my husband too. I'd spoken to Ralph once, only to confirm that I was alive and well. I didn't mention the will or my decision to divorce Alton. I simply said I was fine and would contact him again at a later date.

As I reached for the warm cup of tea near the sofa, I wiggled my toes under the soft blanket covering my legs. Beyond the windows the sky was gray with clouds that threatened snow. And yet I was warm and happy. I was sober and clean. I was growing stronger in a home I'd only heard about, dreamt about.

Oren and I studied my father's will. Deciding to divorce Alton was similar to the consequences of taking the pills, the ones Jane confiscated from me. And yet now with the knowledge of the codicil, it was different.

I could live and other than the corporate structure of Montague going public, the assets would be evenly divided between the heirs: Alexandria and I, the way it always should have been.

The activity on the television screen caught my attention. I'd muted the sound, but now reached for the remote control and allowed the reporter's voice to replace the soothing snap and crackle of the fire.

"…pleaded not guilty to felony murder in the death of Melissa Summers. As you may recall, her body was found on Edward Spencer's family estate on Saturday evening. The coroner has not released any details of her death at this time other than the time of death is believed to have been only hours before her body was discovered."

I tucked the blanket around me as I listened to a videotape of Melissa's parents. My heart broke as they talked about their daughter, shocked that she'd been alive for all these months. Her mother cried as she begged for justice, afraid to speculate on how her daughter had been living and under what conditions.

My breath caught in my throat, a lump forming as they played another video of Alexandria and Chelsea entering the police station. I didn't know one of the men with them, other than that Alexandria had told me it was her new attorney. The screen had their names, even Isaac's.

I'd never felt overly attached to most of the staff at Montague. There were only special ones who'd stayed with us through the years: Jane and Brantley. The tea bubbled in my stomach at the thought of Brantley purchasing drugs for Alton's plan.

It was the memories of Jane that brought me relief. That was the same feeling I had seeing Isaac following Alexandria. Relief and gratitude. I'd been so close to pushing her into a life with Bryce, with a man who could murder someone in cold blood and show no remorse.

His picture came on the screen. He was leaving the jail, flanked by Ralph Porter and Suzanna. I scanned the crowd for Alton. Surely he'd be there, but he wasn't.

"*Amore mio.*"

I turned away from the television to the loving gaze, the one that saw what no one else had seen, had tried to see.

"You're sad?"

I nodded, unaware that my cheeks were damp.

"Talk to me."

I looked down into the mug. The warm golden liquid moved as my hands trembled.

Oren reached for the cup and placed it on the table as he sat beside my legs, his warmth against me. "I'm listening."

I lifted one of his hands to my cheek and tilted my face into his palm. Closing my eyes, I felt the dampness as more tears fell. "I don't want to be sad."

"I don't want you to be sad." He looked at the television. The reporter was speaking about the penalty for murder in the state of Georgia. Felony murder carried the possibility of death, or to life in prison with the possibility of parole in 25 to 30 years. "I can't believe a young woman is dead. I can't believe I'm alive. I can't believe any of this."

Oren's cheeks rose as small lines formed in the corners of his eyes. "Death is sad."

I nodded.

"Being alive shouldn't be. My dear, we have a whole life to live."

"I think I'm ready."

His smile grew. "Then we will live."

My lids fell, my lashes damp as they closed. "First, I need to talk to him. I need to talk to an attorney."

"Not in that order."

"What?" I asked as Oren came back into view.

"An attorney first."

"I know you're right, but I owe him…"

"No, you don't owe that bastard a thing. You don't think he knows. He knows where you are. He even knows who you're with. Adelaide, this is a game of chess, or if you like, make it a game of Battleship. I don't care." He grinned.

A memory of the two of us playing Battleship came back to my now-clear mind. We'd met at a small bed and breakfast in the middle of the Ozarks. It was hidden away in the dead of winter. How I made it up the icy roads I'll never know. When we woke, we had another foot of snow. The roads were closed. Other than the caretakers, we were alone in a winter wonderland.

The cabin where we stayed had electricity and a fireplace. The shelves were filled with books and games that had been used by hundreds of other guests. Somehow one of us pulled out the box.

I was sad to say I'd never played the game. My daughter would probably have loved it, but I'd never played it or any games with her. Instead of demeaning me for my confession, Oren admitted that he too had never played. Never as a child or an adult.

In the middle of a cabin, isolated in what looked like a snow globe from the window, we sat on a shag rug in front of a fire and played Battleship. We didn't play one game. Over the course of our three-day reprieve, we played it over and over. Each game was more strategic. Each game became a new challenge, because we had knowledge and experience. We learned one another's strategies and weaknesses.

I took a deep breath. "He knows me."

Oren nodded. "And you know him."

"I do."

"I agree it's time. I didn't want to rush you, but you need to make a move. What will he expect?"

"Submission. Acceptance. For me to acquiesce to whatever he demands."

"Can you imagine his board, the way he has his ships aligned?"

Another tear fell. "Do you think I can?"

"I know you can."

My chin fell forward as I tried to stop the ache in my chest. The pain was intense. Could it be my heart? No. It wasn't physical. It was fear, terror as I'd never felt. And in my life I'd been afraid.

"You stopped talking," Oren said as he lifted my chin.

"I'm not who you think."

"I beg to differ. I'm very good at reading people. It's served me well."

I shook my head. "No." And then I reconsidered. "Perhaps. I believe that you excel at many things, Oren Demetri, but you have one serious flaw."

His neck straightened. "Do tell. I've not been told."

A grin threatened my sad facade. "Or perhaps you haven't listened."

"Adelaide, you're wounding me."

"You see what you want to see, not what is there. I'm not a strong woman. I'm a woman who submits, acquiesces, and accepts. I always have been. It's how I was raised and how I survived. My father thought no more of me. If he had, he wouldn't have sentenced me to a life with a man I didn't love. Alton has never thought more of me." I shrugged. "And I've never given him reason to."

Oren reached for the remote and turned off the television. When he turned back, the glow of the fire as his backdrop, I stared deeply into his eyes. The blue glistened with the reflection of the fire as the gray beyond the windows grew darker.

"In all the years, did I ever tell you about my mother?"

I sat taller, pulling my legs closer, confirming our physical connection. I shook my head. "No. I don't even know her name."

"Paola. It means small."

I held my breath as he spoke. His timbre slowed as his mind went back through the years.

"And she was—small. A petite woman, like you. My father was big, a giant in my eyes when I was a child. He worked hard, physical labor. He was a longshoreman, Adelaide, manual labor on the docks of New York. I've never spoken about my parents, not because I'm ashamed, but because I don't deserve you. You weren't raised for the likes of me."

I leaned forward, my ribs aching as I kissed his lips. I'd endure the pain to take away his. "Please go on."

"My father worked hard and made it to supervisor. That was an accomplishment for a first-generation American." His smile came back to life.

"But it was my mother who was really the strong one. She was the one who took his paycheck and created a life and a home. He made what he considered good money, but it came at a cost. At the end of the day, she was the one who kept it together. I didn't realize how vital she was until she was gone."

"What happened to her?"

"There were protests. They didn't call them that. The union was in charge. There were rumors of a strike. One night…" He took a deep breath. "…my father went to the shipyard. There had been threats. It was his job. Not that he made enough money for something like that. My mother heard a rumor. She'd overheard something at the market. I didn't learn the details until I was older. She went to warn him, a little feisty five-foot-tall woman. Because her husband was in danger and she wouldn't sit back and let fate have its way."

I waited as he stared out the window, his hands still holding mine.

"My father came home, battered but alive."

"Your mother?"

"She washed ashore two days later."

"Oh my God."

"My father lived only another year. He drank himself to death. I was in college, because that was what she wanted me to do. Neither one of them saw my success or my choices. I'm not sure if they would have approved. They never met Angelina or saw their grandson. They worked hard and taught me to do the same." Oren squeezed my hand. "My mother lost her life fighting for what she believed, for the man she loved. She was strong. I see that strength in you.

"You have always been strong and little," he added with a grin. "She had what you didn't. She had the strength of those around her. It fed her. It fed me. Let me share that with you."

"I-I don't…"

"Adelaide Montague, you have survived death. That is more than Paola was able to do. I see a woman who can do anything."

"Why?"

"Why what?" Oren asked.

"Why do you see that? Why have you loved me?"

"Because you let me, because with you I wasn't just a longshoreman's son.

With you, I'm *someone more*, just like you are with me. You're more than a name and a company or an heir. I just wish you'd see yourself as I see you."

"Call him?"

Oren shook his head. "The attorney first."

"I've only ever worked with Hamilton and Porter."

"No, *amore mio*, you have worked with Stephen Crawford."

A smile came to my lips. I had. "He isn't an attorney."

"Not yet, but he can help you with Preston, Madden, and Owen. Daryl Owen has started representing Alexandria and Chelsea."

"Do you have his number?"

The lines were back in the corners of his stunning blue eyes. "As a matter of fact, I do."

CHAPTER 27

---•O•---

NOX

"I AM READY to get out of this fucking town, this fucking state. They've all gone mad," I said to anyone and no one. The only one to hear was Charli. Thankfully we'd finally been left alone. It seemed like forever since we had. Not that a hotel suite was the same as our apartment, but the relief that accompanied the solitude was revitalizing.

Chelsea hadn't stopped crying since we'd left Hamilton and Porter. Maybe she had. Now that she was in her own suite, I didn't know. For the longest time she didn't want to leave our sides. I couldn't blame her reaction after the number Porter had done on her. Charli even offered to stay with her; however, honestly, I was more receptive to Isaac's offer. He promised not to leave the front room of her suite. She could sleep and he'd make sure no one entered. Though she'd been hesitant to accept his offer, it was obvious he was more of a deterrent to unwanted visitors than Charli.

Chelsea hadn't been sure who she feared more would knock on her door: the Savannah-Chatham police or Spencer.

Deloris recommended restraining orders to protect both Chelsea and Charli. While it seemed like a smart legal move, I knew there was no way anyone was getting through my people or me. It wasn't happening. I'd lay down my life for Charli.

We had eyes on Spencer. So far, after leaving the jail, he'd stayed put at Carmichael Hall. According to aerial news footage, the house was clear. It was a nearby building—Charli said they were garages—that was roped off as a crime scene.

Deloris had Charli's phone, the one Fitzgerald had given to her. Everyone already knew she was in Savannah; it wouldn't be that difficult to pinpoint her location. Other than her clandestine rendezvous with Jane and our legal meetings, we'd been imprisoned as much as Spencer. It wasn't only the press that was hounding both Charli and also Chelsea, but also their concern over meeting Fitzgerald or Spencer.

Charli huffed as she settled on the sofa with her laptop. "I want to leave too, but Daryl said that if Chelsea left before giving the police a chance to question her again, it could look suspicious."

"She has Isaac. We can even leave Deloris. I could whisk you back to New York."

"I want that too." Her golden eyes lit with happiness. "My mom sounds... good. I'd like to see her."

"Did she really say she was going to call Daryl about a divorce?"

"Yes." Charli looked down at her screen. "It's after seven. She may have already done it."

I sat beside her, the sofa bowing to my weight as I let out a long breath and fell against the soft cushioned back. "Come on, princess, let's go back to New York." I reached for her sock covered feet as her toes burrowed against my leg. "Not even Rye. Let's go back to our place. We won't tell anyone and..." I pulled her feet until her legs were straightened over my lap. "...I'll show you my cape."

A stunning smile widened across her lips as I rubbed the arches of her feet.

"That feels so good," she cooed. "You better stop or I may fall asleep."

"That's not exactly what I had in mind."

"Your cape?" she asked. "Really? I was beginning to think it didn't exist."

"It's all part of the myth, the legend. If I'd shown it to you too soon, you wouldn't have truly appreciated it."

Charli laughed. "There isn't anything you've shown me so far that I haven't appreciated."

"I like the sound of that."

She shook her head and looked back at the laptop. "I know I should be working on schoolwork, but I'm trying to see what I can find. I mean, the state has charged Bryce. They can't charge Chelsea too, unless it's as an accessory."

I laid my head back and closed my eyes. "She has a solid alibi. She was out, all over Savannah, all day."

"And she was alone."

"But Deloris has obtained more than a few of the stores' surveillance. Chelsea was on the footage. It's all dated and time stamped. Deloris is working on the timetable. Traffic, distance, time spent in each establishment."

Charli nodded again. "I know it's her. You know it's her, but with the big sunglasses she was wearing, it's not exactly conclusive. In the pictures, in all honesty, it could be me." She shook her head. "Daryl said Ralph could just be blowing smoke, but I think establishing an ironclad alibi is her best defense. She signed for some of the merchandise. Deloris is securing all the transactions."

I lifted my head. "Why would he show his hand?"

"What do you mean?"

"He could have had Chelsea on the stand and taken that line of questioning. If he had, he could have, at the very least, established a shred of doubt in the prosecution's case, made the jury question her alibi, especially with the sunglasses. Instead, he showed his hand. He's giving us time to refute him long before this thing goes to trial. It doesn't make sense."

Sighing, Charli closed the laptop and sat it on the carpet near the sofa. "Shit. He has another angle, doesn't he?"

"I don't know what it is, but I think he does."

"I want to leave too," she said wishfully. "How about if I meet with Ralph one last time tomorrow about the will and then we can go?"

I sat up. "No. Why do you need to go back to that snake's office?"

"Because I'm not coming back. I don't want to... until I'm subpoenaed. I might as well get this over with, especially if my mother is really going to talk to Daryl and leave Alton. It's not going away. Their divorce is a stipulation of the will."

"You're not leaving my sight."

Charli pulled her feet from my lap and climbed up on her knees. Leaning over me, she kissed my cheek. "I like the sound of that." Her kisses rained lower over my ear and my chin. Each contact created a chill that ignited a flame. "What is it... exactly... that you... want to see?" she asked between kisses.

I shook my head. "Oh, princess, you're playing with the wrong kind of fire right now."

Her long, untethered hair flowed over her shoulders, tickling my nose as she continued to pepper my neck with soft kisses. Her petite hands moved over my shirt to the buttons. "I think you're... the exact fire... I need to forget... this shitty day."

I lifted the platinum diamond-dusted cage hanging near her collar. "Did you hear that, Deloris... or is it Isaac... Clayton?"

"Fuck!" Her cheeks glowed red. The crimson was bright enough to rival her hair as she reached behind her neck and undid the clasp.

As she laid the necklace beside her laptop, I seized her wrist. In one quick move, she was flattened and pinned between the couch and me. "What did I tell you about taking that off? Are you planning a swim?"

"No," she giggled. "If you'll let me up, I'll go get the other one. It's in the safe."

"The same place as your wedding rings?"

It took her a minute—during that time visible questions swirled in her golden gaze. And then, all at once her lips parted and laugh filled the room. "Yes. Right where I left them, dear." She shrugged. "But that time, I was planning a swim."

In the living room of a Savannah hotel suite, we were transported back to Del Mar. "You were the most beautiful woman I'd seen. I came out of the water and there you were. So sexy and sophisticated." I ran my finger over her lips. "And your mouth. Witty and smart. Yet young and innocent.

"My cock is getting hard just thinking about that bathing suit."

Charli wiggled beneath me, her round curves and hard planes rubbing against all the right places.

"Hmm. You were very sexy and mysterious. All tough and protective."

"I was? I'm not anymore?"

"I've seen under the mask."

"Only what I've let you see."

"What are you hiding from me, Mr. Demetri?"

"If I told you, I wouldn't be mysterious."

"You'll always be..." Charli's words faded as her cell phone chimed from the table across the room.

"It can wait," I said.

She pushed against my shoulders. "Not if it's my momma."

Sighing, I sat up. "I remember when you used to avoid her calls."

She shot me a grin over her shoulder as she hurried toward the phone. "I remember when you wouldn't talk to your dad. Look how things have changed."

"Momma," she said into her phone. "Is everything all right?"

Standing, I bent down and lifted the pearl necklace from the floor. Giving Charli a moment of privacy, I carried it into the bedroom. Inside the large closet was the standard-issue hotel safe. I exchanged the audible necklace for the other one, closed the safe, and carried it back to the living room. Charli was still talking as I draped the chain around her neck and secured the clasp.

Though she shook her head, she didn't try to stop me. There was no way she was getting out of my sight. Not her or her blue dot.

"I'm so proud of you," she said into the phone. "Really. It'll be all right. Nox said the Demetri Enterprise legal staff is looking into Montague Corporation. Nothing will happen overnight. They're corporate attorneys. They'll help... Not in person? You're not coming here, are you?"

The panic in her tone made me stop and stare, as if by standing still I could hear Adelaide's response.

Charli let out a deep breath. "Good. We're hoping soon. Probably tomorrow... I love you too."

She swiped the phone and laid it back on the table. "I can't believe it. She's really going to do it."

"Did she talk to Daryl?"

"Yes. He's agreed to represent her in the divorce."

"I hope she's letting him tell your stepfather."

"No."

"No?" I asked.

"She wants to do it. She says she *needs* to do it."

"Not in person?"

Charli shook her head. "No, thank goodness."

"When?" I asked as my phone buzzed with a text.

Deloris: **"ADELAIDE JUST CALLED MR. FITZGERALD IF YOU WANT TO LISTEN."**

My eyes grew wide. "This may be inappropriate."

Charli's cheeks rose. "Oh, I'm intrigued."

"No. The text."

She placed her fist against her hip. "Who's sending you inappropriate text messages?"

"No…" I shook my head with a grin. "Deloris is listening to *everyone*. She has your stepfather's phone tapped. I can tell her to stop listening, but she wanted you to know that your mom just called his number. They're talking right now."

"Can she hear what they're saying?"

I nodded. "And you can too if you want."

Indecision washed across her features, a cloud of morality. Right versus wrong. Curiosity versus privacy. And just like a gust of winter wind, the hesitancy was gone. "Hell yes." She rushed toward the door. "Let's go. I can't wait to finally hear her tell that bastard off."

I hurried to keep up as Charli ran down the corridor toward Deloris's room.

She may have been quick, but my strides were longer. I reached her just as she slid through Deloris's slightly ajar door. She came to a dead stop, her heartbeat quickened against mine as I pulled her toward my chest. The room vibrated with the thunder of Alton Fitzgerald's voice.

"…after nearly four days! Four days!"

Her body trembled, the joy from moments earlier was gone as her eyes filled with scenes Deloris and I couldn't see.

"Princess, let's go. Deloris will let us—"

She covered my lips with trembling fingers as her head moved back and forth.

Adelaide was speaking. "Stop and be glad I called you now."

"Be glad? I'd ask where in the hell you are or who you're with, but I know."

"I know you know."

"If that criminal thinks he can come between us…"

"Us, Alton? There's never been an us. There's been a you and a me. That doesn't make an us."

"Come home and we'll work this out. Surely you've seen the mess—"

"The mess your son has created?"

"What?" Charli gasped as she stumbled, reaching for her stomach.

Her complexion paled as I wrapped my arms tighter around her, also trying to make sense of what had just been said. Did Adelaide just admit that Bryce was actually Fitzgerald's son?

"Come on—"

"No," Charli said. "I need to hear this."

"…I've seen it," Adelaide continued. "Not that you wanted me to. While in that awful place, I couldn't see anything or anyone—"

"Because you were drunk. You always have been. We put you in that hospital, a very respected facility, for your own good. Do you have any idea how much that place cost?"

"I'm better. I'm calling to let you know that I've contacted an attorney. Expect to be served with divorce papers."

"Have another glass of wine, dear. You're delusional."

"And leave my house."

"How dare you! I've built this house, this fortune…" he continued to bellow.

Charli pulled away and sank to the edge of the sofa. "Can you turn that down?"

Deloris nodded as she adjusted the volume.

"…your father expected this out of you," Fitzgerald continued to bellow. "He knew you'd ruin another marriage. He knew you were never going to keep any man satisfied—"

"Was that why you killed him?" Adelaide's calm tone resonated as even Fitzgerald had difficulty finding the right words.

"Delusional. I have medical records. I have proof. The doctors will all testify to your incompetence."

"That's wonderful. I have doctors, too. I have proof, too. They ran tests. I won't say more because I won't waste my breath. Just know that I've seen the entire will, including the part you didn't want me to see.

"You knew that though," she continued. "That's why you drugged me, poisoned me. You're not as untouchable as you think. Push me on the divorce, Alton. Please.

"Because when you do, I'll enjoy watching you fall. The codicil says everything goes to the rightful heirs. Guess what? That's not you."

"We had a prenuptial agreement. The wealth I added to this company, this family…"

"Maybe you and Bryce can share a cell. From Chelsea's bruised face, it's easy to see that the apple doesn't fall far from the tree. Or because of that, maybe you would rather room with someone else. That boy has quite the temper. Maybe you could find out what it's like to be on the receiving end."

"There's no way I'll allow—"

"Goodbye, Alton. Let me give you some parting advice, the same you gave me: remember to swallow and grin and bear it."

Though Fitzgerald continued to speak, the line had obviously been disconnected.

I reached for Charli's hand. The trembling had stopped, but her cheeks were wet.

"Princess?"

She took a deep breath and stood. "What did she mean about Alton's son?"

Deloris's eyes widened. "I really don't know. I can try to find out."

"Eww," Charli said, turning a small circle. "His *son*. Suzanna and Alton's affair has been going on for nearly thirty years?" She took a deep breath.

"I think I feel ill."

"You didn't marry him. Even Porter isn't claiming you did."

Her head moved back and forth. "B-but he wanted me to. Alton was pushing me to."

"So Spencer would have access to everything Montague."

Charli sat back on the edge of the sofa. "That would make sense, but did my grandfather know? Is that why he stipulated Bryce in the will?"

"We're jumping to conclusions," Deloris said.

"And... my grandfather? Did Momma accuse Alton of killing him? What the hell?"

"It's because of the date on the codicil," I volunteered. "The law student who used to work for Hamilton and Porter and now works with Daryl told us about it last week. Your grandfather approved the codicil the day he died. Stephen thought it was weird."

Charli's eyes opened wide. "My whole family is fucked up."

A grin came to my lips. "And I thought I had the market cornered on that family trait."

She stood again and reached for my hand. "Tell me we'll go back home soon. My mom deserves a hug."

"Your stepfather is going to fight her," Deloris said. "He's calling Ralph Porter right now."

Charli shrugged. "She knows that, but did you hear her? No matter what he says or does, she'll always have that." Her smile returned. "I'll always have it." She tugged my hand, pulling herself toward me and looked up. "Hi, I'm Alexandria Collins. I'm twenty-four years old and I just met my mother. She's kind of kick-ass."

I kissed Charli's forehead. "I think I know how you feel. And I'd say her daughter is even more kick-ass."

"I hate to be the one to break up this tender moment," Deloris said. "But go back to your room and let me monitor..." Her eyes widened and nose scrunched as she lifted the earphones now replacing the speakers toward her ears. "...this tirade."

Even through earphones the tenor of Fitzgerald's voice could be heard.

"You might want to adjust that volume again," Charli said.

"Batplane? Our apartment?" I asked, hoping for an earlier exit.

She shook her head. "Our suite for tonight. The dust hasn't settled for Chelsea."

My gut twisted with the apprehension Savannah induced in me. "Twenty-four hours."

"Yes, Mr. Demetri."

CHAPTER 28

———•O•———

ALEXANDRIA

THE CLICK OF the old-fashioned elevator slowly moving upward was replaced by loud voices arguing as we ascended to the second floor of Hamilton and Porter.

I reached for Nox's hand, recognizing the loudest voice. Nox didn't ask. He knew the voice too. He'd heard it last night in Deloris's suite. I envied his limited exposure. I'd heard it most of my life.

"What the hell?" Nox said. "You asked her to be here, set up this appointment knowing that he'd be here?"

"No, sir," Natalie said, "Miss Collin's appointment was set first." She opened the cage-like door. "I didn't know they'd be so loud. Let me take you to another room. He won't know you're here."

"The entire will, Ralph. You told me she knew about the codicil, but not the entire will!"

I stood taller, my feet unwilling to move as Alton's voice echoed down the corridor.

"Alton, she's lying. I have the records from when she was here. They concentrated on the codicil."

"Fix it! She wants a divorce. It's not happening. She agreed to no divorce. We'll fight her at every turn."

"Calm down."

"Calm down? You want me to calm down as everything I've worked for vanishes? It's not just me. You've helped. You know what you've done. I'm not losing everything without..."

Nox tugged my hand, pulling me toward Natalie and Mr. Owen as Isaac stayed by our sides. The voices faded as we turned a corner and entered the conference room.

No one spoke as Natalie shut the door.

"I'm sorry," she said. "Mr. Fitzgerald wasn't on Mr. Porter's schedule. He just showed up."

"Showed up?" Nox asked. "You're sure he doesn't know that Alex is here?"

"No, sir. If you'd prefer to reschedule?"

My heart beat rapidly as I increased the pressure on my clenched teeth. I shook my head. I didn't want to reschedule. I wanted to get on the Batplane and fly back to New York. I wanted to talk to my mother about the accusations she'd made during her telephone call with Alton. I wanted to know why she suspected that Alton had a hand in my grandfather's death. I wanted to know why she referred to Bryce as Alton's son and why he didn't refute her.

I took a step back and sank to one of the cushioned chairs at the table, my stomach twisting with each thought. I had questions. I needed answers.

Sleep had been evasive as I mulled over Mother and Alton's conversation in my head. Sometime during the night I'd made a mental leap. If Momma blamed Alton for my grandfather's death, could he also be responsible for my father's?

"Miss Collins, are you all right?" Natalie asked.

"What?" I looked up into her concerned expression. I was sitting at the table with my head in my hands. Her question brought me back to present.

Nox squatted near my knees. "You're suddenly pale. Are you sure you don't want to reschedule?"

I shook my head again. Breakfast had been less than appetizing. I was ready for Lana's cooking or even Silvia's. The hotel room service didn't even come close. "No. His voice just caught me off guard. If we reschedule we need to stay here longer. I don't want to do that."

"Can I get you something? Water or coffee?" Natalie asked. "I-I'm not sure how long Mr. Porter will be."

Mr. Owen pulled back the sleeve of his suit coat and looked at his watch. "Mr. Porter will be here in less than five minutes, because that is the time we scheduled."

"Sir, I-I'm not—"

Nox also stood. "Our appointment supersedes a walk-in, Ms. Banks."

"I-I'll see what I can do."

"Miss Collins," Mr. Owen said as he sat. "I've read over and over your grandfather's will regarding my phone call with your mother. The way I interpret Article XII..." He pulled a printed document from his briefcase. "Right here." He pointed.

As is now the case, it is essential that Adelaide Montague remain married to Alton Fitzgerald for the remainder of their earthly lives. As Adelaide's husband, Alton Fitzgerald will have all rights set forth as the primary stockholder in Montague Corporation. If either party files for divorce or attempts to end the marriage, all Montague holdings revert to Alexandria Collins.

"So it's all mine. End of story?"

"That would be too simple. Look at the next section."

This wasn't the first time or even the tenth time that Nox and I had mulled over this document. I knew I wasn't an attorney yet, but some of the wording seemed inconsistent to me, at best.

Once the age or degree completion has occurred, in order for A. Collins to inherit the Montague holdings and assets and to fulfill the requirements set forth in this legal document she must adhere to the following:

Being of the legal age of twenty-five (or having completed her college degree), Alexandria Collins must agree to a legal union with a husband who too will represent her and their biological children's shares in Montague Corporation as well as in the running of private Montague assets.

"And this is where we get into the bullshit about Spencer," Nox said, leaning back in the chair beside me, no longer reading along.

"Yes," Mr. Owen confirmed. "I do believe he's no longer a viable option. Thankfully, your grandfather put the qualifier in that he must prove himself worthy."

"But the codicil changes everything anyway, right?" I prayed we'd interpreted it correctly.

"It qualifies, but quite honestly there's room for interpretation. If contested, it could go before a judge and be reheard."

"The codicil says that the assets will be equally divided between the heirs. That's Alex and her mom," Nox refuted.

"Yes. I've been reviewing your mother's prenuptial agreement. Your grandfather may have entrusted his daughter to Alton Fitzgerald, but he didn't his fortune or his company. The wording is complex legalese. Just like the portion of the will pertaining to you, the prenuptial agreement is vague. In essence, your grandfather forbade their divorce. I'd assume he was concerned that Mr. Fitzgerald would be the one to initiate it. That was why he stipulated the assets going to you. He even made that stipulation in the case of either of their deaths.

I nodded. "Alton told me that Momma wouldn't die. He said some things are worse than death."

"Unbelievable," Nox muttered.

Daryl Owen looked up from the document, his dark eyes swirling with both disbelief and pity as he shook his head. "Okay, well, I interpret your grandfather's wishes as no matter what, Montague will stay in the family. His stipulation for liquidation and assets going to Fitzgerald Investments was nullified by the codicil."

"So we're good?" Nox said.

"Where it gets complicated are the stipulations for Alexandria's inheritance. He states twenty-five years of age or the completion of a degree."

"I have a degree."

Mr. Owen nodded. "And a legal union with a husband who too will represent her and their biological children's shares…"

"Misogynistic." I shook my head. "Come on, even the monarchy of

England is now recognizing female heirs in lines of succession. If this goes before a judge, he or she would recognize that times have changed."

"Get out of my way!"

My breath caught in my lungs at Alton's demand. His voice was coming from right outside the door.

"No, sir," Isaac responded.

"I said get out of my way. Alexandria is in there and I need to see her."

We all waited, the entire room holding its collective breath, but Isaac didn't respond.

"Alexandria!" Alton's voice boomed from the other side of the door. "If you want your mother to have any chance of a divorce, get out here."

Nox put his hand on my arm. "Don't move. You heard your mom on that call. She can handle him. Let her."

The dread I'd felt at first hearing his voice as we ascended the elevator shaft morphed. Nox was right, my mother had stood up to him. Alton's world was crumbling and it was time I stopped bowing to his every demand.

Disobeying Nox's demand, I stood. "I'm not going out there, but if he wants to talk to me, he can come in here, in front of all of you."

"No," Nox said. "You don't owe that pig anything."

"I don't. I want him to know I'm done listening to him. I want him to hear it from me."

Nox narrowed his gaze, scanning me from head to toe. "Are you sure?"

Rolling my upper lip between my teeth, I considered my decision. As I did, I turned to his reassuring light-blue stare. His presence overwhelmed me as it had from our first meeting. It wasn't stifling, like Alton's or Bryce's. I didn't disappear in his presence. I became more.

With Nox I was safe and strong. It wasn't the knowledge that he could fight my battle, but knowing that I could. I could stand against the injustices in my life and I'd be supported, because Nox understood that my power didn't threaten his control.

Nodding, I reached for Nox. As we touched, I stared at the contrast in our hands.

His was larger and stronger, and had given me so much.

His hands had held me, caressed me, and given me delight. They'd taken me where no one else had gone. They'd teased me, bound me, and even spanked me. They'd brought me to tears and to ecstasy.

Nox had taught me to trust with my whole self. It was a gift. With him I knew who I was. With his hands, he'd shown me strength, not in him, but in myself.

"Alexandria!"

Last night on the phone Momma had lit a match to Alton's world. I heard the panic in his voice. It was time to fan the flame.

Straightening my shoulders, I lifted my chin. "I am. I'm done cowering at the sight of him. I'm done being a scared little girl. Montague is Momma's and mine. If he wants anything after the divorce, he needs to learn who's in charge. The scepter has been passed. It's time for him to bow."

Giving Nox's hand a squeeze, I moved mine to the table and steadied my stance. Though my entire body trembled as if the room had suddenly dropped twenty degrees, I did my best to appear confident.

Alton's demand came again, this time with threats to Isaac and everyone keeping him away from his daughter.

Nox's warm hand covered one of mine as he lowered his voice. "You want to do this?"

I swallowed and nodded.

Nox looked to Mr. Owen. "You heard the lady. Open the door."

When Daryl pulled the door inward, only Isaac's back was visible. He literally filled the doorway. By the way his jacket strained I could easily imagine his arms crossed over his chest, his protruding brow beneath his shaved head, and the same scowl he'd worn in front of Montague Manor.

"Isaac," Nox said, "Miss Collins will see Mr. Fitzgerald."

"Sir?"

"Alexandria, come out here," Alton demanded. "We'll talk in private."

"Isaac," I said calmly, "if Alton wants to speak to me, he can come to me."

Instead of stepping aside, Isaac pivoted into the room. His back flattened against the wall. His arms were still crossed just as I'd imagined, and his expression was as intimidating as I'd ever seen. Though it was meant to cause fear, his sneer made me smile.

I turned back to the open door. "If you have something to say, come in here and say it."

"Alexandria, this is a private family matter." ·

With Suzanna by his side and Ralph behind him, his face glowed a deep shade of crimson.

My smile grew. "Suzanna isn't family."

"Alexandria?" She elongated my name, each syllable dripping with Southern guilt. The tone alone said she was hurt by my comment and insulted by my audacity. It was the way proper ladies condemned one another, verbal cues that spoke more than words. Usually they were accompanied by a smile on their face and a drink in their hand.

I tilted my head innocently as my eyes met hers. Then straightening my stance, I turned back to Alton. "This is your last chance. Speak now or forever hold your peace. We're leaving today and won't be returning until we are needed to testify."

"On Bryce's behalf... right?" Suzanna said. "Dear, he needs you. He's distraught. Come to Carmichael Hall. You know—"

"Mr. Fitzgerald?" Mr. Owen interrupted.

Alton's chest puffed as he took a step through the doorway. "Alexandria..." The restraint in his voice was impressive as he kept his gray eyes on me. "You always have been a spitfire."

"What do you want, Alton? What could you possibly say to me now that your marriage is over and your world is crumbling?"

"No, that's where you're wrong. It's your world and your mother's that is crumbling. My world is intact. This is Savannah. I rule Savannah."

I shook my head. "Every dictatorship comes to an end."

"Really, Alexandria. The Montagues aren't a dictatorship; they're an American monarchy and your reign doesn't need to end. Don't let your mother's delusional and irrational decisions stop you from what was at your fingertips." He took a step closer.

Though Nox's shoulder was against my side and his woodsy scent soothed me, my vision was beginning to narrow. My heart beat faster as the red faded and Alton's confidence grew.

Fighting my childhood training, I maintained my ground. "My mother isn't delusional. She's clearheaded for the first time."

"No, dear. It's too late for that. I filed papers long ago." He tilted his head toward Ralph. "He can show you. Your mother signed them. She can't file for divorce. She's not mentally stable. She lost the legal right to make that or any other decision years ago. Her behavior recently, her stay at Magnolia Woods… it all supports how truly ill she is."

He twisted the figurative knife, doing what he did so well. He planned and plotted. He prepared for every turn of events. Yet if that were the case, why had he been yelling at Ralph?

I shook my head. "No. She's free from you. She'll never come back."

"That's up to you."

"I'm not marrying Bryce!" My declaration came out louder and shriller than even I liked.

Alton nodded, a smile gracing his thin lips. "You've made that clear. I have an alternative for you, a way to give your mother the freedom she thinks she wants without allowing her to end up destitute."

"She will never be destitute," Nox's deep voice infiltrated my nightmare. "Neither will Alex."

"Alexandria, you are the heir to more money than these criminals can fathom. If you think that either one of them is interested in anything other than your bank account, you're mistaken."

His tone was slow and calm. He'd moved closer and closer until only the shiny table separated us.

My hands slid on the table's surface, perspiration leaching from my palms despite the goose bumps on my skin.

"That's not true," I countered. "I love Lennox and…" I took a deep breath. "…for the first time I've seen what Momma looks like in love."

He shook his head. "Delusional. I wonder what drugs she's taking now. Is she washing the pills down with wine? It's her favorite pastime."

"Stop it! She's not. She's strong."

"The choice is yours, Alexandria. I'll let her go. I'll even give her some money in the settlement, so that when that criminal gets tired of her, when he learns how truly boring her company can be in and out of bed, at least she'll be able to afford a roof over her head."

I didn't try to hide the disgust from my face. "You're the one who's delusional. You're the one who will be without a roof."

"Alexandria," Ralph said. "I have the medical and legal power of attorney. If you'd like Daryl to look at it, that can be arranged. The documents support what Alton is saying."

I shook my head, trying to keep my thoughts straight. "You wanted me to marry…" My stomach twisted, bile bubbling at the words I was about to say. "…your son!"

Alton's eyes opened wide as Suzanna's closed.

"That is not common knowledge. I did, but I was wrong. It isn't too late," Alton said.

"Too late? It is. He's going to prison. He killed a woman."

"Dear, he didn't." Suzanna's words faded away as Alton and I continued our stare down.

"Hear my proposal."

Straightening my neck allowed much-needed air to fill my lungs. "Make it quick."

"I'll give your mother the divorce. I won't make a public spectacle out of her mental state. We'll keep it a family matter. You don't need to marry Bryce. However, you will need to marry. Without a marriage you can't inherit. I've generously decided to allow you to maintain your inheritance. Instead of marrying Bryce, once the divorce is final, you'll marry me."

CHAPTER 29

ALEXANDRIA

THE SMALL ROOM exploded in a chorus of retorts.

Suzanna's skin paled until it filled with red, her blood running to parts unknown and then rushing to the surface. She wobbled on her too-high heels until she found her voice. "What the hell? Her? What the hell?"

Her distaste for foul language was forgotten as she spewed and sputtered. She repeated the question, each time louder, though no one answered. She wasn't alone. Nox was on his feet, rage permeating his words and oozing from his stance. He wanted Alton out of the room, demanding that Daryl file an immediate restraining order.

Isaac's eyes were wide as shock registered on Ralph's and Daryl's faces.

It was chaos, yet through it all, Alton stood steadfast, his hands now on the table, his beady gray eyes seeing only me. With each passing moment, his thin lips moved to a smile as he slowly scanned me up and down, seeing as far as the table would allow.

My flesh quivered as if his gaze could literally touch me, could see beneath my clothes.

"As I said, a spitfire."

I reached for Nox as he lunged forward. "Everyone, stop."

The turmoil quieted though it hung thick in the air.

221

"Alexandria, it's your chance to keep what you should never lose and help your mother in the process."

The first laugh was more of a cough. I feared that it might be filled with the bile that his proposal had produced. It wasn't. Instead the ring filled the room. With each breath my laughter grew until it poured from my soul. I was manic as tears of hilarity filled my eyes. "Delusional? You're the one who's delusional."

Alton straightened his shoulders. "I've always said it would be fun to tame you. Bryce couldn't handle you, but I can."

"Out!" Nox yelled. "Get the hell out of here and stay the fuck away from her. If you get within fifty feet, screw that—one hundred yards—you're a dead man."

I reached out to Nox's arm, stilling his words and his threats.

"Ralph can draw up the agreement," Alton said.

"No." I turned to Mr. Owen. "You and Ralph take care of whatever needs to happen. We're done. Obviously it's my mother's husband who is in need of medication or maybe hospitalization. I think both medical and psychiatric evaluations are warranted." I turned back to Alton, doing my best to ignore the glare coming from Suzanna. "You're a desperate man and desperate men do desperate things. Here's my advice: go fuck your whore and visit your son before he's put away for life… or sentenced to death."

The crimson returning to his cheeks was oddly comforting.

"My mother and I are done." I reached for my purse as Nox placed his hand in the small of my back.

When Alton didn't move, Isaac stepped forward. "Sir, step aside."

As Alton turned, I saw my stepfather in a different light. He wasn't the monster I'd allowed him to be. He was a pathetic tyrant, a bully of a man. When faced with Isaac's girth, his wrinkles deepened and he shrunk into his expensive suit.

"Alton?" I heard Suzanna say as we stepped from the room.

I turned to Mr. Owen. "As soon as you can, evict him from the manor."

Nox's hand didn't move from my back as we made our way outside.

THE SCENES BEYOND the windows of the SUV brought back memories, both good and bad. Nearly nineteen years of my life had been spent in this city and more accurately on the grounds of Montague Manor.

I gripped tighter to Nox's hand.

"This won't be the last time you're here," he said as the large iron gate moved open, allowing us to enter.

"I kind of feel like if it is, I'm all right with that."

"It's yours. You heard Daryl. You've read the will. No judge is going to deny you your rightful inheritance."

Sitting taller I leaned close and kissed Nox's cheek. "It's the money, isn't it?"

"What?"

"That's why you put up with me."

Nox's smile grew. "No, princess, it's because I like the way you scream when I—"

Deloris cleared her throat. "TMI. You're not alone."

We weren't, not that that had ever stopped Nox before or his comments or actions. However, it wasn't only Isaac or Clayton this time. Deloris was with us today.

"This won't take long," I said. "Jane said she had our passports ready. My mother didn't trust the mail."

Deloris nodded. "I feel better being here with you."

"Jane promised that neither Bryce or Alton were here."

"Daryl got the restraining order signed," Nox said. "Your stepfather can't be within one hundred yards of you." Nox's grip tensed. "The things he said. Fuck. I don't plan to let him get that close. Then again, I wish he would."

"Lennox," Deloris warned.

"I should have hit him harder. I will next time."

"I'm impressed," I said.

"I'm impressive," Nox replied with a grin.

"No, I'm impressed that Mr. Owen got the restraining order filed. I can't believe a judge actually signed something against the great Alton Fitzgerald."

"Also one stopping Mr. Spencer from going near Chelsea," Deloris added.

Even without Chelsea pressing charges, her cheek gave reason for a restraining order against Bryce. Mr. Owen hadn't requested an order for me with Bryce or one for Chelsea with Alton, but between the two of us, we had them both covered.

Clayton brought the car to a stop and I peered up and out of the window. The pristine walls, spotless windows, and expansive stately porches were exactly as they'd always been, yet knowing that my mother's nightmare as well as my own was about over, gave them a new sheen.

Clayton opened the SUV's door. As I climbed out, Nox followed behind me.

"You don't need to go in."

He lifted his brow. "We discussed the rules. I still haven't reddened that sexy ass. For the record, going in what is still his house without me is the same as one of his cars."

My behind tingled and grin returned at his threat. It wasn't just the warning but the way the talk of his spanking my ass made his blue eyes shimmer. "Yes, Mr. Demetri."

Nox's lips quirked upward as he reached for my hand. Together we ascended the steps to an opening door. "Magic?" he asked in a whisper.

"It's like Hogwarts," I said. "No, seriously, the Montague staff is magic. They can appear and disappear. I'm not sure how they do it."

"Alex!" Jane's welcoming voice echoed in the foyer as we stepped inside.

I wrapped my arms around her and then took a step back. "Jane, this is Lennox Demetri."

Nox offered his hand. "Very nice to meet you, Jane...?" He allowed her name to linger in the air.

"Peterson," I said. "Jane Peterson."

She nodded and scanned Nox up and down. "My my, I see why Alex is smitten with you."

A hint of pink dotted his cheeks. "She speaks very highly of you too."

"That's good to hear." She leaned closer. "I like that smile on your face. It makes you even more beautiful than you always are."

"I like it too."

"Beautiful on the inside too."

"Maybe one day you could tell me some stories about Alex when she was young?" Nox asked.

"She still young, but yes, sir. I have stories."

"Alex said you've been here her whole life?"

"That's true," Jane said. "Mostly because I'm older than dirt. It seems like my brother and I been here since before time."

"Your brother?" Nox asked.

"Yes, my brother, Brantley. He been driving Montagues before I had diapers to change."

I shook my head. "When I was little and learned Jane's last name, I thought they were married."

Jane's laugh warmed the room and filled my soul. I could listen to it forever. "Ain't no man out there who can handle this." She swept her hand down herself.

I laughed. "Keep looking. There are some good ones out there."

"Yes, child, I'd say you might have found you one. Besides, Brantley and me ain't never been that close."

"But you've worked together... forever?" Nox said.

"This place is big. We came here at the same time 'cause our parents worked for Mr. Charles and Miss Olivia."

My tone turned serious as I scanned the otherwise-empty foyer and allowed my gaze to linger on the hallway that led to Alton's office. "Tell me again that he's not here."

"No, ma'am. He's at work. I know from Brantley's phone, Mr. Fitzgerald's not left Montague Corporation all day. When he's here, he's locked in his office or up in his room."

"Thank you for helping us. We'll be heading back to New York soon." I reached for Jane's hand. "What are you going to do?"

She shrugged. "What can I do?"

"Come to New York. Momma would love for you to be with her, and so would I."

"I'd like that. I'd like Miss Adelaide to come home too. This is her house. It's yours."

I took a deep breath as I looked around the foyer, taking in the marble floor, the large staircase, and the ornate lighting. It wasn't as scary as it had been, but it also didn't fill me with the warmth of Rye. I turned back to Jane.

In her gaze was the warmth, the feeling of home. I smiled. "Who knows? Maybe someday."

I reached again for Nox's hand. "While we're here, let me show you my room."

His brows rose in question. "You do know that we have a car full of people waiting."

"Two people. It's hardly a crowd. Besides, when did you worry about Deloris or Clayton?" I tugged his hand toward the stairs. I'd never imagined having Nox at Montague Manor. I'd never wanted to bring my worlds together, but with his hand in mine, the steps seemed less daunting. The doors weren't soldiers ensuring my obedience. The keyholes weren't portals with eyes watching my every move. The corridor was only that—a hallway.

I opened the door to my room.

"Very girly," he said, taking in the frill.

I hurried toward my bed and bounced on the edge. "It is. Flower wallpaper and a canopy bed."

Nox sat beside me. "I like it."

"You do?"

"I like learning more about you." He ran his hand up the smooth wooden post that held the canopy. "And I like what we could do with these posts."

Heat filled more than my cheeks as my insides twisted and legs squeezed together. "Car with people, remember?"

He leaned over me, pushing me back to the mattress. "Just imagine you tied to these posts, your legs spread wide and sexy tits vulnerable."

"Nox?"

He ran his finger along the neckline of my dress down to my breast and circled my covered nipple. His smile grew. "Your nipples are hard just thinking about it. Think what I could do to them if we took off this dress?"

He was right.

"They aren't the only thing that's hard." He reached for the hem of my skirt. "Come on, princess, let's be naughty in your bedroom."

"I…"

"What do you have here that I could use to tie your—"

A knock came on the doorframe, its sound stopping the rest of his question.

"Excuse me."

My cheeks warmed as Nox and I turned to the open door and Jane's smile. "Umm, yes?"

"The gate just called."

I sat up as Nox sprang to his feet.

"It ain't Mr. Fitzgerald."

"Bryce?" I shuddered at his name.

"No, ma'am. It's Mrs. Spencer." When my eyes narrowed, Jane went on. "This is your house. You shouldn't let that woman push you out."

"I know, but I'm done with confrontation for now."

"Then you best be going." She extended her hand with two small folders. "Here's yours and your momma's passports. I sure hope I see her before she goes far away. I ain't never been to New York."

Nox extended his hand. "Miss Jane, we need to rectify that very soon."

She nodded. "I think I'd like that, Mr. Demetri."

Standing, I smoothed the skirt of my dress. "I know Momma would like that too. Thank you, Jane."

"Thank you. I knew you would save her. I prayed you would."

"I wasn't alone." I glanced up at Nox.

"Thank you," she said to both of us. Her big brown eyes glistened with unshed tears.

I wrapped my arms around her. "Come now. With us. There's nothing stopping you."

Jane patted my back. "How do you know? I happen to be a very busy woman. I have business. Remember, I'm the house manager? What do you think would happen to this place if I just ran off? Then when you and Miss Adelaide come back, it would be a mess. I can't let that happen."

"I love you," I said, kissing her cheek just before Nox and I hurried down the stairs and out onto the driveway. As we slipped into the back of the SUV, a black sedan turned into the circular driveway.

Deloris nodded toward the car.

"Suzanna," I offered.

"I was concerned."

"Jane said he wouldn't be here. I trust her."

"Nice woman," Nox said, adding with a grin, "with terrible timing."

Even though winter was approaching, most of the giant oak trees held tight to their leaves. The moss never went away. It was the other trees on the property that stood like skeletons, their flesh gone, leaving only the naked bones. I sighed as the tires bounced upon the cobblestones. A glance out the back window revealed only dried leaves blowing in our wake.

I turned back around and leaned against Nox's shoulder. "Thanks. I liked having you there."

"Do you think your mom will ever want to come back?" Nox asked once we were off the grounds.

I shrugged. "I wouldn't blame her if she did. She's never lived anywhere else."

"Never?" Nox asked.

"I think she and my dad had an apartment before they were married while they both attended Emory. They married right after she graduated and moved here."

"That would have been intimidating."

"You think so?" I asked, surprised that Nox would think anything was intimidating.

He nodded. "And your grandfather. I don't know anything about him, except his will. Princess, that is the document of a narcissistic egomaniac. I'd venture to guess that Bill Gates' last will and testament isn't as detailed."

"And yet, it isn't," Deloris said. "It's wordy and specific while at the same time vague."

As the SUV moved closer to the hotel, I asked. "Do you think there's any merit to my mother's accusations that my grandfather was killed?"

"Like Lennox said the other night, it's the date of the codicil," Deloris said. "Your grandfather added it the day he died. That isn't enough to warrant an investigation."

"It's enough to be suspicious," I agreed.

"We need to hurry," Deloris said, looking at her phone.

"What is it?"

"It's Isaac. Our eyes outside the hotel contacted him: Mr. Spencer just arrived."

CHAPTER 30

OREN

I'D MADE THE drive from Westchester County—Rye to Brooklyn—hundreds if not thousands of times. Through the years I'd seen the changes, the improvements. The roads had become highways. The highways expanded. Theoretically it should have lessened the time needed for the commute. That was in theory.

Through the years the traffic had grown, tripled if not quadrupled. It didn't matter if I took the Throgs Neck or Whitestone Bridge, there were always backups. Always cars. One of the problems were people like me—people who drove alone rather than carpooling. One person. One car. I wasn't like Lennox—I rarely used a driver. I was more of a solo man. Always had been. Tonight, as my headlights reflected off the wet pavement and the sky spit flakes of snow, I was alone.

Adelaide was doing better by the day, growing stronger.

I'd been proud of her the other night as she spoke to Fitzgerald. I'd heard his responses. Each one reinforced my desire for his demise. It wasn't like the idea was in need of support. I'd wanted it for nearly fourteen years, since the Christmas party.

The thing I needed to clarify, the reason I made up an excuse to leave Adelaide with Silvia, knowing they were safe and protected, was that Alton

Fitzgerald's demise was my request. When he no longer took a breath—because I knew it would happen—it would be my debt to pay.

That was why I'd again called Vincent, why I'd requested a second audience with him in a single week. That was why as the temperature outside the car dropped, my skin was warm and prickling with anxiety.

Instead of meeting at Vincent's home, he'd asked me to join him at a little restaurant off the beaten path. It wasn't the same one where we'd met years ago, but the interior was similar: dark wood-paneled walls with a wooden floor, tables covered in red-and-white checkered tablecloths, and each table lit by a single candle flickering in a red jar. If it hadn't truly been authentic Italian, it would look like it was trying too hard to be.

The aroma of delicious Italian spices beckoned as I opened the front door.

Places like this didn't employ young girls to welcome customers. The hostess was closer to my age with eyes that had seen a lot and a quick tongue that would happily send tourists fleeing. The elite clientele served here didn't play well with outsiders.

"Mr. Demetri, it's been awhile."

"Sophia, you're as beautiful as ever."

Her sexy but dangerous veneer cracked and her smile blossomed. "The eyesight, they say it's the first to go."

I leaned forward and kissed her cheek. "I have a meeting."

"Yes, Mr. Costello is waiting."

I looked down at my watch. He'd told me nine o'clock. It wasn't even 8:30.

Sophia must have seen my concern. "He's been here with the family. The others left."

"It's just Vincent and Luca?"

"No, Luca took Bella, Gabriella, and the baby home. Cute little thing. Not so little," she said. "He has the cheeks of his grandfather."

I shook my head. "Poor guy."

"Your words, not mine."

She pulled her black sweater over her breasts. Ever since the first time I'd met her, they hadn't changed, not in thirty years. They were still full and perky and accentuated her small waist. It was amazing the work doctors could do.

"Come with me," Sophia said with a wink.

Her heels clicked on the wooden floor as we passed tables filled with patrons and those completely empty. That was the way places like this worked. There were always tables available for the regulars, even if that meant turning down others at the door. It wasn't a restaurant: it was a home, a dining room always available for family.

Delicious scents wafted through the air as I spotted Vincent and Jimmy. As usual, they were seated with their backs against the far wall.

"Your guest," Sophia said as she gestured toward the table.

"Thank you, Sophia." I turned to Vincent and placed my hand on the back of an empty chair. "Thank you for seeing me, Vincent. I hope I didn't disrupt family time."

Vincent nodded toward the chair, his way of telling me to sit. "No, Carmine was ready to go home. He's not yet learned to appreciate the finer Italian cuisine."

"Jimmy," I nodded, taking the seat. Turning back to Vincent, I unbuttoned my topcoat. "I won't keep you. I wanted to talk to you about my requests."

"My men? Is there a problem?"

"No. They've been excellent. It's my other request."

"Eva. Her father is glad she's back home."

"Yes, she's a remarkable girl."

"A doctor," Jimmy corrected.

"Yes, she is. An excellent one. I can never repay what she did. I'm here about the most recent request."

"Oren, it's time to cut the apron strings."

I took a deep breath. "Your men—"

He lifted a hand. "You know how this works. It takes time."

I did know how it worked. That was what bothered me. "I'm not recanting or asking you to renege."

"No, why would you? You've loved her for many years. It must feel good to have your son make the request you've wanted to make. What happened? Did she ask you to spare him?" He waved his hand. "Women, they can be so

232

emotional, even when it's not warranted."

We stopped talking as a waitress dressed all in black arrived with a tray holding three glasses of amber liquid. "Straight up?" she asked as she distributed the whiskey.

"Thank you," I said. I lifted the glass and swirled the liquid. The strong aroma felt good as it burned my nose. It would be the first alcohol I'd even inhaled since moving Adelaide into my house.

When she walked away, I sat the glass down. "You knew. You knew who was at my home and didn't say anything."

Vincent shrugged. "I was waiting for you."

"Chelsea Moore is real. She was there and she'd been injured. Now she's with Lennox in Savannah."

He shook his head. "It's unusual, the whole situation. I agree." His eyes closed. "Your first." His eyes opened again, his gaze seemingly seeing the past. "You never forget. Someone else's first, it means nothing." He took a drink of his whiskey and grinned. "I almost forgot, but then it came back. The bar. Race fan. It was the surveillance that brought it full circle."

"I didn't… I never intended."

"It happened."

I lifted the tumbler to my mouth and tipped the glass. Like liquid fire, the heat scorched my lips. Without drinking, I placed the glass back on the table. I wouldn't do it. I couldn't.

Taking a deep breath, I confirmed his assessment. "It did come full circle. She did. He was an abusive fuck. You remember the surveillance. It was because her old man finally figured out he'd sold his daughter to the devil. I didn't know until recently what that meant. I hope now it meant he made a last-minute change to his will. That didn't spare her the years of degradation."

"And yet it took Lennox…"

"Alexandria Collins is her daughter, is *his* daughter… the race fan." When Vincent didn't respond, I went on. "None of this is news to you."

"No, Oren, but it's good to hear it from your lips."

"I won't say it got easier. I will say I never made the mistake of getting to know the families again after my first job."

Vincent lifted his hand toward the waitress. "Quite a coincidence, your son, her daughter."

I shrugged. "Guilt combined with hope."

"Hope?"

I nodded. "Not much. I don't deserve it, but a small kernel. I took the man who should have helped her. I stole that from her. She's young and smart."

"Columbia and Stanford," Vincent said.

I wasn't sure why it surprised me. It shouldn't.

"Yes, but Fitzgerald, he had plans for her. They needed to be stopped. If they weren't, she'd have been sentenced to the life her mother endured."

The waitress sat another glass in front of Vincent. After she left he lifted it, like a toast. "Knight in shining armor, you are."

"No. We both know that isn't true."

"Six years."

I tilted my head.

"It's been six years. Eight since Angelina's funeral. You weren't at Jocelyn's."

"You were?"

"Didn't Lennox tell you?"

"No," I admitted. "We weren't talking much at that time."

"Now you are?"

"Yes. I've been honest with him—mostly."

"And he's being honest. He's understanding his family."

I shook my head. "Angelina and I didn't want that. She didn't want that."

We sat in silence as Vincent finished his current glass of whiskey. Though the air was still strong with the aroma of garlic and oregano, my appetite was gone.

"Jimmy," Vincent said, "go get the car. Bella is blowing up my pocket."

I smiled. "I always liked her."

"She and Angelina were tight. They would cackle like hens in a chicken coop."

"Luca has become a good man. He's ready. You made him that way." I leaned forward. "I thank you for Lennox. He's a good man too."

"We miss Angelina," Vincent said.

"I do too."

"You love this woman, the race car fan's wife?"

I huffed. "I do. I'd give her back that man if I could."

"The other husband?"

"He should have been the one in the car. Even old man Montague figured that out. He just never got the chance to make it known."

"But he did," Vincent said as he stood. He moved his head from side to side. "And he didn't. He contacted me. Left a message and asked to be called back. Times were busy. Business, life, and death. Two days passed until I returned his call. When I did, I couldn't reach him. He'd passed away. I didn't pursue it." He shrugged and grunted as he pulled on his overcoat. "Never even gave it much thought until recently. Lennox's request reminded me."

My request, I wanted to repeat, but I didn't. Instead, I asked, "The message?"

"Asking for a favor."

CHAPTER 31

ALEXANDRIA

"THERE'S A RESTRAINING order," I said to everyone in the vehicle as I found my phone and called Chelsea. "Are you all right?"

"Yes, why? Is something wrong?" Her initial tenor slowed as a new panic infiltrated her question.

"Chels, we're on our way. Where's Isaac?"

"Alex, you're scaring me. Isaac was here. He read something on his phone and stepped out of the room for a minute. He said he'd be back."

"Okay. Don't open the door for anyone but us."

"What do you know?" she asked.

The speed of the SUV increased as the bare trees along the road blurred. I shook my head and covered the phone. "We're at least fifteen minutes away."

"I'm calling the police," Deloris said. "This is a direct violation of the restraining order."

I lifted the phone back to my ear. "Isaac called. He's probably not wanting to scare you, but Bryce is at the hotel."

"He's here and Isaac left?"

"No," I said, "Isaac didn't leave. He's checking it out." I took a reassuring breath. "He's taking care of it. That's what he does."

236

"Do you think Bryce knows I'm alone? Do you think he knows you aren't here?"

"I don't know what he knows." I lowered my voice. As Deloris began speaking into her phone, Nox's hands balled into fists and the vein in his neck as well as the one on his forehead pulsated. "Deloris," I said to Chelsea, "is calling the police. Chels, Bryce was released on bail. There's a restraining order. If he comes within one hundred yards of you he's in violation of that order and risks revocation of his bail."

"They'll put him back in jail?"

"Yes, theoretically. It would be grounds to revoke his bail."

"And he won't be able to get back out?"

"I suppose. I don't know for sure."

"He's not that dumb, is he?" Chelsea asked.

We all leaned one way and then the other as Clayton swerved around slower moving vehicles as he continued speeding toward the city.

"Let him."

I turned to Nox. He was now on his phone too.

"Let him," he repeated to his phone. "Keep her safe, but let the asshole hang himself."

"No," I pleaded.

Nox hung up his phone and covered my knee with his hand. "It'll be all right. Isaac won't let anything happen to her. If Isaac keeps Spencer away, when the police arrive they'll just talk to him and he'll still be free. If he's at the room, his ass will be back in jail."

I shook my head. "No. Chelsea isn't a pawn in some damn game. You can't keep using her to get what you want."

"What I *want* is for you to be safe. What I want is for both of you to be able to sleep at night without nightmares. What I want is Edward Spencer to be someone's bitch behind bars for a very long time. I want him to suffer for what he's done to you."

I lifted the phone to my ear again. "Chels..." I tried to sound strong. She didn't answer. "Chelsea!" Still no response. I tried one more time. "Chelsea!"

I turned to Nox and Deloris. "Call Isaac. She isn't responding."

Nox reached for my phone and looked at the screen. "The call's still connected."

"I know. I'm not hanging up."

"Alex," Deloris said, "the police are already on their way."

"Deloris, do you have that other phone? The one Alton gave me?"

"It's back at the hotel. It's turned off. They aren't tracing it, if that's what you are concerned about."

I shook my head. "No. I was hoping you had it. I'd call Alton and tell him that his son is about to violate the restraining order and risk his bail. If anyone could get Bryce to listen, it's him."

"Do you remember turning off the location on that phone Saturday night?"

I tried to remember. "No. I knew it was on. It was part of the reason Alton gave it to me. He didn't even try to hide the fact that it was one of his ways to keep track of me."

She shook her head. "The location was off when I found the phone at Lennox's house. I heard the chatter from Mr. Fitzgerald. They knew exactly where you and Chelsea were. I'd assumed it was through your phone, but I was wrong."

"What does that mean?" Nox asked.

"It means that just like we have eyes on them, they have eyes on you."

"Do you think they knew she was alone?"

Deloris nodded. "I think it's a real possibility."

I lifted the phone again to my ear... nothing... no voices or noise. The small timer on the screen was still clicking the seconds. The call was still connected. "Chelsea!"

A crowd was gathering as the blue lights of multiple police cars flashed near the hotel. As soon as Clayton brought the SUV to a stop, I opened the door and jumped to the sidewalk. Ignoring Nox and Deloris's shouts, my heart thundered as I ran toward the glass front.

There were more police than I'd first realized, some wearing visible vests over their uniforms, and many were conversing in groups.

The driveway in front of the building was roped off, yellow ribbon with the words CRIME SCENE blocked my way. I slowed just enough to duck under the tape when an officer in uniform stopped me. "I'm sorry, miss, no one in or out."

My breathing stammered my speech. "I have to get in. It's my friend in there."

Nox came up behind me, also catching his breath. "Officer, we're the ones who called this in. Let us enter."

"I'm sorry. I have my orders. The hotel is on full lockdown."

I shook my head faster with each of his words. "Lockdown. No. What happened? I can't reach her."

Nox also hadn't been able to reach Isaac since their last call.

The officer reached out and touched my shoulder. "We have a possible hostage situation."

The ground beneath my feet tilted as fear strangled the muscles of my throat, seizing my response. Nox was speaking to the policeman. His words grew fainter and fainter until my knees lost tension. I reached for his arm, but it was too late. The world went black.

"Miss Collins. Miss Collins…" My name repeated as I blinked away the haze.

There was a woman in a uniform with a very bright light. I squinted my eyes as I tried to make sense of where I was. There was equipment around me—medical things, but it was cramped. The bed below me was soft and narrow. There was a large opening, near my feet allowing daylight and noise to enter.

An ambulance.

I was in an ambulance.

"W-what happened?" I asked. And then I remembered. Struggling to sit, I pushed against the blankets. The back doors of the ambulance revealed a surreal scene of lights and uniforms. It was as if the doors were a screen and beyond was a movie. But it wasn't fiction or even dramatization. It was real life.

"Miss Collins, you fell. You hit your head."

I looked around as I sat taller. "My head?" I reached for my own hair and tenderly pushed. The back of my head was sore to the touch but I didn't have a headache. "Where's Nox?" When the woman's gaze narrowed, I explained.

"Where's my boyfriend? He was with me."

"Oh, yes, he's outside talking to the SWAT team."

SWAT?

"I need to get to him."

She encouraged me to lie back on the gurney. "Miss, you shouldn't be up and about. We need to run some tests."

I pushed back, throwing my feet from the gurney. "I'm fine. Let me go." I yelled toward the open door, "Nox!" My volume rose. "Deloris! Nox!"

"Miss..."

The most handsome face with the lightest blue eyes turned the corner, rounding the open doors and bringing every inch of his six-foot-plus body into view. His smile melted my heart and brought hope to my soul.

There had to be good news. That was why he was smiling.

"Is she all right? Do they have him? Please tell me she's safe."

Nox reached for my hand and ignoring the pleas of the paramedic, he helped me down from the tailgate. "How are you?" He ran his hand over my head. "You dropped like a rock before I even knew what happened."

I winced as he came into contact with the sore spot. "That hurts... a little, but tell me about Chelsea."

Reaching for my hand, he kissed my forehead and spoke as he led me toward a group of policemen in SWAT uniforms. "You haven't been out that long. The paramedics want to take you to the hospital for a scan."

"I'm not dizzy... just my head is sore."

"Princess, you're growing a goose egg on the back of your head."

"Fine, I'll get a scan—later. Chelsea?" I asked.

"At first they thought Spencer went to her room. They sent officers up there. The door was open." He paused. "They found her phone sitting on the table."

I stopped walking, unable to do anything but listen.

"I'm not sure how or why," Nox went on, "but she left the room and went down to the coffee shop on the first floor."

"Why?"

"I don't know. Our guys spotted her before the police, but so did Spencer. He's telling everyone that he's armed. Isaac is there too. Spencer is holding everyone in the coffee shop. He's threatened only Chelsea. Well, and Isaac."

"Miss Collins?" an officer wearing a Kevlar vest asked as he approached.

I eyed his uniform, the vest, the hat, the ammunition. "Yes, is this really that serious?"

"Has Mr. Demetri filled you in on what's happening with your friend and fiancé?"

"He's not my fiancé anymore." I looked up to Nox. "He's told me that my friend is safe?"

"Currently. Edward Spencer just made a demand."

"What?"

"We need to take you to the negotiator. Mr. Spencer said he'll let everyone else in the shop go. There are seven other people, including three children. He says he'll let them all walk out, if you'll go in."

"No," Nox said, pulling my hand closer.

My stomach twisted. "Children? There are children in there?"

"Three children, two women, and two men as well as your friend and Edward Spencer."

"I can't believe he'd do this." I turned back to Nox. "What does he have? What kind of weapon?"

"Isaac has been our eyes inside. He's managed a few text messages and even a picture. He's one of those men, one of the two. Spencer has said he has a gun. Isaac has only seen it through Spencer's coat, the outline. Isaac was ready to take him out when he grabbed Chelsea, but Isaac was afraid that if he did, Chelsea would be hurt."

"Oh my God. Why didn't she stay in the room?"

"Miss Collins. We wouldn't ask you to do this, except our profiler believes that the gun is fake. Mr. Spencer's profile doesn't include weapons."

"He's accused of murder. A body was found on his property," Nox said.

"Yes, sir. And I can't release any details about that, but a weapon was not the cause of death."

I let go of Nox's hand, covered my stomach, and whispered, "He beat her to death."

"Miss Collins?" the officer asked.

"Bryce doesn't use weapons; he uses his hands and verbal threats." I pointed to the hotel. "This isn't him. I mean, I think your profiler is right." I turned to Nox. "Isaac said he *grabbed* Chelsea?"

"Yes."

"That's what he does. Brute force is his thing, not a gun."

"I don't care, you're not going in there."

"He won't hurt me like he will Chelsea."

"No," Nox said definitively.

I turned to the officer. "Can I try to talk to him? On a phone?"

He nodded. "We have his number. That's how he made the demand. He called us. We've set up a line of communication. Our negotiator can ask him if he'll speak to you."

"Can you take me to the negotiator?"

A few minutes later, Nox and I were in the back of a large van talking to more of the SWAT team. "Our profiler is usually right," the negotiator said, "but if she's wrong? I don't recommend going in, not until we have more information on Edward Spencer."

I leaned forward with my elbows on the makeshift table, trying to calm the nerves that currently felt like bats or maybe dragons in my stomach. "What do you want to know?"

"We've contacted his mother. She's on her way."

"How about his father?" Just asking... saying it aloud... caused my dragons to take flight.

The officer looked at a tablet in front of him. "Marcel Spencer? He's deceased."

"What?" My eyes grew wide. "He's dead? When?"

"It says here, he died eight years ago."

"No," I said, shaking my head. "Bryce never said he'd died. He would have told me."

"Ma'am, it says right here that Marcel Spencer died after a self-inflicted gunshot wound. Apparently he had a history of mental issues. I can't be more specific."

I looked at Nox. "Mental issues? What if Alton isn't his father?"

"What if he is? They need to tell him what's happening. You said yourself that he's the one person that Spencer might listen to."

We sat back on the small chairs as the negotiator called Alton. Part of me was surprised he wasn't already on his way. If Suzanna was, why wouldn't Alton be?

"He's not far away."

I took a deep breath. "Umm, I can't be near him."

"Excuse me?"

"I filed a restraining order against him yesterday. I think he can help, but we can't be within one hundred yards of each other."

The negotiator shook his head. "Lady, you're not making this easier on us."

"And you're not putting her in danger," Nox said.

"Will you agree to stay in here?" The officer asked, motioning around the van.

"As long as I'm with her," Nox answered for me.

The officer looked at me and again at Nox. "Fine, let's get the call set up."

"I'll do whatever you think is best to keep my friends safe."

CHAPTER 32

———•○•———

NOX

"MR. DEMETRI?" ONE of the policemen asked, sticking his head in the van. "Can you come out here for a moment?"

Though Charli nodded her encouragement, I didn't want to let her out of my sight. "Don't do anything, no call, nothing, until I get back."

"Yes, Nox."

I shook my head as I made my way out the small door.

"Sir, your man on the inside. You said he's armed?"

"Yes, but he hasn't made that known to Spencer. He didn't want to push him."

"That's good. Our team needs to know what they're up against. Right now, your man could be working with Edward Spencer. We have to be prepared."

I clenched my jaw. "He's not working with him. His job is to protect Chelsea Moore. He was doing that until she left her room."

"He left her alone."

"To find out what was happening," I refuted. "He's inside that shop with her and if he needs to, hell yes, he'll show his weapon. Right now Chelsea is his priority."

"Can you get word to him?" the officer asked.

"I can try."

A few minutes later, I was back inside the van holding Charli's hand. "Princess," I whispered, "you don't look well. I want that bump on your head checked out."

"I will, once Chelsea is safe."

"Are you ready, Miss Collins?" the policeman asked.

Charli took a deep breath and nodded. "Is Suzanna here?"

"She is. I'd like to bring her inside so she can hear the call. She might be able to help."

"Okay."

There wasn't much room as the small door opened and Suzanna climbed in. Her eyes immediately went to Charli.

"Why are you here?" she asked. "Haven't you caused enough problems?"

"He has Chelsea."

Suzanna shook her head. "This is ridiculous. She testified for him. He just wanted to talk to her about doing it again. Why does everything have to get blown out of proportion?"

"He beat her!" Charli said.

"He wouldn't do that," Suzanna retorted, her neck growing straighter by the minute. "Officer, will I be able to talk to him?"

"Yes, ma'am. We're about to connect the call."

Charli reached out to Suzanna's hand. "I saw it." Her voice was tense and low. "He did it in front of me. He hurt me too. He needs help."

"You don't know or care what he needs." She looked my direction. "I mean, look at you, men falling all over you. Bryce, him, and even Alton."

Charli's expression paled. The way her lips contorted, she looked as if she'd eaten something sour. I reached for her leg as words collided on my tongue. This was Charli's fight. I was here for her. That didn't mean I didn't want my turn in the ring—in the octagon.

The sound of a phone ringing filled the van.

"This is on speaker," the negotiator explained. "Let me talk first. He'll be able to hear you both."

The women nodded.

"Where is she?" Spencer's voice filled the van.

"Mr. Spencer, Miss Collins is right here." He nodded at Charli.

"Bryce, please let them all go. There are children."

"Witnesses, darling…" Chelsea's scream sounded in the background.

Charli leaned forward on the table. "Oh God, Chelsea. Bryce, please."

"She's fine. Just waiting for you to arrive. Remember how this works?"

"Bryce," Suzanna said. "Honey, I'm here too."

"Mom? Why are you here? Where are you?"

"We're here, dear, right outside the hotel."

"Both of you come in. Mom, you can be a witness too. Remember, Alexandria," Bryce said, "you said you'd say yes in front of witnesses?"

Charli's face fell forward as her body shuddered with tears. "Bryce, please."

"Oh, darling, you know how I like begging." His voice moved away from the phone, it was distant as he spoke to Chelsea, telling her she could beg. He wanted her to. He demanded it.

"Motherfucker," I muttered under my breath.

"Bryce," Charli said. "Let the kids go. I'll beg if you want."

My teeth clenched tighter, listening to her words, her fear.

Fucking impotent was how I felt.

"You come in here," he said, speaking again into the phone. "And they can leave."

"Why are you doing this?" Suzanna asked. "Why? We know you didn't hurt that girl. You will be found not guilty. Honey, why?"

"I can't spend another night in jail. I won't." His volume rose. "Get on the fucking ground, all of you."

Screams rang out, echoing through the van from the speakers.

"Darling," his voice was again soft. "There's a guy in here, a priest, minister… or something. Fuck, he could be a rabbi… I'm not sure. It's not the Presbyterian Church, but he can marry us, just as you promised. Five minutes. Pretend I'm that asshole who you can tell time for. I'm hanging up. Be in here in five minutes or… well, you know how this works." The line went dead.

"What the fuck?" I asked.

"I'm going," Charli said as she stood.

"Like hell you are!" I pulled her back to the seat. "Get your sharpshooters. Isaac got the message. He's working on getting Spencer near a window."

"What?" Suzanna cried. "No, you can't hurt him."

"Lady," I shouted, my finger pointed in her direction, "did you not just hear him? He's psycho!"

"No!" She stood. "He's distraught." She turned on Charli. "And it's your fault. It's all your fault."

We all stilled as the sound of a small explosion sounded in the distance. A car could have backfired, perhaps fireworks popped, or had it been a gunshot? The negotiating officer reached the door first as Suzanna slid back to the chair, dropped her head to the table, and cried.

"Suzanna," Charli said, "I'm so sorry. I never wanted—"

"Suspect apprehended..." The announcement came loud and clear.

Apprehended. Not down. Not shot.

Charli's eyes opened wide. "Chelsea?"

We pushed past Suzanna and climbed from the truck. A multitude of officers were converging upon the front of the hotel. I scanned the windows. They were all intact.

Maybe we hadn't heard a gunshot?

Deloris stood outside the roped-off area; her eyes met mine as she nodded.

"Oh, Nox," Charli exhaled as she dropped my hand and ran forward.

With his arm around her shoulder and Chelsea buried against his side, Isaac was leading her toward us. Charli met them first.

"Chelsea..." Her words weren't forming as they hugged and cried.

"What happened?" I asked.

"I got the shot, the one I'd been waiting for," Isaac said. "When he hung up the phone, he was angry. Before that, it was weird. He was calculating and methodical. No emotion. But after hearing Alex's voice, he lost it, enough to turn his back. He'd made everyone lie down."

"Dead?" I asked.

"Sir," an officer said to Isaac. "Sir, come with us."

Isaac nodded and turned to me. "No, sir. Wounded."

A moment or for twenty years? Deloris's question came back.

Twenty years.

"My private security license is in…" Isaac began to say as he handed his gun to the policeman.

I turned back to Charli. She and Chelsea were surrounded by uniforms. I turned to Deloris. Somehow in the mayhem she'd made her way to this side of the tape.

"Six o'clock," she said.

I pivoted, my gaze meeting Alton Fitzgerald's. He was being held back by the police who were no doubt upholding the restraining order Charli had mentioned.

"Nox," Charli called.

As I made my way through the paramedics, I wrapped one arm around her and the other around Chelsea. "I-I…"

I couldn't come up with the words I wanted to say.

"We're good," Charli said. "They want to take both of us to the hospital."

"I'm going with you."

Charli's lips quirked upward. "I thought you might."

"Isaac?" Chelsea asked. "What will happen to him?"

"He's a licensed private-security provider. You were his assignment. He has the right to defend you."

"I'm sorry," Chelsea said.

"Why?"

"It's my fault." As she spoke, my gaze went back to where Fitzgerald had been. He was gone.

I pulled Charli closer. "Let's get you two into an ambulance."

"I wanted him to break the restraining order," Chelsea explained as we walked. "I wanted him back in jail. I never thought it would go this far." She broke down, her steps stalling as we moved toward the open door of the ambulance. "Those kids were so scared…"

Sirens blared as more ambulances pulled forward. They were loading up everyone from inside the shop.

Charli reached for my chin and turned my face toward hers. "Stop worrying. We're safe."

"He was here."

She nodded. "And so are you."

Damn straight. I wasn't going anywhere else.

CHAPTER 33

—•O•—

CHARLI

"MISS COLLINS, IS THERE anything I can get you?"

"Discharge papers," I said to the nurse.

"It's only overnight. After what you've been through and in your condition, the doctor just wants to be certain that everything is okay and monitor you through the night."

I nodded, more tears filling my eyes. I hadn't been able to stop the waterworks since the emergency room doctor gave me the news. I should have told Nox right away.

I didn't.

Now it was a few hours later. I was tucked into a hospital bed and waiting for Dr. Beck to arrive.

The door to my room opened. The flowers were the first to enter. Well, those and the long jean-covered legs I knew so well.

"Look what I found," Nox said as he placed the ridiculously huge bouquet on the table beside the bed.

"We're flying home tomorrow. Don't you think that's kind of silly?"

"No," he said. "After all the shit that's happened, if I want to shower you in rose petals, it's my prerogative."

"I was a little shocked that you and Deloris both left me."

Nox pulled a chair closer. "She's with Chelsea. I never really left. I just thought you and the doctors needed some privacy, but…" He leaned over and gave me a kiss, lifting the necklace from my chest and rolling the platinum cage between his thumb and fingers. "…I never took my eyes off of you. And the two men guarding your door weren't going anywhere."

The necklace wasn't the audible one. If it had been, he'd know what I wasn't brave enough to say.

I exhaled. "Bryce is back in jail…"

"Medical unit. Psych ward. That's what they're saying on the news. His gunshot was only a flesh wound. Isaac knew what he was doing."

I closed my eyes, imagining what Suzanna was going through. Once she'd learned he'd survived, she was elated, only to learn that he was being detained again. Now it was a psych ward. What would that be like for a mother?

"Isaac said something…" Nox said.

I opened my eyes. "Oh, how is he?"

"He's fine. They didn't keep him long. He's legit. I mean I don't employ criminals to keep those I love protected. He has the license and permits. He was within his legal rights."

My cheeks rose. "I never thought you employed criminals."

"Your stepfather did. He has called me and my father criminals in every conversation."

"His world is crumbling. He's the one who's delusional."

"Did you talk to your mom?" Nox asked.

"Briefly. I'm kind of tired. I told her we'd be back tomorrow."

Nox sat in the nearby chair, his ankle crossed over his knee as he leaned back. Seeing him, his calm and cool demeanor after everything we'd been through, tugged at my heart and twisted it in knots. His words from months ago came back to me. They'd been playing on a loop since the doctor in the emergency room explained why they wouldn't be performing the CT scan.

I tried to pay attention as he said something about Isaac, something about Bryce. I was hearing his deep voice and watching the movement of his sensual lips, but I wasn't listening. Instead I was hearing a conversation from a while ago, from the night he'd told me about Jocelyn.

"I want to know how you feel about children."

"I don't know... I think I'm too young." I shrugged. *"I guess my mom had me when she was about my age, but I want other things first."*

"But eventually?"

"I suppose," I admitted.

"I don't."

In my mind the words from another time took on new meaning. His voice became more determined, more emphatic.

He didn't. No discussion, just no.

"Charli, are you listening?"

I shook away the past. "What? No. Sorry."

"Is it your head?" he asked, jumping to his feet. "I don't understand why they didn't do that scan. We could be on our way. I mean, even Chelsea is out of here."

"Nox?"

He lowered the side rail and sat by my side, his weight dipping the mattress and causing me to roll toward him. It wasn't far, but his warmth was there, beside me, comforting me.

"I-I'm sorry." The words stuck in my throat, bubbling up with the sobs I could no longer suppress.

He exhaled as he smoothed my hair away from my face. "There's no reason to apologize. I'm sorry. I should let you sleep. We can talk about Isaac and Spencer, about all of it, tomorrow or never. I don't care."

"Dr. Beck is coming to see me."

"Okay, who is he and I thought you'd already been seen."

I nodded. "I have. He's my doctor, or was while I lived here."

"That's nice." Nox's eyes widened. "Your mom's doctor too, right?"

"Yes."

"I remember his name from all the stuff my dad put together on your mom."

I tried to explain. "I wanted to see him when I first got here, to Savannah, but I never got the chance. If I had, I would have asked—"

"If you had," Nox said, interrupting the prelude to my explanation, "you could have found out all that stuff about your mom. He ran tests and everything. Oren thinks that's why your stepfather changed doctors."

My stomach twisted as my limbs became weightless. It was like I was floating suspended. It was disconcerting and odd.

"Charli, you are sure you're all right?"

I exhaled as I focused on his stare. Feigning a smile, I said, "I think I need to rest."

Nox pushed a button on the control lying beside my pillow. As the bed moved back, he kissed my forehead. "Let me turn down the lights."

"I love you," I said.

"I hope that's not the bump talking."

The tears came back. "I-it's not. I just…"

"Shhh," he soothed. "I love you too. Get some rest. We're going home tomorrow."

"Limits… hard limits?"

His blue eyes shone in the dimmed room. "Get some sleep. You know mine. We can keep looking for yours."

Tears sealed my eyes, the moisture gluing my lashes to my lids as I closed out the world.

The nurse used the phrase: *barely* pregnant. Can a person really be only a little pregnant? Was I ready? I couldn't answer. I didn't know how to answer.

It wasn't planned. I could say that without a doubt.

I'd wanted to get birth control. I'd planned it, but things got out of hand. With everything that had happened, I couldn't even remember my last period.

As Nox settled again in the nearby chair, I heard the cushion exhale.

My head throbbed more from pent-up anxiety than from my injury. Quietly, I allowed the tears to ease down my cheeks. I didn't want Nox to know I was crying, but it was getting increasingly difficult to hide. If only I'd brought my pills. I should have had them in my purse, but I didn't.

Did it happen at the hotel? Maybe in Rye? That wasn't that long ago.

A little pregnant.

The swish of the door against the floor caused my puffy eyes to open.

Nox stood as I focused on Dr. Beck. When our eyes met I shook my head, praying he wouldn't mention in front of Nox the reason for his visit at this late hour.

Oh, please don't congratulate him.

"...Lennox Demetri, Alex's boyfriend."

"Mr. Demetri," Dr. Beck said, "nice to meet you. I've known Alexandria, well, before anyone." He smiled. "I delivered her."

I struggled to push the button, bringing me up to sitting. "Dr. Beck, it's been awhile."

"And look at you, you're lovely." He turned to Nox. "The first time I saw her she was a little tiny pink thing with bright copper hair."

Nox smiled while I continued to pray that Dr. Beck would stop talking about babies.

"I've grown up," I said.

He tapped a small laptop, one I was sure had my current medical records. "Yes, you have." He looked between Nox and I. "Before we begin, can you tell me about your mother?"

"She's doing well. Much better."

"I tried to get into Magnolia Woods," Dr. Beck explained. "I don't have privileges there, but I hoped..."

I shook my head. "It wasn't you, Doctor. It was Alton. He didn't want you there."

"What's going to happen?"

"It's not common knowledge, but she's going to file for divorce." I wasn't sure why; however, Dr. Beck's reaction surprised me.

"Young lady, that's the best news I've heard."

My eyes opened wide. "Well, I'll pass on your reaction to my mother."

"I have years of records. If they could help with the divorce or anything else..." He turned to Nox. "... if that's being pursued, I'm available."

"That's very kind of you," Nox said. "We can pass that on to her. Doctor, Alex is tired. Can we get this done so she can sleep?"

"Yes, if you'll excuse us for a few minutes, we'll proceed."

"I-I..." Nox stuttered, undoubtedly surprised by the doctor's request.

"Thank you, Nox," I said. "I'll be fine."

"I'll be outside if you need me."

Dr. Beck and I both nodded.

Once the door was closed, the doctor came closer and lifted my hand. "You haven't told him?"

The damn tears came back. How could there be any left? Pressing my lips together, I shook my head.

"You were engaged to Edward Spencer?"

I took a ragged breath. "It's hard to explain. I was, but I wasn't really."

"Is this young man the father or are you upset because you don't know?"

"No! I know. He's the father. Bryce and I never..." I didn't finish the sentence, suddenly embarrassed by the conversation with a man who'd known me since I was born.

Dr. Beck smiled. "...*had sexual intercourse*. It's okay. I've been a doctor for nearly forty years. I've learned how it all works."

Warmth filled my cheeks. "Bryce and I never had sex. I know how it works too, and Nox, Lennox, is the father. He's the only possibility. I haven't told him because this is unexpected and I don't know how he'll feel."

"Another thing I've learned in those forty years is never to assume you know the answer to that question."

"It's just that..." I shook my head as I lifted the sheet to wipe my eyes and nose. "I'm not even sure how I feel."

"Well, let's look at the results." Dr. Beck opened the screen on the laptop. "I miss good old paper charts. You never had to wait for those to boot up." He paused. "First, how are you feeling? Your head I mean."

"Honestly, it hasn't been in my thoughts at all."

"No headache?"

"A slight one, but I think it's more nerves."

He nodded. "Let's see here... according to the blood test done in the emergency room..." He looked up from the screen. "Now, you should know this is only an estimate. An ultrasound would tell us more. Based on the hCG level in your blood, you're approximately six weeks along."

His words squeezed my chest. "No, that can't be right. I've been on the pill. It was just these last three weeks I've been without my pills. I've thought about it. It had to happen a little over a week ago."

"Now," Dr. Beck said. "Do you remember me saying that I know how this works?"

"They said *a little* pregnant in the emergency room."

His lips pressed together as he shook his head. "Ain't no such thing. There is and there is not. You, my dear, are. Did you not wonder why you didn't have a menstrual cycle after you stopped taking the pills?"

"No, I-I hadn't thought about it. There was a lot happening."

"Well, let me explain. You didn't have a cycle because you were already pregnant. Your uterus was holding onto that little fellow. This can happen even with oral contraceptives. The good thing is that you stopped taking the pills. It's usually safe, but it's better to be off of them. Have you noticed any weight change?"

"Loss. I've noticed loss. Nerves."

"Could be. More than likely it's your body feeding the little one inside of you."

I leaned back against the bed and closed my eyes. How did this happen? How had I not realized? Nox had said I was too thin. Even Patrick said I looked like *they* were sucking the life out of me. It wasn't them.

Oh God. Alton was going to force me to marry Bryce and I was already pregnant with Nox's baby.

Nox.

His words came back again, the same chorus, same verse.

"I want to know how you feel about children."

"I don't know... I think I'm too young." I shrugged. *"I guess my mom had me when she was about my age, but I want other things first."*

"But eventually?"

"I suppose," I admitted.

"I don't."

I took a deep breath. "I'm too young."

"You're a baby in my eyes. It never ceases to amaze me when my babies have babies. You're only about a year younger than your mother was. But watching babies have babies has been one of my greatest joys."

"My mom was married."

"Alexandria." He set down the laptop and reached for my hand. "I'm not too old to understand. Tell me what you're thinking."

My heart ached, broke. Hard limit. Nox hadn't found mine, but he knew his own.

"I'm a student... I-I don't..." The tears came back with a vengeance. "He said he didn't..."

CHAPTER 34

───●○●───

NOX

I OPENED THE blue dot app on my phone. There she was, right where she'd been when she asked me to leave.

Asked to leave.

Rationally I got it. I did. I understood that the old man's a doctor—her doctor. It's not like Charli and I were married...

Her heart rate was up.

Mine was too.

After Jo, I never thought I'd want to marry again. Fuck, for years I never even dated, but damn my plans all to hell. I wanted to marry Charli. I wanted to be in the room with her right now. I wanted to wake beside her every morning and fall asleep there every night.

The ten days she was with that asshole... that crazy motherfucker... I was beside myself. She's mine and has been since the day I saw her at the pool with that floppy hat and sexy smile. I loved her so much it hurt. I didn't deny it.

I'd told her thousands of times.

Maybe our relationship moved fast, too fast, but that didn't make it wrong. When something was right, it was right.

Theoretically I understood that now wasn't the time to propose. Hell, she'd taken some huge-ass diamond ring off her finger a week ago and thrown it at Fitzgerald. There had to have been a proposal that accompanied it in the first place.

And then there was the other day at the law office.

Fuck!

The mere thought of Fitzgerald and his proposal made me rabid as in foaming at the mouth and ready to kill. The fucking audacity to propose marriage. Like in a million years she'd have said yes?

Then there was the damn will. The marriage stipulation. If I proposed, there'd always be the question of whether I'd done it for the money, for her inheritance. I didn't need her damn money. I didn't want it.

That house… castle. Others would speculate. We'd know the truth, but that wouldn't quiet the rumors. I'd lived with rumors after Jo's death. I didn't want to do that to Charli.

Besides, she had school. We needed to get home. Spencer was locked away and there was the restraining order against Fitzgerald. I imagined Charli in that hospital bed. She'd tried to hide it, and I suck at emotions, so I let her think she had, but she'd been crying. Ever since the night I took her back to New York, she'd been emotional and crying out in her sleep.

I wanted Spencer to suffer, to have a taste of what she'd gone through. Even of what Chelsea had suffered.

It wasn't just emotional. It had taken a physical toll.

Charli needed rest and Lana's cooking. She needed security and routine. She needed to get back to her schoolwork and ridiculously large law books. The last thing she needed was another marriage proposal.

I glanced toward the door to her room. The two men outside her door weren't trying to be inconspicuous. Their black suits screamed bodyguards.

Did I have time to go get coffee? I didn't want to not be here when that door opened.

My mind was all over the place.

Closing my eyes, I recalled Del Mar.

And then it hit me. That was my new plan.

We'd go back. Just the two of us. No business or friends. This time if a resort whore made a move on her, I'd be the one who not only stepped in, but who had the right to do it. Wait, no. No public pool. We'll book the presidential suite again with our own private pool and balcony.

I pictured the whole thing. An evening on the balcony, the sky aglow with an orange sunset, French wine, and a real proposal. Down on one knee. Maybe her mom could give me advice on a ring.

It brought a smile to my face.

I had a plan.

Christmas was a month away. No. She'd want to spend that with her mom. Next summer, after the dust settled.

I closed the app and walked to the nurse's desk. "Excuse me, do you know how long Dr. Beck will be with my... girlfriend?"

The nurse looked up from the computer screen. "Girlfriend... as in a girl who's a friend? You're cute." Her eyebrows jumped. "Handsome, too. Too bad she's engaged. It was all over the news." Before I could respond, she went on. "No. I don't know. He's not usually here this late at night."

"She's an old patient of his."

"He's a great doctor. I mean, most of the younger ones would never come in like that. But I guess this is pretty special, a Montague and all." She lowered her voice. "You hear all kinds of rumors, but she seems pretty normal."

I smiled. "I think she's more special than normal."

"No, I meant that as a compliment. With all the stuff that's been on the news. It's just too bad that she was with that guy." She shook her head. "Crazy. I'm not supposed to say that, but like I said, it's been on every news channel.

"You're pretty special to be helping her out—with him in jail and all. I wouldn't blame her if she decided to get rid of it. He's nuts and that can be hereditary."

A punch to the gut. The kind that knocked you to your knees and made the world go black. Not enough to enjoy the reprieve, but the kind that sent shock and pain to every nerve throughout your body until you screamed just to know that you still could.

That was what this woman had just done to me. I stumbled backward.

"What are you talking about?"

She lifted her hand. "Sorry, man. I figured she'd said something to you.

You two seemed close. Don't tell her I told you. I could really get in trouble."

"She's... his?" I couldn't form a complete sentence.

"Really," she said. "You know nothing. I know nothing. Just a baby. I don't think there's been a paternity test. I was only assuming." She shook her head. "Nothing." Her lips came together. "Remember... .I'm the Jon Snow of information. You heard nothing from me."

I pushed away from the counter, Charli's hospital door the only thing on my radar.

The guards moved aside as I shoved it open. "Charli?"

The doctor was sitting beside her, holding her hand. The tears were back as she looked up at me. Fuck, the nurse was right.

"You said you didn't..." My accusation came out louder than I intended.

"I didn't what?"

"I believed you."

"Young man..." Dr. Beck stood.

"Nox, what are you talking about?"

"You said he didn't touch you... like that. I'll kill him. I'll kill him!"

Charli's head moved back and forth. "He didn't. We didn't."

If I'd been wearing her necklace the heart rate would have been off the chart. They'd be sending a crash cart to her room. Code blue. Was that what they called it?

It had to be a heart attack. That's what happened when the pain was so intense that speech was out of reach. "You didn't...? I took a step forward as the realization struck. "Me?"

She nodded, her lips turning upward into a sad smile. "I'm sorry. I tried to tell you."

"When? How?"

Dr. Beck laughed. "Would you like me to explain the *how*?"

"That's why they didn't do the scan," I said, the pieces of the puzzle sliding into place.

I fell to the side of her bed and clutched her hand. "You didn't know?"

"No, not until a few hours ago." Her chin fell forward. "They say six weeks. I know your hard limits..." She gasped for breath and looked back up. Her golden eyes were clouded with emotions, too many to decipher. "...but I can't. I just can't."

I couldn't understand. Her sentences weren't making sense. "Can't…
what?" And then I heard her words. Six weeks. "Six weeks?"

Charli nodded.

I turned to the doctor. "Is she all right? Do tests. Do whatever you need
to do. Is the baby where it should be?" I jumped from the side of the bed and
began to pace small circles. "She needs to stay here. No, wait. We need to get
her to New York." I ran my hand through my hair. "I know, my cousin is a
doctor. I'll call her."

Dr. Beck put his hand on my arm. "Son, calm down. Alexandria is a
healthy, strong woman. That kid of yours is zapping her energy and will
continue to wreak havoc on her emotions. You're in for a fun eight months,
but physically she's fine."

"You know this because you've done tests, right?"

"No, I know this because she's a healthy young woman."

I shook my head. "No. No. That's not enough. I want one of those things
where we can see it—an ultrasound—and I want it tonight. I want to know
where it is."

"Nox."

Charli called, but I kept talking to the doctor. "Order it. Now."

"Nox."

"Son, where it is… is where it should be."

"We don't know. Not until we see it."

"Lennox!"

"What?" I asked, turning toward Charli.

"Will you please come here?"

Would I come to her? Hell, I'd walk over hot coals. I'd swim through
alligators. I'd do any damn thing I needed to do. What I wouldn't do was put
her at risk.

I took a deep breath and went back to her. The gold of her eyes was
clearer, brighter. I cupped her cheeks. "You're not fighting me on this. I need
to know. I can't *not* know that you're all right."

Charli nodded within my grasp. "Dr. Beck," she said. "Please. I know it's
late and unusual, but can we please have an ultrasound?"

"I can order one for tomorrow."

Nox sat taller. "Tonight."

An hour later, with Charli in a wheelchair as a man in scrubs pushed her toward large doors with a sign that read DIAGNOSTIC IMAGING. Our private parade headed inside: the orderly, Charli, the two guards, and me.

"This could have waited until tomorrow," Charli said for what I think may have been the tenth time.

"No, it couldn't."

After the orderly left and our guards moved outside the door, I helped Charli from the wheelchair onto a long table. "You're not telling me to leave this time."

She kicked her sock-covered feet back and forth as she reached for my hand. "I don't want you out."

"Yet you told Dr. Beck you'd do this alone?"

She moved one shoulder up and down, the neck of her hospital gown falling to the side and exposing her soft skin. "I didn't tell him I *wanted* to. I told him I *would*. I didn't think you wanted this and I couldn't not..."

"Princess, I won't stand by and let anyone... not your stepfather, that asshole Spencer, or even that one..." I nodded toward her stomach. "...hurt you. I can't wrap my mind around this. I really can't, but first, let me have the peace of mind to know you're okay."

She nodded.

As we waited for the technician, we talked. We even mentioned Jo. It was hard not to, and yet it didn't feel wrong. It was almost as if she were beside me, encouraging me to do what I hadn't done before. I recalled what Oren and Silvia had said, saying that my mom had been happy for my dad... that she knew about Adelaide.

Rationally I knew it wasn't the same.

My mom had been alive. Jo was dead.

Nevertheless, I understood what that support must have meant to Oren. I wanted it from Jo. I prayed she was with us, beside me. I longed to let her know that I'd never forget her. I wanted to believe we had the kind of love that transcended loss. I wanted to think that she was happy for me—for us. I wanted her to know that I could do better. I could be the man I wasn't for her. I could be that man for Charli, because in loving and losing her, I'd grown.

I prayed she knew that I was sorry I'd failed her, but with failure came wisdom.

I would have given my own life to save hers. Now I felt the same way about Charli.

Charli pulled my hand as she sat on the edge of the table. Quietly, she wiped my cheek.

I didn't realize I'd been crying.

"It's all right," Charli said, "to think about her and the baby you lost."

I shook my head. "No, I am, but not like you may think."

"I think you lost two important people and now you're faced with the possibility of history repeating itself. It won't. I told you before that I would keep the promise she couldn't. I never intended for this to happen. That doesn't mean I won't work to keep my promise."

My cheeks rose. "About that. I guess the red-ass thing is off-limits for about eight months."

Charli giggled. "I think if everything is the way it's supposed to be, nothing is off-limits. That's what Dr. Beck said."

The door opened and Dr. Beck came in. "It's good to see you both smiling. Are we ready to see this little Montague?"

"Demetri," I corrected.

"Collins, actually," Charli said as she lay back on the paper-covered table. "I'm surprised to see you, Dr. Beck. I expected a technician."

"I told you that my babies having babies is one of my greatest joys. Would you really want me to pass this on to someone else?"

"No, thank you for everything."

The old man smiled and patted her hand. "Let's get this started. This is a little cold and may be uncomfortable. Due to the early stage of your pregnancy we'll need to do this vaginally."

Charli reached for my hand. "Whatever we need to do, we're ready."

CHAPTER 35

———•O•———

ALEXANDRIA

NOX SQUEEZED MY hand as we rode toward the airport. The corner of his lips quirked upward and his light blue eyes shone. Beside me was the man I loved more than I ever thought possible. I'd trusted him with my hard limits and last night, in a small diagnostic-imaging room, he'd trusted me with his.

Maybe it wasn't that together we hadn't discovered my hard limits; maybe instead, it was that as long as he was the one with me, they didn't exist. Or like last night, they faded away. Together we could push the boundaries that when separate were too much for either of us to handle.

In our possession we each had small black-and-white photos of Nox's hard limit. Not really more than a peanut within a black womb—exactly where he or she belonged—the little life inside of me was more precious than any diamond or gem. He or she wasn't an heir to a fortune; the future was yet to be written on what would become of Montague Corporation. There was no doubt that a long legal battle lay ahead for Momma and Alton.

None of that mattered.

This little life was the promise of a future free from ghosts and shadows. This child would never be dressed to perform in a dog-and-pony show, never lie in bed and pray that the yelling down the hall wouldn't come to his or her room, and never have reason to doubt that he or she was conceived in love and loved unconditionally.

The measurements that Dr. Beck performed confirmed the gestational age. I was six weeks pregnant. Our little daughter or son would join us around the middle of July, a mere thirteen months after the trip Chelsea and I took to Del Mar.

I understood Nox's obsession with safety. It was now mine too.

Yesterday I'd been willing to walk into a coffee shop, to put myself in harm's way in order to save my friend.

Smiling at her across the car from me, I would do what I could for her. Putting the little peanut inside of me at risk, though, wasn't an option.

Chelsea tilted her head. "Are you sure you're okay? What did they see in the CT scan?"

Nox and I had agreed that Oren and Mother should be the first to learn our news.

"They said I'm fine. I bumped my head."

She pursed her lips. "You just seem funny. Not ha-ha funny. Weird."

"I'm just happy. We're finally getting out of here."

Chelsea sighed as she looked out the window. "I spoke to my mom last night. I should move back to California. Kelsey and I could get an apartment. I have some work experience on my resume."

"Montague?"

"Yeah. I didn't do much, but I can say I was employed."

"Tell me who your supervisor was. I can try to help."

Chelsea shook her head. "No. I was thinking about going back to school to get my master's degree. Abnormal psychology has suddenly become more fascinating."

"Can't you do that in New York?" I asked.

"There is an apartment on the Upper West side waiting for an occupant," Nox said.

"I thought I might move there," I said with a sideways glance.

"Think again, princess."

Chelsea shook her head at us. "I appreciate all you have done, but I need to stand on my own."

"That's not a bad idea," Deloris chimed in. "You can do whatever you want. The payout from Infidelity should be in your account soon. It would be a nice nest egg if you decide to go back to school. You'll be able to afford that apartment or any other."

"Why don't you check out schools in both New York and California," I suggested. "Then decide what's best for you."

Chelsea leaned her head back against the seat.

"We should be back in Rye by early afternoon," Deloris said. "If it's all the same to you, I think I'll separate from this fun group in the city."

Nox nodded. "Remember when we had weekly meetings?"

"Those were the days."

Clayton turned the car into the same private airport where we'd been nearly a week before.

"Sir?" Isaac said, causing us all to look up.

"No! This isn't happening again," I cried, taking in the sight of numerous police cars.

"Seriously, do Savannah police not have anything better to do?" Clayton said.

Nox looked to Deloris who shrugged. "No idea," she said.

When the limousine came to a stop, Nox didn't wait for either Clayton or Isaac to open the door.

"What is happening?" he called as he jumped out of the car. "We're leaving."

I climbed out behind him.

"Mr. Demetri, Miss Collins," Officer Emerson said.

"Please tell me this is a going-away party," I said.

"No, ma'am. We'd like to take you back to the city."

"No." My head moved back and forth. "I don't care what my stepfather has decided to do. Talk to Daryl Owen of Preston, Madden, and Owen. He represents me. He can deal with Alton Fitzgerald's next power play."

"Ma'am, Mr. Owen is aware we're here."

I opened my purse and pulled out my phone. Though I hadn't heard the notification, I had one text message.

Daryl Owen: **"YOU'RE NOT A SUSPECT. DON'T SAY MORE.
I'LL MEET YOU AT THE STATION."**

I looked up, my brows knit together. "Suspect? What is he talking about?"

"It doesn't matter. We're leaving," Nox said, placing his hand in the small of my back as the stairs to the private plane moved slowly to the ground.

"Mr. Demetri, we must insist."

"No, you must not."

"Stop," I said. "Tell me what Alton has done. What bogus thing has he concocted?"

"Ma'am, your stepfather was found dead in his bedroom this morning."

I fought to breathe. Had my childhood wish finally come true? "What?" I looked up to Nox in amazement and shock. How could we be happy about life with so much death?

"We have a few questions for both of you. There are eyewitnesses who say that you, Mr. Demetri, threatened Mr. Fitzgerald."

"Who?" Nox asked.

"Come down to the station. We'll get your statements and then, hopefully, you can leave."

Nox reached for my hand.

"This can't be happening," I said.

Nox turned to Officer Emerson. "Fine, we'll follow you."

"No, sir. I'm sorry, but we'd like each of you to ride in a separate police car."

"Why?"

Officer Emerson tilted his head. "We need your separate statements."

Separate.

No. We were much stronger together.

"Charli?"

"I just want to go home. If this will get us home, fine."

Deloris came closer.

"We're headed back to Savannah," Nox explained

"Did something...?"

I slowly nodded. "Yes, Alton died last night."

Deloris's hand covered her lips. "How?"

"We aren't releasing any details at this time," Officer Emerson said.

The room was the same. The same concrete block walls. The same two-way window. It was the same room where Chelsea and I had made our statements about Bryce, when we'd come voluntarily. Technically I was again in the room voluntarily. It was just that this time it felt different.

The door opened and Daryl Owen entered. His dark brown eyes were filled with concern. "Alex?"

Leaning against the far wall, I closed my eyes and wrapped my arms around my midsection. "I can't believe it."

"They're going to ask you about Lennox. Everyone in that room at Hamilton and Porter heard him threaten Mr. Fitzgerald's life. Can the two of you account for where you were last night?"

"Yes. We were at the hospital. They didn't release me until this morning. Nox stayed with me."

"There are doctors and nurses who can testify to his presence?"

"And the bodyguards he had posted outside my room. And…" I reached into my purse. After a prolonged look at the small gray peanut, I handed Daryl the grainy picture. "See in the corner. It's dated today and time-stamped at 12:42. Nox and I were at the hospital all night."

Daryl held the small paper. "You're pregnant?"

"I am. We weren't planning on telling anyone, not yet."

"Is it…? I don't have a polite way to ask this…"

I straightened my neck. "I never slept with Bryce. The baby is Nox's. I didn't know, but I've been pregnant since before I came back to Savannah."

"The implications… the will… the divorce wasn't filed, but now Mr. Fitzgerald is dead."

"My baby is not a chess piece to be strategically placed in a plan to win Montague. Besides, if Alton's dead, whom would his assets go to but his wife?"

"His son."

CHAPTER 36

———●○●———

ALEXANDRIA

"HIS *SON* IS in jail. His son is going to rot behind bars after what he did yesterday, not to mention the dead woman on his property. And furthermore, never in all of my life had Alton claimed paternity. You're telling me he's done it now?"

"It was a new will, just signed and witnessed two days ago."

I couldn't think straight. I was sure the topic had come up in some class, but my brain was fried. "That's assuming his will sticks, which you're going to make sure it doesn't, since my grandfather's will already covered what would happen in the case of Alton's or my mother's death. Anyway, assuming his will gets heard, how does that even work if Bryce is convicted? Felons can't run corporations or manage investments."

"Not easily but they don't lose their property or ownership rights. They do lose their civil rights, like voting. But that wouldn't matter. Mr. Fitzgerald made a provision for that."

I sat at the small metal table and exhaled. "Of course he did. What?"

"Edward Bryce Carmichael Spencer's inheritance, if he were unable for any reason to claim it, would go into a trust."

"The named executer of the said trust?" I asked, full well knowing the answer.

"Mr. Spencer's mother."

I shook my head. "You're not talking Montague Corporation or the manor, because those have never been owned by Alton. They've remained in my mother's name."

"The manor is safe," Daryl said.

That was good, because there was no way I'd let that bitch live in my mother's home. "The corporation?"

"It's complicated. The actual corporation is safe, unless the court mandates the changing of the internal structure from a private to a publicly traded commodity. It's the profits over the last twenty years that could be ruled as his—at least fifty percent. This is all open to interpretation. My firm hasn't seen the profit and loss reports for the last twenty years. It will take months, if not years, to get it all ironed out."

I lowered my forehead to my folded arms and laid it upon the table. With a deep breath, I closed my eyes and thought of New York. I imagined our apartment and the aroma of Lana's lasagna. I pictured the view of the city from the balcony, the ribbons of cars and lights twinkling stories below. The door opened with a click and a swish, bringing me back to the stark reality of Savannah.

"Miss Collins," Officer Emerson said. "Same Bat time, same Bat station."

"We need to stop meeting like this."

He sighed, taking the chair across from me as Daryl sat beside me. "Miss Collins, what can you tell me about your stepfather?"

"That's a rather vague question," Daryl replied. "Perhaps you could be more specific in what you're wanting to know?"

"All right, Miss Collins, let's start with your lack of grief upon learning of his death."

I shook my head. "Shock. I'm in utter shock."

"Does that mean you weren't expecting it?"

"How, Officer Emerson, could I possibly have expected Alton's death? I saw him two days ago. He was the same delusional, bellowing maniac he's been my entire life."

Officer Emerson looked up from his legal pad. "Two days ago, when your boyfriend threatened his life."

"Two days ago, before I filed a restraining order against Alton Fitzgerald. It was after that when I took legal recourse against a man who has bullied and manipulated me my entire life. My boyfriend was with me as I filed. Why would he do anything that would jeopardize our going home when we'd put our faith in Savannah's law enforcement and judicial system?"

"Do you know of anyone else who would have wanted to harm your stepfather?"

"There is probably a list a mile long of people who would *want* to. That said, I can't think of one person brave enough to confront him."

"What about Mrs. Spencer?"

I sat back and worked to keep the sneer from my expression. "Mrs. Spencer? What about her? She's going through a lot with her son."

Officer Emerson nodded. "It's a stressful time. Tell me, exactly, if after *bullying* and *manipulation*—your words—your entire life, what made you file a restraining order now?" He leaned forward. "What was the straw, Miss Collins, the one that finally broke the camel's back?"

The bats were back, flapping their wings and stirring the breakfast I'd eaten. "He scared me. He looked at me."

"He looked at you? He's been your stepfather for over twenty years and he'd never looked at you before?"

"Not like that."

"Like what?" the officer asked.

I pushed back the chair and paced, hoping to calm the queasiness. "He proposed. It wasn't even a proposal. It was a mandate. He said that after he divorced my mother I would marry him." My breathing came faster. "He called me a spitfire and said…" I closed my eyes, willing the bile to stay put. "…he'd always wanted to tame me." I collapsed into the chair.

"I was there," Daryl said, reaching reassuringly for my hand. "So were Ralph Porter and Mrs. Spencer."

"And so was your boyfriend, Lennox Demetri?" Emerson asked.

"Yes."

"And Mr. Demetri was upset?"

"Yes, he was upset. So was I. So was Suzanna. She even cursed… multiple times."

"Why do you think she was so upset?"

"Oh," I said, "I don't know. Maybe because the bitch has been his whore for thirty years and she finally thought she'd get the keys to the castle. She was prancing around like queen regent before the engagement party. And when she finally learns that he's willing to divorce my mom, instead of giving her what she's wanted for all these years, he shoved her aside and proposed to me." I let out a long breath.

Shit!

Both men stared at me with wide eyes. Slowly my tirade registered. I'd spewed the answer—the disgust at not only Suzanna's behavior but also the hurt that she'd played my mother. It came out of me. Now I heard my words.

"Oh my God," I said. "I saw her yesterday. They weren't together. She looked at me with daggers in her eyes. She said something about men... Bryce, Lennox, and even Alton."

"Miss Collins, where were you yesterday and last night?"

"Yesterday I was at the hotel and then they took me to the hospital. I wasn't discharged until this morning."

"Before the hotel?"

"I woke at the hotel." The day replayed in my head. "Oh, we went to Montague Manor to get my mother's and my passports."

"So you were at the manor yesterday. What about Mr. Demetri?"

"Yes, he was with me."

"Did you have access to any food or drink, specifically your stepfather's Cognac?"

My head moved from side to side. "We went in, spoke to Jane, I showed Lennox my old bedroom, and we left." And then I remembered. "Suzanna arrived as we left."

"Are you sure?"

"Yes, Jane told us she'd passed the front gate. That was why we left."

"Do the guards at the front gate keep a log of all cars?"

I shrugged. "I don't know. Probably. Alton's kind of a control freak like that."

"He was," Officer Emerson corrected.

"Yes, he *was*."

Once we were done, I waited with Isaac and Deloris in a row of chairs as Daryl Owen and Officer Emerson went into another interrogation room. From along the wall where we sat, we could watch the large room filled with multiple desks. Like worker bees, the people buzzed around, in and out. No doubt the discovery of Melissa Summers, Bryce's episode at the hotel, and now Alton's death weren't their only working cases. Nevertheless, they were big cases.

"Miss Alex."

I stood at the sight of Jane coming into the police station, her eyes filled with tears.

"Jane?"

"Miss Alex, he's gone."

I nodded. "Did you… find him?"

She shook her head. "No, Brantley did. Mr. Fitzgerald wasn't ready to leave for work. He's always ready at the same time. Brantley could've asked someone to go check, but he went up to their room, the one your momma shared with him. He knocked, but Mr. Fitzgerald didn't answer. He said he knocked again."

She wiped her eyes. "Brantley took care of Mr. Fitzgerald, like I tried to take care of your momma."

Tears filled my eyes, not at the loss of Alton, but from the emotion in Jane's voice.

"Miss Peterson," an officer said. "We need you to make your statement now."

She shook her head. "Miss Alex, this is what I was saying. I can't say nothing."

"You can, Jane. Be honest."

"But Miss Suzy, she—"

"Miss Peterson, this way," the officer repeated.

I reached out to Jane's arm. "She what?"

"The other night, the two of them got into a fight something fierce."

"Miss—"

"Officer," I said. "I'm Alexandria Collins. Miss Peterson works for my family."

"Yes, ma'am. We know that."

"She won't be answering any of your questions until Mr. Owen is done with Mr. Demetri. At that time, he'll need to speak to her and sit in with her during your questions."

The officer sighed. "Miss Collins, a statement is all we're asking. A few minutes. We have a lot of your house staff to question. There's no reason to make it more complicated."

"Sir, if you have others to question, feel free to take their statements. Miss Peterson is waiting for Mr. Owen."

"Fine," he said, waving to the chairs. "Have a seat, Miss Peterson. You just lost your place in line."

I took Jane's hand and pulled her toward the chairs. "Are you all right?"

"I am," she said as she sat beside me. "But Brantley, he's heartbroken."

I found it hard to believe anyone would be heartbroken over Alton, and then we all turned to the loud wailing. The crowd parted as Ralph Porter entered with his arm around Suzanna.

"And there she is, the newly crowned heir apparent." I leaned toward Jane and whispered, "Fighting something fierce?"

"Yes, child. I ain't never hear anyone give it as good as he, but Miss Suzy, she was riled up."

"Honest, Jane, be honest. The police and court can make you break your nondisclosure. If you don't, they can find you in contempt."

"No, I don't want to be in contempt of anything."

"Then tell the truth."

"What if they ask about other things?"

"What other things?" I asked.

"Like your momma. What if they ask?"

"Don't volunteer, but answer whatever they ask. My momma is in New York. She had motive but not access."

"Lots of peoples have motive, Miss Alex." Her eyes went to Ralph and Suzanna. "Lots of people."

CHAPTER 37

NOX

MY HANDS SPLAYED upon the metal table. The cool surface helped me focus as Officer Emerson asked me about my threat and my feelings in general regarding Fitzgerald. Apparently, besides my verbal threat at Hamilton and Porter, there were witnesses who commented about the looks I'd given him yesterday, following the standoff at the hotel. I couldn't recall any specific facial expressions. My concern had been keeping Charli safe.

"Did you believe he would cause her harm?"

"Enough that I supported her filing of the restraining order."

"How far were you willing to go to keep him away from Miss Collins?"

There was no limit, but I didn't say that. "She filed a restraining order, and my plan was to take her home to New York."

"Yet you threatened to kill him, in front of multiple witnesses."

"I did," I agreed. "I threatened. I didn't do it." *Not personally.* My jaw clenched, knowing without a doubt that I was responsible. I was the one who'd given his name to Vincent. I was the one who'd signed his death warrant. I'd done that before his grotesque proposal. After that, I was willing to do it myself, but I didn't. I'd found peace in knowing he'd already been condemned.

I wasn't sorry that he was dead. I wouldn't say that I was pleased, but I would say satisfied.

The questions continued with specifics about my whereabouts last night. Had I been with Charli at all times in the hospital? I hadn't. I'd given her privacy to talk to her doctors. I'd bought flowers and gotten coffee. I'd paced the halls and talked to Deloris and Isaac. I'd called Oren and told him what happened with Spencer. I thought it was best he knew about the standoff and about Charli in the hospital so that he could break the news to Adelaide.

"My phone," I volunteered.

"What about your phone?"

"I wasn't with her every minute, but I did stay at the hospital. I made calls and received them. With the locator on my phone, the records will prove where I was."

"And doctors, nurses, and cameras, can they all verify that you were there all night?"

"Yes."

"What about your visit to Montague Manor?"

I tried to recall. It was only yesterday, but it seemed so much longer ago. "We weren't there long. It was before the incident at the hotel. We went in and talked to the house manager, Jane Peterson. Then we went to Char—I mean, Alex's room. And we left. I doubt we were there for more than fifteen minutes."

"Did you have a drink? Did you sample Mr. Fitzgerald's fine liquor?"

I straightened my neck. "It was early afternoon. I'm not opposed to daytime drinking, but no. It wasn't offered and even if it had been, we were planning to fly home."

"But you didn't fly home?"

No asshole. If we had, I wouldn't be here right now.

"You know why. Most of Savannah's finest were with us at the hotel."

"Thank you, Mr. Demetri. At this time we don't have reason to keep you in Savannah." Officer Emerson turned to Daryl. "Mr. Owen, you have Mr. Demetri's contact information?"

"I do."

"Mr. Demetri, will you be willing to return to Savannah if we have further questions?"

"If they can't be handled over the phone, I will. I do have a business to run."

"Thank you for delaying your departure. We'll be in touch."

I thanked Mr. Owen for coming to our aid again as we made our way into the large desk area of the station. Turning the corner, the vision across the room caused me to stop, mesmerized by the sight. Between Isaac and Jane sat the most beautiful redhead I'd ever seen. Her face was close to Jane's as they talked. With Charli's hair pulled back in a low ponytail her porcelain profile stood out, a stark contrast to the rich mahogany of Jane's. In that moment I understood what people meant when they talked about pregnant women glowing.

Could everyone else see it?

How could they not?

Like a beacon of brilliance in the crowded police station, my Charli glimmered. She didn't need designer gowns, jewels, or an exclusive luxurious surrounding. Simply being herself in slacks and a sweater, she was luminous.

It was then she turned and our eyes met. Instantaneously her lips curled upward and her cheeks rose. Her smile lit her entire expression and her golden eyes shone with the light of a million stars.

"Can we go?" she asked.

"Yes, princess, let's go home."

Jane sat straighter, narrowing her gaze my direction as she tilted her head. "Mr. Demetri, what did you just call her?"

"Princess, but in all honesty…" I reached for Charli's hand. "…she's my queen."

Jane shook her head. "Child, you hold on to that man."

"I don't plan on letting him go." Charli turned to Mr. Owen. "I know we've monopolized your time, but Jane has worked for Montague for the length of my entire life. She's more than an employee—she's part of my family. When Montague employees are hired, they are required to sign a nondisclosure agreement. The police have questions and she's unsure of what she can and can't say. I've told her that you will sit with her and help her during her statement."

"Miss Peterson," Mr. Owen said offering her his hand. "I'm Daryl Owen.

I'd be happy to assist. It's nice to meet you."

The two shook.

"Thank you," I said. "This time, we're really leaving."

"Go and congratulations."

Charli's cheeks filled with pink. I hadn't mentioned our baby during my statement, only the hospital, but it was obvious she had.

Though Jane's eyes questioned, Charli simply accepted his congratulations and kissed Jane on the cheek. "I hope you know that you're always welcome in New York. Call me."

"Child, you call me, and give your momma a big hug."

"I will. I promise."

A car ride later, along with Deloris, Isaac, Chelsea, and Clayton, and with my hand in the small of Charli's back, we ascended the stairs of the private plane. At the top of the steps, I stopped and scanned the tarmac. The Georgia blue sky shone overhead as small tugs moved planes from here to there. Aircraft of varying sizes sat inside hangars. There were even a few poised and waiting for takeoff.

"Nox?" Charli asked.

"I'm just enjoying the view."

Her gaze scanned the same scene. "Am I missing something?"

"Not one police car."

She grinned. "Let's leave before one shows up."

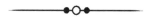

CLAYTON PULLED THE black sedan up to the gate in front of the house in Rye.

"I'm nervous to tell them," Charli said.

"We don't have to, not yet. It can be our secret."

"And Daryl Owen's and Dr. Beck's..."

"I'm confident those people are legally bound to keep secrets."

"It was hard not to tell Chelsea." Charli sighed. "I hope she likes the apartment."

Deloris and Isaac stayed with her in the city to take her to Charli's place on the Upper West Side.

"At least she's willing to give it a chance. Tomorrow we'll be back at our place. You'll see her."

The gate opened and Clayton moved forward as Charli nodded. "I'm ready for it to be just us again. And," she said enthusiastically, "I can't wait to see Pat. He was so great and then for the last week I fell off the map again."

"You've talked to him."

"I have," she said as Clayton opened the door. "But I haven't told him. I didn't know, when we spoke."

Cool wind whipped auburn wisps of Charli's hair around her face as she pulled her coat tighter and stepped out.

"I-I…"

I pulled her to a stop and brushed my lips over hers, stilling her words. Pink from the wind colored her cheeks as we stood on the sidewalk. "I'll follow your lead. I won't tell if you don't."

Charli took a deep breath and nodded. At the same moment, the door opened wide.

"What are you two doing? Come in," Silvia called.

For the first time that I could recall, my home welcomed me, truly welcomed me, from the flowers on the table to the sunlight shining in through the back windows. Impulsively, I kissed Silvia's cheek. "I have a secret."

Her eyes sprang wide only a second before Charli's.

"Follow my lead?" Charli asked.

"Alexandria!" Adelaide's voice came from the sitting room.

As Charli skirted away, Silvia reached for my arm. Narrowing her brown-eyed stare, she asked, "What's gotten into you?"

I was stunned with the response that danced on my tongue, fighting to be said. I wanted to say: nothing has gotten into me; it was in Charli. But I didn't. Instead, I shrugged and said, "I think it's called happiness."

"It's not a secret, Lennox. It shows on your face. You might want to appear a little more grief-stricken when interviewed about Mr. Fitzgerald's death."

"The interview is over. They told me to go."

"Come in here," she said, leading the way. "There's something you should see."

Still wearing my coat, I followed Silvia. Adelaide was lying on the sofa, a blanket over her legs with Charli perched on the edge. Their eyes were open wide. I turned to see the television screen.

PERSON OF INTEREST DETAINED IN THE UNEXPLAINED DEATH OF ALTON FITZGERALD, CEO MONTAGUE CORPORATION.

"Who?" I asked.

"Oh my God," Charli exclaimed.

Adelaide didn't speak as she focused on the screen.

I searched the room. "Where's my dad?"

"His office," Silvia said.

"My office," I corrected.

"Whatever." Silvia joined Adelaide and Charli as the reporter continued to detail the case.

After making my way to the office, I turned the knob slowly, unsure what came next.

My education had paved the way for my knowledge of Demetri Enterprises. It was the foundation. The rest was experience. Though we rarely saw eye to eye, following my recovery after my last MMA fight—the one against Luca—I started spending my time at the corporate offices.

Oren thought it would be a better use of my time than the octagon.

Being the son of the CEO I expected a nice office with a view. That's what I have today. It wasn't what I found when I first started. It might as well have been the mailroom. I was taking classes at NYU. When I wasn't there, my first job had been in the accounting department. They didn't give me important tasks. It was menial and mind-numbing. Through the years I moved from department to department, not as an officer of the company but as an employee.

I hated some of the work. I hated Oren for not recognizing my ability and potential. I hated that he reminded me over and over that the Demetri on the letterhead was his name.

Today I had the perspective to see that my experiences gave me the ability to take over when he moved away. They not only helped me, but the core officials of Demetri knew me and were willing to continue working for the son, the one who'd done more than been born into his position.

During those early years, I could have asked for Oren's advice. I could have talked to him about the tedious tasks that really weren't truly menial. He could have explained his reasoning. There were so many things we could have done. We never did.

That all contributed to the uneasiness of asking for his advice now.

"Oren," I said, entering the office.

His embrace as he stood lingered. He knew what was coming—what my debt to repay the favor of Fitzgerald's death would entail.

I didn't.

"He's gone," I said, speaking of Fitzgerald as I sat in the chair opposite him, no longer obsessed with who was on which side of the desk.

Oren leaned back. In his gaze was a resolution and sadness that ate at my gut.

Finally, I asked, "What happens now?"

Oren leaned forward. "How I wish you'd have asked that before."

Before I asked Vincent for the favor. He didn't need to say the last part.

Everything was different now.

It had been one thing to promise service and repayment when it was Charli that I was protecting. But now, with the baby on the way, I didn't know what I'd promised. I didn't know the time commitment or the duties. Instead of my confident self, I was that twenty-year-old working in accounting, crunching numbers that never seemed to end. The uncertainty terrified me. How would it affect Charli and our baby?

"It's too late for that," I said, trying to appear confident, maybe even knowledgeable.

"First," Oren said, "we go to him, thank him for the service. I can call."

"No. I'll call. Give me his number." I looked out the window. "What about his men?"

"A few more days."

"Why? I have security. We don't need them. Besides, Spencer is locked away in a prison hospital and Fitzgerald is…"

"He's *dead*, Lennox. I never wanted to say this to you, but get used to the term."

My stomach twisted. "How did you do it? I mean, being married and running Demetri, building the company, and having a kid, and this—debts and obligations to the Costellos? How did you do it?"

"I believe you were the one who said I failed at a few of those roles."

Fuck!

My eyes blinked, lingering shut before opening. "Can it be done?"

"Son, I'm proud of you. I'm proud of the qualities I see in you. You're a hard worker. You're tenacious and determined. You're stubborn and resolute in your beliefs. You love with your mother's heart. Vincent is a fair man and so is Luca. I don't know what they'll ask or even when. It may be tonight or not for ten years. But above all they're family. Your blood. They'll take care of you."

"You've never told me specifics of things you've done, things that were required of you."

"And I never will," he said. "I've done my best to keep you out of it. Angelina did too. But I've come to understand that the best intentions aren't enough. Despite what you may be thinking or worried about, the Costellos are your family. They also run legitimate enterprises. They provide needed services. They're respected. That's what you need to give to them. That's worth more than money and time. That's what Vincent saw in you the other day. Respect."

"His phone number?"

CHAPTER 38

———●○●———

CHARLI

"MOMMA? HOW ARE you?" I asked after Silvia stepped away.

Her chest rose and fell. "I'm alive."

"Are you in pain?"

"Some, but it's getting better."

I rested my hand on her blanket-covered legs. "Can you take anything?"

She smiled and shook her head. "No. I'm an addict."

"No, you aren't. They did that to you."

"No, sweetheart. Alton poisoned me or at least we think he did. I guess we'll never know for sure, but I poisoned myself too. No more pain medicine. No more alcohol. I'm thinking clearer than I have in years and I like it."

"But I don't want you to hurt."

"Tell that to the physical therapist who visits every day. He just left. That's why I'm here on the sofa in front of the fire. The man is a tyrant, and instead of trying to help me, Oren and Silvia encourage him."

We'd turned the volume down on the TV, but it was still playing. "I can't believe they've arrested her. Do you think she really did it? The police asked us about Alton's liquor. I think maybe he was poisoned."

"Karma…" Momma said. There was no humor in her tone or her eyes, but the irony was there.

"I wondered if he could have done it to himself," I said. "When the police first told us, that was my first thought. I mean, he was grasping at straws to save his kingdom and it was crumbling around him. Even Bryce." I shook my head. "Momma, he's lost it. Yesterday when Bryce pulled that stunt at the hotel, he proved how certifiably nuts he really is. He solidified public opinion of him. It will affect the murder case. Alton had to know that. He had to see it all dissolving around him."

"I'm sorry," Mother said, "for so many things. I have no excuse, except that I drank the Kool-Aid for so long that I believed it. I had to. I couldn't face each day if I didn't."

I turned back to the television. The screen was filled with a picture of Suzanna. I recognized the sapphire-blue dress. The picture was from the engagement party only a week ago. "Damn, she was prancing around the manor like the queen bee, and now look at her. Did you know she fired Jane?"

"What?"

"I hired her back. There were so many things that happened."

"I think she did," my mother said.

"What?"

"I think Suzanna killed him."

"He changed his will," I explained. "Alton did, making Bryce his heir. My attorney said it was done only two days ago. That was the day he said he'd give you the divorce if I married him."

Momma's lashes fluttered as she slowly moved her head back and forth.

"Jane said they fought—Alton and Miss Suzanna. I saw how angry she was in the attorney's office. She even cursed."

"Saying he'd marry you over her was probably the final blow. She expected more, but she wasn't good enough. No one ever was... he excelled at making people feel that way." Momma's eyes closed. When they opened, they were moist with new tears. "Alexandria... I've thought about his proposal to you over and over since you called. I need to know something. It's true that I turned a blind eye to many things, but the one thing I tried to do, and Jane tried to do, was protect you. Did he ever...?"

"Do anything—sexually?" I asked, finishing her sentence. "No. I never felt that vibe, not until the proposal. And even then, it was a feeling. He didn't actually touch me. It was the way he looked at me, and how he said Bryce couldn't tame me, but he could. I thought I'd vomit right there. Nox went nuts. Suzanna went crazy, as I said, cursing and yelling.

"While I was growing up, he was demeaning and cruel, psychologically abusive. I never knew when he'd blow. He believed in corporal punishment. But no, thank God, he never made sexual advances."

She closed her eyes. By the fire's light, I watched as a tear trickled down her cheek.

"Were you and Suzanna really friends?"

"Yes," she said. "I know that may be hard to believe. It even pains me to think of her arrested for Alton's death. Part of me wants to thank her. She's cleared a path for you with Montague, but the other part of me feels sorry for her. I was married to the man for twenty years, but she was the one who loved him."

I scrunched my nose. "How could you be all right with that?"

"I wasn't. I accepted it. If I'd loved him, I might have been jealous. As I said, I never did. My marriage was a business deal. I was nothing more than a bartering chip for my father to ensure the future success of Montague Corporation."

"Do you think he loved her?"

Mother shook her head. "I'm not sure he loved anyone, except himself and money and power."

"Momma, I'm sorry."

"No, don't be. I don't deserve that. I almost did the same thing to you, and I'll regret that for as long as I live."

"Stop."

Her blue eyes opened wide. She looked too frail. In the fire's light, I could see her cheekbones, and the bones of her fingers as her hands clenched in the blanket's edge.

"We've lived with enough of that. There's been enough regret. Spend your energy getting better, growing stronger. Decide what you want to do about Montague Corporation."

"Me? It will be yours."

"Ours. As I've always said, I don't want it. If you do, make it a success.

Show the world a female Montague is better than the male in her stead. Besides, I'm going to be a little busy."

Before I could go on, we both turned to Oren and Nox coming through the doorway toward us. Though Nox had been happy, perhaps even joyous, when we'd arrived, both his and Oren's expression had turned. Lines cluttered their brows. Even their steps seemed slower, creating a cloud of unease.

"Is everything all right," Mother asked.

"I was about to ask the same thing."

Nox sighed as he sat in a nearby chair. "Everything is fine. Work has been piling up. It's time to get back to the city."

Momma reached for my hand. "I'd hoped you'd stay here a little longer."

"I have a few more weeks of class and finals. There'll be no honors this semester. I'm hoping to pass."

"I'm impressed you've been able to keep up to date as it is," Oren said.

"Yeah, it's been a little difficult."

"You have your life to keep you busy. I understand," Mother said.

I'd been right when I'd told her to stop with the regret. Alton was dead. Bryce was in jail and now so was Suzanna. My mother was sober and clean, and most importantly she was alive. My monsters were caged, and miraculously, we'd survived. It was time to focus on the future.

"Nox?" I asked.

His eyes opened wide as joy returned to his light-blue eyes. "Are you sure?"

A grin covered my face as I nodded. "I am. Let's concentrate on good things."

"Alexandria, what is it?" Momma said.

"Yesterday," I began, "at the standoff at the hotel, I fainted."

"Lennox told us," Oren said.

"You called from the hospital," Momma said. "Were you hurt more than you said?"

"No," I replied unable to contain my smile. "Even though I hit my head when I fell..." I touched the back of my head. "...and it's still sore, they didn't do a scan." I shook my head. "This is really weird talking to both of you like this."

"It is," Nox agreed. "I have no idea what you two plan on doing, but no matter what, Charli and I need to let you know that you'll share a grandchild."

Oren shot to his feet. "Did I just hear you correctly?"

The cloud of death and poison infiltrating our thoughts disappeared as Momma reached for my shoulders. "You're pregnant? My baby's having a baby?"

I lifted my shoulders. "That's what Dr. Beck said."

"Dr. Beck…" She sighed.

"Yes, he asked about you."

"Alex, are you all right?" Oren asked.

It was Nox who answered. "Dad, she's perfect. We had an ultrasound last night. You should have seen…" He pulled the picture from his pocket.

I couldn't stop the tears. My damn emotions were on overdrive. The man who'd told me he never wanted children, the same one who warned me about his father, was oozing joy and excitement, explaining to that same father about the ultrasound and how our child was safe and secure, exactly where he or she belonged.

When I turned to my momma, her eyes glistened with the new tears. For once, they weren't from sorrow or pain. Tears of joy blurred our vision.

"What?" Silvia asked, coming back into the room. "What's happening?"

Nox turned. "How does Aunt Silvia sound?"

Her face paled as she looked from Nox to me and back to him. "It sounds great," she said cautiously. "And you're happy? You're really happy."

"I am," Nox said.

THE BED DIPPED as I cuddled toward Nox's warmth. His cologne filled my senses as he wrapped his arm around me providing his hard shoulder as a pillow.

"That went better than I imagined," he said.

"How is this going to work?"

"What work?"

I lifted my head. "Hi, baby, this is your grandmother and grandfather.

What will our baby think when he or she figures out they're *your* dad and *my* mom. That should make grandparents' day at school interesting."

Nox's shoulder shrugged. "Who knows? It'll work. I don't know how. I have no idea what they plan to do." His nose wrinkled. "I don't think I want to know."

Laying my head back on his shoulder, I giggled. "I agree. Not going there…" Unwanted images flashed in my mind. Things a child never wants to imagine with her mother. "Ewww… now I'm going there. Yuck. Make it stop."

Nox rolled me to my back with a soft laugh. "We could replace those thoughts."

"What, sir, do you have in mind?"

Our lips united, fueling a hunger I hadn't realized I had. He pulled away. "I love you. I plan to say that every day. There's just one thing I need you to do for me."

"Every day?"

"Yes, everyday, and it's not what you're thinking, but I'm good with that too."

I was thinking what he thought I was thinking. I was thinking about wrapping my lips around his cock and the way my big protective, dominant man trembled as I worked my tongue over his velvety tip and ran my hands up and down his hard shaft, but… every day?

"Every day," he said, pulling me from my own erotic scene, one I could enjoy since we were in the starring roles. "I'm going to hold you to your promise. Your only job is to stay safe." He reached down and covered my stomach. "To keep you both safe."

I nodded. "Yes, Nox."

"Are you sure Dr. Beck said it's all right to…? I mean, I don't want to hurt…"

Reaching up, I cupped his cheeks and pulled his lips back to mine. "We already have, multiple times. Remember, I'm six weeks. That means I've been pregnant since…"

His grin grew. "I think it was the night you wore that red dress."

"You do? What makes you think that was the night?"

"Because it was perfect—the garter belt, the lack of panties…" He wiggled his brow. "Fuck, I'm getting hard just thinking about it."

The imaginary blow job I'd been thinking about faded away as memories of that night came back to mind. Instead of Nox between my lips, I recalled the lasagna and bread, the chicken and vegetables…

I sighed. "Oh, the food at that restaurant was so good. We need to go back…"

"Is that how this is going to be?" he asked with a grin. "I'm imagining you in fuck-me heels, a black garter belt, and sexy stockings with your tits and pussy at my disposal, and you're thinking about food?"

No… and yes.

My core twisted at the memories of not only the sex, but also the prelude. It had been perfect. The sexual tension that he'd built had had me ready to combust. Then again, the food was awesome.

"Well," I said, "I am eating for two now."

He reached to my breast and rolled one of my nipples into a hard nub. Even without his ministration, the other nipple followed suit. It was as his scruffy chin abraded my sensitive skin and kisses peppered my neck that all thoughts of Italian delicacies slipped away. Well, all but him.

"Oh."

"That's it, princess." His skillful hands moved lower, his fingers splaying over my stomach. "I'm going to dominate your body and mind until the only thoughts in that beautiful head are about me and the ecstasy of me inside you. I'm going to make you hungrier for what I can give than what Antonio can."

I giggled. "He makes really great lasagna."

He pointed to his chest. "No more food talk. Me. Mind on me."

"Yes, Nox."

It wasn't difficult to follow his instructions. Lennox Demetri was a man on a mission. As he did as he promised, dominating my body and mind, my legs parted, heels planted against the soft sheets, and back arched. His touch was the music that rocked my world. I was his instrument. Together our song filled the air. My whimpers were the high notes while his growls created the bass.

The flurry of the last few weeks disappeared as we sang, not with our voices but with our bodies. They moved in sync, coming perfectly together. Apart we were half—unwhole. Together we were one—complete.

As I drifted off to sleep my mind lingered in the almost-dream world. It was there I heard the word *marriage*, the word that used to scare me, but no longer did. It wasn't a proposal—maybe it hadn't been audible. I wasn't sure if it came from Nox or from my heart. All I knew with complete certainty as I surrendered to slumber was that I was loved and adored by a man with whom I would willingly spend the rest of my life, the man whose baby was inside of me.

CHAPTER 39

—●○●—

OREN

WE WERE FINALLY nearing the meeting I'd been dreading. It hadn't occurred in a day or even a week. Time had ticked away. Life had moved on, and so had death.

Christmas was near. The houses in Brooklyn Heights were decorated with colorful lights and lush greenery. Wreaths hung on doors, while trees sparkled in windows.

Adelaide was doing better by the day. She still experienced tenderness in her ribs and occasional migraines, but most notably her mind was clear. Five weeks clean. She said it was an everyday battle. Nevertheless, she was winning.

The shine in her blue eyes and the color in her cheeks was what brought a smile to my face.

The case against Suzanna Spencer had built and held steadfast. She was being held without bail. Alton Fitzgerald's funeral had happened and was done. Much to my chagrin, Adelaide went back to Savannah to oversee the arrangements. As she explained, news of her divorce wasn't news at all. The papers were never filed with the court. She was a widow. More than that, she wanted to quell the rumors of her illness.

With Silvia's help, Adelaide had even managed to gain some weight. The therapists who still visited daily were pleased, as were the doctors. Her decision to attend the funeral was her declaration to those who'd wished her harm. She wanted all of Savannah to know that Adelaide Montague was alive and well.

While in Savannah, she'd taken advantage of the current uncertainty of Montague Corporation and as the majority stockholder called an emergency meeting of the board of directors. She spoke honestly, asking them to remain steadfast during this time of upheaval. While the courts were working out the details, she assured them that Montague Corporation was her priority. She didn't want to make any major personnel changes for the time being, relying upon the knowledge of those who'd helped foster its latest success. The only change she stressed was the need to move all legal matters to a new law firm: Preston, Madden, and Owen.

She convinced the board to move fast, letting them know that she would be filing charges with the State Bar Of Georgia to examine the legal practices of Hamilton and Porter. With the current state of affairs, it was in the corporation's best interest to avoid another scandal.

In record time, Hamilton and Porter lost its biggest account. On the other hand, Preston, Madden, and Owen was hiring new associates.

Though I would have liked to have been at her side as she showed Savannah her strength, she opted for Alexandria. Together they spoke to the board. Afterward, with the help of Gwendolyn and Preston Richardson, Alton's sister and brother-in-law, and Patrick, Alton's nephew, they faced the mourners and accepted kind words of sympathy.

She and Alexandria held their heads high, despite the murmuring by the entire country.

After all, the whole nation had watched the train wreck—on social media—as Alexandria's engagement party ended with her fiancé's arrest through the arrest of her future mother-in-law for the murder of her stepfather. The world hadn't known that her engagement to Edward Spencer had all been a sham. Calling Spencer or even Suzanna out on that, at this point, would only add fuel to the fire.

The reporters had only scratched the surface of how the tangled web of intrigue had at one time been orchestrated by the puppeteer strings held by the man in the coffin.

Though I wasn't there, Lennox was. He stayed in the shadows and out of the spotlight. After everything was said and done, he refused to allow Alex to go back to Savannah without him. I couldn't say as I blamed him.

Thankfully after the funeral, Adelaide decided to return to Westchester County, to the home in Rye. I hadn't been sure she would. I'd been too anxious to ask. However, when she did, when she returned to me without the assistance of kidnapping, I couldn't have been happier.

Her strength to face life's challenges with her head high continued to amaze me. I was continually awestruck by the woman who shared my life, my bed, and even our future grandchild.

We hadn't broached the subject of our future. Just knowing it held untold possibility was enough for us both.

Adelaide and I also both waited and hoped for news of our children's wedding, but as of yet, neither Nox nor Alex had mentioned it. It wasn't that we were old-fashioned. If they didn't want to marry, that was their choice. Then again, maybe we were. I wanted the baby growing inside of Alex to be born a Demetri.

At this moment, standing upon the stoop of Vincent Costello's home, the baby's last name wasn't my or Lennox's biggest concern. In our long wool overcoats as the snow flurried about and landed in white flakes on my son's dark hair, my skin prickled with anticipation as our breath materialized in soft white clouds.

The door opened to Bella's bright smile. "Oren! Lennox!" she said, wrapping both of us in a warm hug as she ushered us inside. "When Vinny said you were coming to our house, I had to question his sanity. Just maybe it's still intact," she said with a wink. "You're here. It's so good to see you!"

"You too, Bella," I said.

"Your home is beautiful," Lennox complimented as we took in the lovely woodwork of the classic townhome.

"We couldn't stay out in the suburbs. We both wanted to be close to Luca and Luisa."

"How is Luisa?" I asked, genuinely interested. She'd been the prettiest little girl. "I still remember her first communion."

"The party," Vincent's voice came booming as he walked toward us coming from a back hallway. "You didn't attend the church service."

The man had the memory of an elephant.

I nodded. "Yes, the party was wonderful. She looked like a princess."

"She's doing well. Very well," Bella said as she turned to Lennox. "Like you, she decided to do the school thing. She just finished her bachelor's degree and has started her graduate work in kinesiology."

"There's so much I don't understand," I admitted.

"It's science, sports medicine, and physical therapy," Vincent explained. "Obviously she gets her brains from Bella."

"Luisa's a smart one," I said.

"It would be good to all get together," Bella said. "Family shouldn't spend so much time apart."

"Come back to my office and we'll have some privacy," her husband offered.

I looked around for someone else, for Jimmy or Luca. No one else was there. It was almost as if instead of a business meeting, this was simply a family gathering. For some reason, that didn't fill me with hope.

"Thank you, Bella," I offered. "We'll need to see."

Once we were behind the closed door, Vincent said, "Oren, I didn't know you'd be here. Didn't we discuss apron strings?"

"I asked him to join us," Lennox volunteered. "I'm here to thank you. Sincerely. This is new to me."

"Showing gratitude is new?"

"No, sir. Asking for help."

Vincent smiled as he nodded. "Take off your coats and have a seat. I meant what I said. You're Angelina's boy. You heard Bella; we would like to get to know you. Perhaps your girlfriend too?"

With our coats draped over a chair, Lennox and I found a seat on a sofa, as Vincent settled into a plush chair that reminded me of a throne. His office was regal, fitting of his title.

"You were saying," Vincent said to Lennox, "that asking for help is new?"

"It is. The situation was out of hand. It became even worse before... before—"

"Before Alton Fitzgerald died," Vincent said. "Is that what you're trying to say?"

"Yes, sir."

"And you think my men helped you with that out-of-hand situation?"

I looked to Lennox and back to Vincent. Was this a trick?

"We asked," I said. "Both of us."

"And I told you it takes time. There's a process. The first step is understanding the man. My men needed to know who he was."

My pulse sped up. "Are you saying it wasn't you?"

"Oren, I haven't done that in many years."

Lennox shook his head. "Sir, I came here to let you know that I'm willing to repay the debt."

"After receiving your call, only days after the news of Fitzgerald's death, I assumed as much. You see, Lennox, you were in Savannah when he died," Vincent explained. "You're family. I would never, Luca would never, our men would never, carry out a job and leave one of our own as a possible suspect." He leaned forward. "It wasn't on the news, but I'd imagine that the police... they questioned you? No?"

"They did," Lennox said. "But I had an alibi."

"You see, we wouldn't have been able to guarantee that. You were with the girl?"

"I was. She'd been hurt. She fell earlier that day. The doctors wanted her to spend the night at the hospital. I stayed with her."

Vincent's round cheeks rose. "A good man." He turned to me. "You raised a good man."

"Thank you. I think Angelina gets most of the credit." I still couldn't comprehend what he was saying. "If not you... who?"

He shrugged. "I suspect the woman they have in jail? After all, the police wouldn't make a mistake, would they?"

With the color returning to his cheeks, Lennox said, "I still asked. I'm in your debt."

"No, you're not. I don't take payment for deeds uncommitted. You and I are even, Lennox. I only ask that you call me more. Get to know Luca again. Maybe bring your girlfriend to dinner? We'd like to meet her." He turned to me. "There is something I've been meaning to discuss with you."

"Your men," I volunteered. "Thank you for their time."

"They brought me something," he said, standing.

We waited as Vincent waddled over to his desk and came back with a Ziploc bag containing what appeared to be a burner phone.

I reached out, holding the corner of the bag. "What is this?"

"It's a phone my men found as they escorted someone away from your property."

The phone was small, black, a standard-issue flip phone. "Do they know who the man was?"

"A scum. A leech. The kind with no loyalty."

"Did you see what was on here?" I asked. "Did you get any information?"

"A little from the phone. More from the man once my men helped him find his voice."

"Who did he work for?" Lennox asked.

"A man who will never bother you or your girl again." He turned to me. "I once heard him described as an abusive fuck."

Dread connected the pieces of the puzzle. "Fitzgerald. You're sure?"

"He had Alexandria followed. The man had been doing it for over six months. Have your people look. That phone is full of text messages. Cryptic at best. Luckily my men can be persuasive."

"That's how they knew where she was," Lennox said. "My people figured that Fitzgerald had tracked her phone, but then discovered the phone's locator was off. We'd scoured our own people, but everyone in our loop came up clean."

Vincent nodded. "He's no longer a problem, the man or the one who hired him."

"How can I thank you?" Lennox asked.

"Dinner. Let us meet your new love."

"Yes."

CHAPTER 40

—•○•—

CHARLI

I BALANCED THE shopping bags in one arm as I fumbled with the lock to our apartment with the other. It was hard to believe that Christmas was so close. The year was a blur. With trying to study and pull my grades up, after all we'd been through, I'd finally had a chance to shop.

It wasn't only the studying; I'd been exhausted since Alton's funeral. Not tired. I'd been tired before. This was bone-dissolving exhaustion, the kind that left me weak, the kind that sucked each and every bit of energy from my body. My OB/GYN said it was normal and everything was fine. On the positive side, I hadn't had morning sickness and my appetite was more insatiable than ever.

As a matter of fact, as I turned the key, my thoughts weren't on the Christmas presents I'd purchased or the maternity clothes I'd seen. It was on whatever Lana had simmering in our kitchen. I may have even daydreamed about it throughout the afternoon. Closing my eyes as I opened the door, I inhaled.

Spices and goodness were what I sought.

Instead, the faint scent of jasmine air freshener from the globe plugged into the wall was all I detected. I opened my eyes. The city's lights sparkled through the windows and near the sofa a slender tree twinkled with white lights. Together they were the living room's only illumination. Surprised and bewildered by the lack of aroma, I dropped the bags at the floor, kicked off my boots, and pushed my code into the security system.

"Hello?" I called, wondering if Lana was still here, just running late.

This time of year the days were short, too short. Though the sky was dark, I didn't expect Nox for at least another hour.

Since we'd returned to our schedules, he'd been working hard doing whatever it was he did. I'd told him about the strange meeting that time in Alton's office, the one that included Senators Carroll and Higgins as well as Severus Davis. It seemed as though something had been bothering him, and though I cared if it was related to that, I'd honestly been too tired and preoccupied to ask. Part of me was also scared.

It was last night after I'd been out to dinner with Cy and Pat that I knew that I'd been right. Nox had been worried about something. Perhaps the reason I hadn't asked was because part of me was concerned that the baby had soured his mood. Even though Nox always acted happy when he talked about it and constantly questioned my health and emotions, I was nervous. It was easier to blame his mood on the odd assembly at Montague Manor.

However, last night with my tummy filled with a fantastic meal from my favorite Thai restaurant, I'd come home ready to wait for him and catch up on my pleasure reading. He'd had plans too and had said he didn't know how late he'd be. All I could remember was that his plans included Oren.

When Nox returned home... it's hard to explain but it was as if he were a new person or more accurately his old self. Whatever cloud of concern that had been hanging over his head was gone. He talked about his cousins from his mother's side and said they wanted to have dinner with us.

Even now, as I carried my shopping bags down the hallway to the bedroom, the memory of his change of demeanor brought a smile to my face.

"Good evening, princess."

I gasped as I spun in the darkened bedroom. "Oh my God, Nox, you scared me."

With the light from the windows, I took him in. His suit coat was gone. His bright white silk shirt disappeared into the trim waist of his trousers. The black belt with the silver swirl on the buckle surrounded his hips and made my knees weak.

"I thought you weren't going to be home until later."

He wrapped his arms around me, pulling me so close I needed to crane my neck upward to see the light blue that I adored.

"I rearranged my schedule. You said on the phone you had more energy." His dark eyebrows bobbed as his lips turned upward. "Don't tell me you used it all up shopping."

I melted toward him, wrapped in his warm embrace as the beat of his heart thumped against my ear. "No, but did you tell Lana not to cook? I didn't smell dinner."

He nodded. "I did. I made plans."

I exhaled. It wasn't that I didn't enjoy going out, but I'd been out. I looked back up. The gleam in his eye gave me the zap of energy I needed. I wouldn't ruin his plans. "What did you have in mind?"

"I got you something to wear."

"You did?"

He tugged my hand, pulling me into the closet. On the center sofa was what appeared to be a soft pair of leggings, fuzzy socks, and an oversized sweater. "What?" It wasn't what I'd expected.

"Princess, I'm cooking dinner for you. There's a warm bath in the tub. You rest."

"You? *You're* cooking? Why didn't you let Lana?"

Holding both my hands he pulled them to his chest. "Oh, are you doubting me?"

I laughed. "No, hell no. A bath and comfortable clothes sounds amazing. I was expecting heels and a garter."

"We still have the ones from that night. If you'd rather…?"

I kissed his soft lips. "After walking around Manhattan with Clayton all afternoon, I'd rather the fuzzy socks."

"That's my sex kitten," he laughed as I practically skipped to the bathroom.

As I opened the door, warm, humid air redolent with the sweet scent of jasmine filled my senses. That was what I'd smelled as I entered the apartment. It wasn't the air freshener. I grinned at the rose petals floating on the water's surface.

I peeked my head back out to the bedroom. "Are you sure you don't want to join me?"

Soft music was the only response.

Sighing, I quickly stripped out of my clothes and eased myself into the warm, scented water. It was heaven as I laid my head back, my hair pinned on top of my head in a messy bun, and allowed the warm bath to lap over my growing breasts.

I wasn't sure how long I'd been in there, but as the water began to cool, I forced myself to move. The leggings were new and covered in colorful pictures of shoes. The sweater was loose and hung from one shoulder. The fuzzy socks weren't sexy, but since there were no panties or even a bra accompanying Nox's chosen ensemble, I decided to go without. It was my sexy contribution to the outfit.

I could be a sex kitten if I wanted.

Still trying to decipher Nox's culinary skills, I slid my stocking feet along the hallway and quietly entered the kitchen. For only a moment, I stood in the doorway and watched as Nox stared down at the stovetop with a spatula in his hand. His protruding brow and clenched jaw told me that whatever he was cooking was receiving his full attention. It was completely out of character and surprisingly arousing.

Sneaking up behind him, I wrapped my arms around his waist and peered around his body. "Grilled cheese?" I laughed. "That's your culinary skill, the reason you cancelled Lana?"

"Yes, now don't disturb me. I need to show you that I can cook them without burning them."

"That's not fair. You distracted me."

The devilish grin I loved sparked to life as he connected the dots of the spatula in his hand and me by his side. Before I could squeal and run away—I blame the lack of traction on the socks—the spatula came down with an audible swat to my behind.

"Oh, Mr. Demetri, now I plan on distracting you."

His blue eyes went to my long hair as he gently tucked a stray strand behind my ear and pushed the length over my shoulder. His touch lingered as I tilted my head, giving him full access to the exposed skin. His voice rumbled, becoming thick. "You seem to be missing a strap."

I shrugged, the thunder of his voice rolling to my core. "You said to wear what you had out. You didn't have a bra out. I always obey your commands, Mr. Demetri."

He dropped the spatula to the counter and cupped my behind, pulling me close. "I didn't have panties laid out either." His fingers splayed as a brow rose. "Fuck. No panty lines?"

Slowly, I shook my head as I lowered my eyes.

Leaping out of his grasp, I grabbed the spatula and flipped the sandwich, just as the butter turned to the perfect toasted brown. "I saved it!"

"Oh, no. This is my meal. Give me that spatula."

My eyes widened. "Why?"

"Because distracting me is a punishable offense."

I handed it back with another kiss. "Guilty as charged. What's come over you?"

"I was thinking a nice quiet night at home sounded good."

I couldn't agree more. I opened the cupboard and reached for the plates. "We're missing the California wine."

Nox bent down and kissed my stomach. "No wine—California or French—for a while."

"The doctor said a glass now and then is fine."

"My rules overrule the doctor."

I shook my head as he took the plates from my hands and carried them to the table. I filled two glasses with ice water. "Yum, grilled cheese and water."

"Oh, I have salads in the refrigerator. Can you grab them?" he asked.

I opened the door and on the top shelf were two bowls filled with greenery and carrots. Nothing else registered, because all I noticed was the blue velvet box atop of one of the salads. "Nox?"

"Can you carry them to the table?"

With trembling hands, I did as he said, setting down the one with the box at my place.

"Open it," he said.

I could barely grip the soft exterior as I lifted and pried back the lid. The hinges moved, revealing the satin slot where a ring would be. "What?"

I turned as he fell to one knee with a diamond ring in his hand.

"Oh, Nox." Tears filled my eyes.

"I've thought of thousands of ways to make this moment special. I imagined the Eiffel Tower bright with lights. I thought of whisking you off to Del Mar. I even had a plan with a sunset and the balcony of the presidential suite. I considered a Broadway show and a carriage ride in Central Park.

"And then I realized that the setting wasn't what mattered. The only thing that mattered was you and I and your answer."

I couldn't form words as he went on.

"I remembered a night, the first night I brought you here. I remembered the promise of frozen meatballs and the presence of burnt sandwiches. I recalled your gorgeous eyes…" He reached up and wiped a tear from my cheek. "…the ones that are now clear, even with tears. I remember the way they clouded as you opened up to me, telling me about your family. And I remembered wanting to take those clouds away forever.

"Oh, Nox…" He touched my lips.

"Charli, you are my forever. You've brought love back into my life. Not just between us, but with our baby and even our parents. In the short time we've been together, you've given me back a reason to live, to wake, and to move." He leaned forward and kissed my stomach again. "Together we've created a new family."

Navy swirled in his light-blue orbs as he looked up. "I'm not the most romantic person. Truthfully, I'd be better at this if you were the one on your knees."

I giggled.

"The most important thing is for you to know that whether we're in an exclusive resort eating caviar or at home with cheese sandwiches, I'm so fucking in love that I can't stand another day without your saying you'll marry me, that you'll agree to let me be your forever."

I pried my gaze from his eyes, from his protruding brow and chiseled jaw. I looked at the ring he held between his finger and thumb. The band was platinum, dusted in small diamonds like my necklace. There was one center stone. It was round and sparkled, standing high on prongs.

It was simple and elegant.

It was classy and understated.

It was perfect.

"Yes." It was the only word I could say as my soul flooded with emotion and I sunk to my knees before him.

He cupped my cheeks as his warm, possessive lips met mine. And then with our faces close, he said, "I asked your mom."

"You did?"

"I did." He slid the ring over my finger. "I know it's old-fashioned. I drove to Rye this morning and asked for her daughter's hand." He shrugged. "She said yes. I'm glad you did too."

Splaying my fingers, I stared down at my hand. "Nox, I love you. That was the best proposal I've ever heard."

Standing, he reached for my hand and pulled me to my feet and into his embrace. "Well, the bar was set kind of high. I mean, I heard the one proposal: *You'll marry me*. It was a tough one to beat."

My smile grew so big my cheeks ached. "It was close, but for the record, yours is the only one I accepted."

"Good to know. Let's eat these delicious sandwiches and explore that kneeling thing a little more."

"Oh, Mr. Demetri. Whoever said you weren't romantic?"

CHAPTER 41

---•O•---

ALEXANDRIA

FOR THE MIDDLE of March, it was unseasonably warm in Southern California. We'd enjoyed days in the mid-seventies. Today was no different as the sun was about to set over the Pacific Ocean.

"Damn, little cousin, you're stunning."

I smiled at Patrick through my lashes. "You know, I think you said the same thing right before my interview with Karen."

"Well, what can I say? I need to work on expanding my vocabulary. I should get one of those word-of-the-day calendars."

"You're very handsome yourself. Wait until Cy sees you in that suit."

Patrick reached the lapels and puffed his chest. "I know. I know. It's a curse."

We stood together before the full-length mirror in the master bedroom of the presidential suite in Del Mar. Yes, the same suite, the same resort. I wasn't sure how Nox was able to schedule it. Spring recess was a busy time at all the beachfront resorts around the country. It was also the first time since the semester break that I'd had the time to go away. Thankfully my grades were improving.

Patrick pressed the palm of his hand against the white satin, below the empire waist of my wedding dress. "Hey, teeny-tiny cousin, this is your favorite cousin, Pat. Just checking in. How you doing in there?"

I shook my head.

"That bump is getting bigger than teeny-tiny."

"Thanks, Pat," I said. "Just what every girl wants to hear before she walks down the aisle."

He stood behind me, his chin at my shoulder. "You should see what I see."

I shrugged.

"Oh, no." He pointed to the bottom of the mirror. "Listen to me. Start at the floor. Look down there."

Taking a deep breath, I did as he said.

"What do you see?" Pat asked.

"Shoes."

Pat shook his head. "I'm getting *you* that calendar. Look again and let me tell you what I see: I see Louboutin white crystal-encrusted pumps peeking out from under a ballgown satin skirt that's covered in shimmering white organza. As I look higher, the empire waist keeps my tiny cousin hidden, while the scoop neckline accentuates those glorious growing ta-tas.

"My God, Lennox won't be able to get higher than that neckline. And above it, above them…" He wiggled his brows. "… is the beautiful pearl necklace that never seems to leave your graceful neck."

He lifted my chin.

"And higher, now that's the most stunning of all. I see the perfectly painted lips, permanently stuck in the most sickeningly sweet smile, cheeks that are tinted by the sun, and golden eyes that sparkle at the mere thought of the man out there on the balcony. Above it all, luscious auburn hair with highlights of gold and lowlights of mahogany that has been styled into the perfect 'do."

He reached for the diamond tiara on the nearby table and lowered it to my head.

"Pat, I wasn't sure if I was going to wear that."

As he secured the combs to keep it in place, he asked, "Then why did you buy it?"

"Because I wanted to be his princess."

He kissed my cheek. "You always will be."

I turned, the skirt pivoting with me. "Thank you."

He took a step back. "And for the record, I'm only walking your pregnant ass down the aisle. I am not now giving nor never will give you away."

"I love you."

The door opened and Patrick jumped in front of me, his arms spread wide. "Hey, no seeing—"

"Keep your panties in place," Chelsea said. "I've seen her. Hell, I dressed her. Babe, it's time." She winked. "And I know you can do this."

"What would Chelsea do?" I said, reminding her of the imaginary bracelet she'd told me to wear on my first date with Nox.

"Oh, no. Hell no. Charli with an *i* has this thing covered."

She came behind me in the mirror; only a small bit of her navy maid of honor dress showed behind my wide skirt as she brought her face next to mine. Our resemblance was gone. Her hair was now a lovely shade of blonde with blue tips that covered the last six inches. The soft blue curls were colored specifically to match her dress. It worked.

I reached up and hugged her face next to my shoulder. "I love you too."

"Well, I hate to break it to you," Chelsea said, "but if you don't get out there soon, I think you'll have some stiff competition."

"Really?"

"Yes, Jane is in total love with your guy."

"I know." I laughed. "She's told me at least a thousand times. She's so excited about the baby."

"We all are. Now…" She reached for my hand. "…are you ready for the show?"

"No, I'm ready for the real thing."

"Then it's time to go get him. Your mom is so nervous that I think she may take flight. You know, that thing she does with her hand by her throat."

I shook my head. "Yes. It's better than a wine glass."

"Well, Mr. Demetri is holding on tight, keeping her from becoming airborne."

"Come on, cousins," Pat said to me.

I nodded to Chelsea who picked up her bouquet and handed the larger one to me.

"Let's do this!"

Placing his hand at his waist, Pat offered me his arm. "Striking, astonishing, dazzling, and eye-catching."

We paused before the entry, still hidden from all the people on the balcony, as Chelsea walked before us. I leaned closer to Pat and whispered, "Tell me you didn't just Google synonyms for stunning."

Winking, he patted my hand as the music of the harpist grew louder. It was the wedding march, very traditional and old-fashioned. It was perfect— ideal, wonderful, and picture-perfect. I didn't need a calendar.

I closed my eyes as Pat led me through the glass door to the balcony. In front of the pool, a small arrangement of chairs, flowers, a harpist, and an altar had been assembled. We didn't have a *his* side and a *my* side, just a grouping of chairs that held my momma, Oren, Jane, Aunt Gwen, Uncle Preston, Cy, Deloris, and Clayton.

As my gaze lifted, my breathing hitched. With the orange glow of the setting sun sending prisms of light dancing off the waves below, the other guests, the minister, Isaac, and even Chelsea disappeared. All I could see was the man in the silk suit. Holding his own hands in front of him, he shifted slightly from one foot to the other, causing his suit coat to shift, accentuating his wide shoulders and the V of his trim waist. His dark hair was gelled back and his tie matched his eyes. His chin was covered with only a hint of stubble and his smile shone like a beacon beckoning my approach.

My steps stuttered as Nox scanned me from my Louboutins all the way to the diamond tiara. Like the first time he'd seen me at the pool, his light blue eyes burned my skin, sending a rush of heat and leaving goose bumps in its wake. I was covered in satin and shimmering organza, yet under his approving gaze I was stripped bare.

My princess, he mouthed.

My Batman, I returned.

Our endearments weren't audible, though our hearts heard every syllable. In his, I heard his deep timbre. It rolled like thunder to my soul until I searched the horizon for the clouds. There weren't any. The sky was clear and darkening by the second, making the white twinkling lights decorating the balcony and below the pool's surface sparkle like fireflies.

Stopping before Nox, Pat lifted my hand and placed it in Nox's. "Take care of her or I'll have to kick your ass."

We all laughed.

"What?" Pat said as he sat beside Cy. "I could... if I wanted to."

"Dearly beloved," the minister began.

I suppose I'm supposed to remember every word, but the phrases, combined with the gentle breeze and ocean's surf, faded away. Our marriage wasn't about words but about us and about what together we could never be alone. With my hand in Nox's I was filled with love and hope. I was part of a family. I loved and was loved.

Were they butterflies that fluttered in my tummy as Nox said the words *I do*, or was it our baby?

With tears of joy pooling on my lids, I turned to the minister as he asked, "Alexandria Charles Montague Collins, do you take this man as your lawfully wedded husband?"

This time in front of witnesses there was no hesitation. "Yes, with all my heart I do."

OUR RECEPTION WASN'T held until a week later at a large hall in Brooklyn, New York. It was Nox's cousin Vincent Costello and his wife Bella who'd planned it all. They insisted, understanding our desire for a small, intimate wedding.

"Fine, fine, I get it," Vincent had said. "You've had enough news coverage, but Alexandria, you must allow us to celebrate. Not just us, but *all* of us." He emphasized the word *all*.

I'll never forget his boisterous laugh and welcoming smile. From the first time Nox took me to their home, I was welcomed. Not just by Vincent and Bella, but also by the entirety of the Costello clan and that encompassed a lot of *us*.

In a way, being with this part of his family made me feel as if I were meeting his mother. After all this was her family.

How could I say no?

And now surrounded by cousins and more cousins, my small family had grown by leaps and bounds. There were so many women, all anxious to give me their marriage and mothering advice.

I wanted it, every word. I also wanted to accept the invitations to learn to cook. They told stories of family meals preceded by full-day cookathons. It was a life I'd never experienced, but one I was anxious to try, not only for me, but also for our child. He or she would only know love, so much love.

"Alex," Eva, Nox's cousin who was the doctor, asked, "How are you feeling?"

"Good…" As I spoke I glanced over at my mom. She and Vincent seemed to be in an in-depth conversation. It amazed me how the family had welcomed her as well as me, and not only as my mother, but also as Oren's significant other.

Nox was speaking with his cousin Luca, laughing and jabbing playfully at one another. And then I spotted Oren. If I didn't know better, I'd have thought he looked concerned as he watched my mother with Vincent from afar. What did he possibly think Vincent would say to my mother?

"Princess."

I turned to the deep voice of my husband. "Yes?"

Nox reached for my hand and pulled me close. "Our first dance is coming up, but I was wondering…" His lips quirked upward and his blue eyes shone.

I looked around the room full of people. "What were you wondering?"

"There's a gas station down the street. I thought maybe you and I could go there before our dance, because, Mrs. Demetri, I'm dying here, not being able to touch you like I want to. You're the most stunning bride I've ever seen and as much as I appreciate all that my family's done for us, right now I want to get you alone."

My cheeks warmed and pulse increased at the memory of Nox and I at a gas station along Highway 101. "Get me alone?" I wrapped my arms around his neck as our bodies came together. "And, pray tell, what would happen if we were alone?"

His warm breath skirted my neck, leaving goose bumps in its wake as he leaned down and whispered, "Trust me, another standing ovation."

CHAPTER 42

———●○●———

OREN

SINCE THE NIGHT we brought Adelaide to New York I'd gone without alcohol. I'd taken the whiskey to my lips the one night I'd met with Vincent, but I never drank. That said, throughout those months, I'd never craved it as much as I did at this reception. Watching Vincent speak to Adelaide was about to do me in. Maybe I should find Eva and ask her about a tranquilizer. Hell, being part of this family, she surely carried a bottle in her handbag.

It wasn't that the reception wasn't going well, or even the inclusion of the Montagues with the Costellos. Angelina's family had embraced Alex and Lennox in a way I'd never envisioned. It was Adelaide who concerned me. I couldn't imagine her mix of emotions.

"Oren," she said, her sweet voice pulling me from my thoughts. In my worry, I hadn't even noticed that their conversation had ended. "Are you all right?" she asked, reaching for my hand.

"I am." I eyed her up and down. "Are you?"

"I'm simply overwhelmed by Angelina's family. The way they've welcomed not only Alexandria but me as well." She shook her head and took a sip of some pink punch. I wasn't sure what it was, but it was the same thing the children were drinking. "They're lovely people."

Taking her hand, I led her to a back hallway.

Her eyebrows danced. "Oren Demetri, are you planning to make out with me at our children's reception?"

"No, well… not here." I added the last part with a grin.

She looked about at the empty, secluded space. "What is this about?"

"I should have told you. I'm sorry. You should know that Vincent—"

She touched two fingers to my lips. "I know who Vincent is. You told me his name many years ago."

"You know?" I couldn't believe my own ears. "And yet you're here talking to him?"

"He threw our children a wonderful party. Why wouldn't I talk to him?"

"Adelaide."

She lowered her voice. "Stop, Oren. Never again." She looked around the hallway to make sure that we were alone. "You and Vincent aren't the only ones to blame for what happened." Before I could speak, she went on. "I'm not the victim I played so well. I knew full well what I was doing when I told my father that Russell was leaving me, that he was planning not only to divorce me but also to take Alexandria with him. I knew, and I chose his fate over allowing him a safe escape and me suffering the consequences of divorce and disgrace." Her blue eyes widened as she spoke, her words slow and message filled with determination. "I knew. That makes me equally culpable. I played a part. My father was the one who initiated the request. There is no *one* responsible party."

"You know how it works?"

She shrugged. "I understand a little. You see, a long time ago, I dated this man. I think it's still called dating when you do what we did. Anyway, this man fascinated me. He told me stories. Some were dark, but all were sugarcoated with enough sweetness to make them palatable.

"I wanted to know more. My knowledge is from books, TV shows, and movies. In my head the theme song from the Sopranos will be the kids' first dance."

I laughed, shaking my head. "And you're here. With me. With all of us."

"Again, Oren, why wouldn't I be?" She brushed my lips with hers. "I love you. You've said you love me. You're divorced. I'm widowed. Isn't it wonderful how life works out?"

In the distance music filled the hall.

Adelaide reached for my hand. "Okay, so it isn't *Woke Up This Morning* or even *Speak Softly Love*." She gave me a soft kiss. "Sir, may I have a dance?"

The lights had been dimmed with only a spot on the newly married couple. Lennox and Alexandria had everyone's attention as the whole room watched. Alex's dress shimmered as she waltzed in Lennox's arms. It wasn't their attire that held everyone's interest, but the expressions on their faces. The way they stared into one another's eyes.

In a room full of people, old and young, happy and sad, Alex and Lennox were alone. No one else mattered as they moved to their own private melody.

"What do you wish for them," I asked. "If you could wish anything."

Adelaide smiled as her eyes stayed glued to our children. "That in their young lives they've already experienced all the pain they will. That now and forever they only know joy." She turned to me. "And you? What would you wish?"

I scanned the crowd, my gaze meeting Vincent's. He nodded.

Had he told us the truth? Had he orchestrated Alton's demise and then selflessly refused Lennox's debt?

I wasn't sure I'd ever know. I smiled and returned the nod, my gratitude, and my respect.

"*Amore mio,*" I said, whispering toward Adelaide, "I pray that together they know the joy of fidelity, the joy that only comes with fealty, loyalty, and support."

Adelaide lifted her glass of pink punch. "To fidelity."

THE END

But I couldn't end it... not yet.
Please turn the page for a glimpse into the future—
for the epilogue to the Infidelity series.

EPILOGUE
CHAPTER 1

———●O●———

Christmas Eve
Nearly Four Years later

CHARLI

STANDING NEAR THE window, I watched as the snow continued to fall. The light from the pool house's windows illuminated large, fluffy flakes dropping steadily through the dark night sky. It had been snowing for hours. Each frozen crystal added to the growing sparkly blanket of white. Inside, the fireplace snapped and crackled as voices murmured and laughed, keeping the cold at bay.

"What are you thinking about?"

The deep voice questioned me while at the same time strong arms encircled my once-again enlarged waist. Nox's hands splayed over our growing baby, our second little miracle. I leaned my head back against his wide chest and took in our faint reflection. From the top of his dark hair I started to scan, and inch-by-inch my gaze lowered. As I always did, I hesitated as my gaze met his mesmerizing blue eyes. He could speak volumes with them and never say a word.

Down I moved to his sensual lips and chiseled chin. It was resting atop my head, covered with just the right amount of stubble. We fit together perfectly. Nearly four years married and I doubted I'd ever tire of the way he held me or looked at me. Even from across the room, he made me feel as if no one else mattered, no one else existed.

Through all we'd experienced, his love and concern never wavered nor had his desire—make that our desire. In his arms, I was alive. With only his eyes he could set my skin ablaze. With his touch he could accelerate my heartbeat or calm a wild sea inside me.

The first time we'd created life while death had been all around us. This time, the life inside me was a planned joy, an anticipated addition to our family. Nox's hard limit was gone.

"I was thinking," I said, "about something Silvia told me a long time ago."

I spun in his arms, craning my neck upward and relishing his light-blue gaze. Even surrounded by family and friends, Nox had a way of cutting through all the noise to see me, deep inside me.

"If it's making you sad, stop."

Despite the moisture in my eyes, my lips turned upward. "It doesn't make me sad, not really."

"You, Mrs. Demetri, have never been good at lying."

"I'm not lying. I'm not sad. I'm reminiscing. The first time I was ever here in our house, Silvia told me about your mom. She said how much she'd loved this house and how she'd always wanted it filled with family."

Together we turned toward the Christmas tree, aglow with colorful lights. From our position we could see the back of Oren's and my mother's heads as they sat together on the sofa. Silvia, Cy, Pat, Uncle Preston, and Aunt Gwen were also near, some refilling their plates with more of the amazing food that I'd help Silvia prepare. The chatter was light and festive as Christmas music played in the background.

I'd not neared Silvia's level of culinary genius; however, frozen meatballs were no longer in my repertoire. With hers and the help of many patient Costello ladies, I'd made enough strides to keep my husband from starving— well, when Silvia wasn't around.

Nox nodded. "It feels good having them all here. I think she'd be happy."

I turned back toward the window. "I'm glad it feels good, because if the snow keeps falling as the weather people promise, we may all be together for more than tonight and tomorrow."

"Luckily we have some extra rooms, plus the guest house, and Silvia will keep everyone well fed."

"Mommy!" Angi squealed as she ran ahead of Jane. "Will Santa still come?"

Nox squatted to the floor, capturing our daughter only seconds before she tackled me—and her baby brother in the process. "Whoa, slow down, princess. Have you been good?"

Her lips thinned as she gazed up at her daddy, peering her big light-blue eyes through long lashes. "Mostly."

"Mostly?" he asked, tickling her sides.

"Daddy, stop!"

The entire room quieted as Angelina became the center of attention.

"If you've been *mostly* good," Nox asked, "why are you worried about Santa?"

She pointed out the large windows. "Because the man on TV said the snow is coming. He said lots and lots. He said no driving. What about Santa?"

"Child," Jane said, "I told you, Santa flies a sleigh. Snow's a Christmas miracle."

I leaned closer. "Jane's right." I glanced at her smiling brown eyes, winked, and looked back to my daughter. "She always is. Santa's sleigh flies better in snow."

Angi tilted her little head. "But when you were little, you lived at Grandma and Grandpa's big house. It doesn't snow there. Did you still get Christmas miracles?"

"Baby, you're my miracle."

She reached out and laid her small hand on my tummy. "And my baby brother, too?"

"That's right."

"So Santa will still come?"

"Now how old are you?" Nox asked.

"You know how old I am! I'm three and a half!"

"Has Santa ever not come?" he asked again.

"No."

"There is one thing you have to do," I said.

"What?"

"You must go to sleep."

"It's the rule," Nox added with a wink.

"No," she declared with all her daddy's finality. "Grandpa said I could stay up with him and watch for Rudolph. Santa needs his nose in the snow."

Nox's shoulders straightened. "Grandpa said that, did he?"

"Yep." Auburn curls bounced as Angi's little head bobbed.

When she was first born, her hair was copper, just as Dr. Beck had described mine. But with time it's grown darker. I wouldn't be surprised if one day it was as dark as her daddy's. I still have my hopes set for some red highlights.

"Angi," Oren called. "You weren't supposed to tell. That was our secret."

Her little eyes opened wider as she covered her mouth. "Oh, Grandpa, I forgot!" She took off toward him and my mother. "Can we still stay up? Please? I won't tell…"

I shook my head as she landed directly between our parents.

"He never told me I could stay up for Rudolph," Nox muttered.

"Mr. Lennox, some Christmas miracles take longer than others," Jane said.

With my hand in Nox's, we watched as both Oren and Momma nodded and agreed to whatever diabolical plan Angi was hatching. Though they'd decided marriage wasn't in their future—or more accurately, my mother had decided she'd spent most of her life as a man's wife—she and Oren were rarely apart. Whether they were in Savannah, London, or visiting us in New York, they were together.

When Momma had explained her reasoning, how after years of marriage, first to my father and then to Alton, she wanted to live for herself, I understood. It had been my plan when I'd left Savannah after academy and gone to California. I'd wanted to know what it was like not to be Alexandria Montague, what it was like to be Alex. And then I'd become Charli with an *i*. Now it was Momma's chance to live as Adelaide Montague. She'd dropped the Fitzgerald and embraced being herself.

Not being married didn't lessen Mother and Oren's obvious love for one another. While at first the whole idea had seemed strange, it no longer did.

With Oren by her side, I witnessed a mother I'd never known, one who was fiercely loyal and intensely driven. After the court agreed to uphold not only my grandfather's will, ruling that Alton's recent revision had been made by a man who was not of sound mind, but also our shares of Montague Corporation—together we maintained the majority vote—she asked Oren to help her, to teach her. She set out to learn what her father and Alton had told her she could never do. With Oren beside her, and with the help of Nox and Oren's people, the board of directors was thoroughly vetted. Those loyal to Montague, to the belief in the company, were retained. Those loyal to Momma's deceased husband were relieved of their positions.

New faces, both men and women, were brought on board. The misogyny of the past was over. It wasn't always smooth. Change rarely was. The value of Montague stock fluctuated. Some of the subsidiaries sought other backing and support. However, Montague wasn't alone in its struggles. The entire country had seen the shifts. The country as a whole was in a state of flux.

That had its advantages. We were no longer front-page news. Alton's murder was in the past, as was Suzanna's conviction. The press had called her a scorned lover. She'd received a life sentence with the possibility of parole after twenty-five years. Bryce's plea was not guilty by reason of insanity. After his stunt at the hotel with Chelsea, it seemed plausible. However, the state didn't accept it. The prosecution took the risk of taking his case to trial. Melissa Summers had been murdered on the Saturday of our engagement party. Hundreds of people saw and spoke to Bryce that night.

Cold and calculating were words used by the prosecutor. The trial went on for a lengthy period of time. Chelsea and I attended every session. The jury deliberated for days. Finally we received word the verdict was in.

Guilty of murder exercising malice and aforethought.

His sentence was for life with no possibility of parole.

Over time the association with Montague faded away. Despite my grandfather's antiquated way of thinking, he had built a company that fostered success. As other headlines took precedence, the CEO or majority stockholder of Montague Corporation was no longer an issue.

Momma never took the position of CEO. She recognized her limitations. That said, she helped to fill the position with a person she could trust, and now she was an active member of the board. Even from London, she managed to stay on top of the pressing matters.

Jane ran Montague Manor until Angelina was born.

I wanted Jane in New York and thankfully she wanted to be here.

She didn't raise our daughter the way she had me. Nox and I were too hands-on for that, but she helped. She and Silvia both. Together they sat with us during long nights of crying and colic. They gave advice and cared for all of us. Jane held my hand while Silvia kicked Nox's behind. She was his voice of reason when he became too obsessed.

It worked. Together we were a family.

As Oren had said many times: family was family.

No longer did Nox and I need our apartment in the city. It didn't make sense with Angelina. We both wanted our child to have a home with a yard, surrounded by love. That didn't mean Nox and I didn't still work in the city. Until just recently, I had a part-time position at Demetri Enterprises in their legal department—the job Nox had offered me years ago. With Dominic Russell almost here, I was officially on a leave of absence.

"I'm sorry Chelsea and Isaac couldn't be here," Nox said as we continued to watch the scene around us unfold.

"I know how you were looking forward to seeing him."

Nox shrugged. "After all those years of having him around every day, it's weird."

"Don't you speak to him daily regardless?"

"I do. Security isn't all hands-on. He's lightened some of Deloris's burden."

"I think it's kind of cool that he and Chelsea finally realized there was something between them."

Nox reached out to my stomach. "It's about time since their little one is due in three months."

I laughed. "I know. I was so looking forward to seeing Chelsea. She wasn't showing the last time we were all together." I smiled, recalling their wedding.

"Well, not all brides look as beautiful as you did with a baby bump."

"Speaking of brides… Uncle Preston seems to be doing well with Cy."

Nox sighed. "I'm so glad they're out of Infidelity and now married."

I narrowed my eyes. "I am too, but what's going on?"

"Why would you think something is going on?"

"The way you said that. I know you hate the company."

Nox shrugged. "Demetri pulled out."

"I hate when that happens."

His blue eyes shone. "Oh, princess. We can rectify that right now. You, me, upstairs."

I laughed. "That's almost as tempting as a trek to the gas station restroom."

He leaned close, his warm breath near my ear and whispered, "We'll do it in the bathroom, you can hold the vanity, and I'll watch your golden eyes in the mirror as you scream about my cock."

I shook my head. "Dick. You're avoiding the subject."

"I'm not. You want it. Just admit it."

"I want to know what's happening with Infidelity."

"It dodged a bullet, a big one, with the Melissa murder. It's not worth the risk. We're no longer involved, not Demetri Enterprises, not you, or Chelsea, or Pat and Cy."

"But, Nox, hundreds or thousands of people are, from everyday people to movie and sports stars. I wouldn't want it made public for any of them."

"Princess, I'm not exposing it. Deloris was a huge asset for the company. But we're out. She has more important things to do than watch their firewalls. I'm not saying it'll happen, but if it does, we're clear. Even their..." He nodded toward Pat and Cy. "...records were deleted."

"Chelsea's?"

"Yes, that happened before asshole's trial."

I knew it had. It was just good to hear it.

"Lennox," Oren called. "Angi and I have a proposition for you and Alex."

Nox's smile grew. "Do you know how much trouble we're in if she learns her negotiating skills from him?"

EPILOGUE
CHAPTER 2

—•○•—

Christmas Morning

ADELAIDE

"SOMETHING SMELLS WONDERFUL," Oren said as we made our way down the stairs and toward the kitchen.

"I have your coffee poured, and the calzones are almost ready," Silvia said.

"Silvia," I said, taking in the counter filled with sweets. "You always outdo yourself."

She grinned. "I like having people around again. This place was too quiet for too long."

A squeal came from the way of the corridor to the pool house.

We all laughed. "It's not too quiet now." I nodded toward the hallway. "I'm guessing Angelina is already awake?"

"That girl's been up for hours. It's taking every bit of her parents' persuasion to stop her from opening the presents or passing them out. Lennox told her she could as soon as everyone was there."

"Just imagine what it will be like when there are two of them," I said.

"Oh, Lordy, Miss Adelaide," Jane said, coming from the direction of the excitement. "I think I'm getting too old for this."

"Nonsense, Jane," Oren said. "You're young at heart where it counts."

Silvia carried a tray of coffee mugs toward the pool house. "Most everyone is already there. Come on and enjoy the fun."

Oren reached for a tray filled with delicious-looking pastries. "I'll take this out there. If you'll bring my coffee?" he asked with a kiss to my cheek.

My lips rose. "We'll be right there."

Jane shook her head. "This, all of this, is a dream come true. I always prayed that one day I'd see you and Miss Alex happy, really and truly happy." Tears filled her eyes. "It's a blessing."

I knew exactly what she meant as small lines formed near my eyes, my cheeks rose, and my voice became lyrical. "It is. I mean, look outside."

We both turned toward the window. The scene beyond the glass was of a winter wonderland. Familiar shrubbery had been transformed into glistening white mounds and the pool and lawn were all one snow-covered plain.

"Look at us," I said. "Two fine Georgia women in the middle of a frozen tundra with smiles on our faces. Who would have ever predicted?"

"Me," Jane said. "I didn't know how, but like I said, I prayed. I believed."

I reached for her hand. "Thank you for praying. I never thought it would happen. I never imagined…"

"Can't never give up hope," she said, her shoulders growing straighter. "Nope."

A scene from years ago came back to mind. A glass filled with small white pills and the decision to wash them down with fine Montague Private Label. I lowered my chin. "I almost did. I was mighty close to giving up." I swallowed and looked into Jane's beautiful brown eyes. "I never properly thanked you for what you did that night."

"That's not true, Miss Adelaide. I'm thanked every day. I'm thanked every time I see you smile. Everyday Miss Alex has her momma and Miss Angi has her grandmother. My heart is full of thanks."

"I hope you know how much we love you. You're our family."

"Oh, I know. You're mine too."

I laughed. "Oren always says that family is family. No matter what."

"Yes, ma'am."

I reached again for my cup and Oren's, but before picking them up I turned to Jane. "Before we go out there, I have a question that I've been meaning to ask. Whatever happened to those pills?"

"Why? You don't need them."

"No," I agreed. I'd been clean for over four years. "I've just been curious. Angelina visits the manor. Soon we'll have little Dominic. I wouldn't want them or anyone else to find them."

"Not a thing to worry about, Miss Adelaide. I wouldn't let those pills hurt you. I'd never let them hurt those babies. Besides, I got rid of them about four years ago. They're gone now."

My stomach twisted as I digested her meaning. "Four years?"

Jane reached for my arm. "That's all over now. Ain't nothing to think about."

"Jane?"

"Ma'am, they go much better with Cognac than they do wine."

"B-but Suzy?"

Jane shook her head and straightened her neck. Her usual smile flattened into a straight line. "No, ma'am. That woman wasn't living in your house, not as long as I had breath in these lungs. No, ma'am."

I stared for a moment into the mugs of coffee still sitting on the counter, unsure what to say. There were too many things, too many memories, scenes where despite what I'd claimed, Jane had known the truth. She'd seen. She'd listened. Taking a deep breath, I reached out, laid my hand on hers and lifted my gaze.

She winked as her cheeks rose. "No need to talk about that anymore, Miss Adelaide. Now, let's go out there to the pool house and watch little miss open her presents. I've been out there. Lord a mighty! Santa definitely made it. I'd say he needed a backup sleigh for all them presents."

"Remember, he's magic."

"Ma'am, magic happens all the time. Sometimes, we just need to help it."

"Thank you."

Jane shook her head. "Keep being happy. That's all I ever wanted." She nodded toward the mugs. "I can help you with those."

"No, thank you. I've got them," I said as I picked up Oren's coffee in one hand and my own mug in the other, and Jane and I began walking together down the corridor. Beyond the windows the sun in the bright blue sky was almost blinding, shining on the snow with new intensity.

"Miss Adelaide," Jane asked, "Are you and Mr. Demetri going back to Savannah or to London?"

"Savannah, for a while." I stopped. "He's there, Oren is... in my house..." I wasn't sure what I was saying. Maybe I was seeking Jane's approval.

"Yes, and he makes you happy?"

"Yes, very much."

"And he's good to you?"

I nodded, swallowing the lump forming in my throat.

"And you love him?"

"I hope that's obvious."

"It is. And because of all that, your house... that's right where he belongs."

Swallowing the lump, I said, "Well, I like having him there, filling the manor with new memories. I also love his flat in London, but it's cold there, even colder than here. Oren and I are working out a pattern that keeps me away from too much snow. Nevertheless, we're not going anywhere until Dominic arrives."

"That little baby boy..." Jane shook her head. "...it shouldn't be long now."

"Grandma," Angelina called as we stepped through the doorway into the pool house. "Finally. Now can we open presents?"

"Yes," the room said together with a collective sigh.

Warmth filled my cheeks as Oren wrapped his arm around my waist. I handed him his mug.

"Your arrival was greatly anticipated," he whispered.

"I guess it was. I didn't realize."

He nodded toward the windows filled with a winter wonderland and winked. "I have a gift for you."

"You do? What do I need? I have you and the kids. I have Angelina and soon little Dominic..."

Placing our coffee on a nearby table, he reached for a long, slender box, wrapped in beautiful white and gold foil paper.

"Hmm," I assessed as he handed it to me. "It's too big for jewelry."

"If you're telling me you'll wear a ring if it's a present, I can be back in an hour."

I laughed. "On Christmas?"

"Don't doubt me. I have connections to some of the best jewelry stores in the city."

"I'd never doubt your connections." I shook the box to the sound of rattling. "Is it broken?"

"Perhaps you should open it and find out."

"Momma," Alexandria said from near the tree, "what do you have?"

"I don't know." I pulled the ribbon and slid my finger under the tape. As the paper bowed backward, I read the box and grinned.

"Battleship?" Alexandria said. "Since when do you play board games?"

Oren smiled, his eyebrows dancing. "Your mother has many secrets."

Both Lennox's and Alexandria's hands flew into the air.

"We don't need to know more," Lennox said with a grin as he turned to Angelina. "Now, my little princess, which package do you want to deliver next?"

"This one," she said, pointing at a small red gift with a green bow.

Lennox read the tag. "That one says it's to you from me."

"It does?" She wasted no time ripping the paper and opening the hinged box. "Oh, look, Mommy, it's a necklace like yours."

Alexandria smiled and nodded. "It's just like mine. Your daddy's kind of overprotective."

"Does that mean you love us?"

Lennox secured the chain around Angelina's neck and kissed her forehead. "It means I love you very much."

"Because we're your princesses?"

"Yes!"

"But what about my brother?" Her little face scrunched in question. "Will Nic get one too? Boys don't wear necklaces like this."

Lennox shrugged, giving Alexandria a smile. "I'm sure Deloris can figure out something. And when you, Miss Angi…" He pointed to her nose. "…are a teenager, we'll make you a necklace like your mommy's other one."

Alexandria laughed and she shook her head. "I don't know. There might be a few things we'd rather not hear."

EPILOGUE
CHAPTER 3

——————●O●——————

After the New Year

NOX

"DAD, ARE YOU sure it isn't time for you to go back to London or maybe Savannah?"

"You're stuck with us until our grandson arrives," Oren said with a grin.

I eyed him up and down. "I do admit, this family-man thing is looking good on you."

"I know... I should have tried it sooner."

I shrugged. "Better late than never."

"Now back to what I was saying. Higgins lost the reelection, but Carroll is still in. That finance bill we fought five years ago was pocket change compared to some of the shit they have ready to be heard."

"It's good that Higgins is out. He was dirty anyway. I'm surprised he made the last term."

Oren shook his head as he leaned back in the chair across the desk from me. "I'm learning more and more about Georgia politics. There's some good people, but the old guard is hard to oust."

"One at a time, I suppose."

"Have you spoken to Carroll?"

"I have," I admitted. "The distribution centers we opened a few years ago are working three shifts a day. But you're right, the new national bill could seriously hurt us by taking away the tax breaks we were given."

"Those were guaranteed for ten years."

"What is that in political years?"

Oren nodded. "I think it's time to court the new elected officials. We need to concentrate on the states that have supported business in the past. We have more than Demetri now. We have Montague now too."

"I don't feel right…"

"Why? It's your wife's company. We're not at odds. We want the same things."

"Lennox," Silvia said as she opened the door. Her brown eyes were wide with concern.

I jumped to my feet. "What is it?"

"Alex didn't want me to say anything, but I can't keep quiet any longer. She needs to get to the hospital."

My gaze met Dad's as we both rushed toward the doorway. "Have you called Clayton?"

"Yes, he's getting the car."

I stopped and looked at Silvia. "Will that be all right or do you think we should call an ambulance?"

"He's here now. Go. Jane and I have Angi. You all go up to Mount Sinai and keep us posted."

Charli held tightly to my hand as Clayton navigated the wet roads, getting us all closer to Mount Sinai Hospital. I'd called her OB/GYN and he was meeting us there.

"You're going to be just fine," I said for the hundredth time.

Charli exhaled in puffs as she nodded. "This happened faster than last time. I was barely feeling it and now…" Her words trailed away as her eyes closed and she blew again.

I peered out the windows. "We're almost there."

"Oh, Nox." She reached for her stomach.

As she did, I did too. It was hard, rock-hard. "Princess, it's a contraction. Squeeze my hand and blow."

"I know what it is!"

Oren and Adelaide's eyes grew wide as they pretended to watch the passing traffic.

"Clayton!" I called, not knowing what to say to my wife, the woman who was about ready to break every bone in my hand. I'd used that hand to break bones. I'd used it to give pleasure. I'd even rocked our daughter holding her in that hand.

All I could think about was that I'd never be able to do any of that again. Not with the pressure she was applying. I'd be rocking little Nic with a cast around my fingers.

Finally, the car came to a stop outside the emergency room doors. Lying in wait was a team of orderlies and nurses. "Mrs. Demetri?" one man in scrubs asked.

"Yes," I answered as I helped Charli from the car to the waiting wheelchair.

"Sir, come with us," he said as he reached for Charli's wheelchair. "Mrs. Demetri is already registered. Let's get you all up to Labor and Delivery."

A few minutes later, I paced back and forth while Charli's doctor performed all the necessary steps. I expected him to say we had a long haul in front of us. I expected the speech we'd gotten with Angelina about how babies have their own sense of urgency.

That wasn't what he said.

"Ladies and gentlemen, Alex's water just broke and your son is crowning. It's show time."

Charli's head went back and forth. "No shows. This is real."

I smoothed her beautiful hair away from her face. "I think that means there isn't time for any pain medicine."

"I-I don't know if I can do this."

"Trust me, princess. You can do anything."

Her eyes closed. "Doctor, it's so fast. Is it all right? Will he be all right?"

"Don't worry, Alex, your son has his mind set. He's ready to meet his mom and dad. There isn't anything we can do to dissuade him."

"He's a Demetri, all right," Charli murmured.

"When did the contractions start?"

"Not that long ago. They weren't even strong until suddenly they were."

"How fast are they coming?"

"We were timing every four minutes in the car," I volunteered.

Suddenly the room was filled with people in scrubs as someone covered me with a paper gown.

Charli peered at me with wide eyes. "You need to tell Momma and Oren."

A new wave of uneasiness washed through me. "I don't want to leave you."

"Are they close?" the doctor asked.

"Right outside, I think."

"Go. Hurry back. You have time."

As Charli nodded, I let go of her hand and weaved through the crowd of people. The hallway seemed quiet compared to the mayhem within the delivery room. I didn't have to look far to find our parents' concerned expressions.

"The doctor said everything is fine," I reassured. "But things are moving fast."

"How fast?" Adelaide asked.

"He's crowning."

She gasped as Oren nodded. "Demetri men are determined." He patted my shoulder. "Go. We'll be right here."

"Lennox," Adelaide said, "tell her I love her... *we* love her."

I smiled. "I will."

I rushed to Charli's side as her neck strained and back arched. Her feet were up and the doctor was in place. "I'm here. You're doing great."

Charli nodded with tears in her golden eyes.

"Squeeze my hand. Let me take some of the pain." She reached for me, her petite hand falling into my palm. As she squeezed my skin blanched. "Do you trust me?"

"Y-yes."

"Then believe. You've got this."

"Talk to me," she said.

"What do you want to talk about?"

"The story you tell Angi. Tell me."

My chest tightened as I concentrated on my wife, doing my best to block out the other voices. "You want to hear a bedtime story?"

Charli nodded as her expression contorted.

"Okay… listen to my voice. Don't think about anyone else."

She nodded again as her shoulders relaxed and grip loosened. "There once was a princess…" she began.

"There once was a *beautiful* princess," I went on, "with flowing hair of red and eyes of gold. She lived in a castle with shadows all around. They darkened the corridors and rooms. They'd fly all around while soldiers stood guard, but the princess wasn't scared. She was the bravest princess of them all.

"She was so much smarter than her evil captors that she even escaped. While free from the castle's shadows and resting in the sun, she met a man. Little did she know that the man she'd met also lived in darkness, in the blackest of night. Unready to show the world his face, he kept it hidden by a mask and cape. His disguise was work. He wrapped his days and nights with it and kept the rest of the world away.

"One day, the mean dragon with beady eyes and fiery skin lured the princess back to the castle. Knowing her kind heart, he tricked her."

"Push, Alex," the doctor said. "We're almost there."

"Keep going," Charli said as her face grew red. "This is my favorite part."

"Did Prince Charming save the princess?" one of the nurses asked.

"No," I said, kissing Charli's forehead. "Batman did. And she saved him, too."

With my cheek near hers, we both turned toward the ringing cry of our son and watched as the doctor lifted Dominic's little body. A fine layer of dark hair covered his head as his arms and legs flailed in time to his healthy wail.

"And the best part," Charli said with a smile as tears rolled down her cheeks. "They all lived happily ever after."

THE END

Never stop believing

COMING SOON...

Just announced: **RESPECT**, a stand-alone Infidelity novel by Aleatha Romig chronicling the life story of Oren Demetri, a reluctantly made man. Release date to be announced.

Aleatha is also excited to announce more additions to the world of Infidelity with Kindle Worlds. In March of 2017, in conjunction with Amazon, the Infidelity World will be added to Kindle Worlds as other authors will have the opportunity to write within the world you've come to love… the world of the Montagues, Demetris, Spencers, and Fitzgeralds… the world of Infidelity.

Please follow Aleatha Romig on social media for information related to RESPECT, the Infidelity World, and more exciting surprises and releases.

WHAT TO DO NOW...

LEND IT: Did you enjoy *FIDELITY*? Do you have a friend who'd enjoy *FIDELITY*? *FIDELITY* may be lent one time. Sharing is caring!

RECOMMEND IT: Do you have multiple friends who'd enjoy *FIDELITY*? Tell them about it! Call, text, post, tweet... your recommendation is the nicest gift you can give to an author!

REVIEW IT: Tell the world. Please go to the retailer where you purchased this book, as well as Goodreads, and write a review.

STAY CONNECTED
WITH ALEATHA

Do you love Aleatha's writing? Do you want to know be kept up to date about Infidelity, Consequences, Tales From the Dark Side, Light series, and what's coming next?

Do you like EXCLUSIVE content (never-released scenes, never-released excerpts, and more)? Would you like the monthly chance to win prizes (signed books and gift cards)? Then sign up today for Aleatha's monthly newsletter and stay informed on all things Aleatha Romig.

Sign up for Aleatha's NEWSLETTER: http://bit.ly/1PYLjZW
(recipients receive exclusive material and offers)

Join Aleatha's Facebook group for updates, trailers, teasers, and events.
http://bit.ly/2c4bYYr

You can also find Aleatha@

Her website: http://aleatharomig.wix.com/aleatha
Facebook: https://www.facebook.com/AleathaRomig
Twitter: https://twitter.com/AleathaRomig
Goodreads: www.goodreads.com/author/show/5131072.Aleatha_Romig
Instagram: http://instagram.com/aleatharomig
Email Aleatha: aleatharomig@gmail.com

You may also listen Aleatha Romig's books on Audible.

BOOKS BY NEW YORK TIMES BESTSELLING AUTHOR ALEATHA ROMIG

INFIDELITY SERIES:

BETRAYAL

Book #1

(October 2015)

CUNNING

Book #2

(January 2016)

DECEPTION

Book #3

(May 2016)

ENTRAPMENT

Book #4

(September2016)

FIDELITY

Book #5

(January 2017)

RESPECT

A standalone Infidelity Novel

(TBA)

THE CONSEQUENCES SERIES:

CONSEQUENCES
(Book #1)
Released August 2011

TRUTH
(Book #2)
Released October 2012

CONVICTED
(Book #3)
Released October 2013

REVEALED
(Book #4)
Previously titled: Behind His Eyes Convicted: The Missing Years
Re-released June 2014

BEYOND THE CONSEQUENCES
(Book #5)
Released January 2015

COMPANION READS:

BEHIND HIS EYES—CONSEQUENCES
(Companion One of the bestselling Consequences Series)
Released January 2014

BEHIND HIS EYES—TRUTH
(Companion Two of the bestselling Consequences Series)
Released March 2014

TALES FROM THE DARK SIDE SERIES:
(All books in this series are stand-alone erotic thrillers)

INSIDIOUS
(October 2014)

DUPLICITY
(Completely unrelated to book #1)
Release TBA

THE LIGHT SERIES:
Published through Thomas and Mercer

INTO THE LIGHT
(June 14, 2016)

AWAY FROM THE DARK
(October 2016)

ALEATHA ROMIG

Aleatha Romig is a *New York Times* and *USA Today* bestselling author who lives in Indiana. She grew up in Mishawaka, graduated from Indiana University, and is currently living south of Indianapolis. Aleatha has raised three children with her high school sweetheart, Mr. Jeff, her husband of thirty years. Before she became a full-time author, she worked days as a dental hygienist and spent her nights writing. Now, when she's not imagining mind-blowing twists and turns, she likes to spend her time with her family and friends. Her other pastimes include reading and creating heroes/anti-heroes who haunt your dreams!

Aleatha released her first novel, CONSEQUENCES, in August of 2011. CONSEQUENCES became a bestselling series with five novels and two companions released from 2011 through 2015. The compelling and epic story of Anthony and Claire Rawlings has graced more than half a million e-readers. Aleatha released the first of her series TALES FROM THE DARK SIDE, INSIDIOUS, in the fall of 2014. These stand-alone thrillers continue Aleatha's twisted style with an increase in heat. In the fall of 2015, Aleatha moved headfirst into the world of romantic suspense with the release of BETRAYAL, the first of her five-novel INFIDELITY series. Aleatha has entered the traditional world of publishing with Thomas and Mercer with her LIGHT series. The first of that series, INTO THE LIGHT, was published in the summer of 2016.

Aleatha is a "Published Author's Network" member of the Romance Writers of America and PEN America.

Manufactured by Amazon.ca
Bolton, ON

12584702R00208